Mad Honey

Mad Honey

Katie Welch

This is a work of fiction. All characters, organizations, places and events portrayed are either products of the author's imagination or are used fictitiously.

Published by Buckrider Books
an imprint of Wolsak and Wynn Publishers
280 James Street North
Hamilton, ON L8R2L3
www.wolsakandwynn.ca

Editor for Buckrider Books: Paul Vermeersch | Editor: Jen Sookfong Lee | Copy editor: Jen Hale
Cover design: Michel Vrana
Cover image: Engraving of bee from above, Grafissimo, iStock
Interior design: Jennifer Rawlinson
Author photograph: Kevin Bogetti-Smith
Typeset in Cambria and Ohno Blazeface
Printed by Rapido Books, Montreal, Canada

Printed on certified 100% post-consumer Rolland Enviro Paper.

10 9 8 7 6 5 4 3 2 1

Canada Council for the Arts | Conseil des arts du Canada
ONTARIO ARTS COUNCIL
CONSEIL DES ARTS DE L'ONTARIO
an Ontario government agency
un organisme du gouvernement de l'Ontario
Canada

The publisher gratefully acknowledges the support of the Ontario Arts Council, the Canada Council for the Arts and the Government of Canada.

Library and Archives Canada Cataloguing in Publication

Title: Mad honey : a novel / Katie Welch.
Names: Welch, Katie, author.
Identifiers: Canadiana 20220159386 | ISBN 9781989496527 (softcover)
Classification: LCC PS8645.E4395 M33 2022 | DDC C813/.6—dc23

to Will Stinson, for everything

and to my daughters, Heather Saya and Olivia

The busy bee has no time for sorrow.

– William Blake, *Proverbs of Hell*

Prologue

When he came back to himself he was inside the cabin, stretched out on the narrow mattress where he had closed his eyes, the folded ridges of a scratchy wool blanket pressing into the thin membrane of his skin. There was a musty smell of damp pillows and wet wood, and the distant sound of tires whooshing along a gravel road. So he had ears, and a nose, and long limbs that extended from his torso, and sensitive nerves sending information to a brain that processed information in words. In those first moments, he remembered an altogether different sensory experience, and he dwelled on the details of the dream before abandoning himself to wakefulness, catching fleeting images in his memory like butterflies in a net before they became lost to him.

Beck was whole, but he could feel his pieces. They flew like miniature striped dirigibles, coming and going from the mothership of his hive-body. Instinctively he understood the hum and thrum of life, a pulse that moved not slick red blood, but sweet amber honey. Reflective thought was absent, but he was conscious, in a way humans are not, of the building up and breaking down of things corporeal. Each of his cells was a bee performing one specific duty, the task each bee was created to do: clean, eat, build, come or go. If he sensed his core overheating, he initiated the fanning of wings, maintaining the comfort of his queen. Beck quivered at the thought of her, unique piece of his pieces, part of his parts, reigning over the glorious ordered chaos of the hive, thousands of segmented black legs shuffling up and down aromatic waxen walls, nurseries of white larvae, and perfect hexagons of heavenly honey, sweet honey, rich honey, perfect food of light and love! For a few seconds Beck remembered what it was like to sense the dawn of the sun-day and reach outside himself, sending wavering lines of gold to every fragrant receptacle, every colour-exploding flower. There, inside the flowers, parts of him slipped along silky coloured petals, cushions of fuchsia, yellow, lavender, crimson, rose and white. Inside flowers, all those bits of him sipped, with ten thousand tongues, the nectar he needed and desired. Then he called his pieces back to himself, and deep in his core, waggles spread ripples of promise and pleasure.

The plywood walls of the cabin came into focus. His eyes slid right, toward the brilliance of sun glaring through a window, then left, to a cottage kitchen. A blue enamel kettle, flecked with white and blackened around its base from the propane stovetop, reminded Beck he had a mother who often prepared hot beverages in the emptiness of this space. Glossy photographs thumbtacked above the sink were evidence of a father whose habit it was to capture two-dimensional images for contemplation at some future time. Awareness of these people, his parents, came complete with a history Beck recognized as being his own: shunted from Canada to Cuba and back again a dozen times in his school years, a perpetual stranger, a friend who like a favourite toy got lost, only to turn up again in the yard, faded from weather and stained with mould.

His four limbs were jointed in the middle. He folded them at these junctures and redistributed his weight until he sat on his bottom, facing a chipped mirror screwed directly to the wall. A face Beck recognized as his own wavered in the mirror's imperfections, toffee-coloured skin, long dark hair and beetle-black eyes. He remembered that kids in his Toronto neighbourhood used to call him *Black,* and sometimes mistake him for a girl because he was skinny and pretty, with big lips and long eyelashes. In the Havana suburb where his mother's family lived, kids had called him *white*. He'd never risen to the bait of juvenile racial slurs, or used name-calling to start a playground fight, but he'd never complained or run away, thus avoiding a reputation as a coward. He had stayed quiet and peaceful, deflecting punches with his elbows in eerie silence, cementing his reputation as Beck Wise, weirdo.

He had been conscious for only a few minutes, but Beck's identity was galloping back into the paddock of his flesh. He rubbed his eyes, amazed by the squishy resilience of eyeballs, and marvelling at the hard knobs of his knuckles. Little by little he shifted his centre of gravity from his bottom to his feet, straightening the ladder of bones inside his body. Pain ran along his muscles and shot complaints through his fingers and toes. His ability to be ambulatory returned and he took unbalanced steps, coaxing an unfamiliar anatomy closer to the window. Outside, the poplars along the road were shedding brilliant yellow leaves, and the grass around the cabin had the faded look of autumn. It had been early summer, late June, when he had come to the cabin to be alone and had reclined on the rickety bed. Where had he been?

One

The day Beck came back, Melissa was trying to take a day off. It was September 14, her birthday. Daphne had insisted she would do all the morning chores, so Melissa was lying on her side in the grass beside the flower garden, pushing away a dynamic, omnipresent mental list: *harvest pears and tomatoes, clear out bean rows, check on the chickens, feed the goats and the donkey, get an oil change on the truck, clean up the outdoor canning kitchen, go over the farm financials* and on and on.

It was a breezy day, and the way the grass moved was mesmerizing – swords of pale green clashing silently, battling against a backdrop of white and blue. The breeze blew strong enough to sway individual blades of grass but not the stalwart orange poppies beyond the lawn. The world was sideways from where she lay, the clouds tall instead of long. Orange poppy petals exploded around pointillistic black centres suspended on hairy, pale green stems perpendicular to her body. The weight of her head pressed into the bent elbow of her warm, suntanned arm. A dark lock of hair tumbled across her line of sight, and she tucked it slowly, neatly, behind one of her prominent ears, the fleshy earlobe triple-pierced and adorned with three silver rings. Her broad hands were proportionate to her taller-than-average height and perennially dirty. She wore a creamy white sundress that day – unusual, because she eschewed dresses; they weren't farming clothes. Daphne, who rocked splashy, multicoloured sundresses in the fields, would disagree.

Melissa was blissing out on poppies painted against deep blue sky. The centre of each poppy was made up of tiny, delicate petals arranged in ever-tightening concentric circles, swirls of orange deepening to a red that was almost black. A rivulet of drool escaped the low side of her mouth and descended, slow and glistening, to her outstretched arm. She observed one poppy in particular, the most splendid flower. The breeze settled, and her whirring thoughts settled too. For a few seconds she experienced the illusion of suspended time, achieving meditative success, the elusive quiet mind she'd heard yoga enthusiasts brag about. She felt and saw only the perfection of the tableau: border of spiky grass, vermilion floral profusion, hemisphere of sky extending to the limits of her vision.

A sound broke the spell, the characteristic buzzing of a honeybee, a high, soft pitch, not the guttural rumbling of a bumblebee. She heard the insect approach but didn't look for it, focused as she was on the epitome of an orange poppy in all its resplendent stillness. When the bee flew into her sight, she pinpointed the little creature's location by its insistent hum. Every hair on the bee's body stood out in sharp definition. Melissa imagined she could see the mosaic of its compound eyes, thousands of iridescent surfaces creating pixelated sight. Quivering in anticipation, the bee navigated the forest of orange flowers and, improbably, chose to land on the very flower she observed. Six black legs twitched, extended and contracted as they assumed the insect's weight: landing complete.

Melissa broke her meditation, reminded again of yoga classes she had once attended, and how she used to lie still during savasana, waiting for the all-clear so she could get going. She sat up slowly, abs contracting bottom to top, and the universe righted itself. In the distance, the back side of a stone farmhouse loomed up behind the flower garden, erupting out of the earth's crust, but she kept watching the bee, zeroing in on the delicate filigree of veins in its wings. The flicker of something human in an upstairs window, an arm waving, caught her eye. She tore her gaze away from the poppy and its fascinating striped occupant. *Why would you interrupt me now?*

Daphne was waving frantically from a bedroom window. Her hair, which she either twisted into tidy braids or allowed to puff out freely, defying gravity, was big that day. A halo of tight brown curls filled the window, and the whites of outsized eyes shone like searchlights in the middle of this mane. Her mouth opened and closed in a pantomime of a spoken name – wide, narrow, wide, repeat.

"Melissa! Melissa, *Melissa*!"

The faraway voice was an itty-bitty insect noise by the time it reached Melissa, but there was no mistaking the urgency in the swing of Daphne's arm, or the too-round aperture of her mouth. In an easy movement Melissa levered her nearly six feet of muscle and bone to its default upright position. She reached down and snatched a pair of mirrored sunglasses from the grass, catching a glimpse of her distorted features in the lenses – broad lips, roman nose, black caterpillars of never-plucked brows like thick bridges over hazel eyes. Genetic gifts from her father, mostly; nobody believed her short, blond, snub-nosed mother was biologically responsible for her Amazonian frame and glossy dark-brown hair. She didn't hurry back, but sauntered, relaxed for the first time in weeks and loath to get uptight again. Daphne and her arm disappeared from the upstairs window, then emerged with the rest of her springy, lithe limbs from the kitchen door at the back of the house. She had the knack of being beautiful, and could do it in ripped pyjamas with a head cold. On the day Beck came back Daphne was especially striking in a green tie-dyed tank top, frayed jean shorts and bare feet. She pursed her lips and arched her eyebrows; Melissa could tell that she'd regretted yanking the birthday girl away from the repose that was supposed to be her present.

"Sorry. It's Beck. I wouldn't have interrupted you for anything less."

"Beck – here? Now?"

"Not yet. On his way."

Beck had departed one evening in spring, leaving a short note saying he would be back, but taking his toothbrush and his favourite jeans and shirts. As ever, Melissa had been busy. A week had gone by before she'd wondered if he would keep his written promise to return, and at a month she'd known he wouldn't. She supposed he had broken her heart; Daphne assured her it was definitely broken, but there were ways to shut off inconvenient feelings. When she was young Melissa had found a toggle switch in her chest. Flipped to *ON*, the switch opened a circuit and allowed pain to course through her body like electricity through a wire. In the *OFF* position, the current halted. With her heart switched off she could still profess love, nurture animals and mourn sad news. It was as simple as saying the right things, pantomiming feelings, playing emotional charades. But hurt accumulated behind this electrical gate, and there were nights when alone in her room, she flicked the switch and let pain circulate, wiping away the weakness of tears with rumpled bedsheets. As time passed she'd found she could live without Beck her lover. But he was also her beekeeper, and he cared for the livestock: a dozen chickens, Hotay the donkey and goats Jeffrey and Edna. She had muffled romantic sorrow when Beck had evaporated, but business-wise, his departure had been a letdown and a big inconvenience, and it had pissed her off. Ironically, when Beck vanished, he had been trying to protect the Hopetown Farm beehives from colony collapse disorder, a mysterious plague marked by vanishing bees. In the crispy, stifling last weeks of August, the rest of the farm staff had cobbled together what they knew about beekeeping and honey extraction, and planned for the imminent honey harvest. When Melissa had cursed and complained and worried out loud about the bees, she'd overheard sticky sympathy: *This is so hard for her – she misses Beck so much.*

Daphne chewed her bottom lip and shifted her weight from side to side in an impatient dance, waiting for a reaction. Melissa stifled a germ of excitement – *he's back, he came back* – and concentrated on summoning up the bitter taste of Beck's betrayal.

"Do me a favour? When he gets here, tell him to go away."

"But don't you want to know where he's been?"

"Not really. I stopped wondering a long time ago. Please tell him to leave."

Daphne narrowed her eyes and folded her arms. "Maybe he got amnesia," she said. "You don't know what happened."

"Oh, give me a break. How do you know he's on his way – did he call?"

"Natalie called. She spotted him on the road and pulled over to talk to him. He told her he was coming over here today to check on Hotay."

"Check on Hotay? How does Beck know Hotay's still *alive*? What is he thinking, that he left just yesterday? Wow. Just, *wow*."

Melissa pushed past Daphne into her favourite room in the farmhouse, an oversized, sunny, butter-yellow kitchen with a blue, red and green Mexican tile splashboard running along spacious wooden countertops. Scooping an apple from a big terracotta fruit bowl, she took an aggressive, juicy bite, chewed vigorously and swallowed hard.

"I don't want him here. Deliver that message for me. Come on, it's my birthday – please?"

Daphne picked up her own apple from the bowl and crunched into it, her bite matching Melissa's in intensity. She spoke wetly, around a mouthful of fruit.

"Nuh-uh. I'm not going to deliver that message." Daphne wiggled a remonstrative finger. "You need to tell him yourself."

Melissa didn't have a problem delegating chores on the farm, or *bossing everyone around*, as her mother would say, but there was a tendency for that directive energy to spill over into her personal affairs. She had once told – told, not asked – Beck to do her banking while he was in town, after making the farm deliveries. She remembered the wave of indignation she had felt when he had laughed at her. She had opened her mouth to give him a lecture on insubordination, and realized what was so damn funny. Melissa Makepeace, queen of her little realm. Daphne and Beck knew the boundary between their employee and friend roles, and defended it valiantly. Melissa sighed.

"All right, fine. Would you check on Hotay, then, please? And the chickens, and Jeffrey and Edna? I'm going to change, grab a sunhat and attack the weeds."

"So much for your holiday. You're supposed to be chilling out beside the lake, remember?"

"Thanks, Daph. You're sweet, but I can't sit down now. I'll get wound up."

The women swung their apple-free hands together and clasped them, Daphne's delicate fingers inside Melissa's big calloused palm. Daphne was Melissa's adopted sister and understood her better than anyone else; she leaned in, kissed Melissa on the cheek, then whirled and left, letting the wood-framed screen door bang shut behind her. And at that precise moment, it started up again: *the old puff-and-tuck routine.* Pushing her broad lower lip out past the curved bow of the upper, Melissa forcefully expelled three breaths, blowing errant strands of hair toward the sky. Automatically she tucked this hair from her face, roughly, three severe tugs on each side, anchoring it firmly behind her ears.

Time rocketed back to thirteen-year-old Melissa, kicking the cheap carpet in her therapist's office, a nubbly brown surface that yielded to the toes of her black army boots. She puffed and tucked compulsively. There was also a thing she did with her tongue, touching all her teeth in turn with the fleshy pink tip. Under no circumstances could tooth-touching be interrupted. At school, her teachers became impatient, and her classmates mocked her. After tooth-touching came thigh-scratching, fingernails gouging at the same spot on both sides of her jeans until she wore holes in the denim. A sniffing pattern was the last straw, the tic that made her mother seek professional help.

"It's because her father left, two years ago," Jill Makepeace told the therapist, a sensible woman who wore tailored pantsuits and patent-leather ballet flats. "He just walked out on us, the unenlightened bastard."

Jill Makepeace favoured creative New Age insults. Teenaged Melissa slouched beside her mother, carpet-kicking, puff-and-tucking, tooth-touching, scratching and sniffing.

"Thank you, Mrs. Makepeace. I'm going to ask your daughter some questions now."

"Is it Tourette's Syndrome? It is, isn't it? What can you do for her? Is there something she can take, Valium or something?"

"I think if we stay calm, Mrs. Makepeace, and discuss the –"

"She's getting bullied at school! Do you know what that's like for her?"

In the end, mother and daughter had to have separate sessions, back-to-back half-hours with the same therapist. The problem wasn't Tourette's, after all, but *an excess of nervous energy and a lack of self-worth*. The therapist taught Melissa techniques for *taking back power* and *being in control*. Her mother's therapeutic journey was learning to *stay calm* and *remain centred*. As Melissa settled into being a proper sullen, opinionated teenager, her mother claimed she had learned her therapy lessons a little too well.

"You shouldn't boss your friends around, Lissy. No one's going to want to hang out with you."

"I took my power back, and now I'm supposed to be a doormat? Whatever, Mom."

Time and maturity had eventually taken care of Melissa's nervous tics. On the day she turned twenty-three, she was running the farm. She took care of the scheduling, managed staff, distributed produce and balanced the books. The re-emergence of her tics was baffling – if Beck's departure hadn't triggered her old compulsions, how was it his return had brought back spastic adolescent anxiety? In the sunny kitchen Melissa spun on her own axis, describing a slow circle, soaking up the comforting familiarity of the heart of her home. She ran her dirty fingernails along wooden chopping-block counters, wiped clean of crumbs, and flicked her eyes over objects she had known forever, as far back as she could remember: orange-and-white ceramic bowls, a crystal butter dish, black cast-iron pans, quilted pot holders embroidered with daffodils and a painted rooster, strutting on the highest shelf beside the copper pots. Loved things, solidly in the places they ought to be. Once, when Melissa was a little girl, her mother had rearranged everything in the kitchen. Arriving home from school, Melissa had surveyed the chaos, all the things in wrong places, and burst into angry tears. She needed to be the instrument of change in her environment.

Beck's exit would have been easier if she had kicked him out.

She strode from the kitchen down the first-floor hallway to solid wood, double front doors. Grasping a latch in each of her hands, she swung both doors open at once, her hair fanning backward with the power of the gesture. What a fabulously cinematic moment it would have been, had Beck been approaching the farmhouse. In the film it would be springtime, the elegant porch roof draped with cascades of pale lavender wisteria blossoms. Lingering shot of Melissa, standing proudly in the entranceway, wisps of hair lifting gently in a breeze, her expression imperious. Cut to Beck, stopped in his tracks by her beauty and supremacy. His mouth drops open a little in awe. He releases a dirty valise from a gloved hand, removes a weathered fedora and holds it to his chest, observing her lady-of-the-house glory. Slow pan back to her, shaking her head sadly, regretfully. Quick shot of Beck's black, imploring eyes. Cut back to her, pushing the doors shut with a majestic, ambidextrous swoosh of long, muscular arms. She recites her line: *Regretfully, we can't abide fly-by-nights at Hopetown Farm. Fare thee well, Beckett, and better fortune in your future endeavours!*

But there was no one in sight. No one on the gravel path leading from front steps to lawn, or on benches placed like hyphens between maple and blue spruce lining the entrance walkway. Perpendicular to the trees, a cedar hedge filtered out grit and noise from the road beyond. A small gap in the hedge revealed a sliver of this road, a secondary route, the graded gravel surface muddy in spring and dusty in summer. A squirrel darted across the overgrown lawn and Melissa startled, then felt ridiculous. Somewhere nearby a crow was cawing, over and over, a melancholic complaint.

She closed the front doors and plunged into the farmhouse, leaping by twos up the wooden staircase to the second floor: two, four, six, eight stairs to the landing and turn – then two, four, six, eight stairs to the upstairs hall. Four bedrooms and a bathroom sprouted from the trunk of the second-floor hallway. The master bedroom, to the right at the top of the staircase, sat furnished but unoccupied, though sometimes she rented it out to itinerant farmers, globetrotters looking for seasonal under-the-table work. Her parents used to sleep in there, tactfully removed by the length of the building from her childhood room, where she still slept. The next door to the right opened to the main bathroom, tiled in white, with an old porcelain washstand holding soap and towels and a claw-footed tub with rickety shower surround, stained rust and copper-green below the waterspout. After the bathroom came Daphne's room.

Melissa's mother had adopted thirteen-year-old Daphne through a social-work program for teenaged foster children. Eavesdropping, she had learned her mother had sought both a farm labourer and a companion for her daughter. Melissa had been thirteen too, and instantly jealous of the interloper's beauty and city-girl savvy. Daphne's turbulent past, full of beatings and expulsions, lent her tragic gravitas, and by comparison Melissa felt like a spoiled hick. Jill's adopt-a-friend ploy had eventually worked, but the first year had been forced, the girls slinking around each other like strange cats, tails twitching, hair bristling. To Daphne's disadvantaged eyes, teenaged Melissa knew, she was an indulged whiner, specifying what she wanted in her school lunch box and composing wish lists for Santa in October. From Melissa's point of view Daphne was a usurper, a drainer of resources and an unwanted competitor for her mother's attention. In the end, their adolescent psyches had united them in their contempt for uptight adult particularities, and they had grown close, learning first to understand and then to love their differences.

The last door on the right of the upstairs hallway led to the smallest bedroom, a claustrophobic space scarcely bigger than a walk-in closet. This was where Beck had lived, before he'd started sleeping with her. She resisted the urge to peek into the other bedrooms, and strode down the hall to her sanctuary, the only door on the west side of the hallway. The other rooms all opened out above the lake and offered commanding views of the water. Her room was long and narrow; her windows overlooked the front yard and the road, the maple and spruce trees and the cedar hedge. Long white cotton curtains diffused light onto pale green walls, and the furniture was a nostalgic mash of rustic antiques and thrift store junk. On the day Beck came back, a ceramic vase on her broken rolltop desk held a bouquet of sweet peas – pink, blue and white. The sheets were in disarray, a giant crumpled white carnation against the chestnut baseboard. *Tsk.* She pulled roughly at the quilted bedspread, a quick flattening of fabric, then stepped out of the sundress and into jeans and a T-shirt. A tall closet door hung open, and from a jumble of hats on the topmost shelf she extracted a round straw sunhat.

Her mind was whirring like a pinwheel. *Why* had Beck come back? He might have guessed how badly hurt she had been when he left, how his absence had hollowed out her days. She thumped downstairs and went outside, pressing the sunhat into place, both a shield against the day's intense rays, and a guard against puffing and tucking. The air above the vegetable fields rippled, distorted by unseasonable heat. Passing a compost station, she lifted two stainless steel pails from a neat stack. In the distance she heard the rough clatter of Joseph Sommerton's diesel truck.

Joseph, the farmhand, was an old friend of her father's. He'd worked at the farm since her parents had bought the place, before she was born. When she was eleven Melissa's father, Charlie Makepeace, had run out on her and her mother. She tried not to think about it, but somehow Beck's return was bringing up the hateful memory. One icy February day she had woken up and skittered downstairs. Her mother was having a cup of coffee and her face was all twisted up. "Your dad is gone," she said. Melissa didn't say anything for a while, then her mother said it again, "Your dad is gone," and Melissa asked, "Is he dead?" Her mother shook her head 'no' and said he was still alive, just gone. Melissa asked over and over why he left and the answer was always the same, "Nobody knows but him." Then her mother said, "It's okay, Lissy – we can run the farm without him. We're going to be just fine."

She used to hear them fighting after she went to bed, her mother's voice reedy and insistent as an oboe, interrupted by her father's trumpet-shouts. "If you're so goddamn smart, what do you need me for?" One particular daytime argument was lodged in her brain. The gardens were neglected and overgrown that summer, the shrubs unkempt, the lawn shaggy. She was playing outside when she heard her father yell from inside his work shed, "Nobody's perfect – back off!" Her mother came scuttling out of the shed and walked unsteadily to the kitchen, clenching her fists and talking to herself. Melissa stayed hidden in her tall-grass fort. Years later, she would still remember the sour taste of the stalk she had been chewing, her stomach contracting with fear as she listened to her father curse and kick the shed walls.

Jill Makepeace rose to the challenges of single parenting. She hired seasonal help locally, oversaw the operation of the farm and raised her daughter. Joseph quietly picked up jobs that Charlie had abandoned, the farmhand appearing like magic when strong arms were needed, silently lifting or hauling, restraining a stubborn, aggressive animal or fixing a broken truck. Joseph lived in an ugly brown fifth wheel trailer parked on the northern fenceline. He rolled his own organic tobacco cigarettes and kept to himself. Melissa liked the man's gruff speech, and treated him like a surrogate uncle.

Melissa's mother tried hard to compensate for the missing father in her daughter's life. In summer, they made old-fashioned candle lanterns out of paper bags. The lanterns dispersed a soft, natural light that didn't interfere with stargazing, and at night they would lie side by side on an old sleeping bag, making up new stories about the constellations, Melissa reaching out to touch her mother's pretty profile. They swam together in Bow Lake, a fish-laden oblong of water that lapped on a pebbly shore, a short walk southeast of the farmhouse. On winter nights her mother taught her how to knit bumpy sweaters, the wool purchased in clear plastic bags from the Lanark United Church thrift store in colours nobody wanted – walnut brown, anemic yellow. They bartered, exchanging dark green broccoli heads and orange-yolked eggs for pink butcher-paper-wrapped local beef and sausage. "We're doing it, baby," her mother used to whisper in her ear when they hugged, "we're running the farm."

It bothered Melissa that memories of her father were fading, colour draining from them like newspaper mulch between rows of onion spikes. There was a pleasant memory she revisited over and over when she missed him: Canada geese flew in a V formation against a stormy sky. Her father's long arm pointed at the flock as it passed, the geese honking, flying so low Melissa could hear wingbeats. He explained why geese flew in a V, and she didn't understand what he was saying, but she was content and joyful just being with him. There was also a negative recollection stuck on repeat: she was sitting at the dining room table, homework spread out, photocopied sheets of math problems. Her father was scribbling with a pencil, solving equations she couldn't figure out, punctuating his explanations with impatient arrows and underlining heavily, as if vehemence could force her to understand. There was shouting, a disagreement. She couldn't concentrate, she hated math and her father was frustrated because she wasn't listening.

Melissa walked between rows of strawberries covered in netting, then followed an alley of staked bean plants sending tendrils curling into the air around them, seeking support. The bean alley led to a squash plantation where thickets of shepherd's purse and yellow spears of mullein – hardy weeds that the mulch hadn't prevented from thriving – jutted among broad leaves. Daphne wasn't there. Melissa peered back toward the farmhouse, but saw no one.

She had known Beck for a decade before they became lovers. He was at her high school in Lanark and then he wasn't; he popped in and out of the parochial community, a mysterious, sexy semi-stranger. His parents owned an uninsulated summer cabin about a kilometre toward town. Beck sometimes brought a battered guitar to school, and he was a pretty good singer, especially of his own rambling compositions. His mother, Eurydice, was Cuban. She wore hand-dyed blouses accessorized with large, flamboyant jewellery. She used to visit the farm to buy produce, and Melissa remembered loving the smooth lilt of her Spanish accent. Then, as Melissa embarked on her neurotic teenage years, Eurydice brokered a summer exchange of labour-for-produce with Jill Makepeace, and started showing up with Beck in tow to work mornings in the fields. Gagged by adolescent timidity, Melissa gave Beck a wide berth and tried not to glance at him. He returned her shyness with polite, cool indifference. He made her sick with queasy desire. *He took his shirt off oh my God he took his shirt off.*

After graduating from high school, Melissa completed part of an undergraduate arts degree at the University of Ottawa before deciding she was wasting her time, because all she wanted to do was farm. She came home to a mother swept up in a gusty midlife storm. Jill had a severe haircut, shaved down to her skull above her ears; she had joined a radical feminist group that picketed the local Catholic church, protesting their stand on contraceptives. She spent more and more time in Ottawa and began to rely on Melissa to keep the farm running. Familiarizing herself with the business, Melissa scrolled through old invoices on the office computer and found letters composed by her father. On grimy keys she ghost-typed the letters of her father's name as she read his old correspondence. Here he was, requesting overdue payment from Samantha Wells at Natural Foods in Lanark, and here again, suggesting Balvinder Singh, who owned the Produce Point Market in Almonte, buy up Hopetown's bumper crop of tomatoes.

"Does Balvinder Singh still own Produce Point?" Melissa asked her mother one evening.

"That old coot? He'll never sell, or retire." Jill peered over her reading glasses. "Why?"

"He and Dad knew each other pretty well. I found some letters."

Jill lowered her book and fluttered her eyelashes. "I wouldn't go dredging up the past with Balvinder. Things weren't smooth between your father and our retailers. He ruffled feathers."

"But that was a long time ago." Melissa saw her mother's spine stiffen.

"The police talked to everyone, Balvinder too. Oh, honey, we've been over this and over it. I know it's hard to accept."

"I don't have to accept anything. Dad's still missing, and for the millionth time, unlike you, I don't want to believe he's dead. And now that I'm living here again, I'm going to try to find him."

Jill sniffed indignantly, pushed her glasses back up and raised her book to hide her face. It wasn't long afterward that Jill announced she was travelling to Guatemala and Ecuador on an open-ended ticket, to work on sustainable farms and explore her creativity.

"These are my *wisewoman* years. You'll understand when you get to be my age. Beck will start working full time when I leave, and Joseph and Daphne are here for you. Between the four of you, you'll keep everything running. You and the farm will be fine."

Her mother's departure released an avalanche of toil that engulfed Melissa's days. From before sun-up until she fell into bed exhausted, Hopetown kept her hopping. She let her guard down and befriended Beck, who moved into the little spare bedroom. They talked about farming, about Hotay and the goats, about the bees. Weeding beside him she smelled his dirt-tinged sweat and the private, close scents of skin and hair. Beck loved farming, he said. No better life, he claimed, than to wake up every day where roosters crowed and fields grew food. He didn't need anything else, he lied. One morning he slipped uninvited into her bed. She woke up and found him there.

"Beck?"

He was naked, not touching her, just there, beside her in bed. Pushing up to her elbows, she saw his eyes were open, his lips parted. A quick heartbeat thrummed in his jaw. Though not a virgin, her sexual experience was limited to clumsy tumbles in dorm rooms during parties and nights grappling with men she didn't love, segueing to early-morning confused bus rides home before they woke up. That first time with Beck was the template. She went to bed alone and slept alone, and woke up to find him either there, to her delight, or not there, to her damp and desirous chagrin. Out in the fields they talked about gardening, farming, beekeeping, but never about sex, and they both shied away from public displays of affection. In retrospect Melissa guessed they were hiding their affair, and wondered why that had been so. Maybe because she was the boss and he was her employee, which she knew was vaguely uncool.

It was a perfect arrangement. Then he left. And now, for some reason, he was back.

She pulled weeds with a murderous vengeance, right hand manoeuvring a cultivator, left hand ripping roots free from soil and filling metal pails with limp, lifeless plants. She tried not to think about Beck, but the rhythm of her labour lent itself to a disgruntled refrain, *selfish, selfish, leaving the way he did.* At last the weeding process worked its therapy, and her mood shifted from the jangled dissonance of a jazz drum solo to stuttered acceptance, a classical guitar arpeggio.

Daphne tromped over from the animal enclosures in a pair of battered leather boots. She was ready to weed, armed with a hoe and two more pails.

"No sign of him yet," Daphne said. "Maybe he won't show up."

"I'm not holding my breath. If and when he does, it's Hopetown Farm, not Hopetown Hostel. I'm serious, I'm sending him packing."

Melissa smacked the metal cultivator tines into a fresh patch of weeds. A startled black beetle scurried away, escaping the sudden destruction of its green gazebo. Daphne fell in beside her, and Melissa relished the comforting repetitiveness of their actions, an age-old agricultural camaraderie, two women tilling together. The sun shimmered, toasting air that was alive with the whirrs, chirps, buzzes and swishes of a hundred thousand tiny creatures. A garter snake whispered past dry stalks. The earth spun on its axis, light slanting from a different angle each minute.

Morning became afternoon. Daphne, who kept checking, was the first to spot Beck. In Melissa's peripheral vision she saw him too: a tall silhouette, black hair tumbling to his shoulders, the ropy muscle and sinew of his arms dangling from loose shirt sleeves. He stood in the shade of the house, looking out over rows of vegetables. He didn't wave.

"He's here," Daphne announced.

"I know."

Melissa didn't break her weeding rhythm or acknowledge Beck. The work and the sunhat prevented her from succumbing to an overwhelming urge to puff and tuck.

Two

A large housefly came to life and rammed the front window. The repeated impact of insect body against glass made Beck wince. The fly seemed to be the cabin's only other occupant, though there were sure to be spiders lurking in the corners. Flimsy walls and duct-taped screens answered none of Beck's whispered questions. Signs of the cabin's other occasional inhabitants were forsaken and dated; a shrivelled tea bag in a tarnished tablespoon beside the sink smelled of mint, his mother's favourite; on the bricks-and-boards shelf, an Ursula K. LeGuin paperback, spine cracked and cover faded, had evidently been abandoned by his father mid-read.

Beck's ma and pa rose like monoliths in his mind.

In day-to-day life Beck's mother, Eurydice de Famosa, was intense but taciturn; her large brown eyes could deliver searing, scathing disapproval in a brief glare, or melt into chocolate pools of compassionate love. Eurydice, farmer and mother, was also santera, a high priestess of Santeria. In Canada she kept this esoteric vocation mostly veiled, but in Cuba, she was a front-line responder to urgent matters of the spirit. Neighbours would call her in an hour of need – cancer, gambling debt, unwanted pregnancy – and Ma would hurry to gather sticks, bones, shells and oils, and set off to intervene. Whatever the problem, it was sure to be more manageable after a visit from Eurydice de Famosa; her instincts were uncanny and her intuition bordered on clairvoyance.

Those who witnessed Beck's mother as santera, a medium between the mortal and the sacred, never forgot the experience. Beck's Cuban peers kept him outside their inner circle, a social avoidance that bordered on fear, as if his mother's ability to penetrate to the core of predicaments encompassed him. One time Jorge Torrenos, the best forward in the empty-lot pickup football gang, witnessed Beck's mother channel the Orishas in his aunt's kitchen, and for a week afterwards, until his shock dimmed, Jorge wouldn't pass Beck the ball with its scuffed pentagonal pattern, even when Beck signalled madly that he had a clean shot on goal.

Passive and slow to anger, Beck's pa had his own brand of intensity, a slow-boil stubbornness he employed to outlast his wife's more volatile moods. Matthew Wise was a professional photographer, a man preoccupied with minutiae, the details of capturing images, light and shadow, composition and frame. During Hurricane Ernesto, while the neighbours shrieked and ran around flapping like chased chickens, Beck's father had wandered outside with a waterproof telephoto lens and snapped pictures of airborne laundry, flooding streets, crumbling plaster and arcs of electricity where exposed wires had fallen into pond-sized puddles. Peering from between drenched curtains slapping at the walls, Beck had admired his father's soft yellow aura, the calm disposition that protected him from both hurricane and hysteria. Son grew to resemble father in this respect; Beck was often tranquil, content to observe, easily engrossed in the way sun played in strands of hair, or the progress of a caterpillar on a sidewalk.

As a child Beck had appeared and disappeared, popping in and out of countries at the mercy of his parents' travel plans, a rabbit-and-hat lifestyle that set him apart from his companions with their stable homes and predictable lives. No matter what month was displayed on the calendar, when his parents felt like going to Cuba they would pack up and leave, neglecting to inform anyone, including his elementary school. In Toronto the guidance counselling staff would scramble to find Beckett Wise, leaving desperate phone messages and once, when he was nine, even contacting the police. His Cuban school administrators were more relaxed and worldly-wise, but on semester breaks, bicycles would skid up to the dusty football pitch, and one player would be missing. Beck, the Incredible Disappearing Weirdo, was somewhere over the continental United States, on a flight to Toronto.

Beck was in the cabin. It seemed to be early autumn. He knew who he was, and where he'd come from, but the rest – missing months, absence of his parents, humming half-memories – was a riddle. He ate a can of stew gleaned from a disused drawer, and fell asleep.

In the morning Beck found himself at the farm, fingers trembling and heart tripping along too quickly, as if it remembered another rhythm. His feet had walked there from the cabin without consulting him. *I was a bee colony.* Who would believe him – how could he explain? He had slipped sideways before, but this time he had disassembled and become something foreign, a vastly different living thing. There had been no language when he was ten thousand letters of a wordless whole. And now, inexplicably back inside his mortal coil, he had forgotten how to speak.

Beck stood in the shade of the farmhouse, experiencing his body as a tight, single entity. He cringed at the sight of Melissa's rangy form in the fields. Why had he come? This was where it had begun, the process of – molecularization? There wasn't a vocabulary for what had happened to him; or if there was, he didn't know it. He had felt complete, as a colony, but scattered along invisible bee-lines. Becoming human again was like stuffing the thousand thousand parts of him into a skin bag.

Keeping bees on the farm had been Melissa's idea. Her father had abandoned the farm's beehives when he left, and she had asked Beck to bring them back to life. *Why not*? Beekeeping was quirky, a bit weird, a good fit for him. There was a Beekeepers' Society in Almonte, he found out, a short drive from the farm, and they held monthly meetings at the Lions Hall. Beck started attending, listened, asked questions. About a dozen beekeepers showed up for each meeting, two or three commercial honey farmers and the rest hobbyists. At first he took all their advice – not visiting the bees on stormy or rainy days, for instance, because the experts said bees were grumpy then.

The first time Beck opened a hive, the buzzing sounded hostile, but after a while the persistent drone of bee activity became welcoming, an invitation. He realized he was a benign presence to them. One day he thought, *We're friends. I'm friends with these bees.* He wanted to be with them every day, rain or shine. Half an hour a day with the bees turned into two hours, then four. He tapped into their collective brain, contemplating the complexity of the colony. They were marvellous, each bee a single cell in a hive-body, spread out over space. *How amazing is that?* Everything about honeybees fascinated him: the way they constructed perfect hexagonal architecture, sweet-smelling, bright yellow comb. How they collected ingredients and made stiff, sticky propolis to glue their hive together and protect it. They even grew their own leadership with royal jelly, a white elixir that transformed a standard, plebeian larva into a queen.

And honey. Oh, the honey, tingling on his tongue, sending shivers through his human cells. He ate it at every meal. He kept a jar handy, indulging in little spoonfuls throughout the day. He drizzled honey on Melissa's naked body, amber beads along her clavicles, a sticky line from navel to pubic bone, and then licked her clean.

After a while, he stopped zipping himself into the protective white shell of his bee suit. Why bother? They were friends, he and the bees, and he had faith they wouldn't sting him. It was the same with all animals. Put out calm and loving energy, and that was what came back. He wore a hat and veil for a while longer, then put those aside as well. He moved slowly, breathed deeply. He felt serene when he was with the bees, and they never stung him.

Marjorie Hill thought he was nuts. Beck met her at the Beekeepers' Society meetings. A feisty seventy-something woman, she had kept bees most of her life. She wore her long white hair in two loose braids flopping over pierced ears. Her wrinkled skin glowed, and her eyes sparkled. She was tiny; standing erect, the part in her pale hair barely reached his shoulder. The creases on her face were deepest at the corners of her mouth, parentheses enclosing a lifetime of smiles, he guessed. One evening after a meeting she tugged the sleeve of his jacket.

"They'll know if you're anxious, upset, distant – the bees always know. Go to the hives with your mind, body and spirit, or don't go at all. Why don't you come visit me and my hives?"

She lived close to his family's cabin, Beck was surprised to discover, less than a kilometre away, along the same road. In fact, it was astonishing – she was their neighbour! She had been there all the summers as he'd grown up, putzing on her property and keeping to herself, and he had never known her. Her house was a century old, a funny little wooden box.

Inside, it was modest and a little bit rundown, what you might expect from the country home of an elderly person living alone. The front door opened into a sitting room full of old but elegant polished-mahogany furniture, and lots of mismatched pillows. A faded pink sofa featured antimacassars hand-embroidered with bees. She hustled him through this room and to the right, into her untidy kitchen, toast crumbs on the counter and a leaning pile of dishes. They drank a glass of water together before heading out to the bee yard, tapping a toast, *clink-clink, to the bees*!

Marjorie was a consummate beekeeper. Beck could tell by her hives; fresh white- and yellow-painted Langstroth high-rises gleamed in the sun, and flat grassy paths led to each stack of boxes. They suited up and went in. She used her bee tool to lever open the closest hive, removed a frame and held it up to the sun. It was bursting with healthy comb and covered with bees.

"Doesn't it bother them, when you hold the frame like that?"

"They don't care. They're focused on getting their jobs done."

"I get it." He tried to sound nonchalant.

"You do, eh? Hmm. I wonder. A bee colony is a complex society. It isn't just a lot of bees doing different jobs. It's three different animals, made up of smaller animals."

"*Three* animals?"

"They're called zooids. A zooid is a group of individuals that act like they share a brain. In a bee colony, the zooids are the queen bee, the drones and the worker bees. The queen lays the eggs and gives the orders, pheromonally speaking. The workers do just that – all the work."

"The drones protect the hive, am I right?"

"No, you're wrong. The *workers* protect the hive. The drones, the only males, are harmless, and very nearly useless. They have only one job, but it's important. Their only raison d'être is sperm donation. The drones fertilize the queen, and they do it all in one night. High above the hive, in a wild bee orgy called the nuptial flight. The queen gets all the sperm she needs, for the rest of her life, in that one big gangbang in the sky."

Beck blushed, a rarity for him. An old lady was schooling him on bee sex.

He met her twinkling eyes directly, and they burst out laughing. The rest of the afternoon, she opened his bee-eyes. He learned how to locate a queen bee, and how to use a smoker – *sparingly* – to pacify honeybees. Marjorie knew the history of the boxy Langstroth hives almost everyone used, with their space allowances of precisely one bee-body between frames. By the end of the afternoon his head was reeling with bee facts: propolis, queen excluders, centrifugal extractors, *Varroa* mites, American foulbrood. She backed up her lessons with hands-on demonstrations. That one afternoon in Marjorie's bee yard gave him the confidence he needed to begin keeping bees.

Weeks later, Beck visited Marjorie to brag about his progress. He told her he'd stopped wearing his bee suit, and she was miffed.

"Why would you do that? You might not be allergic, but that doesn't mean the stings are beneficial."

"I don't get stung."

"Oh, the hubris! Well, I'm not going to try to convince you. Experience will be your teacher. Who is stronger, Beck, you or Mother Nature?"

He shrugged this off and proved his theory. Even-tempered by nature, he calmed himself further before approaching the hives, meditating until he was in a sort of bee-trance. He moved slowly, and was careful to never crush or compromise a bee. The happy hum of their buzzing got inside him. It was a frequency he could physically sense, a light vibration all over the surface of his skin. Some days the effect was sexual. Beck felt himself getting turned on, riding a wave of arousal.

Signs of trouble in a hive brought him back into focus, his erection dwindling. Not every larva pupated perfectly. Occasionally he would spot a pale bee missing half a wing, one composite eye askew on her fuzzy little head: damage from *Varroa destructor* mites. There were many other bee perils, but the Hopetown Farm hives were mostly healthy while he was their keeper. He kept a vigilant watch for wasps, which could invade hives, kill bees and take over the space. An electric fence kept skunks, badgers and bears from knocking over the stacked wooden boxes to feast on brood and honey.

In the news, Beck read about a sinister honeybee plague. Entire colonies were disappearing without a trace. No piles of bee corpses, no predator. The bees simply vanished – there one day, gone the next.

"What do you think causes it?" he asked Marjorie. She had come to show him how to uncap a full frame of honey. They were standing shoulder to shoulder in the outbuilding where the farm's extraction equipment, some of it purchased secondhand from Marjorie herself, was kept. She ran the edge of a heated knife along capped cells, exposing the precious honey inside.

"People. Greed. Pass me that metal pan beside you. I'll save this wax and make candles with it this winter."

Hopetown Farm honeybees harvested nectar in fields of natural wildflowers and spray-free crops; statistically, they had a better chance of survival than bees that pollinated factory farms. The beehives were important to Melissa and to her mother, Jill. But Joseph, the grouchy bachelor who squatted in his trailer at the edge of the farm, disliked the bees, and claimed honey-sale returns weren't high enough to justify the labour and investment in beekeeping. He was slouching beside the electric fence one day when Beck was showing Melissa – okay, showing *off* – a full frame of honey.

"Makes no sense. You're wasting your mom's hard-earned money, Lissy."

"Let Beck take care of the bees, Joseph, and stop worrying."

Joseph sauntered away, shaking his head. Beck, disturbed, watched the farmhand leave.

"That guy bothers me."

"Joseph? Don't pay any attention to him. He likes to complain about everything."

Winter arrived. Reluctantly, Beck insulated the hives, stapling cardboard and tarpaper in place, entombing his best friends. Spring seemed a long time away. Compensating for the loss of the bees' company, he borrowed library books and read everything he could about bees. He watched videos about honeybees, and ate more honey than ever. Melissa was relaxed when there was snow on the ground; they went cross-country skiing together, shared blankets in front of the fireplace and had copious bouts of great sex.

One night in January, he woke up shivering. He had been tossing and turning, fending off a nightmare, and his blankets had migrated to the floor. Fuzzy, half-conscious, he stumbled to Melissa's room and climbed into the warmth of her bed. He woke up at dawn to Melissa gently shaking his shoulder.

"Beck, you're *buzzing.*"

"What?"

"You're buzzing. Making buzzing noises, like a swarm of bees."

"My snores sound like bees?"

"No, you're making a buzzy sound, like a beehive."

He rolled over to face her, surfacing from dark dream-tunnels.

"Really? I was dreaming about bees. Sorry."

"It's okay, never mind."

She kissed him softly, then harder, and he re-entered his body.

There were just four of them on the pared-down staff that winter; himself, Melissa, Daphne and Joseph. At breakfast the morning after he buzzed, Beck watched the others stuff themselves with scrambled eggs, toast and jam. His own appetite was missing, and he wondered if he were getting sick with the flu. He was afraid Melissa might tell the story about him buzzing in his sleep, but she didn't. A fine, needle-like snow blew outside the windows, sweeping in horizontally from the northwest. The farmhouse seemed bleak and forlorn. They had boxed up the Christmas decorations, denuded walls and banisters of glitter and greenery. The women planned to bake that day, and Joseph trudged outside, grunting about fixing a fence. For some reason, Beck desperately wanted to press his ear against a hive, but he was self-conscious. He didn't want anyone to ask him what the hell he was doing in the bee yard in the dead of winter. He went to Hotay's shed instead.

Hotay was good company, better than Jeffrey and Edna. Melissa kept Hotay to protect the chickens. Donkeys were supposed to keep coyotes and wolves away, braying and kicking when canines came near. "I couldn't have buzzed," Beck whispered in Hotay's long, furry ear, and the donkey nuzzled him placidly, batting long eyelashes and looking like the star attraction at a petting zoo. Hefting hay into the goat and donkey stalls, all Beck could think about was the bees. He kept glancing at the hives, snugly packed in sheets of black, waxed cardboard. He conjured up the smell of sun-warmed grass mixed with deep yellow wax, and listened to an internal soundtrack of the bees' incessant hum. He missed them way too much. It was shocking how much he thought about them. But he couldn't stop.

Beck began to hibernate, sleeping twelve, thirteen, fourteen hours a night. Melissa thought he was sick. He still slept in the small bedroom, telling Melissa he slept better alone, but in fact he was having bee-dreams. *What if I buzz in my sleep again?*

Spring arrived at last. He pulled winter wrappings from hives and the bees were alive – healthy activity in every colony. Beck was much more than relieved. He was inordinately delighted, proud the bees had survived the winter, the way a parent is proud of their kid's most mundane achievements: riding a bicycle, eating all their vegetables. He visited Marjorie, who indulged his desire to talk about beekeeping exclusively.

"Try some of this honey." She extended a wizened hand holding an old-fashioned silver tablespoon, filled to its edges with dark orange honey. He closed his eyes and accepted her offering. It tasted odd, not wholly sweet, as honey should be, as if it were infused with a savoury spice. It was thick and difficult to swallow.

"It's called deli bal, and it's good medicine," Marjorie told him. "It was discovered in the hives of bees kept far from here, in Asia. This honey has power, boy, let me tell you. It's a tonic, full of vitamins. You should have a spoonful every time you visit me. Now, come see what a full frame of brood looks like."

Beck wanted to be with the bees all the time, and he started resenting his other chores. In May he got sneaky. He sought out Daphne and found her alone, cheerfully sweeping the henhouse steps in a hemp dress and cowboy boots, her hair a magnificent corona. He hated taking advantage of her good nature, but, obsessed, he did it anyway.

"Hey, Beck, what's up?"

"I'm so busy in the bee yard. Do you mind taking over Hotay and the goats until I get the hives settled?" he lied, which didn't feel good, and his father's lectures about values rang in his ears. He believed in the vital importance of honesty and integrity, but he was an addict, and the bees were his illicit drug.

"Sure, I'll manage the animals. As long as there's heaps of honey."

Beck should have run the scheduling change past Melissa, but Daphne said yes, and then his days were free to spend entirely with the bees. He cleaned surfaces, repainted supers, melted wax, washed jars. He sat with the bees, he stared at the bees.

"Bee-brain," Melissa called him one day, a new term of endearment Daphne had coined. "I'm working on a fresh design for our honey jar labels. If the crop is as big as you're projecting, we'll be looking at a wider market."

But Beck didn't chaperone the bees as they made that season's honey. He *became* the bees.

In the days before it happened, his skin vibrated around the clock. He was lost in a reverie, imagining the inside of a hive, dark and busy, fuzzy bodies brushing up against each other, wordless signals arriving from every direction. In waking dreams he burrowed into flowers. Surrounded by petals, stamen tickled his abdomen. He felt what it was to fly, winged and weightless, navigating breezes. He could imagine all these things *simultaneously*. It occurred to Beck that he might have a mental illness, some type of entomological schizophrenia. Fear stopped him from admitting this to anyone. The night before he changed, he packed a knapsack full of clothes and a few toiletries and essentials. He rummaged in the office for a scrap of paper and pencil and wrote Melissa a hasty note. *M, gone to the cabin, hives are fine. I'll be back, B.* He folded the paper over once, tucked it under the computer keyboard and walked the quarter-hour to his parents' cabin. Instinct told him he needed to be alone for some biological process, the way a mother cat finds some secret, quiet place to give birth to her kittens. Beck knew he could slip away. Early summer was busy on the farm; everyone worked long, sweaty days from dawn until sunset and fell into bed exhausted at night. Farm visitors peaked then too – people coming and going, buying produce, petting Hotay and the goats. Melissa was distracted; she had an old school friend camped out in her bedroom.

Beck stretched out on one of three single beds in the cabin, with its scratchy wool blanket and musty-smelling pillow. The sense of wriggling underneath his skin was unbearably strange. Flopping on the bed, he tried to focus on a remedy for his symptoms, but he couldn't think clearly. Bee-thoughts took over his brain. There was a droning in his ears, and then the only sensation was his skin's vibration, a crawling inside and everywhere, as if, as though –

My body is made of bees.

It was the last human thought he had. He took his first flight, hovering three feet above the grass, weaving around tree trunks, wending his way to a new reality. He was compelled by a bee so majestic, so imperious, he knew that it was *She*, his Queen, leading him to the hive. A blink of darkness, and he was inside the comb itself, dense warm air, closeness of hairy bodies, wings whirring in sticky proximity. Then he knew nothing but bees, until a few days ago, when he woke up whole and human, on the same bed where he'd disassembled.

His legs had led him here, to Melissa. Squinting, he could see her long body out there in the field beside Daphne's, two women stooping and straightening, a harvest ballet. It felt right to be there, but what if Melissa asked him to go back to beekeeping? *Oh, God*. He couldn't do it, he couldn't keep bees, not now, and maybe never again. He couldn't risk being sucked into that vortex. He gagged, and tasted a mixture of honey and bile. A crazed desperation came over him. He was a frog prince, and he needed Melissa to kiss him, to break the curse and make him mortal. He wanted to work hard, have robust sex and sleep solidly through the night.

But Melissa could be brutal. Her hard edge had seemed like strength when he first got to know her; she said what she meant, no hints or innuendos, and she could hire and fire employees without sentiment cluttering up her decisions. Later, after they had been lovers for a while, that same ability to be harsh and impersonal had struck him as bitchy. He tried to get her to open up about her father, who had walked out on her and her mother, but she shut him down. She never wanted to hear about his messed-up childhood either. They never clung to each other and revealed their deepest longings, their darkest fears. He had told himself, back then, that her defences were high. He knew what had happened when he disappeared; he could guess easily enough. She had thickened up her already tough carapace and gotten on with the only thing that really mattered to her: operating the farm. He had become another disappointment in the long line of people who had failed to meet her standards.

What had happened – where had he been? Melissa would demand to know. She was walking toward him, proud shoulders pulled back, brown limbs swaying fiercely, green eyes flickering, dangerous.

Three

He was a shadow against the stone wall, like a jagged crevice working its way up from the ground. As Melissa approached, his edges didn't sharpen; by some trick of the late afternoon light he flitted between there and not there. She picked up speed, her footfalls dragging just behind her rapid heartbeat. She was pleased and outraged to see him, and this internal bluster fuelled her like coal in a steam train boiler.

"I don't know why you're here, but I'm busy."

She walked right past Beck into the farmhouse, the screen door slamming behind her. Anger crackled along her arms and burned in her belly. In her revenge fantasies about Beck's return he was more handsome than real life – his dark hair rippling, a gloss on his skin, shoulders broad – and she kicked him off the farm before she weakened. She had never pictured a pathetic, sickly simulacrum. From the kitchen she watched Beck look vacantly across the fields, his posture tense and awkward. She filled two bottles of water and stormed outside.

"Are you just going to stand there?"

"My legs are tired."

"So you've been, what, *walking* all summer? Never mind, forget I asked, I don't want to know. It's probably a long story. A lot can happen in three months, and as usual, we're behind with the weeding."

He didn't say anything, which quickly got creepy. He blinked. His eyes were flat, unfocused. She had never seen him pale but he was. His skin was ochre, fading to green around his eyes and mouth.

"You look terrible, like you need a sandwich and a nap." She softened.

"Eat a sandwich and take a nap. You can tell us what happened over dinner. My birthday dinner, actually."

He stared at her, uncomprehending, as if she were speaking a foreign language. The date itself, September 14, seemed to shock him. She had the distinct impression he hadn't known what month it was, never mind what day, and that he remembered when her birthday fell but was incapable of assimilating the fact that it was that day. Inside Melissa, a summer's worth of anger was dissolving like sugar in tea. Her fantasies of throwing Beck out were wrecked by his glassy eyes and wretched bearing; he was a scarecrow, propped up by his bones. She touched his hand lightly with her fingertips. Heart thumping, she strained against indulging her tics. *I will not puff and tuck.*

"I'll see you later, Beck."

She rejoined Daphne in the fields. "It's a zombie version of Beck."

"Come on, I can't stand the suspense – where did he go? Did the aliens that abducted him beam him back down, or what?" Daphne was bouncing, jigging her shoulders up and down, a dance she performed when her body couldn't contain her enthusiasm.

"We'll find out tonight." Melissa pursed her lips and shrugged.

After work, she found him fast asleep on her bed. The sight of him there, stretched out where they used to sleep together, enraged her. She wanted to shout: *What the hell*? But she had told him to take a nap, and she hadn't specified where. He was gaunt, skin stretched over the fine framework of his skull, ribs poking through his shirt. His breaths were long and calm. There was something convalescent about him; he was sleeping like an influenza patient whose sweaty fever had broken at last. She stripped off her dusty farm clothes, aware of her naked body's proximity to Beck but quite certain he wouldn't wake. She showered, and when she came back to her room wrapped in a towel he hadn't moved. His breathing was so quiet she wondered if it had stopped entirely, and she leaned in close to him. He smelled sweet, like hay and fresh air. Her wet hair dripped on his cheek and he stirred. She leapt away as if she'd been electrocuted, grabbed a shirt and shorts, and went to the bathroom to get dressed.

In the bathroom, she found herself in the mirror. The woman staring back at her was flushed, her eyes flashing, pupils dilated. She evaluated her physical attributes and sex appeal while simultaneously setting her jaw like a boxer getting pumped to fight. Melissa thought she knew the woman in the mirror's upheaval. She was conflicted, confronted with a lover she still loved. But what did she want? Melissa gritted her teeth and turned away from her reflection, disappointed in herself. She had tried to leave Beck behind. Over the course of the summer she had slept with a couple of men – clumsy sexual wrestling marked by pinched skin and barnyard grunting. She had slept with a woman too, a pleasurable erotic experiment but ultimately as unfulfilling as the hetero sex. These encounters were pale imitations of what she had enjoyed with Beck, their easy friendship, their smooth and intuitive coupling.

Beck slept through the pinging and clanging of meal preparation, Daphne's raucous laughter and the racket of Joseph's diesel truck pulling up beside the house. Daphne couldn't wait to tell Joseph the news, and shimmied while she spoke.

"Joe, guess who's back? The prodigal beekeeper!"

Joseph's lip curled. He scratched stubble on his chin, three days' worth of beard growth, and his frown lines deepened. His fingers were tobacco-stained a hepatic brownish yellow. His displeasure was palpable, a silent, acrid condemnation stealing the freshness from the air. He scraped a chair out from the dining table and placed his fists on either side of a place setting. Melissa felt a prickle of irritation. What right did Joseph have to judge Beck, who worked hard, and who had sinned, in Joseph's opinion, not by abandoning her romantically, but by leaving the labour of the beehives behind? She opened her mouth to defend Beck's reappearance and instead she exhaled hard, puffed three times at her loose hair and tucked it firmly behind her ears. *Fuck.*

Melissa helped herself to a plate of food and Daphne followed, serving up both herself and Joseph. The kitchen opened into the dining room via an inside window, a renovation Melissa's father had effected to brighten and modernize the old farmhouse. They joined Joseph at the table and he acknowledged the meal Daphne placed in front of him with a grumpy nod.

"You should be happy Beck's back," Melissa told Joseph. "Maybe he'll start working in the bee yard again. Don't you remember how obsessed he was with the bees?"

"What was that – did you guys hear that?" Daphne's hand hung suspended in midair; a forkful of curry halfway to her mouth fell with a *plop* to her plate. "There's something in the hallway."

Beck shuffled tentatively from shadows into the muted post-sunset glow of the dining room. His nap hadn't healed him; he was pale, translucent, a hologram. A thin white T-shirt hung from muscle and bone. The frayed bottoms of his jeans and dirty, bare feet suggested homelessness, poverty, desperation. Awkward silence, a hiccup in time. Daphne was the first to recover.

"You hungry, Beck? You look starved. Get yourself a plate of this curry and help yourself to the salad too."

"Then sit your ass down and tell us where the hell you've been," said Joseph.

"Relax, Joe. He can tell us when he's ready," said Daphne.

"I can't," Beck said, staring at Melissa. "I don't know."

Melissa felt blood surge to her brain, and the pain-flash of a headache exploded behind her left eye. "For three months? For the whole summer, you don't know where you were?"

"Let the guy eat his dinner before we interrogate him." Daphne smiled gently at Beck.

"Thank you," Beck whispered, and he walked slowly and deliberately to the kitchen.

Light clunks and pings came from the pots and pans while Beck served himself. Around the table they stared at each other, struck dumb. *He doesn't know*? Melissa mouthed at Daphne, raising her hands and wrinkling her nose, incredulous. Her headache throbbed. She watched Beck enter the dining room, balancing a heaping plate and glancing at her guiltily. He sat down and began to eat, slowly at first, then with increasing appetite, until he was desperately scooping up the food. Gradually everyone else started eating again. The clink of utensils scraping on dishes became the only sound in the room. As if to fill the void, the chirping of crickets on the lawn outside the window amplified. Daphne began humming "Hotel California."

"Surprised to see you again, Beck," said Joseph at last.

"Good to be back." Beck spoke around the food in his mouth. He chewed cautiously, as if protecting fresh dental work.

"When you left, you didn't tell anyone you were going," Joseph persisted.

"I didn't know I was leaving, so how could I tell anyone?"

A hot flush of temper rose up Melissa's neck and invaded her face, like mercury in a thermometer. Oblivious, Beck lowered his head to make the feeding process more economical. He ate, and she searched for words to wrap around her annoyance. She put her fork down carefully and addressed him.

"Well, that *is* strange. If you didn't know you were leaving, how do you explain the bag you packed and the note you wrote on the night you left?"

Beck sat up straight and met Melissa's simmering anger with placid matter-of-factness. "What happened was, I was feeling off, so I decided to go to my parents' cabin for a few days. I thought I was getting sick or something. I even thought I might be *losing my mind*." He twirled a finger beside an ear, indicating the kind of crazy he thought he might have been, and smiled hesitantly, looking at each of them in turn, a vulnerable plea in his eyes.

HEE HAW! HEE HAW! HEE HAW! Hotay brayed loudly in his enclosure beside the garden, and still night air carried the bestial mocking into the dining room. Daphne snorted, which set Melissa off, and they laughed while Beck and Joseph watched them soberly.

"But see, you gotta know where you were," said Daphne, becoming serious. "Beck, buddy, you've been gone since the beginning of summer."

Joseph stabbed stormily at the last pieces of yellow potato on his plate, crammed them in his mouth and pushed back from the table.

"'Course he knows. Doesn't have the guts to say. Man up, Beck. And it's honey harvest soon, so get back to them bees. I've had my fill of the evil little beasts."

At the mention of bees, Beck flinched. Joseph wiped his fingers with his serviette, balled it up and dropped it on his plate in disgust. He slammed the back door as he left. Daphne excused herself and went to the kitchen with a stack of dirty plates, popping her eyes at Melissa behind Beck's back.

Melissa glared at Beck stonily. He lowered his eyes. Joseph was right; Beck wasn't telling the truth. What was so terrible that he couldn't tell her? Her mind leapt about, guessing at what Beck might want to hide. The answer, when she thought of it, deflated her. It was sexual. It had to be. An affair with another woman. Or he had become tired of sleeping with her, and hadn't been able to find a gracious way out of their entanglement. His embarrassment was all she needed to confirm her suspicions. The diffuse dining room light pulsed in her vision, and the headache blossomed into pain pyrotechnics behind both eyes.

"I need air."

The front porch was dark, cool and quiet. Melissa curled up in a familiar place, on lumpy pillows stuffed in the corners of a wicker couch. She tucked feet under legs, and hugged herself against a crisp breeze wafting up from Bow Lake. In a few minutes her headache seeped away, diluted by the serene evening atmosphere. A waxing moon cast pale blue light; clumps of white daisies and sprays of nicotiana glowed like old-fashioned photo negatives. Eyes adjusting, she saw the yard was rustling with nocturnal activity. A fluffy grey cat, one of many unnamed feral mousers, slunk across the yard in a hunting crouch. Bats flitted around the maple trees. The cat disappeared into the blackness of a tree well. Moths fluttered in soft amber electric light spreading from the windows. The hedge bordering the road was like a castle fortification, in its centre a gap, a path of brightness, a drawbridge to the world beyond. It was the place she watched for her father to reappear. What kind of advice would he have for his daughter, her Romeo returned in an altered state, confused and compromised? Melissa guessed her father would counsel patience, kindness and tolerance – things they hadn't given him, absences that had driven him away.

Melissa shivered and wrapped her arms tighter around her breasts. She and Beck had come together slowly, held separate by force fields of caution. Even after they were lovers, they had kept a safe wedge of mystery between them. He was guarded about his past. She hated talking about hers too. They had been capable of long silences. Minimal conversation, Melissa now realized, meant she didn't know as much about him as she should. Maybe there were clues in his childhood, hints of what kind of person he truly was. In the privacy of the dark porch, she searched her head and heart for what she knew for sure about Beck.

It must have been a strange upbringing, the only child of eccentric parents who lived in Cuba for part of the year, returning to Toronto, and later their Lanark County cottage, when it suited them, usually in summer. Melissa was wary of his mother. Eurydice often brooded, engaging in unselfconscious, quiet conversation with herself; she could also swiftly become wild-eyed and segue into vehement, rapid-fire Spanish. She dressed with a Caribbean flair for bright colours and bold prints and wore her hair in a vertiginous topknot. His father was a photographer, a keen observer of people and places. Matthew Wise's work hung in a gallery in nearby Almonte. Melissa was impressed by the contrast between the mild-mannered, introspective artist and the harrowing images he captured, like haggard expressions of bereaved revolutionaries and wreckage left by hurricanes. *Pa's a voyeuristic adrenaline junkie*, son assessed father. Beck had been a loner at schools in both Canada and Cuba – "a weirdo," he said – but he had gotten good grades, and played competitive soccer. He enjoyed playing guitar, farming and keeping bees. Melissa smacked her forehead with her palm. Who was Beck, and what the hell had they talked about? Had she been using him for sex, her personal gigolo? No wonder he left; their relationship was as shallow as a carrot-seed furrow.

The front doors of the farmhouse opened and spilled a rectangular carpet of light onto the lawn. Beck padded out barefoot and closed the doors gently, pitching the porch back into silver semi-darkness. He sat on the other end of the couch and stared into the night, his black eyes insect-wide, reflecting pale half-circles and pinpoints, moon and stars. Melissa wanted to stay angry with him. She wanted to shout at him for leaving, then coming back to lie about it. But she also wanted him to put his arms around her, nuzzle her hair, cover her hands with his and press unspoken promises that he would stay into her flesh.

"Do you remember when I first told you about the waggle dance?" he asked.

It was a strange question, but she remembered. She accessed the memory whole, like the plot of a favourite movie. It was another summer night, a starry one. Holding hands, they had gone for a walk along the gravel road, heading south, away from Lanark, warm wind like tender fingers brushing their skin. An owl had swooped over fields beside the road, sound of its soft hoot, glimpse of its flat, menacing white face. A childish euphoria had engulfed Melissa, and impulsively she had pulled Beck close, hummed an invented waltz and entreated him to dance. She had worn a soft, pale green cotton dress, she remembered, he a hippie shirt and baggy hemp pants. In shadows they could have been dressed for a formal event. Sandal-shod feet had crunched on a makeshift ballroom floor. Beck had gotten into it, taken up the melody, spun her around. The dance had ended with a passionate kiss.

"Honeybees dance, you know," Beck had said.

"Sure, they do."

"You've never heard of the waggle dance?"

"*Waggle* dance? Now I know you're fibbing."

"Well, I'm not. It's how the worker bees tell each other about juicy patches of nectar. They orient their bodies in relation to the sun. They point their hairy little butts however many degrees left or right of the sun's position a bee would need to turn herself, to fly out and find a feast of flowers."

"That's not dancing, that's rotating."

"I'm not *finished*. The dancing bee waggles her hind section super fast, and moves in a figure eight. The length of the dance is in direct proportion to how far the nectar motherlode is found."

"I've never heard of dancing bees."

"There are more things in heaven and hell than are dreamed of in your philosophy. Mine too. Now get this: let's say that it's been a couple of hours since the dancing bee has been to the flowers, but she still wants to tell everyone about it. She actually *corrects* the angle of her dance for the rotation of the Earth."

Melissa remembered the night she had learned about bee dances. After their walk they had made love, half dressed, her green dress bunched around her waist, his hemp pants dangling from one ankle. Back in the present on the porch, she grunted an assent, and curled up tighter in her corner of the couch, drawing her knees to her chest, defending herself against Beck's dishonesty.

"You didn't believe me at first," Beck said.

"That's right, I didn't. What's your point?" she snapped.

"If I tell you, will you keep it just between us?"

"Where you were this summer is a secret?" Her voice cracked on the last word.

"Humour me for a minute."

He sat motionless, holding himself steady with his arms, as if a light breeze might topple him. Melissa exhaled hard, and assented with a brief downward jerk of her head. Beck addressed the lawn.

"I woke up in the cabin the other day and I didn't know where I'd been. My brain felt foggy, like I had a bad hangover, and I had these – snatches, impressions. And they were kind of terrifying. Like when you wake up from a nightmare. And the whole nightmare was based on . . ." Beck glanced at her and stopped talking. He swallowed with difficulty.

"My patience is blade-thin right now," Melissa warned.

"On being a bee colony," he said in a rush. "Like I was inside a beehive, and I was the whole colony. Thousands of workers, hundreds of drones."

"Go on. I'm listening." Her dinner curdled in her stomach. Beck spoke mechanically and miserably, like he was being forced at gunpoint to recite a story he hated.

"And larvae too, always cycling. Older bees dying, larvae hatching, just like the cells in your body. I dreamed there was a voice in my head, a woman's voice, narrating everything I did. I can still hear her now." Beck shuddered.

"You woke up from a dream you were a beehive."

"No, no. I'm telling you, it feels like I *was* bees. A whole bee colony. Like all I did this summer was drink nectar, collect pollen, nurse the larvae, fan the hive, take care of my queen – I was *bees*."

Silence. Even the cicadas fell into a hush. Beck spoke softly into the night.

"Maybe I hit my head, and this is what it's like to have a brain injury? I mean, I guess I could have fallen off my bike, or been thrown from a moving vehicle. I guess I could be imagining bees because, well, you know how I used to think about them all the time. Bee-brain, right?" He laughed nervously. "But it doesn't feel like that. It feels real. I hear the queen's voice in my head, like the narrator in a documentary, talking between my ears. She orders me to send out workers, cap cells, nurse the baby bees and inspect the comb for imperfections. I can feel the brush of bristly forelegs and smell the comb. I can even feel myself throwing up nectar, disgorging honey." He put a hand to his throat. "I'm crazy, right? I must be nuts. Don't tell anyone. Please help me."

He was gaping blindly, blank, white-moon cataracts in his eyes. God, he wasn't lying – he was legitimately scared! He was hearing voices; he was psychotic. Weren't there drugs to treat this kind of thing? She could take him to the walk-in clinic in Lanark, get a referral to a specialist, hunt down a diagnosis and fix him. Melissa heard her mother's pep talk, urging her to action. *We can do it, Lissy. We can run the farm on our own.* Her lower lip jutted and before she could stop herself she sent three puffs of air to the hair around her face, then with three brisk tucks shoved strands behind her ears. Her tongue leapt to the back of her mouth and began its dance from tooth to tooth. While she spasmed, hoping Beck wasn't noticing, the cat darted from the tree well and bolted directly for the porch. It leapt noiselessly up the stairs, then switched gears and walked lazily toward the couch, its bushy brush-tail erect and waving. Winding itself sinuously around posts and chair legs, the cat gave Beck a wide berth and gravitated to Melissa. It lifted soft paw-pads to her knees, a mute request to gain access to her lap, and she unfolded her legs to accommodate the creature. The cat jumped up nimbly, circled twice and settled comfortably. A moment later it began to purr. She finished tongue-tooth-touching without Beck noticing her mouth gyrations and he turned to her, reached across the space between them and put an imploring hand on her shoulder. His touch was thrilling. Her cells responded to his warm fingers, screaming to her brain they wanted more, more, more.

"How can I help you?" she asked weakly.

"Let me come back. I can take care of Hotay, Jeffrey and Edna and the chickens. I'll work in the fields. It's harvest – you must need an extra body."

"But it's not that simple. Daphne works with all the livestock now; you'd be stepping on her toes. Joseph and I have everything else covered. Except for the bees. No one has time for the hives. Do you think you could –?"

Beck retracted his hand, shrinking from her as if she had slapped him. He stared into the night, consulting the shadowy trees, the flitting nocturnal creatures.

"No. Sorry, anything but bees."

The cat stood up, kneaded her lap with its paws, repositioned itself and settled again. The moonlight cast an ethereal aura around Beck's profile. There was an alienness about him. If a savage, pointy-toothed worm had suddenly burst from his chest cavity in a spray of blood, it would be a relief, in a way. An explanation. His hands were on his knees, palms curving over kneecaps, like a mannequin posed in a sitting position. An obscure fear gripped Melissa, and urgently she fought the urge to puff and tuck.

She had almost told him she loved him, before he left. Once or twice, the words had hovered on her lips. How much more devastating his betrayal would have been if she had breathed life into those words. *Turned into bees, sure.* She shook her head to clear it. The cat stopped purring.

"You know it's impossible, right? There's no way you were actually bees?"

"Where have I been, then? Did you call the hospitals when I didn't show up for work? Did you call my parents? I'm telling you, I don't know where I was."

In fact, Melissa conceded inwardly, she hadn't done much to find him. A crowd of excuses populated her thoughts – she had been caught up in farm business, she had had guests. There had been wide bowls of green salad peppered with nasturtiums to produce; she had been required to flip-flop down to the lake with towels and mason jars of lemonade. She had undertaken to rake chicken shit out of the henhouse, and make balaclavas to protect herself and Daphne from inhaling fine dust that rose up behind the tractor. She hadn't forgotten Beck, but she had assumed he would come back, as his little note had promised. Sure, he had packed a small bag, but his guitar was still at the farm, leaning up in a corner of the littlest bedroom. Books and clothes that belonged to him were stacked against the walls. His return had been a certainty, like the sun rising over the lake, or yellow dandelion heads popping out in spring. Beck would come back, of *course* he would come back – that's what she had believed, at first. A series of hectic planting days had turned into a week, and then two. The midsummer evening thunderstorms had arrived before she had even called Beck's welfare into question, and by then, she had been ignoring the space where he used to be with callous determination. She'd been too busy for kind consideration. Indignant blame had been easier.

The wicker couch suddenly felt bumpy and uncomfortable, and Melissa was glad for the blackness of night, hiding her embarrassment. She squirmed and put her hands under her thighs to keep from scrabbling at her legs. The cat clung to her lap with feline balance and persistence.

"Your father called, about a month after you left. He was concerned, but he said it wasn't the first time you had wandered off. I could hear your mother going off in Spanish. She sounded upset. And they came by the farm once when I wasn't around, looking for you."

Beck tilted his head and peered at the sky, as if the mothership might arrive and send down a tractor beam.

"I missed the stars, when I was bees," he whispered.

Beck sank into a spooky trance, and the crickets crescendoed. Melissa felt his attention pull away from her, his presence recede. This was how it happened. You could be close, as close as a parent and child, and still the invisible bonds of love might not hold fast. People spun off on their own orbits, leaving imperfect trace memories, desolate recollections of the way things used to be. If she let her guard down, if she decided to believe that Beck hadn't intended to leave her, would he stay and win her love and trust, then leave again? She reverted to her professional persona, hardening, and prepared to tell Beck he couldn't stick around and screw up harvest season. Gradually she became aware of the rich, warm smell of beeswax. At first there was only a hint of it, then the aroma flooded the front porch. She inhaled deeply three times, perplexed. The bee smell was everywhere, all at once. Opening her eyes wide, she searched the porch for a source, a melted candle, a discarded hive frame, anything. Reluctantly, she turned her gaze to Beck.

"It's me, Melissa," he whispered. "It's coming from me." He slid closer to her on the couch, inviting her to confirm he was the source of the sweet, unique scent.

The reaction from the cat as Beck came near was violent and immediate. It sprang into a crazed posture of defence, hissing and spitting, and produced an extended, anguished yowl from deep in its throat. Four paws planted in Melissa's legs, perforating her skin with twenty sharp, extended claws. The cat metamorphosed from feline to porcupine, back arched in a stiff parabola, every hair erect and trembling. Melissa leapt to her feet, shoving the cat from her lap with such force that it landed on its side with a thump. In a split second it righted itself and disappeared, a grey streak of feline speed.

"Damn it, I'm bleeding."

Beck sat perfectly still, like a statue of a man perched on a couch. "I missed the stars," he whispered again.

Melissa rushed into the house and upstairs. In the bathroom, she cleaned up the cat punctures, puffing strands of hair from her eyes. Hurt and confused, she didn't return to the porch, and Beck didn't follow her inside, solicitous and worried about her injuries, like a normal person. She retreated to her room. The hours of that night were long; they dripped like honey from a spoon. Compulsively, she touched slippery dabs of disinfectant cream on her thighs. She tried to meditate, stretched out on her bed, her upper body propped up with pillows, mimicking her therapist's chaise longue. The moon stared through the window, its pale surface a moronic happy face. Midnight passed, and one day became the next. Woolly ideas leapt like sheep over a fence. The claw puncture pain was welcome, something real and immediate, not Beck's vaporous story, or her father's fading ghost. She pressed sore spots on her legs in order, left to right, again and again. Exhaustion eventually slowed her racing thoughts, and she slept.

Four

Melissa woke up early, blearier than usual, and out of sorts. She blinked out the window. The sky, cold and pale, foretold winter. Birds squawked and chirped fretfully. With a cautious fingertip she traced dots of dried blood, the claw tattoo decorating her leg. Why had the cat been afraid of Beck? It reminded her of movies about aliens, the way domestic animals always sense an extraterrestrial before the people clue in. Beck's bee fantasy was ludicrous, so obviously an invention, but she didn't doubt his confusion, or that he wanted her. He had sought her out to listen to speculation that he had been spirited away by dark forces, and held against his will, all the while wanting to come home. It was the naive scenario she clung to about her father. One day, Charlie Makepeace would extricate himself from whatever circumstances were keeping him lost.

She pulled a shirt over her head and stepped into a pair of jeans. The bedroom across the hall where Beck used to sleep was unoccupied, bed stripped, blankets folded in the centre of the mattress. The bathroom tile was cold under her bare feet. She heard Daphne rustling in her room, drawers opening and closing. At the end of the upstairs hallway, the master bedroom door hung open, and she surveyed her mother's domain, white lacework pillows, pressed flowers hanging in frames and identified in loopy cursive writing, *Queen Anne's Lace, Lavender, Lily of the Valley*. On the wall above the bed, similar frames held dead butterflies pinned to white backgrounds. Her mother's perfume lingered. She closed her eyes, pictured Jill Makepeace and wondered how her mother would react to Beck's preposterous explanation for his absence. She could imagine the toss of blond hair as Jill affirmed everything Beck claimed, drinking up the outrageous details of his story. Melissa was the skeptic. Mom said she could see auras. She was a Gemini, and claimed that this astrological category, comprising a twelfth of the world's population, defined her. *I'm a Gemini – flexible, good-natured and an excellent communicator*! And selfish, Melissa found out. Geminis were supposed to be selfish and duplicitous.

At the bottom of the stairs she hesitated, hands hovering over the front door latches, and decided to make coffee before going outside. She detoured first to the right, into a library/office where she did the farm's paperwork because they couldn't afford an accountant. Floor-to-ceiling shelves were crammed with books about gardening, mushroom harvesting, composting and other esoteric farming lore. There was a fiction shelf too, filled with her favourites from childhood to the present. It was her habit to reread books she loved; some of the paperbacks were ragged with use, their spines splotched and tatty. *Charlotte's Web*, everything by Tom Robbins, *The Shipping News*. The computer was dusty and surrounded by stacks of paper, reminding Melissa that she had neglected receipts and accounts payable for far too long. She powered up the computer, wiped off the keyboard and opened the mail program, then the invoice folder. Scrolling idly, months and years whizzed backward in time, until a long-forgotten name popped up: *Balvinder Singh*. She tapped the mouse, looking for her father's old letters to the owner of Produce Point. They weren't there. Chewing the inside of her lip, she entered Balvinder's name in the search bar – nothing, not even in the trash. Unconsciously she puffed at her hair, and caught herself before the tucking began. She clicked the computer off.

Across the hall was the living room. Beck wasn't in there either. A cozy space no one used from spring thaw to first snow, it had a cracked red leather couch, a wooden rocking chair, an overstuffed armchair, a stone fireplace and an invitingly shaggy hearth rug. It was the only room that contained a photograph of Melissa's father – an autumn portrait of her happy little childhood family, before it disintegrated, was propped up on the mantelpiece. Charlie Makepeace, tall and relaxed in a lumberjacket and jeans, wore a slanted smile. Jill filled the right side of the frame, in a fall sweater and cashmere wrap; she was stylish and self-aware, pouting for the camera. In a broad space between her parents stood the child Melissa in a knitted poncho, purple stretchy pants and ladybug rubber boots, an outfit her six-year-old self must have chosen. She was grinning, poised to take a step, the top of her mussy brown head at her father's hip level, her mother's elbow. Her mother had tried to put this picture away over the years, and every time she did, Melissa had a tantrum. *One family picture, is that too much to ask?*

She went down the hall to the kitchen, flicking her head to the right as she passed the dining room. Beck wasn't there, of course. No one had wiped the table after dinner; flies were feeding on grains of rice and splotches of saffron-hued curry. She *tsked* in disapproval. In the vivid kitchen, she ran warm water and a dribble of dish soap onto a cloth while the kettle boiled, then scoured the dining table, generating the indignant drone of thwarted flies. She poured thick, bitter coffee from a French press and carried her mug out the back door, feet slapping in an ancient pair of leather Birkenstock sandals. Bow Lake sparkled below the fields. A loon ululated in the distance. She made her way to the front of the house, passing first the boat launch road, then her father's old work shed, where these days Joseph repaired broken vehicles and jury-rigged irrigation systems.

Melissa rounded a maple tree, and almost dropped her coffee. Beck was stretched out in textbook Warrior II pose, one knee bent deeply, arms stretched out in a line perfectly parallel with the surface of the earth, his gaze trained meticulously over the middle finger of his left hand. His body was oriented directly toward the bee yard, some thirty metres distant. She must have gasped, because she broke his concentration and he stepped out of the pose.

"Why are you here?" she blurted.

"I was too tired to walk home, so I slept on the porch. I didn't think you would mind."

She went to him where he stood on the grass, glancing at the beehives in the distance as she walked. There was no one else in sight. She heard chickens squawking in the henhouse, and the thrum of a tractor in the farthest fields. A cloud of brown dust roiled above green crops. A buzzing insect zoomed beside her left ear and hovered until she waved it away. She handed Beck her coffee and he smiled, took a small sip and handed it back.

"Melissa, let me help with harvest season. Please. Let me mow the lawn, drive the tractor and plough a field, stack bales of hay in Hotay's lean-to. I know it doesn't make sense, but this farm feels safe – safer than the cabin."

Beck pressed his hands into prayer position on his breastbone, literally begging. When Melissa didn't answer right away, he reached out and touched her arm, squeezing it lightly, imploring. Just that, his skin in contact with hers, unseated her, and her brain released a host of hormonal activity that had lain dormant.

"What really happened?" she asked softly.

Beck cringed and snatched his hand away. He was traumatized. Why hadn't she seen it yesterday? He hadn't turned into a colony of bees of course; that was a construct, a story shielding him from some other unspeakable horror. He rotated, presenting his back to the bee yard.

"I'm telling the truth. I know it's outrageous, but it's all I've got." His shoulders collapsed. "I need to talk to my parents. Can I stay until I've talked to them, at least?"

The tiny spare bedroom leapt into her mind's eye. She could invite Beck to stay, feed him and help him gain weight. She could allow him to help out with harvest and maybe he would take over his beekeeping duties again. His stay would be on her terms, and they wouldn't necessarily wind up in bed together. He couldn't keep up this bee pretense for long; the truth would emerge and they would confront it together. But the invitation got stuck in her throat.

Beck's smile was a thin enigma. She gulped her coffee and set the mug down on the path. Beck fished her cellphone out of his jeans pocket and held it aloft. "I found this on the porch and left a message for my parents."

She grabbed the phone and tossed it to the ground. He stepped in close and took her hands in his. The rising sun crested trees on the eastern horizon and poured pinkish-orange light, illuminating the stone farmhouse facade, making grass and trees glow, releasing energy stored inside every blade, every leaf. The sun healed Beck's pallor in an instant, washing over his black hair and toffee skin, restoring his humanity. He eased his face closer to hers, and she fought both the gravitational pull of his lips and the overwhelming urge to start touching each of her teeth with her tongue in turn.

The phone rang in the grass at Beck's feet, and the charm was broken. Their hands separated. Melissa scooped up the phone, wiped beaded moisture from the screen and answered the call. It was an international number she didn't recognize; the connection beeped, popped and fizzled before a confident woman's voice broke the pastoral serenity.

"Buenos días, Melissa – Beck, he is with you now?"

She passed the phone to Beck. He took it, grinning like a circus chimpanzee rewarded with a banana. She wheeled away from him, puffed three times and tucked hair severely behind her ears. From behind the house came a distinct rough engine idle, and the gate between the yard and fields squealed. A rusty secondhand truck bounced along parallel dirt ruts between house and shed and slowed to a stop beside her.

Jill had bought this replacement utility pickup for the farm after Charlie left. "We need another beater," she had said. The truck had since merged in Melissa's memory with her father's old vehicle, a jalopy he had alternately cursed and praised, once upon a time a flat white, the top of the cab weather-worn to a silver sheen, metal corroded around the door handles, dings and scuffs along the body, lovable in its imperfections and predictable for the way it would break down at the most crucial junctures. Melissa glanced at the muddied licence plate, letters and numbers jumbling dyslexically for a second as her brain tried to rearrange them to form a plate she still watched for, one the local police assured her would pop up on their screens in lurid red, signalling it matched the plate in her father's missing person's file.

Behind the wheel Daphne smiled, a blue bandana tied around her forehead, gold-rimmed aviator sunglasses flashing. Waxed cardboard boxes, dotted with holes to aerate perishable produce, were stacked in the back of the pickup.

"Ready for market day? Hey, Beck – is he coming to help out? Just like the old days!"

Melissa leapt onto the duct-taped bench seat and slammed the heavy passenger door. She leaned out the window. Beck had wandered to the gap in the hedge with her phone pressed to his ear, his free hand clutching a handful of his hair. He spoke in a loud, insistent tone, then fell silent and nodded while the person on the other end took their turn.

"He's not coming; he's not well enough to work. Hey!" Melissa shouted at Beck, and as he turned she felt a lightness in her chest, a momentary giddy happiness he was really there, before the weight of his betrayal extinguished the spark of joy. "Leave my phone on the porch when you go."

Melissa saw the implication he should go back to his family's cabin settle on Beck like a jail sentence. She had imagined this moment as satisfying and triumphant, but instead it felt miserly and cruel. After a long pause, he gave her a thumbs-up and went back to his call.

Daphne stepped on the gas and cranked the radio, tuned to a crackly local Top Forty station. Melissa stared out her window as they whipped past trees and fields, grateful for Daphne, who sang scraps of songs, kept the energy in the truck buoyant and left her alone with her thoughts. Once in Lanark, Daphne slowed the truck to an urban chug and palmed the steering wheel, whistling. Wrenching into reverse, she backed into their spot at the weekly farmers' market, a ten-foot-wide slot of public real estate.

They had their market routine perfected, erecting the canopy and table, unloading the truck and piling the week's produce in an artistic, enticing display designed by Jill. Vegetables and fruits tumbled from straw-lined baskets turned on their sides, colours mixed carefully, carrots beside broccoli, then beets, lettuce, tomatoes and kale. There was barely enough room for everything, but extra space destroyed the cornucopia effect, Jill claimed. Week after week, their competitors watched enviously as customers flocked to the Hopetown Farm market stall, and Melissa was grateful for her mother's business acumen. Jealous or not, the other farmers hailed her and Daphne warmly as they unloaded their truck, and jokes about the week's hot weather shot back and forth across a well-trod aisle of brown grass between two rows of stalls.

"Whoa, Melissa, you're Queen of the Market again. Damn, what are you fertilizing with these days? That broccoli is un*natural*. I don't know how, but you're cheating," said Natalie from the farm next door, who was also their neighbour at the market. "Hey, did Beck finally get back to you? He looks terrible."

Melissa glanced at Daphne, whose sunglasses hid her expression.

"He'll be okay," Melissa said. "We're using our rocket-fuel mushroom compost, the stuff my mom invented. So yeah, basically cheating."

Natalie winked at them, laughing, before her attention was pulled by a customer.

"So where was he – did he tell you?" Daphne lowered her sunglasses with a finger.

"Later," Melissa said, feeling the double burden of keeping her promise to Beck and being less than honest with Daphne. She thought about Beck's beehive hallucination and shuddered. A cog had slipped a wheel in his psyche; he had come unglued. She felt silly for not seeing it coming. His obsession with the bees, his agoraphobic tendencies, the dearth of intimacy between them – how close she had come to professing love for a lunatic! But as she fumbled in her apron for a customer's change, Beck flooded her senses, his lean limbs and bright eyes, and she felt a wriggling in her guts, a churning of excitement and hope.

"Well, if it isn't Melissa Makepeace. Long time no see. Good to see you're keeping things shipshape for your mom."

A woman moved in front of the stall, eclipsing the market with her bulky presence. Sleek blond hair was combed into a ponytail pulled tight behind a round face, and navy-uniformed arms hung akimbo, primed to grab sidearm, two-way radio, pager or baton. In spite of the heat she wore a jacket, with crown-and-flag embroidered Ontario Provincial Police crests on the sleeves. Her blue trousers bunched between legs thick as concrete pilings.

"Oh, hey, Constable Hickey. Can I talk to you for a sec? Daphne, you got this?"

"You bet," Daphne said.

Susan Hickey had been a rookie cop in Lanark when Charlie Makepeace went missing. It had fallen to the young female officer, by intention or orders Melissa never knew, to comfort the eleven-year-old girl as police interacted with her distraught mother. Over the years Constable Hickey had graduated from provider of lollipops and pats on the shoulder to Melissa's chief liaison with her father's case. She followed Melissa around the produce stand to the front of the old truck, rubbing a stick of waxy balm on her lips and smacking them with satisfaction.

"What can I do for you, Melissa?"

"I've been meaning to come by the station, but it's been crazy busy at the farm. I was going through old emails, and I found some between my dad and Balvinder Singh."

"Singh, the pharmacist?"

"No, the Almonte Singhs. The family that owns Produce Point Market."

"Oh yeah, sure. I know who you mean. So what did these emails say?"

Constable Hickey extracted a small spiral-bound notebook from a back pocket and flipped it open. She licked a finger and riffled through pages covered with scribbled notes until she came to an empty one, poised a pencil between her fingers and waited, one eyebrow raised.

"Not much. They were mostly like, friendly reminders of invoices and questions about what Balvinder stocked in his store. I just couldn't remember if anyone ever talked to him about my dad, back then," Melissa finished lamely. She wondered if she should admit the emails had been inexplicably deleted from the farm computer.

"Balvinder Singh, eh?" Constable Hickey printed the name deliberately, finishing with a final flourish-and-stab of her pencil. "I can't recollect offhand. Been awhile since I looked at it, but I'll check your father's file when I get back to the station. You never know. Colder cases than his have been solved. Have to follow up on every lead." She closed the little notebook, jammed it in her back pocket and patted it three times, as if to reassure Melissa the name was safely tucked away. "You hang in there, okay?"

"Wait, there's one more thing."

"Oh yeah? What's that, now?" The police officer folded her arms across her chest, and made a show of vigilantly peering around Melissa's truck toward the market, signifying she was on duty, watching for trouble, and couldn't be waylaid for much longer.

"I probably should have talked to you before. You know Beck, who was working for me?"

"Beck, you mean your boyfriend Beck?"

Melissa winced. "Yeah, sure. Well, he was gone all summer. Did his parents call you, wondering where he was, or anything?"

"That sounds familiar. Yes, his father came by the station. But we decided he was a young man, and it was summertime, and there was no reason to suspect foul play. His dad didn't want us to open a file. Didn't you know he was going away? I seem to remember something about Beck leaving a letter for you." The police officer put a hand on her back pocket, ready to jot more notes, if necessary.

"Yes, but also no. Sort of. Well, he just got back yesterday."

"Oh, he's back. Great. Is that all?"

Constable Hickey stepped out from behind the truck and surveyed the market, shielding her eyes from the sun with her hand. "Duty calls," she said, and clapping Melissa on the shoulder, she left. Melissa watched Constable Hickey's ponytail sway as she wove through the thickening market crowd, swivelling her head from side to side, patrolling her enviable beat.

"Uh, boss? If you're done? We got a situation here," Daphne called out.

Startled, Melissa saw Daphne struggling to serve customers who crowded the Hopetown stall, clutching bunches of carrots and fanning the air with green twenty-dollar bills. Her thoughts had drifted far away, like dandelion seeds searching for fertile ground.

Five

Alamar, Cuba
twenty-five years earlier

There was a fine mist that morning, a translucent veil pulled over the dark green fronds of palm trees. Mist shrouded the pink, yellow and orange blossoms of lush flower gardens (a shame these were hidden) and masked the concrete apartment buildings (a blessing to have their grey ugliness cloaked). Eurydice heaved an expansive yawn that stretched the skin on her cheeks. She was sleepy, in spite of the big cup of black coffee she had swallowed at dawn along with a thick wedge of buttered bread. How was it December already, almost the day of the Procesión de San Lázaro? Had she let so many days slip by without pausing to consult the grubby pages of the calendar tacked up in the kitchen?

By midmorning the mist had dissipated, evaporated under the Caribbean sun and puffed away by salty ocean breezes. She knelt in her flounced white cotton skirt and pink tank top, a mat of woven palm fronds placed under her knees. She was trying to keep clean in case Matthew Wise, the Canadian photographer, came back to the organopónico today. He wasn't there to photograph her, of course, but to document the burgeoning independent farming movement. She knew what kind of photos Matthew wanted because Pedro, Matthew's translator, told Emilio the mechanic, who told Rita the housekeeper, who passed it on to Eurydice. He wanted images of leafy vegetables, succulent yellow fruta bomba, rows of waving green onion stalks, colourful butterflies, tiny iridescent hummingbirds and masses of shiny wet worms like the ones she scooped up now with deft fingers, shaking off black clods of rich earth. And of course, he wanted pictures of the Santeria shrine at the west gate of the organopónico. Foreigners always hung around that shrine, squinting at it, poking their fingers into the eyeholes of the skulls. Matthew Wise had snapped pictures of the shrine from all angles, zooming in on the little heap of blood-spattered sacred stones, brightly painted cow skull and strands of coloured beads draped over the frame. So far Matthew hadn't photographed people, and he certainly hadn't taken a picture of her, Eurydice Maria Lopez de Famosa, because she would have noticed. In her fantasy, Matthew captures an image of her on film, develops it in darkness and suspends it for processing in a windowless room with a scarlet glow. The image sharpens, and he is struck by her beauty.

But the world doesn't want to see pictures of healthy Cubans like me, Eurydice thought bitterly, people with meat on their bones, round fleshy bottoms and thick arms with dimpled elbows. *They want to see us starving.*

If Matthew Wise had been there two years earlier, he could have taken a prizewinning picture of an emaciated Cuban. In her room, Eurydice kept a black-and-white Polaroid image of herself tucked in her desk. In the picture she is twenty, sitting on the edge of a threadbare mattress. A sheet is bunched in her naked lap, and she is examining her reflection in a cracked, dirty mirror. Her breasts are thin, ending in two stark aureoles, and underneath them, the camera has captured shadows cast by her ribs. Her cheekbones throw similar places of darkness on her blank, resigned expression. The photograph transports her back in time, to the old Cuba.

Everything had changed beginning in March 1992, three months after the dissolution of the Union of Soviet Socialist Republics. No one made jokes anymore, or maybe they did, but Eurydice didn't understand them, or they weren't funny. Gloomy faces bored her. It was as if everyone had forgotten how to dance, how to have a little fun. The flat, banal muttering of politics followed her everywhere, big words that meant little, the blabbering of old mouths sitting on porches and sucking on cigars. "Embargo," "industrialization," "petroleum exportation" – fussy words detached from the triumphant rising of the sun each morning, far removed from the butterfly-fluttering of youth in her chest.

"Papá, let's drive to the beach," she begged her father, Luis de Famosa.

"No seas ridícula, niña," Luis said, laughing cheerlessly in his daughter's bemused face.

Eurydice retreated to the kitchen, stung, where her mother, Rosa Veronica Lopez, explained things to her.

"There is no fuel, mi hija, and things are changing too quickly. We must pray to Elegua, the god of opening paths."

Rosa Lopez, priestess of Santeria, led her daughter into the sacred space in the Lopez de Famosa home. Inside was an altar bearing shrines to the Orishas. Small chiselled wooden figurines leaned against peeling blue paint, their faces wearing permanently surprised expressions. Scattered among the figurines were conch shells, little bundles of herbs, painted rocks and a few wilted white flowers sagging in a water glass. Several faded pictures were tacked to the wall, curling at the edges. Rosa's brother Ernesto, who died in a barroom knife fight, was there, as was Charo, Eurydice's cousin who'd died of an infection when she was five. A postcard depicting a distressed Virgin Mary rolling her eyes heavenward hung in a frame above the altar. Rosa and Eurydice bowed their heads. Rosa spoke fervently, drops of moisture collecting along her hairline.

"Elegua, you who provide opportunity, we praise you and we honour you. Today, when circumstances are taking so much away, we respectfully ask that you help us to open doors. We ask that you help to show us the possibilities that are hidden. Elegua, we pray that you will bless us and lead us into a new day, full of opportunity."

Eurydice did as she was told. Every morning and night she dropped to her knees on the floorboards beside her bed and prayed as hard as she could. But the yellow Lada pickup truck stayed parked in the driveway, rusting, collecting leaves and bird droppings. There were no trips anywhere. Her father sat with his friends, stubble crusted on their drooping, mottled cheeks, the old men talking about gas in the past tense, how it used to be cheap and plentiful, and how their cars were useless now. Everyone was riding bicycles, even old people, even fat people. The first sight of her father on a bicycle made Eurydice laugh, her giggles stifled by the warning pressure of her mother's hand over her mouth.

Food became a luxury, and Eurydice's empty stomach made her forget about abandoned vehicles. She hated being hungry. How was the collapse of the former Soviet Union connected to the fact that there was nothing to eat? Russia was on the other side of the planet, a million miles away from Cuba, and as if geographic distance didn't make the place foreign enough, the country, as far as she could tell, was light years away in habits, lifestyle and culture from everything Eurydice knew. Russia meant snow, evergreen trees, wintry fashions made from the skins of furry animals and rigid dancing with the body's extremities – pasty-white pointed fingers and toes. Cuba, her home, was all sun, leafy plants, loose scraps of cotton casually draping brown bodies and sexy, sweaty dancing from the shoulders, chest and hips.

"Go stand in line with your mamá, and help her carry home the rations," ordered Luis de Famosa. New furrows had appeared on her father's face as healthy flesh melted away, and his forehead creased with worry. The old people talked about *Russia, Russia, Russia*, and then one day the refrain abruptly switched to *America, America, America*.

"Donde están todos los barcos, Papá?" There were no more big boats in the harbour, the ones she used to count while waiting for her father to finish his business at the docks.

"No more big boats, my beautiful one," her father told her. "Americans think any ship docking here is contaminated with the stink of communism."

Eurydice sniffed the air, trying to detect the perfume of an imposed socialist society.

Shortages impoverished her life, and the life of her family, as swiftly as an evil curse. One day they were laughing around a dinner table crammed to its corners with every imported delicacy, shreds of slow-cooked meat in sauce, salads thick with pale green avocado flesh, mounds of herbed rice cooked in butter. The next day, it seemed, they scowled at each other, scrounging crusts of bread. Day after day Eurydice stood in line for rice and cooking oil, clutching her family's libreta, their ration book. Skin began to hang from haggard features, fear strained the bonds of friendship and the hours of the day were as empty as the cupboards. She heard her parents whispering after she went to bed, worried tears wetting her pillow. She guessed there were worse days to come, and she was right. The stark monochrome morning came when a neighbour took her picture with a Polaroid camera, documenting the plight of the Cuban people. He snapped two, and gave her one. She didn't have the energy to cry when she couldn't recognize her dejected, starved self in the photo.

The evil curse was lifted with fairy-tale speed, gone as quickly as it had been cast, swept away by magic wands in the form of Chinese bicycles, Australian permaculturists and innovative Cubans turning tractor-trailers into buses and factories into farms. Urban gardens erupted on every scrubby vacant lot, sunny staircase and rotting rooftop; small farms dotted the countryside. Because of the climate, crops grew quickly; harvests filled empty stomachs, and neighbours proudly and generously shared their homegrown bounty. The food was better than before, Eurydice thought – a riot of colour on every plate, an abundance at every street-corner market.

"Gracias, Elegua, we praise your favour!" Rosa Lopez's body shook with raptures of gratitude. When it dawned on Eurydice that they had been saved – she, herself, had literally been saved – she had an epiphany: this wasn't good luck, and this was no coincidence. Elegua had shown Cubans how to heal their society, so Elegua had answered their prayers. Faith flooded Eurydice's body. She knelt on scuffed floorboards before the family altar, wounds of fear healed by the soothing balm of belief. If gods truly answered prayers, then the weight of problems and anguish could be transferred, and the future was full of promise. Her mother bought her a new white dress with a delicate lace yoke to celebrate her glorious confirmation into Santeria.

This was how Matthew Wise found her, in youthful, hopeful bloom. *Math-thew.* His name was awkward in her mouth, too much tongue and teeth. He couldn't pronounce hers properly, either. *Nice to meet you, Your Idiocy,* Matthew had said, when Pedro introduced them. But what did it matter if they couldn't say each other's names? She watched him wander around the farm, now kneeling to better focus his camera on a flower, now tilting his head to laugh.

Eurydice knew why this was happening, why she was falling in love with a stranger. Her mother had been casting love enchantments in her name. Three nights before the photographer had arrived, Rosa Lopez had prayed to Oshun for a harmonious, lasting love to come to her daughter. The stone of Oshun had glowed that night, slick with the blood of the best hen Rosa could buy. Eurydice had whetted the sacrificial knife, sharpening the blade's gleaming edge, and held the chicken expertly, so the bird was motionless as Rosa slit its throat. Crimson liquid had shot in a strong stream from the chicken's neck, and the head had flopped over, almost but not quite severed. The candle had burned high, and a pure, white smoke had issued from the flame. The love spell had worked, but her mother, Eurydice knew, was too eager for her to find a husband, so the enchantment had fallen unluckily on a white Canadian man. Her mother was an accomplished santera, and there was a high concentration of ashé, cosmic energy, in the prayer-stones of their altar.

In other words, Matthew Wise didn't stand a chance.

The day that had begun in mist was brilliant now, sunlight glimmering on wet surfaces. The gardens were looking especially abundant. Eurydice placed both her hands on the soft, smooth curve of her lower back, pressing the kinks out. When she finished her stretch she startled, then flinched in shock – Matthew Wise was standing in front of her, eating a banana. Where had he come from? She looked around wildly.

"Your back must get sore, with all this gardening," Matthew said.

His thin gold-rimmed spectacles sat slightly askew on the long bridge of his nose, and his light brown hair was combed across his forehead. He wore a beige linen shirt with the sleeves rolled up, and khaki pants on his lanky legs. A professional camera protruded from his midsection, suspended by a canvas-and-leather strap. Eurydice sucked in a double-breath of air, craving oxygen to still the jangle of stimulated nerves.

"Sí, back gets sore. I am not working in the garden, but pulling worms," she said, showing him the plastic bucket and its slimy contents.

"¿Por qué – los gusanos?"

"Why no speak English? Is better for me to practise English."

"Okay, so why the worms?"

"Sell to fishers – no waste, nothing."

"Yes, it's very good, how you don't waste anything here, and everything has a purpose."

His eyes slid down to her heaving chest. Eurydice was shocked by his bold gaze, until she noticed she had inadvertently placed her hands on her breasts as she spoke. Aghast by this accidental immodesty, she pulled at the pink fabric of her tank top, pretending to rearrange it on her body, and disciplined herself to be an adult: the Canadian was here to learn about organic farming.

"You would like me to explain the gardens, sí?"

"Well, I . . ." Matthew began, then stopped and sniffed the air hungrily, as if he had detected a luscious aroma. Eurydice sniffed too, but she could smell nothing except the salty ocean, mixed with the warm earthiness of plants and dirt.

"Cassava, muy importante," Eurydice said. She squatted close to where she had been harvesting worms and dug energetically, producing a long, thick tuber in seconds.

"This we grow and eat as an every–kind of food. It is making like rice or potatoes, or dessert."

Matthew took the root and held it delicately in an open palm. He looked back and forth between the rigid carbohydrate and what she hoped was the attractive face of an intriguing woman. She wetted her lips, thinking about the creamy sweetness of her grandmother's cassava cake. The photographer gazed down the smooth slant of his white nose at the bumpy tuber in his hand. When he spoke at last, she heard a recklessness in his words.

"I haven't even been to the beach since I arrived in Cuba. Is there an easy way to get there from here? I'd like to put my toes in the ocean."

"Sí, sí! Podemos llegar en bicicleta." In her excitement, Eurydice forgot to be demure. She grasped one of Matthew's hands and pulled him toward the fence of the organopónico, where half a dozen communal bicycles leaned in a jumble of rusty metal and worn rubber.

Eurydice rinsed black earth from her hands and splashed cold water on her flushed face.

As they rode bikes to the coast, she pointed out sights, the pockmarked facade of la Iglesia Adoradores de Cristo, the muddy waters of Río Cojímar. Matthew kept his camera slung over his shoulder, and she admonished him to ride carefully so he wouldn't fall and smash it. At the beach they leaned the bicycles up against the hairy trunk of a palm tree. The surf was up, clean aquamarine waves smashing into a line of white sand, running on little foam feet up as high as they could reach, trying to escape inland. Matthew rolled his pant legs up to his knees. She watched him survey the postcard-perfect shoreline, feeling proud to offer him so grand a gift. They walked, Matthew stopping every twenty metres to take a photograph. She touched his hand, grazing it lightly with her own, hoping to share the current of her excitement. But he was already under the influence of a love spell, and she was powerless too, her actions controlled by the great, invisible forces that govern unobservable things. They kissed, a roaring embrace, and their fates were wound together, tied securely as the knotted rope around an oracular chicken's stiff, dead legs.

He proposed at twilight, on the Malecón in Havana. Eurydice accepted immediately. In a week-long delirium of lusty euphoria they consummated their engagement in hotel rooms, on the organopónico and on deserted beaches. Matthew felt beguiled by his future. Tight restraints of his childhood were unzipped, loosing flesh, thought and feelings. Over their short courtship, he had come to know Eurydice as a kindred spirit. She was wild without being reckless; a visionary, but with healthy respect for practicalities – she was more practical than he.

"Let's live in Cuba full time," Matthew suggested, drunk on rum and high on the heady fragrance of mariposa jasmine in bloom.

"¿Estas loco?" Eurydice, unimpressed, assumed a withering expression of displeasure that he would come to know intimately. "Who will buy your photographs here – how will you do business? No one, and you will not," she answered her own questions emphatically. "Sometimes we live here, okay, but not always. I do not marry a mainland norteamericano and stay in Cuba."

Matthew settled into a comfortable back seat while Eurydice organized their binational lifestyle, planned for the upcoming wedding and budgeted for their future, sensitively orchestrating the involvement of her sprawling family and his few living Canadian relatives.

Matthew and his sister Sylvia had endured a banal and tedious childhood under the strict watch of conservative parents. While his elementary school classmates sparkled with brilliance and excelled at athletics, Matthew was chosen as an afterthought for team sports, and overlooked when party invitations were handed out. He faded rapidly from thought and memory. Teachers looked away when he spoke. He was boring, knew it, but didn't know how to be otherwise. Things changed when, as a gangly, introverted teenager, he joined his high school photography club, and gutsy pictures he took of his scintillating peers and their exhilarating pursuits won him praise. He applied himself to becoming the best photographer at his school, and for his efforts he was awarded a golden ticket to a compelling, vibrant life. He immersed himself in the excitement generated by fascinating people doing remarkable things. At university, his closest friend and confidante was Barbara Beauchemin, a notable campus character, a ragged goth whose gifted scholarship in quantum physics launched her career into the stratosphere. In his senior year Barbara left him behind, and Matthew consoled himself by riding the coattails of a rollicking gang of pre-med students, tagging along for their fierce parties and fulfilling weekends – until he discovered there were ghastly ways to be interesting.

His parents were killed in a car crash during an ice storm. He shrank from a new sort of popularity, borne of sympathy, and wished to be colourless once more, easily ignored and forgotten. Sylvia, by nature cautious and afraid, turned inward. The accident proved her myriad fears were justified, and one by one she eliminated friends and activities, until she was alone with her neuroses. Perversely, watching his unfortunate sister become a social isolate helped Matthew heal. He would not live, as Sylvia did, to avoid death; he yearned to feel the thumping pulse of life. Photojournalism brought him to Cuba, where he met Eurydice.

Where his fiancé's spiritual beliefs were concerned Matthew was, he thought, extraordinarily patient. Faithless, he threw out vague prayers to a nonspecific God when he was in trouble, and once the issue was resolved immediately forgot his desperate request for divine help. Other people had faith, and that was fine with Matthew – personally, he had never needed it. He appreciated Santeria's drama, the intrigue it lent to commonplace concerns, and observed the faith's trappings, its shrines and altars, like a tourist admiring magnificent displays in an anthropology museum or a couch potato watching a riveting National Geographic documentary. At first Eurydice's relationship with Santeria seemed that of a benign hobby, like quilting, or maybe something more complex, with props, like geocaching.

It came as a baffling surprise when Eurydice explained that she had been "called" – by the gods, Matthew understood – to be initiated as santera, a priestess of Santeria. Surprise morphed into unpleasant shock as his bride-to-be explained the process would take a year. Yes, for a full year she would wear only white garments, keep her head shaved, abstain from alcohol and be celibate. At the end of the year there would be a week-long induction ceremony, a formal production involving costume, guests, special food and drink – almost like a wedding in itself. Wasn't this exciting, was he excited for her?

The white clothes, the teetotalling, the big ceremony, even the shaved head – all of these Matthew could accept without significant personal compromise. After all, his attraction to Eurydice included her culture. His life had become meaningful in ways he had never imagined it might. Not that he espoused a different identity; he couldn't, for example, clap a clave beat. Rhythmic complexities in Cuban music voiced a nuanced perception of the human condition his anemic suburban upbringing had lacked. Santeria's mysteries were beautiful, and to him impenetrable, but he had no need to penetrate what was innate to another. He was content to be the moon to Eurydice's sun. Live and let live. Still, *celibacy*? Matthew asked her to explain a second time, and then a third.

"For a whole year? But – why?"

"Sí. Then I will be santera, and we can make love again."

It wasn't something he could understand or appreciate. He agreed to the deprivation and spent a year secretly wishing he hadn't, biting his tongue when he wanted to beg her, *come on, have mercy, no one will ever know.* He masturbated more than he had at sixteen, his cock perennially hard and pressed against the fly of his jeans. Using work to stay busy and help the protracted time pass, he accepted photography assignments in South Africa, Nepal and France. He stayed on his sister's couch in Toronto for two months. Severe Sylvia was poor company, and he had nothing tangible to pursue professionally in his hometown, but he couldn't stand to be with Eurydice and be chaste.

Finally – *finally* – the year of sexual withholding came to a close. Matthew's frustration was acute. At Eurydice's initiation ceremony he was at best a distracted observer, at worst an obstacle and a nuisance, constructing sensitive Spanish phrases in his mind, delicate ways to ask Eurydice when it would finally be okay for them to tear each other's clothes off. He should have been more respectful of her desire; when at last they were alone together it was clear she had suffered greatly, and longed for physical love as much as he had. It was the only time in his life he literally saw fireworks, flashes of purple and green that popped and crackled as every nerve ending in his body, it seemed, exploded with pleasure.

Beckett Stephen Wise was conceived.

Late June in Ontario, and the sun was relentless. Eurydice was outside gardening, chanting a lighthearted, repetitive melody, a metronome for the rhythm of her work. The Wise family trio was carving out a summer homestead in rural Canada: a plywood shack on an inexpensive, rocky three acres. An inheritance from Matthew's parents, cleverly invested, meant they could live without steady income as long as they were thrifty, and Eurydice specialized in thrift. After the hardships of Cuba in the Special Period, she knew how to stretch every penny. Their annual budget included an airfare fund, their only extravagance – an allowance to travel back and forth once or even twice between Cuba and Canada. In between trips they lived with self-imposed frugality. Matthew was rehanging the screen door at the back of the cabin, a task complicated by the vagaries of his three-year-old son. Beck rose each morning from his little cot, his sturdy body dotted with angry red mosquito bites, scratching furiously and crying in vexation.

"Mux skee toes bite me *'gain*!" Beck screamed, raking at tender skin with dirty, miniature fingernails, tears welling in round, dark eyes and spilling over thick black lashes. Each evening, Matthew shrouded his son's bed in netting, which the toddler then pulled down in the night, annoyed by the high-pitched drone of the insects, and determined to slaughter them all with his pudgy brown fists. Matthew had accepted that Beck was too young to grasp how the netting protected him, and set about replacing the cabin's window and door screens, hoping to keep the tiny nuisances from entering. The screen door he was working on wobbled, the hinges loose and rusty. He removed the entire door, then unscrewed the wooden assembly holding the torn screen in place. The wood was old, silvery-soft and unprotected, like a pigeon's wing. Matthew sighed; the door would have to be stained or painted before it was reassembled.

Peak mosquito hours were at dawn and dusk, when they hovered in clouds around anything warm-blooded; the whiny parasites avoided the scalding midday sun. It was lunchtime. Beck was playing outside, shepherded by Conchita, a golden Labrador retriever that Matthew and Eurydice had bought as a companion for their son and protector of their property. Beck adored Conchita, and the dog returned the little boy's zealous affection with gentle loyalty. Matthew had once observed Beck holding one of Conchita's soft, floppy ears aloft, whispering, *Chita, you is me friend. Me loves you, Chita.*

A nightly sentinel beside Beck's cot, Conchita growled softly when anyone approached. At dinner Beck surreptitiously introduced morsels of his own meal past docile black dewlaps, a transgression Matthew pretended not to notice because when Eurydice caught Beck table-feeding the dog, she ranted about waste and germs. Once she had made Beck cry, telling him an animal as fat and spoiled as Conchita would have been slaughtered and eaten for dinner long ago in post-Soviet Cuba.

The screen door lay in pieces across two paint-stained sawhorses. Matthew began sanding, *chhh-ch, chhh-ch*, fresh yellow wood surfacing from beneath weathered shreds. Beck threw a tennis ball for Conchita. The hot pink sphere bounced a scant couple of metres from the boy, and the patient animal retrieved it. Two large maple trees at the east end of the yard cast shade, dappling the brilliance of emerald lawn with wavering dark splotches. It was a peaceful summer day, grasshoppers clicking, pine cones snapping open, hum of bees. The rhythm of Matthew's sandpaper strokes matched his wife's gardening chants, so he noticed the sudden quiet when Eurydice stopped singing.

His wife was staring into the fringe of trees surrounding the cabin on three sides. Following her gaze, Matthew saw a black bear standing on the lawn. The bear's attention was focused on Beck and Conchita. Matthew wondered if a breeze was blowing the bear's scent away, or if Conchita was worthless as a guard, because the dog was intent on the pink tennis ball in Beck's hand and oblivious to the adult, roughly four-hundred-pound bear. The tableau lasted three or four seconds before Eurydice raised her chin and released a loud, threatening ululation.

"Aya laya laya laya lay! Aya laya laya laya lay!"

The bear slowly tipped its heavy head toward Eurydice with the bored indifference of a creature secure in its advantage. Glistening black nostrils flared, and reddish eyes considered the yelping human. Not a threat, the bear must have decided, because it swung back to examining boy and dog, and ambled its hindquarters out of the shrubs. With all four shaggy paws on the lawn, the bear might have been a kitschy life-sized ornament, posed there to frighten intruders. Now that the bear was within pouncing distance, Conchita finally noticed it. She barked and growled, blond fur bristling along her back. Matthew dropped his sandpaper and spread his arms, shouting, "Go on – go away!" Eurydice, arms akimbo, added: "Aléjate de él!"

The bear loped off unhurriedly; the crisis had passed. But when Matthew turned to Beck he saw not one but *two* barking dogs. Conchita was closest to him. Beyond her was a hazier, darker canine, camouflaged by the shade of the maple trees. Beck was nowhere. Matthew panicked, scanning the lawn for his son and yelling at Eurydice, "Where the hell is Beck?" Sickening seconds passed. Hot air warped reality. Waves of fright crashed over him until Matthew blinked and saw not two dogs, but Conchita and Beck once more. His son was on his hands and knees, pretending to be a barking dog.

Matthew took off his glasses and inspected the lenses.

Eurydice opened the garden gate and ran to Beck. She snatched up her son and carried him, still barking, onto the porch. Conchita woofed into the treeline for another hour, atoning for her lack of vigilance.

"Did you see that?" Matthew asked, his heart pounding.

"Of course. Didn't you hear me? I cried out against this bear."

"Not the bear."

Beck was emitting a convincing growl, baring his square little baby teeth.

"Shhh, mi hijo, shhh . . ."

"The dogs," Matthew persisted, "did you see them?"

"Conchita is a good dog," Eurydice said, stroking Beck's hair.

Matthew knew she'd also seen two dogs, but wouldn't acknowledge it, and he wasn't sure he wanted her to. Eurydice actually believed in magic, powerful magic, including shape-shifting, teleportation and miraculous healing. Discussing these phenomena with her made him uneasy, and usually ended in an argument about where the border lay between the physically provable and the supernatural. Beck was safe, and Eurydice could believe what she wanted. Matthew's practical mind was already filing the incident away as a heat-induced hallucination.

Beck was nine years old, hanging onto his mother's apron strings, restive, skinny and smudged. To avoid the worst of the Canadian winter they lived in Cuba with Eurydice's parents, Rosa and Luis, and worked on the organopónico. Matthew's intention was to teach his son about heavy work – ploughing and fence-building – but the boy clung to his mother like an infant. Matthew believed himself an open-minded, contemporary kind of guy, but his son's preference for what he thought of as women's work – weeding and harvesting – rankled. The boy plainly preferred his mother's company, which insulted Matthew, and inspired in him a sulky envy of his wife.

"Come on, Beck. The men are in the fields today."

"No, Papá – quiero quedarme con Mamá."

"Suit yourself."

"He is still a boy," Eurydice consoled her husband. "When he begins to be a man, he will choose to go with you."

A socialist foreman decided who worked which jobs each day, and though he had no experience, on the day of the accident Matthew was assigned to clear brush. The organopónico was expanding. Everything they grew was sold and eaten; more land had to be cleared and ploughed, and fresh fields planted. The foreman asked a Cuban boy of fifteen to show Matthew how to use a scythe. The kid started with a demonstration, wielding the scythe with grace and precision, swiping the hefty blade in great arcs and felling tall, dry grass in neat bunches. Matthew watched idly, reminded of a Van Gogh painting, a dark-haired peasant cutting down golden wheat.

When it was his turn to try, the scythe was heavier than Matthew had expected. At first he held the tool with its blade aloft, mimicking the Grim Reaper's macabre instrument for harvesting the dead. Then he lowered the blade and swung the scythe back and forth, exploring its trajectory. Sun, reflected on the tool's mirror-shiny surface, blinded Matthew for a moment. A bird screamed nearby, and a scrap of cigarette smoke drifted over from the next field. Matthew took tentative swipes, but the blade struck the grass at the wrong angle, and stems bent, then sprang back.

"Sharp, sharp!" the Cuban boy warned.

Matthew tried again, and failed to cut even a single stalk.

"No," said the boy. Once again he demonstrated his prowess, cutting several square metres in half a minute. They passed the scythe back and forth, Matthew's frustration building. *Simple as a hammer, what's wrong with me?* The sound of the smokers from the next field faded into the distance. The voices had belonged to the Cuban boy's friends; he shielded his eyes from the sun and searched for them. Matthew sensed his instructor's impatience to leave and redoubled his efforts. At last, circles of sweat staining the underarms of his shirt, he succeeded in mowing down a scant handful of grass.

"Bien," the boy said, and he ran off to find his friends, leaving Matthew alone.

He practised in the grass for a few minutes before moving to the field, where the brush was rigid and stubbornly resisted the blade. Again and again Matthew sank the scythe into green, woody stalks, where it stuck fast. He reached down and pulled half-cut plants from the blade with his left hand, while awkwardly grasping the smooth scythe handle in his right. In one day, he was supposed to clear the vegetation from an area the size of a soccer field. At the rate he was going, it would take him a month.

Irritated with this failure, Matthew's thoughts veered to the pessimistic. Usually imperturbable, when he lost his equanimity, Matthew lost it entirely. Would Beck ever grow up and stop following his mother around? And Eurydice! Those meals she used to make, succulent herbed chicken flesh, delicately arranged around the tastiest moros y cristianos in Cuba, a fresh, crispy salad on the side – where had they gone? Thin, tasteless soup, stale bread, vegetables lazily hacked up and plopped onto plates – was this how it was to be for the foreseeable future? Under a perfection of blue, amidst a riot of tropical flowers, Matthew longed for the Canadian boreal forest. He wanted the sharp, clean smell of spruce on a cold spring day, the soft descent of snow, rocky shorelines and lakes full of fish. Self-pity mixed with anger and fuelled his increasingly wild thrashing with the long, sharp blade. He swung the scythe in a reckless arc, amplifying the force and aiming at verdant stems of a plant he hadn't yet encountered. The tool went through this new shrub like butter, and Matthew couldn't stop its swish. The scythe blade sliced through his calf muscle and lodged in his leg.

Matthew teetered. He opened his mouth to call for help and produced only wheezes; breath and sound were trapped in his chest. He stared in disbelief at the archaic farm tool embedded in his body. There was no pain, but the gory spectacle below his knee made him giddy, and he toppled backward in slow motion, arms flailing. The scythe twisted under its own weight; the blade rotated and agony arrived. Blood spilled and seeped into the ground. He grabbed his calf with both hands and pressed slippery red flaps of flesh together on either side of the metal wedge. *I'm going to die out here.*

From nowhere Beck's face appeared and floated above him, framed by the bright Caribbean sky. His vision blurry and fading, Matthew saw his son's mouth open and close, but he heard nothing. Blackness grew over Beck's features, and the whites of his son's eyes receded, leaving behind two shiny black dots. Beck's mouth elongated. Two arms that were not arms thickened and stretched. Coal-coloured feathers flapped and carried Beck, now a crow, up and away. Matthew remembered only snatches of the next hour. Laid out on the ground, his three uninjured limbs held down firmly by farmers, a clean jerk, the silver sickle snatched from his leg, the sound of his own scream. Jostled on a makeshift stretcher through fields of vegetables, tropical trees bumping by. The shock of waking, not to the comfort and security of a hospital bed, but to a Santeria circus in the organopónico's main kitchen, a nightmare of rattles, smoke and chanting, his wife presiding.

Because of blood loss it was days before Matthew could ask about what had happened after his accident, and over a week before he saw his son. His leg was heavily bandaged with white gauze, but Matthew could move his toes, and no blood soaked through the dressing. He looked out the window while Rosa changed the gauze. His mother-in-law prayed quietly. Beck sidled into the sickroom.

"How did you know where I was? Why did you come?"

Beck shrugged, looked down, probed a nostril with an index finger.

"You looked like a bird to me, a black crow. Then you flew away."

Beck spun around and ran out of the room, his cheap sneakers slapping the linoleum. Rosa rolled her eyes at Matthew, threw her hands in the air and followed her grandson. Moments later Eurydice entered, her face stony.

"What did you say to him?"

"He was there, in the field. He found me."

"Leave him alone."

"But he found me – I know it was him."

"Just leave it."

"Pero, no lo entiendo," Matthew said. Eurydice shook her head and held a finger to her lips.

He unwrapped the gauze himself the next morning. There were metres of the stuff; it took several minutes of carefully passing a growing wad of white over and under his left knee before his leg emerged. The smell of an herb he didn't recognize, zesty and acetic, mixed with the sharp pungency of alcohol. Closer to his leg the gauze was stained a saffron yellow, like pollen, and though he felt no pain, Matthew braced himself to see evidence of an infection.

But the wound was healed. It was as if the accident had happened decades before, in his childhood. A faint white line snaked around his calf, and that was all.

Six

In the days after Beck had materialized with his insane metamorphosis story, triggering her tics, Melissa couldn't catch a break on the farm. Codling moths threatened the apple harvest and there were signs of a blight on the Roma tomatoes. One of the laying hens mysteriously dropped dead. The irrigation pipe to the squash field was blocked, so she asked Daphne to connect a series of hoses and water the pumpkin, zucchini, acorn, butternut and spaghetti squashes by hand. Someone needed to do a grocery run; they were down to the last two loaves of bread in the freezer, and there was no salt, sugar, soya sauce or cat food. Melissa yanked her hair into a rough knot and started up the rusty farm pickup. It coughed a puff of bluish exhaust, a classic symptom of engine trouble.

Beck had finished his phone call and then retreated to his family's cabin a few kilometres down the road. Three days had passed without any word from him or any sign he was around. Peeking into the little room where he used to sleep, she was distressed to see that he had taken his guitar. She thought about him incessantly while never mentioning his name, not even when Daphne pressed her to talk about his miraculous reappearance. At last, even though a dozen jobs clamoured for her attention, Melissa decided to go check on him. Joseph snarled at her for abandoning the farm in harvest season, but she had already lost Beck once. She didn't want him to disappear again under her watch. She was rolling past her father's work shed in the old truck when she caught sight of Joseph in the rear-view mirror. He lifted a grubby hand to stop her from leaving. She put her foot on the brake, propped an elbow on the window opening and waited for Joseph to saunter up. When he spoke Melissa recoiled from his breath, *eau de ashtray.*

"Why isn't Beck helping out around here? Not like him to be so lazy. Tell Marjorie Hill he's back. She's not all there, upstairs," Joseph tapped his forehead, "but she lives near the Wise place. She can check on him so you don't have to."

Joseph spat in driveway dust beside the truck and walked away. Melissa wasn't the only person who liked giving orders on the farm. Grudgingly, she agreed with Joseph. She had plenty to do, and visits with Beck would steal time she couldn't spare, but where was he – lying in a feverish stupor at his cabin? Just this once, she would make sure he was okay. The truck rattled over loose gravel and banged into potholes. She glimpsed herself in the rear-view mirror, eyes wide, cheeks red. Who was she kidding? This was a chance to be alone with Beck before his parents got back, away from Joseph's resentful glare and Daphne's knowing smirk. Melissa reminded herself of a sly teenager sneaking out to the bar with fake ID. She knew precisely what she was hoping would happen when she got Beck alone, and she squirmed on the stained upholstery of the bench seat. She was close to the Wises' cabin when, at the last possible second, she spotted Marjorie's disused driveway, its existence obscured by overgrown shrubs. Melissa cranked the steering wheel hard and pulled in aggressively, spraying gravel, and raising a cloud of thin, brown powder.

Dust settled and dispersed around sunflowers towering over a low, forlorn fence that defended a humble white house. There was no lawn; the front of the house was all garden, a profuse green chaos of raised beds, red polka dots of fruiting tomato plants, wild thickets of white globe thistles and explosions of magenta coneflowers. She picked her way over collapsed cardboard boxes and antique rubber hoses to the porch, and tapped on the screen door. From behind her, a scratchy voice spoke.

"I'm not in there. I rarely am."

Melissa couldn't see anyone in the vast tangle of leaves and flowers. She searched the yard, confused, until at last she spotted a wizened person perched on a ladder, tucked inside the branches of an apple tree. White hair hung in a messy braid down the woman's back. She wore an old set of tree-planting bags; soiled, once-rainbow shoulder straps held up three dirty white cylinders of rubberized canvas, drooping with the weight of picked fruit.

"I'll come down."

"Sorry to interrupt your work. I can come back."

"Nonsense. You're here now, and you won't be interrupting my work if you help me with it. Grab a couple of baskets from the pile on the porch and we'll pick tomatoes while we talk."

Melissa obeyed, and returned to find Marjorie at the bottom of the ladder, wincing as she tried to remove the planting bags.

"Here, I'll help."

"I'm fine!" Marjorie yelped, clearly in pain.

Melissa ignored the lie. She lifted the planting bags by their straps from the old woman's stooped shoulders and set them down carefully on the path. She saw Marjorie sneak a surreptitious look at her left hand, then hide it behind her back before clucking disapproval.

"Not there. Put them up on the porch, in the shade. These apples are overripe as it is. I don't need them sitting in the sun."

"Sorry." Melissa moved the bags of apples to the porch. "What's wrong with your hand?"

"Nothing, it's nothing, just a cut. Ambitious pruning project." She waved the hand briefly beside her hip, the thumb puffy and purple-blotched.

"Looks like it's getting infected."

"Well it isn't. It's full of honey and cayenne, best wound disinfectant around, and a cure that has always worked for me. Now, hand me a basket and we'll talk. Let's get the niceties over with first. How is your mother?"

"She's fine, thanks. She loves Guatemala, but she's coming home for the harvest festival."

"Good. And your bees, any sign of Beck?"

"He's back."

Marjorie flinched as if she'd been stung. "That's interesting – where the hell has he been?"

Melissa cleared her throat. "He says he doesn't know. Can't remember."

Marjorie's hand rested on the tomato she was about to pick. A sparrow trilled.

"You don't say," she said at last.

"Between us, I'm worried about him. I think he might not be right," Melissa tapped her temple with a ripe tomato, uncharitably mimicking Joseph's assessment of the old woman, "upstairs. Hey, you were visiting our hives right before he left – did you notice anything strange about him? He says he was getting sick."

Marjorie jiggled her left hand, grimacing.

"Anything strange? About Beck? Well." She smacked her lips. "Let me tell you about Beck and me right from the start. I met him at the monthly meeting of the Beekeepers' Society. He had a pencil and a scrap of paper and he was writing everything down, scribbling away. There was bad advice by the armload, as usual – amateurs and hobbyists who learn in front of a computer instead of out in the bee yard. Drives me crazy, especially the advice about hive smokers. Good heavens, it isn't rocket science, you know, keeping a small fire smouldering away, using a bellows. *Cavemen* did it. Smokers are useful as far as they go, but common sense is more important. Move slowly, if you don't want to get stung. Feel the mood of the bees. If you go stomping in there with your smoker, impatient and aggressive, well it's your own damn fault if you get stung then, isn't it?"

Melissa sensed Marjorie settling into a protracted monologue. She surveyed the robust tomato plants, heavy with fruit, and sighed.

"Don't look at me like that – I'm getting to Beck. I saw him writing down hogwash at the society meeting and I asked if he wanted to learn from me hands-on. Experience is the best teacher, everyone knows that. But I don't invite every vagabond who thinks they want to keep bees over to my place. Beck was special. I was impressed by his looks, I will admit. Tall and dark, with high cheekbones. I've always had a weakness for high, strong cheekbones in a man. Arnold, my husband, had very prominent cheekbones, but then he was an Algonquin, of the Pikwàkanagàn First Nation. Arnold had long black hair too, a lot like Beckett's, but not quite as wavy. Yes, I guess you could say I'm partial to Beck because he reminds me of Arnold."

"But he doesn't know where he was all summer." Melissa tried to steer her back on track. "I'm wondering if he's, you know, *crazy*."

"Crazy? He never struck *me* as crazy. He's a gentle soul – different, I'll give you that. What do you expect, the only child of peculiar parents? Just take Eurydice. She's a good neighbour, but she believes in voodoo and magic, a load of crap from Cuba. Offered to do some mumbo-jumbo in my living room, clear out evil spirits. Well – I said no thank you; if there're evil spirits in my house, they're keeping me company. And his father is an artist, a photographer. But you know all this. Weren't you two sleeping together?"

"Uh, yes. Yes, we were."

"I see," said Marjorie with disdain, as if Melissa had clarified a nasty suspicion.

Marjorie stopped picking tomatoes, set her basket down and wiped the back of a hand across her forehead. Melissa didn't see Marjorie often, and the elderly woman's brusque manner took her by surprise every time. Marjorie had the habit of avoiding eye contact, and her attention was darting from the shabby little building where she lived, out to the road past where Melissa's truck was parked and then up into the fruit trees. In the abstract, Marjorie's situation was sad: widowed long ago, living alone out here without a community of friends. But up close, in person, she was a lot like Joseph, Melissa thought, an aging single person with antisocial behaviour.

"Jiminy, it's hot for September, don't you think?"

Melissa didn't think so. In fact, the day was noticeably cooler than its predecessors, but there were small beads of sweat in the wrinkles around Marjorie's mouth, and the white hairs sticking to her temples were wet. Melissa wasn't around old people very much, so she couldn't tell if the sallow look to Marjorie's leathery skin augured ill health, or if it was normal geriatric decay.

"Beck's an only child, surely you know *that*," Marjorie said, implying Melissa had fucked him without bothering to learn much about him, precisely as Melissa feared she had done. "He was brought up on stories about miraculous cures, dark curses and weird rituals. He had no siblings to bounce that stuff off, so he grew up believing all the hocus-pocus. Beck believes things you and I would find . . . unbelievable."

"For example?"

"For example." She lifted her basket and starting picking again. "Well, okay, I'll give you an example. I keep a dozen laying hens, and I let them into the garden sometimes. Beck asked if I would sell him one. I said no, but I would sell him *two*, so they would be company for each other. He said the chicken was for his mother, and her plan was to kill the chicken. Beck's grandfather Luis was unwell, back in Cuba. Cancer, if I recall. Eurydice believed Luis had an evil spirit inside him and she wanted to sacrifice the chicken to cast the evil spirit out of her father. Of course, I asked a lot of questions at that point, and then I told him no, he couldn't buy one of my good hens so his mother could slit the poor creature's throat for some claptrap, some religious nonsense. Beck tried to laugh it off but I could tell he was disappointed, and he asked again. He explained they would be eating the bird after the bloodletting, the deranged sacrifice thing. So I sold him a chicken. As long as they weren't going to waste the meat, what did I care if they wanted to play with it first? Beck promised the slaughter would be humane. I asked him if his father believed in saints, spirits and slitting the throats of perfectly good hens. I was hoping the poor boy had one sane parent, at least. He said his father didn't used to believe, but then saw a lot of powerful Santeria things he couldn't explain. Gosh, I have to take a layer off, it's so warm."

Marjorie set her basket down and fumbled with the buttons of her long-sleeved work shirt. She was braless. Her pink sleeveless tank top had a hand-painted *Om* symbol, and was splotched with dark sweat stains. Skin was draped over her bones, loose and crinkled, like crepe.

"Are you okay? Sit down. I'll keep picking tomatoes."

Melissa scouted around and spotted a rickety wooden chair leaning against the sorry old fence. She set it in the shade of the sunflowers and indicated to Marjorie that she should sit. Marjorie opened her mouth to argue, then grunted and sat down, dabbing her face with her work shirt. *Too old to be doing all of this work on her own*, Melissa decided, flashing guiltily on her own employees. She could pick the old lady's tomatoes, at least. She grabbed a tomato in each hand, twisted them from the vine and put them in the basket.

"Be careful – don't just drop them in there."

Or maybe she would just finish harvesting this one plant.

"Oh, okay, gotcha. I'll be careful. Hey, did Beck ever give you an example?"

"An example of what?"

"Of, you know, a powerful thing his dad couldn't explain?"

"Oh, yes. I forgot what we were talking about. Yes, he did. Seems that his father had an accident on a farm in Cuba, when Beck was about ten years old. Cut his leg open and passed out. No one knows how long Matthew lay unconscious and bleeding, but when they found him, they didn't take him to a hospital. They cured him with herbs, and killed a goat or something to close and heal the wound. His father's leg was healed in a matter of days, Beck told me. Not even a scab. He wanted me to come over and look at the old scar on his father's leg. *No thank you*, I told him. I didn't need to see Matthew drop his pants."

"Beck never told me about that."

"Listen. I can recognize liars, and Beck's no liar. I taught him how to keep bees, and he helped me in this garden. He says he keeps to himself mostly, prefers animals, but somehow we came to be friends. There were times I wished I were half a century younger. But there you go, time isn't always kind. I'm seventy-two and he's twenty-three."

"He says he can't remember where he's been. For three months."

"I just told you he's honest," Marjorie snapped. "If he says he can't remember, let it go at that." She closed her wrinkled, purple eyelids, tilted her head back and groaned, then sat up again with a start and smiled. "If you want a liar, you don't have to look far to find one."

Melissa's patience with Marjorie had expired. Her thoughts returned to the dead chicken, the broken irrigation line and white, cottony codling moth tents in the orchard. She set Marjorie's tomato basket down and brushed off her hands.

"Okay, okay. Will you check in on him, until his parents get home? He's just next door."

"Nope." Marjorie leaned her head toward a shoulder and closed her eyes again. A fly landed on her age-spotted forehead and rubbed its front legs together.

"Sorry, what?"

"Beck owes me a visit and an apology. I won't go and play babysitter for him unless he shows his face around here first."

"Marjorie, I'm asking for a favour," Melissa heard herself wheedle. "I have the whole farm to run. We're swamped with mechanical problems – we're understaffed." *And furthermore, I just picked your damn tomatoes.* "Could you just walk next door, once a day, for me?"

Why wouldn't she do this? The walk would probably do her good.

"Listen to *you*, princess. Sounds like you're used to getting your own way. I'm not on your payroll, and as you can see, I have my own garden to take care of. And don't *tell* Beck to come and see me either. Let him come of his own accord. I want him to figure it out himself."

Melissa managed to make it back to the truck before puffing, tucking and touching every tooth with the tip of her tongue.

The Wises' cabin was in disarray. To keep track of the passage of days, Melissa saw, Beck was prison-chalking the wall beside his bed, four vertical lines with a horizontal bar struck through them. Her arrival had woken him up; she stood at the threshold while he rubbed his eyes, gathered his wits and put on a threadbare T-shirt inside out. He shuffled dispiritedly outside and stood beside her, squinting in the sunlight.

"Are you okay?"

"Not really. I'm still having bee thoughts. It's freaking me out."

As if on cue, a bee buzzed nearby. Beck grabbed Melissa's arm and pointed.

"Can you see that, or is it just me?"

Melissa tilted her head, trying to find the spot Beck meant. All her attention was focused on his hot fingers wrapped around her bicep.

"I'm sorry. See what?"

"Her path – the direction that bee flew! Like a golden thread, leading back to her hive, do you see it? I know where all these bees are coming from. I can see their trajectories." Beck released Melissa's arm and threw a brief, suspicious glance over his left shoulder. "You know what's weird? I don't even know what day it is, but I always know exactly how many hours and minutes of daylight are left. Also, in the daytime I feel sick, but after dark I'm starving. I've eaten every can of soup and bag of stale pasta in the cupboards, but the only thing I can keep down is honey. What's wrong with me?"

"I don't know," Melissa said softly. "It sounds like you should see a doctor."

"That's what Pa said. He wants to take me to this guy he knows, some doctor in Toronto he went to school with." Beck stretched his arms overhead, and Melissa peeked at him in her peripheral vision, at once loving and resenting his influence, the way he lit a conflagration of desire in her without even trying. "He'll probably put his foot down, and I might even have to go. Pa doesn't get worked up about much, but when he does, it's hard to argue with him. Even Ma has caved this time. He's obsessed with getting me examined by his doctor pal."

"Okay. Well, I guess I'll see you when you're feeling better."

Walking back to her truck, Melissa felt Beck watch her go and sensed him wanting her to stay. But she had torqued up resistance to his charms while he was away. It was up to him to release the tension.

That night she lay spread-eagled in bed, the curtains floating gently in and out of the window. She thought about departure and homecoming. Maybe her fond wish for those who left her to come back included an ingenuous hope that everything would be the same when they did. She thought of resurrected people, like Lazarus, and zombies – a shell of flesh returns, but the soul is long gone or irreparably damaged. Beck was deeply altered from just a few months in exile. What would her father be like, if he returned after all this time? Her mother might be forever changed too, after her time in Central America. "This is going to be a life-changing experience," Jill had said when she was leaving. She would be home soon – who would she be?

Seven

A pale orange dawn crept across a sky that reflected in her bedroom mirror. Melissa kicked away the blankets, rolled over and sat up. There, camouflaged against the pale green wall, was the cicada that had kept her up half the night with its deafening *cheeeerrrrup*. It waved an insolent antenna, pointing it at her, accusing. *You're not fooling anyone, you know. Beck has crawled inside you like an earwig. Even* I *can see it, and I'm a mere bug, hanging out on your wall.*

Who was the fool in all of this, and who was being foolish? Beck was insane, and he was fooling himself into believing this bee colony thing. Or Beck was telling the truth, and she was the stubborn fool, the person whose narrow mind couldn't encompass an idea so grand and implausible as a Beck-to-bees transfiguration. Or maybe Beck was lying, and again she was the fool for lending credence to his outrageous excuse, a fool for welcoming him back with open arms after he'd hurt her, inconvenienced her, embarrassed her. If he was making a fool of her, why did she feel guilty? When Beck's parents arrived from Cuba, Melissa invited the Wise family to the farm for dinner.

"But why?" Daphne asked, throwing up her hands in exasperated disbelief.

"He was working for me when he left. I feel a certain responsibility."

"That's ridiculous."

"No, it's polite."

Daphne nodded slowly. "All right. It's what Jill would do – make them a welcome-back dinner. I'll help you, but warning: this is going to be awkward."

While Daphne was out collecting eggs, Melissa paced in the kitchen, puffing strands of hair off her face, tucking them behind her ears and chewing gum to keep from tooth-touching. Later in the afternoon her apprehension worsened. Would Beck's parents blame her for what had happened to their son? She stood over a steaming pot of quinoa, picking at her jean shorts with ragged fingernails.

They showed up early. Beck trailed behind his parents, smiling sheepishly. Matthew and Eurydice looked as if the summer had aged them. A frowning Matthew shook Melissa's hand gravely, his forehead creasing with earnest concern. Eurydice, traceries of white shot through the black hair at her temples, enveloped Melissa in the folds of a voluminous orange-and-green caftan. Beck hovered in the background like a hooligan called to the principal's office, as if his parents' sudden spurt of aging was his fault, a sophomoric prank.

"He has amnesia. That much is obvious," said Matthew, running fingertips over a diminished hairline.

"Pa and the police figured I was partying in Ottawa." Beck rolled his eyes at Melissa. "You know, because I'm such a wild party animal."

"You've couch-surfed there before," Matthew said defensively. "When that band you like was gigging all the time at the Mercury Lounge. And before we left, you were talking about some music festival in the Gatineau Hills, begging us not to worry if you dropped off the map for a while." Matthew touched Melissa's arm in solidarity. "He doesn't understand how hard this was for us. Eurydice's father has cancer, or we would have been in Canada for the summer as usual. It's been a very stressful time."

"I didn't mean to make life hard for you guys," Beck muttered, and Daphne patted his back in unspoken comfort.

"You have to admit it's strange," Melissa said. "Not knowing where you were."

"Beck is a soul-traveller in the spirit world." Eurydice floated her hands gauzily to demonstrate her son's ethereal journeys. "We may never know where he was, and it doesn't matter. He is home now."

Silent nodding, Melissa found, was the best response to Eurydice's murkier explorations. But Matthew looked livid, his complexion plethoric, and he exploded in a vehement and unusual-for-him outburst. "Damn it, Eurydice, there's a limit! She accuses me of disloyalty," he indicated his wife with an annoyed gesture, "when all I want is to take my son to the fucking doctor."

"And what about your injury," Eurydice puckered her lips wryly, "in Cuba?"

Matthew grimaced and glanced apologetically at Melissa. He wanted to keep arguing, she guessed, but was embarrassed by his outburst and didn't want to make a scene. Beck regarded his father as if seeing him for the first time. Daphne had been right; this was awkward.

Reading Melissa's mind, Daphne licked her lips and smiled bracingly. "Come see what we've done with the herb gardens," she chirped. "Raised beds were my idea, and then we decided they'd look cool if we built them in graduated levels." Daphne steered Matthew and Eurydice outside, winking at Melissa as she closed the screen door, *take some time alone with Beck*. As soon as his parents were out of earshot, Beck touched Melissa's shoulder and leaned in close. His breath smelled of honey.

"I'm sorry I haven't been in touch. Ma saw how thin I am and went ballistic. She's forcing me to sleep and eat. Pa grills me ten times a day and concocts these insane theories."

To hide her hurt, Melissa tipped her head and flicked a hand, *no big deal*. Her eyes stung in the corners. When she spoke, she aimed for flippant, and was appalled to hear herself sound petulant and tearful.

"You were gone, again. I'm kind of getting used to it."

"I'm a weirdo, I know. I've always been strange – do you remember me telling you that?"

Beck sought her eyes, and Melissa ducked her head to conceal a brief puff-and-tuck episode. When she was done she smoothed her hair and raised her chin, trying to seem composed. "You used to be a weirdo who knew how to operate a telephone."

"Ah." He made a fist, and pounded the air. "I knew I should have called. But when you came by the cabin the other day, I thought something was bothering you. You seemed preoccupied and I didn't want to pester you."

"Something *was* bothering me, but it wasn't you. I stopped by Marjorie's place first."

Beck's eyes widened, even as the light in them dimmed.

"What did she say to you?" His voice was quiet, as if he were afraid Marjorie could hear him.

"That you're honest, and if you say you don't know where you were, I should believe you. But she's so strange. The whole time I was there, she talked a mile a minute."

The sun disappeared behind a cloud, and Beck seemed to shrink in the reduced light. The swirl of his parents' voices carried up from the garden, and echoes of Daphne's laughter returned to the kitchen. Beck twitched like a horse ridding itself of bothersome flies. He glanced out the window before speaking.

"Marjorie's probably upset I went away. I used to visit her and help in her bee yard, every day, almost. I felt sorry for her, and she knows so much about beekeeping. But since I, you know, woke up or whatever, I haven't felt like going over there. Her bees, though – I know they're just foraging, but it seems like they're, I don't know, investigating. Spying on me – is that nuts?"

Eurydice pushed the back door open and breezed into the kitchen, followed by Matthew, holding a limp bouquet of leaves. Daphne entered rhapsodizing about a soothing mint tea she would steep after the meal. Beck's interest drifted to the back window; his body stopped but his attention carried on through the glass. Melissa was acutely aware of him as she cooked. Eurydice asserted her culinary preferences, liberally sprinkling hot sauce in the stew. At dinner, Beck fell on his food like a vulture on carrion.

"Apparently your appetite is intact," Melissa observed.

Beck swallowed, and paused to answer. "It was shaky when I first got back, but now it's better than ever. I'm ravenous." He returned to the desperate business of feeding himself.

"At this rate, he'll eat us broke," Matthew said.

"Why doesn't he come back to work? It's harvest, and I could use another field hand."

Hearing false nonchalance in her offer, Melissa cringed. She expected Beck to agree right away, but he hadn't heard; he was intent on eating. He was reminding her of Hotay, the way the donkey bellied up to his trough.

Matthew frowned. "I don't know that's he's strong enough to work yet. Eurydice, I understand you don't think it's necessary, but Beck needs to be examined by a medical doctor. This unexplained memory loss is worrisome to me."

"Our son is here. He's right here – look, Matthew." Eurydice clamped a silver-bedecked hand on Beck's wrist, preventing a spoonful of nutrition from reaching his mouth. Patiently, Beck extricated his arm from his mother's grasp and returned to his dinner. "Flesh and blood and bone, right here. Food and rest are what he needs. I will do a consulta with him, when he is ready."

"A consulta – what's that?" Daphne asked.

"A spiritual reading," said Beck briefly, between bites.

"Oh, like a Santeria thing." Daphne nodded.

"Well, you could do that too," Matthew addressed his wife with patronizing kindness. "Couldn't hurt. But I insist on a doctor. I have a physician in mind. An old friend from university, a guy in Toronto I used to hang out with, Max Griffen. He thinks outside the box, and I trust him."

"Pah – your doctor friend. His mind is closed *inside* a box," said Eurydice, and she pressed her palms together vertically then horizontally, demonstrating a square shape.

Daphne, hypersensitive to conflict, jiggled in her chair and tried to change the subject. "Maybe you could help out with harvest again, Eurydice? Everything's ripening at once, as usual, and we're not quite keeping up with it."

It wasn't what Melissa had in mind. But she had just finished saying the farm needed help. She drilled a meaningful look into Beck's skull, hoping he would interject, but he was busy eating and impervious to her glare. Matthew nudged his wife, prompting her to respond.

"I guess we could use the food." Eurydice inclined her head.

"Good," said Matthew. "Beck and I will leave for Toronto tomorrow, or the day after. We can stay with my sister – your aunt Sylvia, Beck. I haven't seen her for ages." He clapped cupped hands, *thwuck*, and looked around the table, challenging anyone to disagree with him.

Melissa almost laughed. Beck's father normally came across as diffident, hiding behind his camera lenses; this striving to convey authority was more funny than convincing. She waited for Beck to refuse the trip, but he scraped his fork across his plate, indifferent to autocratic decisions being made about his activities. Melissa's shoulders slumped. Why was Beck content to acquiesce so gormlessly to his father's wishes? It was discouraging. He was back, but he wasn't all there. This new Beck was insecure; there was a nervousness about him she didn't recognize.

A conversational pause sagged uncomfortably, and Daphne began whistling into it.

Beck surfaced from his meal. "I could start working here as soon as Pa and I get back," he said, trying to catch up on the action. "I'm already getting better."

Melissa shrugged, indulgent and noncommittal. "We'll see. I hope there's nothing seriously wrong with you."

A shadow passed across Beck's features. He got up and helped himself to seconds.

At the end of the evening, Beck lingered on the front porch while his parents wandered out to their car, entertained by a gracious Daphne. Melissa glanced right and left, ensuring Joseph wasn't skulking about, smoking and spying. Satisfied they were alone, she turned to Beck. He passed a hand around her waist, placed another behind her head and drew her into an impassioned kiss.

"Do me a favour," he said when they stopped to breathe, and Melissa's heart throbbed with expectation. *Will he ask me to wait for him? To believe in him, to believe in us?*

"Don't ask Marjorie to help you with your beehives."

Oh. "Why not?"

Beck's face crumpled, as if he smelled something repugnant. "It's just – I don't know. She's kind of frail. It won't be too late to harvest the honey when I get back from Toronto. And hopefully by then, I'll be able to handle being around bees."

"Fine. I won't ask Marjorie to help. But I can't promise you that Daphne and I won't harvest the honey ourselves before you get back. It's getting late in the season. The bees will start consuming their stores if we leave it too late." Beck arched his eyebrows, surprised, Melissa thought, that she knew this about honeybees. "I was getting ready to do it myself. I didn't know if you would ever come back."

Beck bent over the porch railing, leaning his top half toward the bee yard. A clump of hyssop growing beside the porch was in bloom, a profusion of pink-and-cream blossoms, and in spite of the late hour a few diligent bees were visiting the flowers. "We're so close to your hives," Beck said. "I can even see fat drones, milling around the hive entrances.

It feels like they're pulling me over there. Like I'm hooked up to a fishing line and they're reeling me in."

Melissa held her breath. For a moment she thought she could see it too, a filament stretching out between Beck and the beehives.

"Sparkling streamers, floating in the air . . ." Beck thrust an arm toward the hives. "There – Melissa, can you see them now, with the sun shining on them? They're like gold ribbons, running between the bees and the hives – like little bee highways, see where they come together like that?"

Obediently she looked, but although she squinted and strained her eyes, Melissa couldn't see any bee vectors. Instead she imagined Beck's trust as a simple, invisible gift, suspended in the autumn air without ribbons or wrapping. He gawked and hallucinated beside her, as honest and innocent as a child. He was handing her his faith, trusting she wouldn't betray his strange secret, his conviction he'd been communing magically with bees all summer. Caring for people meant sticking by them through their issues, Melissa thought, even their full-blown delusions. She set her jaw, determined to wait out Beck's recovery.

"Beck? We're on our way!" Matthew shouted from the other side of the hedge.

Beck tore his attention from the bees and hugged her. They shared a final, firm kiss. Melissa propped herself up against the porch's corner post and watched him slip out through the gap in the hedge.

The next morning Melissa and Daphne drank their coffee outside, watching sunlight spread across the lake. The air was cold enough to reveal breath, and they were surrounded by their own misty exhalations. Hotay, harnessed to a cart, stamped his hooves. Melissa inhaled scents of autumn: earth, wet hay and decaying plant matter – carbon in complex arrangements, rich and comforting.

"Man, I miss Jill," said Daphne. "This time of year she should be here, you know?"

"Why? We've got everything under control." Melissa was worried her mother's return would unbalance the new equilibrium on the farm. She liked being in charge, and the thought of Jill calling the shots again made her uneasy.

"I guess. Harvest festival's coming up though, and we've never organized one before. Is there a template or something, a master plan? I don't even know where to start." Daphne sighed.

"Well, I do. I've done harvest festival my whole life."

Eurydice ambled around the side of the farmhouse and greeted them with a distracted wave. Daphne went to feed the goats and Melissa motioned for Eurydice to follow her. The plan for the morning was to harvest squash and stack it in the straw-lined donkey cart. Beck's mother was in an introspective mood, and Melissa was grateful for a quiet beginning to the day. Hotay followed them placidly down the furrows and they got to work. Melissa found harvesting squash a satisfying job – slicing thick stalks, collecting hundreds of pounds of food in a short time. The vegetative part of the plant conveniently died and shrivelled up, exposing the fruit. Bend, slice, *thump*, the squashes piled up fast. An hour slipped by before Melissa struck up a conversation.

"You must have been so worried about Beck when he was gone." Bend, slice, *thump.*

"Sí, and no. Beck has travelled in the spirit world since he was a small boy."

"Spirit world – what does that mean?"

"He sees ghosts and talks to animals."

A childhood recollection slammed into Melissa, whole and vivid. Hallowe'en was coming. She was eight years old, and knew definitively what costume she wanted for the holiday: a scarecrow, with a red-and-white checkered shirt, denim overalls, straw poking out of sleeves and pant legs, convincing makeup and a wild wig. Using one satisfyingly crinkled side of a paper bag, she drew a detailed picture of her proposed costume, rendering each aspect in coloured pencil and labelling the items she would need to realize her vision. She presented it to her parents at the dinner table one evening. Her father accepted the schematic formally and studied the picture, nodding and making the noises of a person engaged in thoughtful reflection. "You can use straw from Hotay's shed, and glue it to the clothes so it doesn't fall out. I think I have a shirt like that in my closet you can wear. You can walk like this," her father said, and he stood up and paraded stiff-armed around the dining room. While he scarecrow-marched, and Melissa giggled, her mother snatched the drawing. "Oh, Lissy – this is an ugly costume. Why don't you want to be something pretty, like a butterfly?" Melissa objected. She wanted to be a scarecrow, not a butterfly, which would be a stupid costume. Her father defended her. Jill and Charlie fought about it, and she took her drawing to her room and cried.

The next day Melissa and her father walked to Hotay's enclosure, holding hands, exclaiming at the size of the pumpkins and squash. In the pocket of his plaid jacket her father had tucked a tube of contact cement; a ball of fabric in his fist turned out to be the checkered shirt from his closet. They made her costume under Hotay's gentle supervision, and stashed it in the work shed until the end of October. After school on the thirty-first, while her mother clattered and banged in the kitchen, Melissa's father helped her draw makeup-stitching on her face and arrange her coveted scarecrow costume. She trick-or-treated on the cold dark streets of Lanark, counting mini chocolate bars and giving her father his favourites. They stopped at a haunted house bedecked with toilet paper streamers, the front yard littered with cardboard gravestones, a spooky organ soundtrack amplified on front porch speakers. At the end of the evening Melissa lay in bed, flattened with disappointment and frightened by a spectre more sinister than any Hallowe'en ghost: the disagreement between her parents ran much deeper than scarecrow versus butterfly.

Eight

Beck was impatient to get back to work, push his missing months into the past and live in the present, but his father was adamant they go to Toronto and see the doctor. Beck pleaded a case for getting on with his life and begged for recuperation at home, but his father wasn't buying it. Usually dreamy and compliant, Matthew was standing firm, demanding answers. Beck was having feverish, sticky dreams featuring Melissa. The human adult male part of him was waking up after a summer's absence and clamouring for attention. Leaving now, he told his father, when Melissa needed help with the harvest season, seemed like a colossally bad idea. But Beck's father arranged for them to stay with his sister Sylvia, and found the address of his doctor friend's clinic. Matthew became single-minded and obsessed, making lists and talking exclusively about the upcoming trip to Toronto. In the end, Beck gave in. The only compromise he brokered was to convince his father that they should take the bus instead of driving.

"There's a climate catastrophe happening. We don't need the car."

"Your aunt Sylvia doesn't live anywhere near Max Griffen's office."

"She lives three blocks from the subway."

His father always ranted about how progressive Cuba was, energy-wise, and loved to explain how after Cuba experienced artificial peak oil, bicycling and public transportation had inevitably evolved, borne of necessity. Beck listened to enthusiastic lectures about Cuban ingenuity and common sense, about the country's low waste output and its advanced environmental consciousness, and then his father came back to Canada and drove his car, used plastic drinking containers and left the porch light on at night, as if Canada were on a different planet than Cuba. At least when Beck called him out on these hypocrisies, Matthew usually relented.

The bus station in Lanark was dingy, bordering on foul. The walls were bile-coloured, the floors polka-dotted with smears of chewing gum and splashes of spilled coffee. Beck's father settled into a torn vinyl chair and became immersed in his e-reader. Beck watched a parade of dismal people shuffle to the ticket counter dragging shabby luggage, resigning themselves to the fate of mass transit in a private-car culture. The bus that pulled in to take them to Toronto was from an outdated fleet. A faint odour of stale vomit clung to green-and-blue polyester upholstery covering narrow, uncomfortable seats. The driver was outdated too: white-haired, mumpish and grim-jowled. He stared out the windshield indifferently as his passengers settled behind him. Their bus pulled out of the dreary station on time. The engine was loud, and the frame creaked and groaned around sharp corners.

Beck was surprised at how much suburbia had encroached on what used to be wilderness between Lanark and Toronto. He remembered the drive as having long stretches of deciduous forest interrupted sporadically by cleared agricultural land and clumps of cows chewing in pretty pastures almost all the way south to Lake Ontario. He stared through the scratched bus window at muddy construction sites featuring the half-built, flimsy boxes of particle board–framed row houses swimming in lakes of dirt. Gone, too, were hundreds of fallow fields full of nectar-laden native flowers, shaggy pink bee balm, spiky purple fireweed. Beck interrupted his father's reading.

"Really bad for bees, these housing developments," he shouted over the roar of the bus as they hurtled along.

"How so?" His father peered at him over the top rim of his spectacles.

"Think about it. When they build these developments, the first things to go are the natural nectar and pollen sources, then the topsoil. Once the houses are up, hardly anyone bothers to put in a garden. If they grow anything, it's a plastic planter full of geraniums."

"So geraniums aren't palatable to bees?"

He had piqued his father's interest. "Absolutely not. The floral equivalent of dumpster diving. Geraniums and marigolds are stinky. And roses are infuriating. They smell good, but they're all swirled up, and completely unnavigable. Chrysanthemums are dry as forgotten toast."

"Those are all popular flowers."

"Exactly, exactly. There are fewer and fewer options for honeybees, but I think things are starting to change. Melissa talks about a movement, people planting bee-friendly gardens, that kind of thing."

"Clear something up for me: Is Melissa Makepeace your girlfriend?"

"She was my girlfriend, before this summer. I'm not sure about now."

Behind his glasses, his father's eyes bulged a little, and he went back to reading his book. For some reason Beck started thinking about when his father used to read to him at night before bed, sitting inside the cabin's mosquito-netting porch enclosure, or in his grandparents' humid kitchen in Cuba. He supposed he would be a different person without those stories occupying his imagination: *The Jungle Book*, *Treasure Island*, *Harry Potter*. His mother had told him stories too, Santeria legends about people growing wings and flying off to find their true loves, and enemies vanquished and villains dying mysterious gruesome deaths, felled by the power of prayer. Beck spent more time with his parents than normal kids did; it was part of what made him an oddball. He already had friends – his parents – so he was poor at initiating friendships. He didn't know how to be Melissa's friend, and he had never told her he loved her, an omission that now struck him as serious.

The bus rumbled along. Beck rested his forehead on the cool window. Approaching Toronto, he saw clumps of houses interspersed with strip malls and big-box stores, extended white rectangular buildings surrounded by black parking lots full of shiny cars. Traffic converged on the bus from nowhere, merging left and right, surrounding them and zooming too close, like hornets mobbing an abandoned picnic. He felt a hammering in his chest, a rapid flutter – wasn't that too fast to be a heartbeat? He closed his eyes and pretended to sleep, trying in vain to calm down.

The bus puked them out into the insanity of the Bay Street terminal, thousands of determined travellers trampling over cigarette butts and sandwich wrappers, trundling suitcases, bumping into each other's backpacks, skirting newsstands crammed with glossy gossip magazines, gum and shrink-wrapped factory-made snacks. A busker squatting on a plastic milk crate played a frantic polka on a shiny blue accordion – mayhem music.

"Been years," said Matthew, nervously pushing his spectacles up his nose, as if getting them closer to his eyes would help him navigate the kinetic shudder of cars and people in downtown Toronto. Heading to the subway, they descended steps that were caked with urban grime. In a concourse at the bottom of the stairs streams of people merged, funnelling in from underground mall entrances and bus transfer stations. It was a hive entrance, arrivals from every direction, departures to the wider world, the coming-in and going-from a sun-deprived box. Startled, Beck stopped moving and became an obstacle. Bodies flowed around him, left and right.

"Are you okay? We have to keep going," his father said gently, and he steered Beck by his elbow through silver turnstiles, down more stairs and into a hurtling tube of humanity.

Matthew wanted to visit an old friend of his, a quantum physicist named Barbara Beauchemin. It was already after noon, and they were better off going to the medical clinic first thing the next morning, in Matthew's opinion, before it got too busy. The way his father talked about her, Beck guessed Barbara was an old girlfriend, a lover from a time before his mother, but he didn't ask if this were so. They rode the train to Museum Station and climbed up to the street. The Royal Ontario Museum was a Frankensteinian building, jagged glass angles jutting out of an old stone behemoth. Beck stared up and up, reeling with vertigo, eyes sliding along impossible lines of slanted steel. His father rotated, pointing out street names and compass points.

"Where is it, now? This way, I think." Matthew set off determinedly.

As they skirted Queen's Park, aggressive squirrels shot between their legs, black beady eyes glinting, mangy tails missing clumps of fur. They swung right and entered the historic part of the university. It was quieter here, with knots of smiling students threading their way through lofty ivy-covered archways, stone walls dotted with leaded windows, and little grassy squares featuring birdbaths, fountains and topiaries.

It was his father's party. Beck allowed himself to drift, and be directed by his father's purpose. From Hoskin Avenue they climbed an imposing staircase, and passed between ornately carved Oxford-style wooden doors into Trinity College, *the still-beating Protestant heart of campus,* his father announced, shuffling up to an old directory affixed to a granite vestibule in the college's imposing lobby. The directory, a glass case enclosing horizontal rows of black ridges, showed the location of various offices with little white plastic letters and numbers clipped into place. *Professor Barbara Beauchemin, Room 247.* Matthew poked a finger at his old friend's name, grinning like he'd solved a tricky puzzle, and motioned Beck up a gloomy flight of stairs.

The second floor was a row of office doors, more solid wood, more archways, the hallowed halls of academia. There was even a suit of armour, dusty and neglected, leaning in an alcove at the end of the corridor. A pinched, grey-haired woman emerged from one of the stone arches. She was at least a foot shorter than his father, who rushed forward and hugged her delicately; she looked breakable. Neglecting to introduce his son, Matthew followed her into her office. This was his usual absent-minded-professor fashion, and hers also, Beck guessed. He didn't mind being ignored, but he was curious about the woman, who seemed more Middle-earth than Metrotown. He wandered along behind them, stepping into an old-world study finished in European scholarly style: leather furniture, hardwood floor, cloth-bound books crammed on shelves stretching from floor to ceiling. Small-paned leaded glass windows overlooked a quiet quadrangle, wrought-iron benches set in its four corners, flanked by tufted flower beds bursting with lavender.

On the polished oak desk was an anachronism, a silver laptop. The computer was surrounded by stacks of paper, magazines folded open to pages marked with sticky notes, newspaper cuttings, pens and pencils. A stained-glass lamp was perched on a corner of the desk, its golden pull-chain swaying underneath an octagon of ornate green-and-gold panels of stylized flowers. The lamp wasn't on, but Beck touched a glass section with a fingertip, and it was warm, as if the lamp had been recently extinguished.

"And this is . . . ?" The little professor scuttled over to him. Her complexion was whitish-grey, as was her straight, shoulder-length hair. Her hand when Beck shook it was limp and clammy. They introduced themselves, he as *Beck,* she as *Professor Beauchemin,* and she hastened back behind her desk. Father and son settled into black leather-upholstered chairs across from her.

"It's so good to see you again, Matthew, and lovely to meet you, Beck. Time seems to roll along without mercy these days. I'm working on a documentary film and it consumes a good deal of my stamina. How are things for you?"

Matthew launched into a description of life on the organopónico. The professor listened eagerly and asked questions. Beck tried to focus on the conversation, but outside the sun was slanting over the rooftops into the quadrangle, illuminating flowers and neatly mown grass clumped up around clover. To his amazement, Beck's eyes picked up the golden vectors of bee travel, and then he saw the bees, each individual as bright as a firefly. He gaped out the window in wonder.

"Enough about me." Matthew's ears were flushed, and he rubbed his sideburns self-consciously. "What's your documentary about?"

"It's an examination of the plight of the honeybee," said Professor Beauchemin.

"Ah, bees. Fascinating creatures," said Matthew.

Bee vectors converged on the southwest corner of the quadrangle. Could there be a hive nearby? Beck imagined he could hear the buzzing, and then he *could* hear it. A single worker picked her way through clover and arrived at a flower, hairy abdomen rubbing powdery pollen, bent black legs loaded with orange globs of nectar.

"You're a beekeeper? But how wonderful!"

Professor Beauchemin was addressing Beck. Flexing all the willpower he could summon, he ripped his focus from the bee.

"Are you interested in the navigational capabilities of the honeybee, Beck? On a quantum level?"

Beck stared at Barbara Beauchemin for a long moment, astonished by her ability to climb inside his thoughts. The humming of the bees blended with sounds of traffic whizzing by and distant student voices. "I don't understand what you mean by 'quantum level.' I think it's supercool that bees use the angle of the sun to find nectar lodes," he said.

"Let me share with you an interesting theory. It was dismissed as rubbish years ago, but it is the crucible in which I conceived my current project. Over a decade ago, an American mathematician was playing with two-dimensional representations of a flag manifold."

"Sorry, a what?" Matthew asked, setting his chin on his fist.

"A flag manifold. It's a six-dimensional field that mathematicians use for making hypothetical calculations." The professor turned abruptly to her desk, yanked a drawer open, located a scrap of paper and a sharp pencil, and started drawing. "Mathematicians, always postulating." Barbara Beauchemin waved a miniature white hand in the air. "We don't have to jump down *that* rabbit hole. It isn't as impenetrable as it sounds. I can draw *this*," she quickly drew a perfect circle, "and tell you to see a sphere. It's a two-dimensional representation of a ball, which is a three-dimensional object. You see?"

Beck nodded. Matthew frowned.

"A flag manifold, a *six*-dimensional field, looks like this on paper." She drew a hexagon. Beck spasmed at the sight of it, and she smiled.

"Yes, it's a honeycomb cell, not surprising of course, six sides of equal length. But the thing is, this mathematician plotted the way quarks would behave in this field. Quarks, do you know what they are? They're tiny subatomic particles. And, um, these are the shapes that emerged, over and over again." The scratch of her pencil, briefly.

"Oh, the dances!" Beck exclaimed, and his father raised his eyebrows.

"Precisely." The professor beamed at Beck, right answer, gold star. "The mathematician who conducted this experiment didn't delve any further, as far as I know. She was roundly ridiculed for this research, by the way. The scientific community reacted very harshly. But I saw the appeal of her idea. It has a lovely poetic symmetry, doesn't it? Honeycomb shapes, waggle dance shapes. It points to honeybees having some perception in a quantum dimension, a perception we humans lack, or perhaps cannot yet perceive."

"I'm in the dark, over here," said Matthew, squinting at the pencil marks.

"See this, Pa, this thing that looks like a coffee bean, or a figure eight?" Beck jabbed the paper. "That's the waggle dance, essentially. That's the precise shape of it. And this small circle? That's the round dance. When the nectar is closer than, like, about fifty metres, we use the round dance, because we only need to communicate the direction of the nectar, not the distance travelled to get there. The distance is conveyed by the length of the dance, in circuits. There's a tremble dance too, for when a bee is desperate to offload nectar in the hive. What she's saying is, the bee dances happen in a quantum dimension, and bees use quantum physics to transmit information. Something like that, right?"

"Something like that," Barbara Beauchemin echoed, batting purplish eyelids. "You said *we* just now, as in the royal *we*. How strange. That pronoun came out of you so naturally. You identify closely with your bees, I suppose."

Outside the window, bees whipped and zipped around the quadrangle. Beck wanted to ask Professor Beauchemin about the gold ribbons, the lines of energy he could see snaking around the courtyard, and the spots of concentrated light where a bee worked in a flower, but he knew how bizarre the question would sound. His dreamy hesitation lasted a moment too long.

"Beck, are you entirely well?" the professor asked. "You've gone a bit pale."

Matthew sighed. "Beck works on a farm. This past summer Eurydice and I were in Cuba. When we're away, we'll go two or three weeks, sometimes even a month, without hearing from our son. He takes care of the cabin for us, and there's no phone service there, so if he doesn't answer his cellphone, it's not unusual. He can't afford a new phone, and when his malfunctions, he's incommunicado. In the middle of the summer I called the farm where he works, and they said they hadn't seen him in a month."

"Where were you?" Barbara Beauchemin asked Beck reprovingly.

"I don't know. I can't remember." Telling the lie, Beck squirmed.

"I flew back to Ontario," Matthew continued. "Our cabin was unlocked. Beck's backpack and a few of his things were in the middle of the floor. One of the beds was messed up. Really messed up, not from sleeping, more like there had been a fight on it. I walked the whole property, three acres, looking for him and calling his name. Melissa, his boss, was furious. His absence was a big inconvenience. All those beehives, and no one to help her with them. My wife, Eurydice, instinctively felt our son was fine, but she was also preoccupied with caring for her father, who was undergoing various treatments for cancer. Well, a couple of weeks ago, Beck showed up at our cabin again, with total amnesia. He has no recollection at all – no idea where he's been. I'm taking him to a doctor tomorrow."

Hearing it matter-of-factly from his father, Beck understood for the first time how his departure had hurt Melissa. He felt a heaviness in his chest and pressure behind his eyes. He ran his hands over smooth skin on his forearms, and reassured by their solidity, he looked out at the sunny quadrangle, where golden vectors converged and spiralled up toward him. A sensation he was being reincorporated into a colony, a wriggling that began in his core and spread through his torso, overwhelmed him, and Beck stood up and walked to the window, touching hot fingertips to cool glass. A shuddering spread up his arm and across his shoulders. His vision began to fragment, and then he was plunged into darkness.

Professor Beauchemin had grabbed opaque curtains and swished them shut in front of Beck's face. His breath stalled between his mouth and his lungs. He staggered from the window and collapsed in one of the leather chairs with a *whump*. His father loomed; with his long arms hinged at knobby elbows and his round glasses he looked like a praying mantis, head angled down, eyes bulbous. The professor pulled the chain dangling from the stained-glass lamp, and electric light illuminated the room, compensating for the closed curtains.

"You'd better get him to a doctor," said Professor Beauchemin.

Beck let his father guide him down the Trinity College steps. Afternoon sun shone evenly on the pavement, toasting the fallen maple leaves, supple oranges, reds and yellows crisping to a uniform light brown. Buses rumbled by. Clumps of collegiate young people navigated the sidewalks in sweaters and jeans and leather shoes, toques and tams and striped scarves. The episode had passed, but Beck was reeling – was he poised to become bees again? What was wrong with him? He peeked at his father, who, on his own, could have passed for a professor walking from cafeteria to lecture hall, his spectacles, tie and jacket identifying him as a pedagogue. Instead, Matthew Wise resembled a care aid, leading a semi-catatonic charge by an elbow. They shuffled toward Spadina Avenue.

"Let's see if we can get you into the clinic today."

Nine

Oh, man, I don't know," said Daphne. "Can we do this?"

"I've watched a honey extraction before, and I understand how the equipment works. How hard can it be?" Melissa asked breezily, stepping into a muddy pair of ankle-high rubber boots.

"Tell me again why we're not waiting for Beck to get back."

"Because after his disappearing act this summer, I don't trust him to get here in time. The weather is turning, and this job needs to be done. And also," Melissa searched for a way to explain without breaking her promise, "I don't think it's a good idea for Beck to work with bees right now."

"Beck loves the bees. He's crazy about them." Daphne did jazz hands beside her ears, miming Beck's unbalanced passion.

Melissa laughed uneasily and put an arm around her sister's shoulders. "True, but I think it's better not to rely on Beck. We can do this ourselves. Anyway, we're not going to start extracting tonight. We're just going to poke around, check out the hives and make sure we have everything we need to start tomorrow."

Dzzzzt, dzzzzt. Melissa's phone vibrated in her front pocket. She dug it out, examined the number on the screen and, giving Daphne a look of bemused resignation, answered. A brash, confident voice invaded the still atmosphere.

"Melissa? Constable Susan Hickey here. I stopped by Produce Point Market today and had an interesting chat with Balvinder Singh. Do you have a few minutes?"

"Yes, sure." Melissa waved at Daphne to go ahead without her, and went back inside the farmhouse.

Daphne stepped off the front porch and inhaled deeply. Melissa had built the first fire of the year in the living room's stone fireplace, and the smell of woodsmoke puffing from the chimney gave her a thrill of contentment. The evening was unusually pretty, rich autumn light electrifying the greens and softening the blues, lending the farm a fairy-tale glow. Soon it would be Thanksgiving, and gratitude surged through Daphne, as it had since Jill Makepeace had become her adoptive mother and brought her to Hopetown Farm. Every day that passed took Daphne further away from the motherless squalor and violence of her preteen years, dank apartment hallways crusted with broken glass and nights cowering on a bare mattress, hoping the door wouldn't open and admit another predator. It was useless and wrong to compare her life and Melissa's, but sometimes Daphne couldn't stop herself, and the disparity between them made her want to grab her sister by the shoulders and shake her until Melissa appreciated her inherited paradise.

In some ways she and Melissa weren't that different. They were both fatherless. Melissa had known hers; Daphne's had left while she'd still been sporting diapers. Both mothers had tried their best for their daughters. Celia, Daphne's biological mother, sashayed into her memories at night, performing a step-ball-change shuffle that meant *I love you* in their private dance language. For some reason, Melissa resisted the notion that Daphne's mother of slaps and mean boyfriends had also been a shy, gentle, dress-up-and-dance-your-heart-out Mama. There had been plenty of love and good times before a tainted dose had taken Celia's life. Some seriously bad shit had gone down after that, and yes, she felt lucky that Jill had stepped in. But Daphne would trade away the farm in a heartbeat if doing so would bring her mother back.

She hated seeing Melissa and Jill disagree. She wished mothers and daughters could always love each other completely, with a love that encompassed strengths and flaws. Jill's eccentricities, her New Age double-speak and lofty ideals, seemed to nettle Melissa the most. But those same qualities had inspired the woman to reach out and help a thirteen-year-old stranger, and for that Daphne thanked God, the devil, the universe and anyone else who had reached out a divine hand and steered her here.

Sun glimmered along a wire past the corner of the farmhouse, and caught Daphne's eye. It was the electrified fence of the bee yard, studded with triangular neon-yellow signs that featured black lightning bolts outlined in red. Beyond the fence, hive supers rose among bunches of weeds and grass. Impulsively, she stepped off the porch, and followed the tamped-down trail to the beehives.

She stopped at the gate, beside a shed containing beekeeping equipment. In the height of summer, clouds of stinging insects here intimidated her, but on this cool evening there wasn't much activity around the hives. Only a dozen or so bees zipped around the entrance of each rectangular stack of boxes. Daphne had twice donned the white jumpsuit, netted hat and leather gloves of a beekeeper. The first time was for curiosity's sake. Beck had been her guide and teacher, and she hadn't enjoyed it. She wasn't afraid, or allergic, but standing in front of an open hive crawling with insects, she hadn't understood the appeal of the pursuit. In fact, the bees had kind of repelled her. Beck had pulled a frame and pointed out the brood cells, capped with a papery grey translucent film. Inside the cells were hundreds of bee maggots, *disgusting*. The electric fence, Beck had told her, was meant to keep out predators who would eat not only the honey but also the brood, getting a good hit of protein in their diet from bee larvae. Eating maggots – the thought of it made dinner climb back up her throat.

The second time was soon after Beck had disappeared. Melissa had insisted they orient themselves in the bee yard and take turns caring for the bees until Beck's return. An irritable Joseph had acted as foreman that day, doling out jobs and barking instructions. Joseph understood what needed to be done in the bee yard, but the farmhand's disdain for the entire endeavour was obvious. He had shown Daphne how to free up frames of comb inside the supers by using a bee tool, a heavy metal object, sharp at one end and curved at the other. The frames were stuck together with propolis, or bee glue. Propolis was made from the sap of nearby trees, Daphne learned, and processed by the bees to create a stiff orange cement. *Crack*! Daphne had pushed the metal lever into the propolis, and pried the frames apart.

"*Pro, polis*. It means *before, city*. They make their home strong before they reproduce and make honey. Amazing, eh?" Melissa had enthused.

Daphne remembered thinking she would rather be doing pretty much anything else on the farm, and wishing she were scraping chicken shit from the henhouse floor with a shovel. But the beekeeping had to be done and Beck was missing and, well, hallelujah, Hopetown Farm. She had given herself over to the task. Now the honey had to be harvested, Beck was down south in Toronto and Joseph said he wanted no part of the bees. "If it were up to me I'd sell the hives," he grumbled to Daphne again and again, though never within earshot of Melissa. Here was the kind of opportunity Daphne could relish privately, an unsolicited contribution to the farm, an expression of her gratitude. It would be a relief to Jill when she arrived, and to prickly Joseph too, if the honey harvest were complete. Pausing by the fence, Daphne scanned the farmhouse, waiting for Melissa's return. But the porch and front lawn were quiet, and suddenly she felt ashamed of her hesitation to venture into the bee yard alone. Proving she was intrepid, industrious, capable and cheerful had been Daphne's ambition ever since fortune had whisked her away from the wretchedness of her former life. She had forced herself to be relentlessly charming and useful, until being so had become natural, intrinsic to who she was.

Turning off the electricity to the fence was simple, Daphne recalled; you just flicked a switch inside the shed. She did this, then picked up a sticky metal bee tool and slid it into the pocket of her crazy-quilt jacket. Her eyes swept past beekeeping suits, three of them, hanging in a row. But the evening was cool, she reasoned, so the bees were unlikely to sting. Her red cotton dress hung down mid-calf over leggings; surely that was enough fabric to keep autumn-drowsy bees at bay.

Closing the shed door, Daphne picked up a plastic-handled screwdriver hanging by a rope from a post. She touched the top wire with the metal end of the screwdriver, ensuring the fence was disarmed, then entered the yard and wandered between the two rows of hives. The bees were few and docile, and Daphne felt adventurous and magnanimous. It was a privilege to commune with every part of nature, and though honeybees weren't her favourite animal, you had to admire the extraordinary insects and the precious honey they provided. Around the hives, feathery tufts crowning tall grasses swayed in the breeze, nodding encouragement. Daphne grasped the bee tool, turned it sharp end out and began prying gently at the lid of the quietest hive. The sun slipped lower as she worked. Making her way methodically, she loosened the rectangular lid until the last gluey bit of propolis cracked. She dropped the bee tool and lifted the cover free of the super.

Immediately Daphne wished she had put on a bee suit, hat and veil. The hive was quiet outside because all the bees were *in*side, crammed between and massing on top of the frames, their movement kaleidoscopic and disorienting. *These frames are full of honey, their winter survival is at stake – what was I thinking?* Daphne stepped back, alarmed, as bees rose en masse from their invaded home and streamed toward her, compound eyes glittering, segmented legs waving dangerously. Her resolution to stay calm quickly failed, and she frantically swatted bees away. *Zing* – the hot, sharp shock of a sting, in the crease between her right thumb and palm. The dying bee released her pheromonal message – *we are under attack* – and *zing, zing, zing*, Daphne was stung – elbow, clavicle, upper lip, eyebrow.

She sprinted from the bee yard to the farmhouse, flapping her skirt with her hands to flush out any invaders, crying indignantly from the pain, shock and preventability of her stings. Leaping up the porch stairs, she threw the front doors open and thundered upstairs to the bathroom. Her face burned and throbbed. Her top lip was swelling; it already felt puffy and misshapen. She turned the cold water tap on full blast so the sound of rushing water would swallow up her sobs. *Baking soda.* Clawing under the bathroom sink, Daphne found an orange box of baking soda she had placed there herself for cleaning. She plugged the sink and dumped white powder into water, making a paste. Someone was hammering on the door with a fist. Blood roared in Daphne's ears. She bit down on her tongue, forcing herself to be calm. With shaking fingers she spread cool wet whiteness over her stings, slathering it on her forehead, slopping some on the floor. She scratched out stingers dangling from her skin, tiny sacs of venom still pumping poison.

Thump, thump, thump – fists on the bathroom door.

Daphne glanced at her reflection in the mirror and let out a strangled yelp – half a bee was hanging from her upper lip. Pale, viscous bee innards bulged from what remained of the insect's abdomen. She scraped at her face with a fingernail and removed the soft part of the bee, but not the stinger. Around the sting her flesh was shiny, inflated and cinched tight around the bee's miniature posthumous weapon.

"Daphne, it's me."

She opened the bathroom door to Melissa, who sucked in air at the sight of Daphne's bulging face. *They stung me*, Daphne tried to say, but her lips wouldn't make the right shapes to get the words out. She let Melissa lead her to bed and nurse her. Her sister brought her a washcloth, antihistamines, a bowl of ice and some slightly freezer-burned chocolate ice cream. Tears rolled down Daphne's cheeks, leaving wet trails through white smears of baking soda paste. She knew Melissa believed she was crying in pain; her bumpy, swollen lips wouldn't let her explain these were tears of relief. Her biggest fear was that one day her past would trample on her present. The hammer had to fall sometimes; in every life there must be sorrow and joy. Two dozen bee stings were an insignificant toll, a minor dose of misery to balance years of happiness. Daphne would gladly feel this pain if it meant she could keep waking up where swallows darted past her window, their freedom emblematic of her own.

Daphne rubbed away the evidence of her tears. Melissa had gravitated to the window and was staring intently over Bow Lake into the encroaching night. Perhaps it was a trick of dim light cast by an inadequate lamp, but her sister's profile betrayed rare vulnerability and fear. In three short bursts Melissa blew hair from her eyes and raked at her scalp with twitchy fingers.

Ten

Dr. Maximilian Griffen shut the door to his windowless office behind the last sufferer of the day and plunked himself down on one of two modest chairs provided for his patients. Reaching down and wincing, he removed slip-on Italian leather loafers. He leaned back and lifted his left ankle to his right knee, the better to examine the source of painful irritation that had plagued him for the latter half of the day. Holes in his socks, there: the explanation. Holes in his premium silk-and-bamboo socks, purchased by the dozen, what – five, six years ago? Pretty good performance for socks, but Max recalled some mention of a lifetime guarantee. 'Buy quality so it lasts' was a philosophy that had rarely disappointed him, so he examined the red sores on the sole of his left foot with dismay. He switched sides, unfolding one leg and folding up the other. Yes, there was a hole in the right sock as well, just one. Still, he mused, it was strange how both socks had reached the end of their lifespan on the same day. Frowning, he wondered if the sores would interfere with his bicycle ride home through urban Toronto, the highlight of his day.

Max reached out a spider-long limb and clicked on his high-wattage examination light. There was no examination table in this, his private office. The Spadina Downtown Health Clinic was a warren of rooms staffed by just three doctors who saw between them in excess of a hundred patients a day. The waiting room was always crammed, the front desk staff harried by phones that rarely stopped ringing. Max had been at the clinic for seven years of equal parts fulfillment and fatigue. Recently, a paucity of physicians coupled with a greatly increased patient population had begun to get to him. The clinic was a piteous parade of headaches and hemorrhoids. The walls of Max's already cramped office seemed to shrink in closer, and in his mind's eye, he pictured himself as a bolus trapped in a coil of intestine, a confounding trap, a long cylindrical muscle contracting upon itself, pushing him closer and closer to messy oblivion. Depression was sneaking up on him, and low-level anxiety. Six months earlier Max had self-diagnosed a classic case of professional burnout, and in that same week his wife had asked him for a divorce. He poked at the inflammation on his feet and recalled the litany of minor maladies he had addressed this week: warts, sore throats, acne, ear infections, banal requests for prescriptions. The job was becoming a blur of uncomfortable people, in an uncomfortable office, in an uncomfortable building. There was a smart rap on his office door. Rhonda, his office manager, waddled in and slapped a thin chart on his desk. She was still cheery after eight hours of slogging away.

"One more patient, Doctor Max."

"Wrong. No more patients today, as per our clearly defined temporal constraints." Max nodded meaningfully at the wall clock, the minute hand at eight after, the hour hand at five.

"Well, when this one arrived it was before four thirty, and we hadn't started turning people away yet. I guess we got the clinic census wrong. Anyway, he's here, and he's a friend of yours."

"No friend of mine would keep me after five, Rhonda."

"Last name Wise. Patient's his son."

A face loomed up from Max's past, a gawky young man with glasses and a camera who used to hang out with Max's crowd. Matthew, was that it? Matthew Wise. An odd duck, a guy whose intelligent but bizarre perspectives had endeared him to an enclave of rambunctious, spirited pre-med students. Max wouldn't call him a friend. More like a quirky acquaintance from way back when, leveraging his way into a late afternoon appointment.

"Damn it, Rhonda, how many times? This is entrapment, and I won't stand for it."

His anger made Rhonda flinch, and she blinked at him through eyeliner-infused tears.

"I'm sorry, Doctor Max. I guess I messed up. I promise it won't happen again."

"If you are truly sorry, tell Matthew Wise to come back in the morning, and let me go home. I've been looking forward to riding my bike ever since I got here this morning."

"He can't come back – he doesn't live in town. I am so, so sorry, Doctor Max."

"Bloody hell," said Max, peeling the useless socks from his feet. A thin, sour odour permeated the office air. "Send them in. No, wait, give me a minute."

He walked around her and into the exam room next door, pulled open a cupboard and extracted a pair of disposable slippers. Sliding them on, Max walked gingerly back into his office, paper whispering on tile floors. Rhonda looked down at his slippered feet, his empty leather shoes and the discarded socks. Her head tilted back and forth, considering the slippers, the shoes.

"Are you okay?" she asked.

"A matter of opinion. Please send them in, so that I may get the fuck out of here."

Rhonda exited, her step heavier than usual.

Max threw his ruined socks in a stainless steel garbage can, placed his shoes neatly in the closet and retreated behind his desk, sinking with a sigh into his customary throne, a deluxe leather office chair. He nudged the mouse and the computer came alive, shimmered and displayed his screen saver, a sunny tropical beach scene. The picture was from last year's holiday on Maui, taken just prior to the divorce. His three teenaged children cartwheeled on the sand; his grim-faced ex-wife was cropped out of the picture. Max stared forlornly at sparkling sand, brilliant blue ocean and waving palms. He heard Rhonda in the hallway.

". . . Doctor Griffen. If you'll just come in here."

A young man with long dark hair, jeans and a rumpled floral shirt entered, guided by an older man, neatly dressed, wearing glasses. As Max watched the pair enter, the light in his office flickered and the men before him appeared to tremble. He reached over, slapped the side of his computer and turned off the examination light.

"Max, it's so good to see you again. This is my son, Beck. Thanks for fitting us in today. We don't have a family doctor up in Lanark, and I really wanted to see someone I could trust."

"Matthew Wise, right, what a blast from the past. I remember an irresponsible evening or two with you. And this is your son? Have a seat, guys." Max indicated the two patient chairs. His patience felt onion-skin thin. "So, what's going on?"

Father and son glanced at each other. Beck slumped in his chair and Matthew spoke.

"This past spring, Beck was working on a farm as a beekeeper, when we lost touch with him. He was missing for almost three months, and then a couple of weeks ago he turned up at our cabin in Lanark County with no idea where he'd been. And as you can see, he's emaciated."

"Is that right? Is this true, Beck – you don't remember anything at all?" Max watched the young man carefully. Beck averted his eyes and a flush spread across his cheeks. "I need you to be completely honest with me, okay? Otherwise I can't help you."

Beck writhed in his chair and investigated the upper corners of the room.

"Were you drinking, or taking drugs? No judgement, by the way," said Max.

That startled Matthew's son out of his silence. He thrust his feet under his chair and squared his shoulders, indignant.

"No, it was nothing like that. I've tried drugs, but this wasn't – I was straight."

"Have you had lapses of memory before?"

Beck shook his head, negative. Max restrained himself from heaving a great, audible sigh as he clicked his pen and took the patient's unremarkable medical history. Healthy twenty-three-year-old male, Latina Cuban mother, Caucasian Canadian father. A strong genetic combination, by the looks of him. Matthew seemed calm and lucid as he related the details of his son's childhood, which had included plenty of fresh air, exercise and healthy food. They didn't have a family doctor; evidently Matthew's wife was some kind of natural healer who preferred to treat her family's maladies at home. Max deliberately skirted this topic. In his experience, laypeople who dabbled in natural medicine had lengthy opinions about health, and there was still, perhaps, a chance of brevity with this visit. His big blue bicycle frame popped into his thoughts. He could practically smell crisp autumn air, hear the leaves crunching under hard, skinny tires, and feel his cheeks flush with the pleasure of exertion.

Max wrenched himself back into his office. Had there been an accident, he asked Beck, a mishap involving a blow to his head? No, Beck said, no head trauma, and no history of seizures, headaches or depression. No family history of brain cancer or other neurological diseases, as far as Matthew knew. The patient insisted he had been healthy right up until he had lost contact with his family and friends, but he was holding something back; Max could tell by his evasive posture.

"Is there anything else I should know about what was happening right before you developed this amnesia?" Max asked, clicking his pen nervously.

Matthew's son wrestled with indecision, fidgeting in his chair. He seemed bursting to confess, and afraid of what he was poised to blurt out. Max expected the young man to admit drugs were involved, but Beck surprised him.

"Okay, there is something. But this is going to sound mental."

Max clicked his pen, waiting.

"I thought I was inside a beehive," said Beck.

Beside him, Beck's father removed his glasses and rubbed them on his shirt, then replaced them and peered at his son as if he were a stranger. *A psych patient. At five fifteen. Rhonda, you're going to pay for this.* The last patient of the day was often complex. Just when you *wanted* a wart or a sore throat, that final sufferer would walk in with undiagnosed cancer. *This, though!*

"The impression you were in a beehive," Max addressed Beck, who sat peacefully, his hands folded in his lap. "Was it the first time you'd had thoughts like that?"

"No. I was dreaming about bees a lot, before the summer. I was kind of obsessed with them."

"You were working with hives every day," said Matthew. "It's natural he would think about them, and dream about them, isn't that right, Max?"

A bee obsession was a unique complaint, and Max suddenly felt a glimmer of professional curiosity. "Yes . . . sure," he said, leaning forward, interested now in the unusual case. Nothing in the young man's demeanour suggested he was psychologically unsound, and if he wasn't lying about the drugs, then where had he been for three months? Maybe the bike could wait.

"Okay, Beck, let's have a look at you."

Max opened his office door and gestured for father and son to follow him. He could feel them staring at his paper slippers. Rhonda was peeking around the corner down the hallway. When she saw him lead the patient and his father into one of the examination rooms, her cerise-lipsticked pout thickened. Max patted a vinyl bed covered in crinkly paper, indicating that Beck should sit. He began measuring the patient's vital signs.

"Blood pressure, pulse and temperature all slightly elevated. How are you feeling, generally?"

"Tired and hungry."

Max brandished his stethoscope and listened to what sounded like the normal heart and lungs of a regular young man. Reflexes, lymph nodes, strength sensation, all normal.

"Take off your shirt, please."

Max grasped an otoscope and turned it on. The father sat down in a corner. An overall impression of excellent health, thought Max. A smattering of black hair around dark nipples standing out from honed pectoral muscles. Unblemished olive brown skin. Good posture, pleasant demeanour. Underweight, though – very thin.

"Open please, and say *ahhh*."

Had this patient eaten honey just prior to the appointment? The unmistakeable aroma of fresh honey clung to Beck Wise's breath. Otherwise, the oral cavity was unremarkable. Max had a rush of intuition and was surprised to feel his stomach clench into a fist of thrilled anticipation, as if he were standing in line to ride a roller coaster. He swung around to examine the patient's ears, and his suspicion was confirmed: the wax buildup was substantial, and the sweet, light fragrance of beeswax emanated from both of the patient's ears, a scent similar to the expensive candles his wife, or rather his ex-wife, bought at Natural Foods.

It's the power of suggestion, I'm not actually smelling this. It's been a long day. Max reached for his laboratory requisition pad.

"I'd like some blood work done, some routine screening. Also a urinalysis and a couple of swabs. There's a lab on the third floor of this building; it opens at eight thirty tomorrow morning. I'd like you to get these done tomorrow, without fail, and I'll see you back in this office in the afternoon. Rhonda can recommend an over-the-counter irrigation kit for your earwax. I also need some other diagnostic tests – a CT scan and an EEG – but they'll take longer to set up."

Max's pen raced down the page, ticking boxes, then he scribbled his signature at the bottom. Beck slid his arms into his sleeves and tossed his black hair easily, buttoning the shirt over his scrawny torso.

"Max, thanks again," said Matthew, extending a hand that Max shook unenthusiastically. Wise Sr. put a guiding hand on his son's shoulder, and led Wise Jr. out of the room.

Max waited several seconds, until they were out of earshot, to exhale forcefully and hang his head. Though it had kept him late at work, the case was more interesting than anything else that had come through his office door in months. But the image of his bicycle dominated his thoughts: bright blue glossy paint; smooth, aerodynamic lines; feather-light carbon frame. He tore the paper slippers from his feet, tossed them in the direction of the garbage can and strode out of the exam room and into his office to exchange dank polyester-cotton blend trousers for sleek, stretchy spandex. Dressed to ride, Max rushed toward the clinic's exit. Rhonda was sitting meekly at her computer.

"Go home, Rhonda. Sorry. I shouldn't have barked at you."

A quarter of an hour later, Dr. Maximilian Griffen, straddling his beloved bicycle, rolled along smooth asphalt, shaking his helmeted head. The hour of his emancipation had arrived; he was speeding along on two wheels in sunshine under brilliant autumn foliage, just as he had dreamed about all day. The evening spread out tantalizingly ahead of him, but his mind wandered back to the confines of his medical office. He couldn't stop thinking about the boy who had been bees.

Eleven

Melissa woke up on the front porch, wedged on a lumpy couch, the top of her skull pressing into the wicker ridge of an armrest. She had a blurred recollection of moving outside in the middle of the night after tossing and turning for sleepless hours in her bed. On the porch, she had not only slept, but slept in – the day was underway, and she was surrounded by the clacking of outsized autumn insects. She opened her eyes to a jaunty splatter of sunflowers nodding over the railing. A single shiny black ant marched vertically up a hairy green stalk. Closer to where she lay, mottled brown spiders lurked in corners, waiting in dense white webs to trap their meals. A late-season honeybee was nestled in the brown centre of a sunflower, directly in Melissa's line of sight. She gazed at the bee, and stretched under a pile of second-best blankets that, she noted, needed a wash. Sunlight struck the top step of the wooden stairs, where the fluffy grey cat Beck had frightened lounged, its bottle-brush tail flicking. Melissa slid her hands into a pocket of body-warmed air, pressed itchy scab-dots on her thighs and tried not to scratch. She mulled over the previous day's phone call from the police.

Constable Hickey had reviewed the file on Charlie Makepeace and found a statement by Balvinder Singh. In the days right after Charlie's disappearance Balvinder claimed he had seen Charlie's truck, on several occasions, with Charlie inside it.

"But when I talked to Balvinder today, it was a whole 'nother story," Constable Hickey had said. "He's not sure the truck he saw in Almonte belonged to your father, and he's quite certain he never saw Charlie himself.

He's withdrawn his testimony. And I sniffed around a bit. Turns out, we can't place Charlie in Lanark or Almonte at all anymore. Why don't you come by the station, Melissa? I'm thinking we might want to reactivate this investigation."

Uneasily, Melissa thought about the deleted emails between her father and Balvinder Singh. What had made Balvinder believe he saw Charlie, all those years ago? Now he had withdrawn his testimony, so maybe it didn't matter. But why were those emails trashed? The only possible culprit was her mother. Joseph, a Luddite, didn't have the requisite technological skills, and Melissa had never seen him at the computer. Beck and Daphne rarely entered the library and had no involvement in the bureaucratic administration of the farm. Her mother would be back from Central America soon, and Melissa would ask about those emails. It was a mistake they had been deleted, surely; a half-hearted attempt to clean up the old hard drive. But even as she contemplated it, Melissa knew how unlikely this was. Jill Makepeace had her flaws, but her actions were rarely unwitting, and never half-hearted.

Heavy boots banged up the porch stairs. The cat flinched and fled. Joseph clomped into view, his cigarette defying gravity in the slash of his mouth. He stared at her, the pewter crags of his face motionless, until she reacted.

"What?" she barked, grouchy and impatient after her interrupted night's sleep.

"Got some bad news – just checked the bees."

"The bees? Oh *shit*!"

She shoved the blankets from her body and stood up, barefoot, still wearing wrinkled, greasy jeans and a black tank top from the day before. She stepped into rubber boots and followed Joseph to the bee yard, her spine tingling with premonition.

Devastation was visible from a distance. The customary symmetrical skyline of hives, like a scaled-down row of apartment buildings, was wrong. Rooftops were missing, or sitting at impossible angles. They entered the yard cautiously, surveying the wreckage. It was a post-earthquake district, entire hives tipped on their sides, broken super frames, exposed comb. Confused worker bees hovered over dark pools of honey, wasted fruit of their meticulous labour.

They suited up and moved through the disaster zone, astronauts stepping slow motion in space. Melissa felt shattered; the destruction of her beehives was like the air-strike bombing of a strategic city, heartless and incomprehensible. Joseph reminded her that the bees, homeless and confused, were likely to sting. He knelt beside a mangled stack of frames. Such delicate structures, she thought, each thin wooden rectangle reinforced horizontally with just two narrow wires. Frames were fragile things, easily broken, but these had been savaged. Gingerly, with the tips of two fingers, Joseph lifted a twisted frame and held it in sunlight. The edges held undisturbed empty comb, pale yellow, preternaturally even hexagons waiting to be filled, but the centre of the frame was a ragged gaping hole, with just enough papery dark cells left to reveal this frame had held not honey but brood – maturing larvae. Joseph placed the crooked frame on the cracked remains of a hive.

"Daphne?" Melissa said, incredulous, trying to understand what she was seeing.

Joseph shook his head. "It wasn't Daphne did this. This was a bear, or a badger. See? The brood comb's been eaten. Daphne got stung and forgot to close the gate and arm the fence. Not her fault."

Melissa examined Joseph's expression. The beehives were his albatross at the farm, his pet peeve. He seemed happy about this turn of events, she thought; the arduous, sticky job of extracting all the honey from twelve beehives was no longer necessary. Maybe it had occurred to Joseph last night to check the bee yard fence. And maybe he hadn't bothered.

"Is it all wrecked – every hive?" Her breath bounced back at her inside the stifling bee veil.

"Looks like the little one in the corner got left alone." Joseph pointed to a short hive, half-hidden by weeds, with a single super mounted on top of the brood box. Melissa crossed the bee yard and grasped the edge of the hive lid with her bare hand. A brilliant flash of pain exploded in the skin fold between her thumb and fingers.

"Stung?"

"Yes, damn it."

The dying bee had released a defensive pheromone, her call to arms, and the number of bees around the hive doubled, angry buzzing increasing in pitch and intensity. Melissa backed away, flapping her hand, as if that would help the pain go away.

"No checking this mess out now. Let's scram and leave them be, Lissy."

Lissy was what Joseph used to call her, back when she was seven and eight years old, before his black hair was streaked with silver, when her parents were busy night and day and Joseph wore the mantle of a kindly uncle. She used to pester him, blow bubbles at him, follow him around. She used to ask him obscure questions until he barked at her to leave him alone, he had work to do. He hadn't called her Lissy for years. Joseph shut the gate. They stepped out of their bee suits and he hung them in the shed. Melissa blew on a dime-sized red welt, white in the middle where the stinger had been. She was appalled to find herself fighting back tears – crying over a bee sting, how pitiful; she was made of tougher stuff than that. Joseph walked sullenly beside her, extracting his tobacco pouch from a shirt pocket. At the farmhouse he hesitated.

"There can't be a harvest banquet this year. We're swamped. Call it off."

So that was why the demolished bee yard pleased him; Joseph hated the harvest banquet. *Rigmarole*, he called it. Annoyance heated Melissa's face and dried her tears.

"No, Joseph, you're not going to talk me out of it. People love the harvest banquet, and Mom's coming home specially to be here in time for it. The banquet's good advertising, and it builds community. You are literally the only person who doesn't like it. There's no reason to cancel – we have *less* work now that the honey harvest is ruined."

Joseph had been rolling a cigarette as she spoke. He paused to light it, contorting his lips to direct his exhale away from her face.

"I'm not helping with the banquet. Got enough to do around here, cleaning up this mess."

"You never liked the bees." A storm swirled inside her, gathering momentum. "I remember, you know – when Dad first bought the hives. You said they were a waste of time and money. Well, news flash, no matter what, we're going to keep bees. They're not just a hobby, or a curiosity – they're *pollinators*."

And just like that a sparkly, perfect idea descended. This year's harvest banquet would be a fundraiser. They would use the proceeds to repair the hives. And the menu would be specific: it would feature food requiring the bees' service as pollinators. Melissa vocalized the scheme as it occurred to her, but Joseph was already shaking his head, a condescending smirk curling his lips.

"Plenty of pollinators without us farming them. Charlie wasn't thinking straight when he started them hives, trust me."

Joseph rarely spoke about her father, and Melissa pounced on this judgement.

"Why should I trust you – what do you mean, he wasn't thinking straight?"

Joseph's eyebrows sank and his face darkened. He clenched his fists, spat in the grass and scuffed the dirt with the toe of his boot. "Never mind. Forget I said it."

"We never talk about this. We never talk about my dad. I get the feeling there're things you want to tell me. What happened, back then?"

"Twelve years, Lissy. That was twelve years ago. Why ask now?"

"Jeez, I don't know – because I never have? Because you never talk about him, and when you do, it's a mysterious half-insult? Because you were an adult when he left, and I was just a kid? I haven't given up on him, and I'm not going to."

A tractor motor started up behind the farmhouse, and the pathetic bleating of goats quavered in the distance. For a moment, Joseph's jutting lower lip and downcast, half-lidded eyes gave Melissa the impression he was going to answer her question. He finished his cigarette and ground it out, hard, under his heel.

"I don't know nothing."

"You don't know why he left, or you won't say?"

"Lots to get sorted. If you want hives, I ain't the one to keep 'em. Them bees might swarm, you know, and swarms can be caught. I guess you better ask Beck to help out."

Joseph trudged back toward the bee yard. Rumpled and dirty, her stung thumb throbbing along with her pulse, Melissa went inside the farmhouse, where it was cool and quiet. Suspended in the stairway, motes of dust drifted like glints of sand in water. Upstairs, the door to her room hung open and the walls were alive with waves of undulating light. Gauzy curtains breathed – drawn out the window for a beat, then pushed back in for two. Pulling the curtains aside, Melissa stared at the gap in the hedge, the place where her father's red lumberjacket and black toque would materialize one day, the day he came home. She pictured the broken hive frames, felt the sting on her hand and choked up again. She wondered if some things were too broken to fix, and some people too long gone or far away to find their way back home.

Apologizing to Beck in her head for breaking her promise, Melissa went to see Marjorie. Maybe the bees could be found, clustered in trees behind the bee yard, and the farm's loss recouped to some degree. She found Marjorie in her flower garden, looking older than she had only a week ago, her hair whiter, her shoulders more rounded. Her light-coloured clothes were smudged with chlorophyll, and her small body curled toward the earth like a fiddlehead fern. She was bare-headed, messy white braids flopping beside tanned, wrinkled cheeks. The beginning of a bouquet, pale pink late-season rhododendrons, lay in a basket at her feet. She was wielding a pair of shears in her right hand. Her left hand was bound with grubby gauze, the arm suspended in a makeshift sling. At first Melissa thought the old woman didn't know she was there, then she realized Marjorie was ignoring her.

"Hey," Melissa said finally.

Marjorie didn't look up. She kept clipping flower stems. "What do you expect me to do, jump for joy? Throw confetti?"

"Something awful happened to my hives."

Marjorie didn't answer, but her pruning got savage. She snipped random stalks. Petals and blossoms tumbled to the ground.

"The electric fence was uncharged, and the gate was left open. An animal got in and destroyed all the hives but one. It ate the brood, whatever it was. I was hoping you would help me get my bees back."

Tossing her shears onto the basket of flowers, Marjorie shuffled closer. A sour smell clung to her and, repulsed, Melissa took a step back.

"Chickens always come home to roost," said Marjorie. "I knew the luck over at your place couldn't last forever."

"What's that supposed to mean?" What was that *reek?* Melissa breathed through her mouth and tried to hide her disgust.

"I wasn't always this decrepit," said Marjorie bitterly. "Once upon a time I was young, just like you. I used to jog in the summertime, and cross-country ski in the winter. I was fit and strong. You ask your mother; she'll remember. I used to ski through your farm in the winter, up and down those trails. I saw the goings-on, when your father was still around."

Wrapping her hands over her elbows, Melissa shivered. She hadn't worn a jacket. She took another step backward, away from the repellent, organic smell.

"Goings-on?"

"Never mind. Nothing you need to concern yourself with anymore. It's all over and done with. But I will say this. If you're searching, look no farther than your own backyard."

Melissa considered the elderly woman, suddenly appreciating her unenviable situation. Marjorie had no one to enlighten with her half-baked advice on life and living, no children or grandchildren visiting, no one to fill the role of young apprentice. Probably Beck had filled that gap in her lonely life, before he went away. Isolated and increasingly irascible, she bottled up crotchety wisdom, and spilled it on anyone who wandered into her sad little lair.

"Go on." With her good arm, Marjorie swatted at Melissa as if she were a troublesome insect. "Get out of here. I told you, I have plenty to do. Figure out your own affairs."

Melissa started to obey, and caught another whiff of the stench. Wincing, Marjorie glanced into her sling, a length of dirty cotton fabric knotted around her creased neck.

"It's worse," Melissa said gently. "Let me see."

"It's fine, I told you. The honey is doing its job." Marjorie opened the sling with her right hand, exposing the left thumb injury, a long, jagged laceration with puffy red edges surrounded by shiny, swollen skin.

"It's not fine, it's infected. You need to clean it up. Do you want help?"

All of a sudden Marjorie was crying, tears coursing down fissures in her face.

"No – go away, go home."

Marjorie hurried into her house, holding her left arm with her right. Her body was crooked, bent over like a twisted branch. The door hung open for a second, then slammed, kicked shut.

Twelve

Beck watched rain falling outside the window in his aunt Sylvia's small blue kitchen. He listened to the loud, relentless percussion of drops splatting on glass panes and their muted hammering on the roof. Although she too had benefited from an inheritance, his father's sister Sylvia worked full time in York University's busy student aid office. She was single, never married, a slight woman with a gaunt face. The hollows under her cheekbones were so deep Beck could see her skull through her skin. When he was little she had never played with him. In her own words, she had *little tolerance for foolishness or imagination*. She smelled of the lemon cough drops she sucked; hard, sour candies that clicked against her teeth. Beck usually tuned his aunt Sylvia out. She had an unfortunate, nasal voice, and on that rainy morning she was relating her problems at work, the jockeying for position in her dreary office echelon based on petty disagreements: "The shared computer screen saver is always a scene from Anita's holiday. It's not fair." Beck's father nodded and mm-hmm'ed in all the right places, but Beck couldn't pretend interest; because his father was listening, he didn't have to. He wished he were at work, getting muddy in a field with Melissa.

While she spoke, Sylvia briskly folded up the thin, hard futon couch her nephew and brother had slept on. Beck sensed she couldn't bear her apartment disrupted, and resented accommodating them. The heels of her shiny black flats slapped the floor as she navigated around the inconvenience of her guests. She ate toast and drank coffee standing at the sink.

"Back to the doctor today?" Sylvia pursed her lips, and a ring of ridges appeared around her mouth. Matthew shifted in his chair and nodded.

"Yes, right after lunch. Our bus leaves at two, so we won't be back."

"It's been good to connect." Sylvia ripped off a crust with her little teeth. "I sure hope you figure out where you were, Beck. It must be freaky, not knowing." She clattered her plate and cup into the sink, wrapped herself in a baggy black raincoat and departed for work.

Wet weather unsettled Beck. The urge to do something productive prodded at him like an erection, physical desperation to fulfill a basic instinct. Hazy hive memories surfaced. He thought he could remember his hive-body feeling frustrated when it rained. The prime directive was gathering nectar of course – nothing was more important – and rain impeded honey-production progress. *No, don't even think about it.* Indulging bee-thoughts was dangerous; thinking like bees could lead to *being* bees, and he didn't want to be bees, though life had certainly been easier with volition removed. When he was bees he had tuned in, turned on and dropped out of the human race. Beck could understand why Doctor Griffen had guessed he'd been really high the whole time, stoned out of his mind. It was true, his summer had been free from complexities of thought, the web of decisions, the constant interplay of egos. He turned his back on the rainy window and contemplated the glossy, wiped surfaces in Aunt Sylvia's narrow flat, wondering idly if she were gay but not out, the suppression of her sexuality making her uptight and unhappy.

He heard his father talking on the phone in the living room, planning their itinerary. Matthew was the acting queen now, directing the show and providing imperatives. Ah, the blissful simplicity of a hierarchy – it had been such a relief, in the hive, to follow his queen's unquestionable edicts. The hive wasn't a dictatorship; it had never felt like a struggle to align the will of many with the desires of one. It was a social collective, each part working toward the whole's common goal, each happily accepting of their lot. Less choice, more cooperation. Guided by wise, firm authority, Beck had been liberated from the ever-present anxiety inherent in free will. For three months he hadn't been obliged to say yes or no, to choose this or that, and there had been no need to interpret feelings. It was a relaxing way to live, in retrospect. None of this *she loves me, she loves me not.*

His father joined him in the kitchen looking dishevelled, particularly for a guy who had just showered and dressed; he had a habit of pushing his fingers through his hair, mussing it up while he contemplated complex problems.

"Let's get going. The lab opens soon."

His father held his jacket open, and Beck slid his arms into the sleeves like an obedient child. Had he been this easygoing and compliant before he was bees? Beck had a feeling why the bees had chosen him, what had made him a good colony candidate. Naturally he loved bees and understood them, but now he nurtured the distressing suspicion he'd transformed because he was an adaptable fellow who didn't struggle. An easy mark, a biological pushover. *You're so even,* Melissa had said when they were first together, and she had sounded impressed. She had meant he never lost his temper or got emotional about things. Later on, the exact same trait had irritated her. *You're so flat – doesn't anything ruffle your feathers*?

The rainy-day sense of thwarted plans stayed with Beck as he walked beside his father to the Bloor subway line. He summoned the recent memory of kissing Melissa and tried to bask in it, but his mind kept sliding sideways to the disappointed mantle she had worn when he had said goodbye. His father was tuned to an internal wavelength, silently attending to private thoughts. Rain slid down the sidewalks in sheets. Beck hopscotched to avoid stepping on the pink squiggles of earthworms. Cars speeding along the street sent puddle splashes arcing in their direction.

After the discomfort and indignities of the lab work, Beck and his father ate a plain breakfast in a dingy café on Bloor Street, then trudged in the rain through Kensington Market under a low, flat surface of steel, the kind of hopeless, uniform sky that heralds wet misery all day. They got to the clinic early, during lunch hour, in time to watch the doctor wheel his bicycle inside, dripping on industrial green linoleum. His spandex riding clothes were spattered with muddy urban filth.

"Good afternoon, gentlemen. Weeks of perfect cycling weather – sunny, dry and not too warm – all rinsed away. I regret promising myself I'd ride my bike until the snow flies. Give me a few minutes." Fifteen minutes later, when the receptionist led them into his office, Dr. Griffen had changed into a plaid dress shirt and pressed, belted pants. A thin chart lay open on the desk with a coloured tab affixed to the upper right-hand corner: *Wise, Beckett Stephen.*

"That's a great bike you have, Max," said Matthew. "Cannondale, a superior machine."

"Aha! Another cycling enthusiast. I might have known. Isn't that how we all used to get around, back in the day?" The doctor grinned. "How's the riding up in your neck of the woods?"

Beck disengaged from the conversation while his father and the doctor gushed about ideal roads and car-free routes. His dream from the night before returned to him, a disturbing sequence in which he had existed not as a colony, but merely as a single bee. Closing his eyes, images of Beck's dream flashed behind his eyelids: flying toward the crisp right angles of a Langstroth hive, body heavy and wings tired, carrying a big load of nectar. Crawling through a crowded, narrow entrance into a warm mass of bee bodies on a vertical comb. Moving through the hive in an ever-tightening Fibonacci curve, closer and closer to the centre, closer and closer to his queen. At last he had found her, his glorious monarch, but when she turned around she wore a hideous human face, a hissing harpy's visage. He had woken up sweaty and scared. Under the fluorescent lights in the doctor's office he opened his eyes, sharply severing the troubling image. The men's conversation had wandered. The doctor was talking about his failed marriage, how he was hoping to settle with his soon-to-be-ex-wife through mediation instead of going to court, and how his teenagers were taking their parents' breakup hard. Sensing Beck's return to the moment, the doctor abruptly resumed his professional demeanour. He selected a pen from a metal cylinder and started clicking the button repeatedly. *Click-click, click-click.*

"Well, Beck, this lab report was mostly unremarkable. Nothing flagrantly amiss, a couple of minor abnormalities. You're nutritionally compromised, but we knew that. Tell me, do you eat a lot of sugar?"

"I was eating a lot of honey. I'm trying to break the habit," said Beck.

"Good idea. Well, until you get these other tests done, I can't say much more. In the short term, I am going to prescribe a multivitamin, adequate rest and a capsule of valerian root each day." *Click-click, click-click.* The doctor inhaled, on the verge of asking a question, holding himself in check.

"What is it, Max?" Matthew asked nervously.

"You've got me thinking about the cycling in Lanark County. I'm due for some time off. If I come up there for a couple of weeks, would you have time to show me your favourite rides?"

After a shocked silence, Matthew grabbed Max's hand and shook it vigorously.

"Absolutely. I'm afraid we can't offer you a place to stay, though. Our cabin is basically a single-room dwelling, and it isn't winterized . . ." Matthew reddened.

"Not to worry, I'll take care of all that myself. You know what? I might look at real estate while I'm up there. I'm pretty tired of fighting crowds and traffic, and you're a convincing advocate for Lanark County, Matthew. You make it sound like paradise."

Beck and his father joined a stream of black umbrellas, and splashed to the subway.

"I'm not sorry we came," Matthew said, rocking with the train's motion as it whooshed through a black tunnel. "It was good to connect with Sylvia. But it seems your mother was right, and I owe her an apology. I'll tell you something, Beck – you can't shake a sensible upbringing. No matter how many times life shows you a miracle."

Beck slept on the bus ride home from Toronto. The rumble of the motor and whirr of wet tires on pavement made him sleepy; his heavy eyelids opened briefly each time his head slipped off the seat and bounced against the window, then dropped shut again. Close to home, he had an uneasy, claustrophobic dream. He was wedged in a tight space, his mouth forced open by strong, rough hands. He woke up just as the hands succeeded in pouring something sticky between his teeth, cutting off his breath. He spasmed, gasping, and then was comforted by the familiar sight of his father reading, his right index finger perennially crooked, poised to flip the page.

While his father drove from the Lanark bus station to the cabin, Beck pictured the way Melissa blew hair from her face and pulled strands of it behind her ears when she was stressed. Remorsefully, he thought about how his absence this summer had likely contributed to her anxiety.

Lanark was cloudy but dry; they had left the rain farther south. Deciduous leaves were beginning to turn colour, smears of gold against shades of green. Soon the full, glorious autumn display of crimson, amber and bronze would set the forest on flameless fire. In the rear-view mirror Beck watched rooster tails of fallen leaves rise in the wake of their speeding car. His father surprised him by driving straight past their cabin and parking at Hopetown Farm. Inside the hedge, Beck's head instinctively rotated toward the bee yard, and he was startled to see the white smudge of someone in a bee suit moving among the weeds.

Melissa came out to meet them. She was agitated, blowing at her hair and tucking it behind her ears. "I guess you've already heard?" she asked Matthew, her eyes travelling swiftly past Beck.

"Heard what? We haven't heard anything. We drove here directly from the bus station. Is Eurydice working today?" Beck's father craned his neck, searching the fields. Melissa exhaled hard and spoke quickly.

"Daphne accidentally left the gate to the bee yard open. Some animal got in, a bear maybe, and wrecked most of the hives."

The moment Melissa got the words out she began working her tongue in her mouth. Beck stared at her, not assimilating what she'd said. She dropped her chin, and motioned for them to follow her. The white speck was Joseph, wearing a bee suit and sorting pieces of wood into piles. Was he dismantling the hives? There were spaces where hives should have been, empty air above dun dirt rectangles and tawny grass. Melissa called out to Joseph, and he growled a grumpy retort Beck didn't catch. Where were the bees? In the switchyard of Beck's mind, the train of his thoughts shifted tracks, and he could perceive the catastrophe, a great hollow where his cherished friends used to be. His attention was drawn to a clump of weeds, behind which the smallest hive pulsed, healthy and whole. So the devastation wasn't complete – and there were swarms too, in the scraggle of second-growth poplars and maples beyond the electric fence. Beck saw the golden highways of the bees' defection, rippling in another dimension. His father spotted his mother in the vegetable fields and flailed his arms, semaphoring their arrival. Beck tried to speak, but sound died in his throat and his tongue was a rock lodged in his mouth. He pointed at Joseph and raised his eyebrows. Melissa linked her hands on the crown of her head, an exasperated gesture.

"I know, right? Usually Joseph won't go anywhere near the bees. He doesn't want to be doing this, trust me. You should have seen the chaos, after the bear, or whatever it was, got in. I'm glad you didn't see it, the way it was."

"The bees have swarmed," said Beck.

"I figured as much. Listen, I have to ask you again to help me with the bees. Joseph is only cleaning up the mess, then he's done. I think he's relieved the hives are wrecked. As soon as the yard isn't an eyesore he's going to abandon it. And sorry, I asked Marjorie. But she won't help."

The scene was far from the romantic reunion Beck had hoped for, and he had a strong urge to go back to sleep. Out in the fields his mother was moving toward them, the orange-and-blue print of her windbreaker vivid, like the plumage of a tropical bird. Joseph dropped an armful of hive pieces, and the rough, violent sound of wood splintering pierced Beck's head. Homeless bees fed on spots of spilled honey in the grass; watching them, he was overcome with a wave of nausea.

"I can't do it," he said weakly. "Anything but the bees."

Melissa pressed her lips together. She dragged her fingernails across her hips, fraying her jeans.

"Okay, fine. I can handle this on my own," she said, and she strode away, dismissing him.

Thirteen

Catching her reflection in the rear-view mirror, Melissa saw a hawk's beak leaning into the windshield, grimly ferocious, a predator pursuing prey, a reminder her mother would soon be home. If her physical attributes were mainly from Charlie, this train-barrelling-down-the-tracks determined expression was pure Jill. Her admiration for her mother's autonomy was lopsided, pulled askew by her hatred of what had caused it. A woman alone, independently raising a child and operating a business, how bold, how kick-ass! But a man running away from his family and responsibilities was craven, and even after a dozen years, Melissa didn't want to believe it of her father.

Thinking of the ruined beehives, she gritted her teeth. Her plan was for Jill to find, on her return, not merely the same fully operational farm she had left, but a smoother, improved enterprise. A bigger honey harvest had been the keystone of that plan. Beck had insisted on making the honey operation central to the farm; now Melissa's annoyance that he wouldn't step up and fix the bee yard was coupled with growing alarm. He was psychologically unbalanced. Worse, in spite of her best efforts not to, she still cared about him.

She was speeding toward the little town of Almonte, a short drive east of the farm toward Ottawa, a picturesque hamlet enjoying a surge of interest and a new prosperity brought by tourists and young people seeking lives of simple activity. Almonte was built on the Canadian Mississippi River, an energetic rush of black water that dropped through the town in waterfalls and rapids, foaming and splashing under stone bridges that stapled the streets together. Churches, banks and downtown buildings fit together like a model village, and had the comforting permanence of nineteenth-century rock and brickwork. On the steep and winding main street, shopkeepers waved at passersby through the squeaky-clean glass of impeccable storefronts. Dawn was breaking as she drove through town, and on Almonte's quaint streets Melissa half expected to see kids in poor-boy caps and knickers with hoops and balls, and women in full-length dresses carrying wicker baskets.

Driving along, she entertained hazy memories of early morning drives to Almonte with her father. After Charlie was gone, Jill had concentrated all the farm sales on Lanark-based businesses. But these days, with Almonte's burgeoning foodie community, it made sense to check out prospective produce buyers there again, which gave Melissa two good reasons to seek out Balvinder Singh.

Produce Point Market's location wasn't ideal – a bare dirt lot on the corner of an intersection, removed from the hip downtown core. But it was big and airy, its tall windows plastered with low-price specials hastily scrawled in black Sharpie on fluorescent paper. Plenty of parking, an awning covering outdoor bins and wide aisles were all attributes in the market's favour, Melissa decided. She sat in the farm truck and watched employees arrive, tie their aprons on and stock shelves.

After a dramatic rise, the sun had gotten lost behind colourless clouds. A dated four-door burgundy sedan drove up to the side of the building, and an older man emerged from this lacklustre chariot. He was a farmer, Melissa guessed, a plaid shirt buttoned over the swell of a paunch, jeans sagging at the knees, utilitarian rubber boots. His mostly black hair, moustache and beard were shot through with strands of white. Yawning, he stretched, scratched the triangle of skin at his neck and reached into his car for a metal travel mug. Melissa got out of the pickup and jogged toward him.

"Are you Balvinder Singh?"

His mouth fell open and he bobbled his travel mug, almost dropping it.

"Yes, that's me. How do you know my name?"

She stopped beside the grille of his car and drew herself up to her full height.

"I'm Melissa Makepeace. Charlie's daughter."

Instantly he looked toward the market's side entrance, but there was no escape, no one beckoning or demanding his managerial expertise. He lifted his mug and took a bracing sip.

"Well, how do you do? I didn't recognize you, but now I see. Yes, Charlie's daughter. You were very, very small the last time I saw you. Maybe like this." He raised his fingers to his forearm.

"Yep, all grown up now. Do you have a minute? There're a couple of things I want to ask you."

Balvinder checked the entrance again – still no rescuer. He sighed.

"Yes, okay. The policewoman came to see me."

"I know, she told me. So you're not sure anymore it was my dad's truck you saw?"

"I am very sorry, but I cannot be sure. It was a long time ago, and for me it was a very busy time, buying this business, moving my family here, meeting so many new people."

"But back then, you were positive it was my dad you saw. What changed?"

"I told the police. I was very, very clear. I didn't see Charlie's face, only his truck with someone driving. But I was very sure it was him, because it was his truck." Stepping sideways, Balvinder's eyes widened, and he raised the arm that wasn't holding the mug. "This truck, this very same truck, yes?"

Melissa swung around quickly, as if her father's old truck were stopped at the intersection, and if she hurried, she'd catch sight of him before he passed.

"Where, what?"

"This is Charlie's truck you drove here, right?" Balvinder gestured impatiently across the lot.

"That? No! It's a lot like his old one, but my mom bought that one to replace the one my dad was driving when he left." Melissa felt a lump of disappointment in her gut.

Without taking his eyes from her pickup, Balvinder lowered his arm, and took another swallow of his morning beverage. "So many years ago," he said. "I would say it was the same truck."

"And where did you see it?"

"At the Almonte Arms. Your father liked this hotel bar very much. We used to meet there for darts. Many times, we met there. It was a stress relief." Balvinder shrugged.

"So you know my mother too?" Melissa knew her father had socialized in the pubs of Almonte and Lanark, and that he used to drive home from those evenings with too much beer in his belly. She remembered her mother chewing him out when he did, their raised voices in the kitchen reaching her upstairs and down the hall. She would tear up a tissue, plug her ears and find the little twists near her pillow the next morning.

"Your mother, and Joseph, right? Your mother I met very few times. Joseph, he brought the vegetables here after Charlie was gone. Very good prices, for a while, and then his prices went up, and I found cheaper suppliers."

"That was the other thing I wanted to ask you," said Melissa, jumping at the opportunity to address business. "Our prices might be more competitive now. Are you interested in carrying Hopetown produce here again?"

Balvinder frowned and stared at his feet. Melissa waited for him to decline and tell her he already had enough suppliers, thanks. But when he looked at her again his eyes were anguished.

"I am very, very sorry. This is so confusing. But I seem to remember Joseph telling me this is the same truck," said Balvinder.

Melissa turned to her rusty pickup, as if it might have transformed.

"It was winter when Charlie went. I remember this, because there was little fresh produce, nothing local. Only, your farm had early greenhouse rhubarb and radishes. Joseph sold me some, and it was this very truck he drove, I thought." Balvinder peered past Melissa at her pickup. "I asked if it was Charlie's truck and, I'm very sorry if this is wrong, but he said it was. So long ago."

Discouraged, Melissa shook Balvinder's hand and thanked him for his time. She had a faded impression of her father's cantankerous vehicle; it had looked like the pickup she had now, a decaying white Ford. The two trucks were similar, and Balvinder had made a mistake. He had seen a different vehicle – he hadn't seen her father in the days after he disappeared. He also hadn't answered her about carrying Hopetown produce, but she didn't pursue the potential business relationship, because all she could think about was the impact of Balvinder's rescinded testimony on her father's case. She got back in her truck and tugged the seat belt across her chest. Balvinder was staring at her from across the empty lot. She could tell he was still trying to figure out the puzzle of the twin trucks. He gave her a half-hearted wave as she threw the pickup in gear, revved the grumbling engine and drove away.

The police station in Lanark wasn't open yet. Melissa bought a coffee and wandered on foot, cutting through a neglected ball diamond to an embankment overlooking the Clyde River. Long grass soaked with dew brushed dark criss-cross patterns on her jeans, like Chinese calligraphy. The river lay low between its banks, depleted after the hot summer but committed to coursing insistently southward. Mesmerized by the small section of rushing river, she extrapolated, and pictured a map of the entire watershed, a network of circulation: the Clyde was fed by tributaries to the north, flowed south to the Mississippi and then poured into the St. Lawrence Seaway. Love for this land, and knowledge of local geography, had been planted and nurtured in Melissa by her father's deep affection for these things. Estranged from parents who had despaired of their headstrong son's disobedience, teenaged Charlie had run away. He had slept in ditches, trapped beaver, fished and developed a strong bond with the woods and waterways of Lanark County. If he hadn't met a beautiful young entrepreneur in an Ottawa bar, Melissa's father used to say, he'd still be warming his hands over a hobo fire in the bush somewhere.

The day was dull. Melissa slowly drained her coffee, meditating by the river. Estimating it was after eight o'clock, she walked back to the modest brick police station, where two cruisers were now parked. From the sterile front office she could see Constable Hickey at her desk, one hand fumbling in a fast-food chain paper bag. She spotted Melissa and waved her in.

"Come on back. I'm just getting started. Have a seat."

"I went and saw Balvinder Singh just now," said Melissa.

Constable Hickey pointed a censorious finger. "I told you *I* would talk to him. Doubling up on interviews doesn't help us solve your father's case. Detective work is our job, not yours."

"I thought if he saw me, it might trigger a memory. And maybe I'm less intimidating than you guys, in your uniforms," said Melissa.

Constable Hickey took a bite of her breakfast sandwich and spoke with her mouth full. "We're not intimidating if you haven't done anything wrong. Anyway, too late now. What did Balvinder say?"

"He can't be sure it was my dad he saw. And he confused the farm truck I'm driving now with the one my dad owned."

"Yep, that's what Balvinder told me too. And you know what? The other statements placing your father in Lanark and Almonte haven't aged well either." Constable Hickey opened a file folder on her desk and slapped it. "This one fella, René Laliberté, he claimed he was drinking with your dad in Lanark the night Charlie left home. Well, René died a couple months after that, smashed up his car driving drunk. And this waitress from the Almonte Arms who testified, I tracked her down, and she's waffling. Says there were lots of guys that looked like Charlie drinking at the Arms that night, and she was busy, and couldn't be sure."

"But they *were* sure, before."

"Melissa, you know we never found any concrete leads. We developed our search based on cumulative reports Charlie was seen in Lanark and Almonte, at his favourite watering holes, in the first couple of days after he left. Those first forty-eight hours are crucial. After that, the trail goes kinda cold." Constable Hickey crumpled up her breakfast bag and tossed it expertly into a garbage can. Melissa began touching her teeth with her tongue, unobtrusively, she hoped. "Basically we're going to rethink Charlie's case from square one. All this time we've been operating on the premise your father turned left out of the farm. But what if he didn't? I'll come out and talk to your mom and Joseph again, see if they remember anything else. See if they can think of somewhere else your father might have gone."

In bed that night, Melissa stared at the ceiling, thinking about the deleted emails to Balvinder. There had to be a mundane reason her mother had trashed them. A rusty white pickup truck drove around and around in circles in her thoughts, and sleep felt like a faraway land where she would never travel. The bedroom door was open; she could hear Daphne snoring across the hall. Outside her window, the moon illuminated treetops swaying like spectral dancers. Restless, she padded down the stairs, went outside on the porch, curled up on the couch and dragged the pile of old blankets over her knees. Wisps of clouds scudded across a bright night sky. She heard a light crunch of gravel, and the fluffy smoke-coloured cat bolted across the yard.

"We have to stop meeting like this," said Beck, stepping into the light, pushing his bicycle up against the stairs. "On the porch, terrifying the cat."

"Damn it, Beck, you scared me! What are you doing here?"

"Couldn't sleep. Thought I'd come over and see if you were still awake."

Beck climbed the stairs and leaned on the railing across from her, assuming a pose Melissa imagined was meant to be seductive. His refusal to help with the bees grated on her like a deliberate act of non-compliance, but his eyes were lively, challenging.

"I can't figure you out," she said. "You're different, and not in a good way. Whatever the truth is about the bee thing, it changed you. I'm not convinced you're healthy enough to work here."

"I'm fine, really. So much better than I was. The trip to Toronto was grounding. Every day I feel more and more human, and less and less –"

"Like an insect?" Melissa smiled. "You look better. I guess if you feel fine, there's no reason why you couldn't give us a hand with harvest."

"I will be so helpful. You won't regret it. And no pressure for us to, you know."

Melissa cocked her head to one side. "No pressure for us to what?"

"Pick up where we left off," he mumbled.

The night's background soundtrack featured a chorus of croaking; frogs lived in a reedy swamp beyond the boat ramp. Melissa could picture the swamp: cattails and skunk cabbage, spiders skittering across the surface of standing water, dragonflies and red-winged blackbirds feasting on a banquet of bugs. A warmth spread across her chest and she was overcome with a sudden mushy sentimentality. She was in love with it all – the frogs, the porch, the pile of smelly blankets, the broken beehives, the skittish cat and Beck.

"I really missed you," she admitted. "The whole time you were gone."

"As soon as I came back from wherever I was, I missed you like crazy."

Melissa smoothed the blankets across her thighs. Beck pushed off the railing, reached out and snatched the blankets from her. She protested and he shushed her, took her bony wrists in his hands and kissed her firmly.

"Here, put these on," he ordered, snagging her rubber boots from beside the door, and while she did he went in the house and took two big sweaters from hooks on the wall. He closed the double doors, thrust a sweater at Melissa and shrugged on the other. Tugging her hand, he escorted her out to the lawn, around the farmhouse and down the gravel path leading to the boat launch road. She was laughing, lighthearted and puckish, but he was serious and determined, storming down the launch to the lakeshore.

Bow Lake was flat, asleep, its surface a dark mirror reflecting uneven lines of moonlit clouds. Their feet sent pebbles rolling down to the water's edge. Melissa grabbed Beck's shoulders, squared her body to his and leaned in as though to kiss him. Instead she bit his lower lip, wrapped his hair in her fingers and pulled hard. Determined to prove he was really back, she also needed to impress him with the heartache he had caused. She threw her weight, trying to unbalance him, and their feet scuffled on the rocks, waking life on the lake. Startled, they stepped apart and whirled toward the water.

A trio of ducks took off, a frenzy of frantic wingbeats. Webbed feet skittered along the surface, stirring the lake-mirror into ripples that spread toward the far shore. Beck loped to an inexpensive fibreglass canoe stored in a tangle of weeds above the rocks. The canoe was resting upside down, paddles lined up alongside it. With a grunt he turned it over and carried it by the gunwales down to the shallows. He stomped back for the paddles and handed one to Melissa. "Get in," he ordered, and promptly she did, balancing her weight toward the bow and leaving the launch of the canoe to him. He put one foot in the stern and pushed them from shore.

They slipped from land. The canoe was the gliding tip of a lengthening arrow pointing at them from the dock. A euphoria she'd forgotten tingled on Melissa's skin and rushed the pace of her heart. This was more like it – more like them, the way they'd been before. She waited until he dipped his paddle before paddling herself, on the opposite side of the canoe and without glancing back at him. He steered, and instantly she knew where they were going: a grassy clearing, the lawn of an abandoned summer home that was visible in daytime from the dock at the farm, a favourite spot of theirs, private and yet thrillingly open. There was a cabin too, an inexpensive timber-framed square slapped together in the seventies, but like so many buildings in Lanark County it was boarded up and falling apart. In autumn the lawn's lone tree, a stately sunset maple near the shore, turned a dramatic crimson and shed its leaves into the lake. Even in the monochromatic night Melissa could see this vivid leaf-flotilla, as shreds of moonlight revealed their destination. Digging in, pushing the canoe, velocity lifted them higher in the water. They withdrew their paddles simultaneously when momentum would take them ashore. Melissa splashed in the shallows, and scraped the canoe over smooth, flat stones.

Beck spread his sweater on the grass. They tumbled onto it and wrestled, rolling and play-struggling, damp leaves adhering to hair and clothes, pinning down limbs with knees and elbows. She was almost his height, and as strong or stronger since his harrowing summer. Invigorated and powerful, she moved his hands where she wanted them, winning the bout. His laughter broke her focus. It was the first time she'd heard the sound of him happy since his return, and it unhooked something she'd been holding back. They undressed quickly and clumsily, rebuffing the night chill with body heat.

On the paddle back they whispered, pointing out landmarks looming on the shore. Fatigue swept through Melissa but Beck seemed fortified and pushed his paddle harder, proving his vigour. Together they carried the dripping canoe back where it belonged.

She woke at dawn when Beck kissed her forehead. He was leaving, he whispered, walking back to his parents' cabin. He seemed prouder, relaxed and at ease, like the person he'd been before being infected by frenetic hive action. Shoulders sore, hair matted, Melissa's body told the story of the night before. Invaded by a buoyant restlessness, she untangled her limbs from twisted sheets. In the shower, surrounded by a clear plastic curtain secured with clothespins, she soaped herself up with a gelatinous mass of bergamot and lye. Leaf bits and dry grass points swirled down the drain.

The harvest banquet was racing up the calendar, underscored by ripening in the fields and reddening on the trees. There would be time for ardent exhilaration, but not today. She rubbed away the night's giddy pleasure with a rough, scratchy towel on her tanned skin. Beyond the bedroom wall she heard Daphne whistle her way downstairs. Outside Joseph's truck arrived, the diesel engine clunking to a stop, metal door slamming. Belatedly, Melissa remembered the bees.

Fourteen

The pollination-themed harvest banquet would be magnificent, a tour de force, the first of its kind in Lanark County; but it was a bittersweet theme, in the wake of the beehive tragedy. Daphne was heartsick about the wrecked hives, and though she claimed she wanted to help clean up the bee yard, Melissa saw her fear and reluctance.

"I'm sorry. I'll do anything else. I will single-handedly reap all the root vegetables." Daphne pouted, oozing remorse, her still-swollen lower lip protruding.

"It's okay. I'll figure it out," said Melissa.

If bee colonies were going to be recovered, it would have to be done soon. From the other side of the house Melissa heard the white pickup stutter and stall once, then twice, and the distinct growl of Joseph's throaty curses. She found him with his head under the dented hood of the old pickup, a cigarette burning in the corner of his mouth, his bare hands coated in engine grease.

"Is it serious?" she asked.

"Don't think so. Distributor cap probably. Might be a spare in there somewhere." Joseph jerked his head toward the work shed.

"When it's fixed, would you mind working on the hives? If you can put them back together, even one of them, we'll have somewhere to put any surviving colony."

"Already told you. I'm not interested in them bees." Joseph buried his head in the old engine. "And they're gone now. How you gonna get them bees back? Not happening."

Joseph's obdurate refusal fuelled Melissa's pertinacious insistence. Beck and Daphne weren't capable of helping? Fine. She would appeal one more time to the only person nearby who could. Even if she wasn't up for helping physically, Marjorie might be convinced to give valuable advice. It would be neighbourly to check on her anyway, Melissa thought, remembering the old woman's tears and her infected hand. She went searching for the farm's dilapidated communal mountain bike.

The bike had no permanent home; it lay wherever its last ride had ended. It was the farm truck's low-tech twin, old and poorly maintained, with a rusty chain, paint faded to a chipped and muddy umber, its original colour a mystery. Often it was propped up against the front porch or leaning against one of the big trees in the front yard; sometimes it was camouflaged on the rocky lakeshore or stuffed in elderberry bushes beside Hotay's enclosure. Melissa checked all the usual places and still no bike. At last she found it, jammed in the cedar hedge beside the road. She cycled to Marjorie's house, pleased with herself for checking up on the old beekeeper.

Fall was coming. The crunch of desiccated leaves on the road's shoulder was satisfying, and she wheeled along, feeling strangely free. The air was crisp and fragrant. At Marjorie's house Melissa rolled the bike along an overgrown front path, choked with speckled brown squash leaves and splayed-out lavender and azalea shrubs, their flowers dried and spent. Once again, Marjorie was missing from her outdoor landscape. Melissa searched the garden, bee yard and orchard before checking the house. She knocked, then hammered on a worn, sun-bleached front door.

No answer. Maybe Marjorie was asleep, or grumpily hiding from visitors. Feeling unscrupulous – *ewww, I'm a peeping Tom* – Melissa started a circumnavigation, standing on tiptoe at each window, trying to get a glimpse inside. The sides of the house were teeming with weeds and smelled of cat urine. In a recess of her conscience, it occurred to Melissa that perhaps the old woman needed help as much or more than she did. Marjorie clearly couldn't keep up with the maintenance of her place – what was she doing, begging a solitary septuagenarian to help with her beehives? Behind the house, Melissa paused under a screened but otherwise open window, too high for peeking in. She heard a faint, feminine groan.

"Marjorie?"

A pause. Another protracted groan.

"Marjorie, it's Melissa – I'm coming in!"

She scrambled through noxious weeds, thistles pricking her as she passed, and scurried, cartoon-clumsy, to the front entrance. She tried to force the door by slamming it with her left shoulder. Once, twice, three times she launched her weight against the old wood. It cracked and complained, but wouldn't give. Before resorting to kicking the door down, she tried the tarnished metal doorknob. *I'm an idiot.* The knob turned easily, and Melissa let herself into Marjorie's home. It smelled of lavender and laundry, and something less pleasant – a mixture of rot, dust and dirty carpets. The interior had a simple layout. The entire front half of the house was a sitting room, an overfurnished space that included a rocking chair and a faded sofa, needlework pillowcases and shelves of floral teacups and china. Photographs hung in frames between the windows. Behind the sitting room, the back of the house had three rooms. To her right, Melissa glimpsed the kitchen and got a quick impression of dated appliances and stacked dirty dishes. A subdued bathroom separated the kitchen from a single bedroom on the other side of the house. Melissa moved into the hall behind the sitting room. Across from the bedroom there was a shadowy alcove, not much more than a recess in the wall, about four feet deep, with a slanted ceiling. A surface of plywood and two-by-fours topped with a dingy foam mattress filled this peculiar, cramped space. The makeshift bed was messy, cluttered with items that didn't belong on a mattress: spoons, bailing wire, a large syringe, a pair of ripped jeans. It stank too – a repulsive odour she couldn't place – not quite rotting flesh, but close. She stared into the alcove for a moment, baffled, until another moan made her turn around and push the bedroom door open.

Marjorie was sprawled on her bed, half-covered with a thin sheet, white hair plastered to her forehead and sticking to the sides of her face. Pallor and fever had sunk wrinkles deep down to her skull. A frail hand, knuckles protruding between lumpy blue veins, clutched a blood-spotted washcloth. The nightstand was cluttered with a jumble of used tissues, brown tincture bottles and glassware half-filled with various liquids. Cautious, afraid of a slap or a reprimand, Melissa touched Marjorie's exposed shoulder. The woman's skin was tissue-paper thin and dry. Her lips were parched. Melissa picked up her right hand, the one clutching the washcloth, but Marjorie didn't respond. Her breathing was shallow, and her pulse raced. Melissa reached across the bed and picked up Marjorie's left hand, but the thing she lifted wasn't a hand. It was five puffy red sausages, tied together at a too-small wrist. On the pale inside of the old woman's arm, a red line snaked from wrist to elbow.

Bloodshot blue eyes popped open, and Marjorie screamed.

Melissa groped in her knapsack for her cellphone. *This is fucking futile, there won't be any service*, and there wasn't. She had no choice but to bicycle back to the farm, and use the Wi-Fi reception there to call an ambulance.

"Marjorie, listen to me. I'm going to be back really soon with help. Don't try to get up, okay?"

The blue eyes inside the wrinkles had gone flat and sightless. It felt wrong to leave without making an attempt to help her somehow, so Melissa frantically cleared away the litter and glasses on the nightstand and pried the washcloth out of Marjorie's right hand. In the confined, outdated and untidy bathroom, she rinsed smears of blood out of the cloth, squeezed and folded it, then brought it back to the bedroom and placed it on Marjorie's forehead. Where had the blood come from? She wasn't cut, as far as Melissa could see. She must have coughed it up.

"They're all dead," Marjorie whispered.

"Pardon?"

"They're all dead, all of them."

"No, they're not. I'll be back soon. Try to relax."

Who were all dead? Melissa rushed from the little house, mounted the bike and pushed off with a frenzied kick. Riding down the road she stood on the pedals, forcing the wheels to spin faster. At the farm she skidded through the gap in the hedge and tossed the bike with a clatter on the leafy lawn. Downstairs was empty; everyone was outside working. She called an ambulance, gave directions and then reversed the bike trip, barging into Marjorie's house about twenty minutes after she had left and hastening to her bedside.

"They're all dead," Marjorie repeated, when she realized Melissa was there.

"*Who*? Who are all dead?"

"The b-bees."

In spite of her vigorous bike sprints, Melissa shivered. "No, they're not *all* dead. There's a hive still standing, and probably lots of swarms."

"All dead. All of them, all the b-bees," Marjorie whispered mournfully.

"I promise you, they're not all dead. It's going to be okay, we can re-build, honestly."

"They're gone, like they never . . ."

The elderly woman pressed cracked lips together. Melissa poured a sip of water into the black slash of her mouth, but Marjorie had no energy to swallow; excess water drained out and ran along the gutters of her wrinkles, stained pink – she was bleeding in there somewhere, or coughing blood from her lungs. The sausage fingers of her left hand were bundled together outside the sheet, oozing yellow discharge. From outside came the wail of a siren, then the crunching of tires onto roadside gravel. An engine cut out. Footfalls thumped up stairs and into the house.

"She's in here!"

Melissa backed out so two paramedics could enter the small, square bedroom. She felt profoundly relieved at the sight of their crisp white shirts, scarlet badges, navy blue trousers and black cases of equipment. They ignored her and got to work examining Marjorie. Melissa retreated to the fussy front room and puttered nervously, running her fingertips over the knots of doilies and squinting at inexpertly framed photographs. She leaned into a sepia image of a handsome man. He glared at the camera, his smooth dark hair and defined cheekbones eerily reminiscent of Beck. *This must be her late husband, Arnold.* Nearby were out-of-focus images of a young child, a boy, engaged in various activities. Here was the boy on a swing set, kicking his heels over his head, and here he was beside a river, holding a fishing pole. The child had dark hair and skin, like Arnold – did Marjorie have a son? If so, he wasn't around to care for his mother. Melissa considered investigating the strange alcove again, but the bedroom door was open and the paramedics would see her poking around. She stayed in Marjorie's living room, trying to figure out where the photographs had been taken. In some of them, the boy's resemblance to Beck was uncanny.

At last, the paramedics loaded the patient onto a stretcher and carried her through the living room and outside. Marjorie's mouth was loose, her infected hand hidden away under blankets. Melissa gave the paramedics her phone number and answered their questions. *No, I don't know if she has family; yes, it was a coincidence I stopped by this morning*. She followed the stretcher to the back doors of the ambulance and spoke to Marjorie as they lifted her into the vehicle.

"Hey, the bees are all right. I'll take care of them; it's going to be okay."

But Marjorie hadn't heard – she looked as if she had lost consciousness. The paramedics closed the back doors and then the ambulance was gone in a hurry, tires throwing up sprays of gravel, wailing siren fading out of earshot.

Melissa reluctantly returned to the stale, sick atmosphere of the house. In the bedroom, she brushed piles of used tissues into a garbage bag. She tore sweaty, crinkled sheets from the bed, and stuffed them into an ancient washing machine squatting in a corner of the kitchen, then moved glassware from bedroom to kitchen and washed all the dirty dishes. A spotty window over the sink overlooked the bee yard; hands immersed in soapy dishwater, her thoughts wandered outside. *Maybe Marjorie meant all of her own bees are dead*? She could see Marjorie's hives, painted white and cream, surrounded by clouds of raspberry-coloured azalea blooms. The hives looked fine, perfect rectangles all in a row. Melissa wiped counters and tabletops, then paused in the gloomy hallway beside the peculiar alcove, where the odd smell was overpowering. All at once she felt nauseated, and had to get out of the house. She made sure the door closed tightly behind her – she had no key, and would have to leave the place unlocked.

She stepped off the porch. *All dead.* Marjorie's words lingered like smoke. The garden and orchard felt empty, as if they already missed their caretaker. Straw-strewn pathways curved and intersected around raised garden beds. Clumps of herbs grew along the paths – blue-flowered borage and feathery dill. Melissa decided to take a closer look at Marjorie's hives, and followed a path around the far side of the house. A white wooden trellis mounted on the red brick chimney supported a tangle of vines, swirling tendrils that caressed her as she passed. Marjorie's bee yard was protected with an electric fence like the one at the farm. The fence encircled ten hives, the entrances thick with drones and workers. Glossy-leaved rhododendrons, some already packed in straw and covered with burlap in preparation for winter, bordered the bee yard in part-shade of pine trees. Half-hidden in the pines, dwarfed by robust shrubbery, Melissa spotted a shed no larger than an outhouse. She investigated and found it secured with a simple wooden latch rotating on a nail. Feeling like a sinister Goldilocks, she opened the wee door and entered.

The shed was a rhapsody to the honeybee, an apiarist's miniature museum. All the functional necessities for beekeeping were there: a white suit hanging on a hook, topped neatly by hat and veil, and rough wooden shelves crammed with hive tools, jars of wax, a bee brush, leather gloves and extra frames. An old-fashioned smoker's round metal body was perched on a shelf, its pointed lid and spout reminiscent of the Tin Man's oil can. On the walls a careful hand had painted bees – nestled in flowers, dancing on perfect comb hexagons and hovering around conical hives. Small gilded picture frames held black-and-white historical photographs of beekeepers, women in full-length dresses, their broad-brimmed hats and veils polka-dotted with bees that had lived and collected nectar a long time ago. Where the shed walls met its slanted roof, letters spelled out a quote in gold paint. *The keeping of bees is like the direction of sunbeams – Henry David Thoreau.* Three more pictures of the mystery boy from inside the house were tacked to the wall, faded with age and curled at the edges.

Closing up the shed, Melissa stepped outside and blinked in the noon sun. She watched bees come and go, perplexed. If Marjorie's bees were fine, who or what was *all dead*?

Fifteen

October's swift entrance dismayed Beck. No green was left on the deciduous trees; they flamed and raged with colour. Leaves, tugged by the wind, detached from branches and cartwheeled to the grass where they lay spent, like pointy-edged pieces of an autumn puzzle. Spring, and then winter; a season was lost. He had promised to help his parents pack up the cabin, but he would have preferred to stay on the farm with Melissa. Washed-out, leaden remains of a storm that had broken to the east trundled across the sky. Purple light filtered into the cabin, and sun burst through a hole in the clouds. Chopping herbs and mumbling under her breath, his mother shot him a meaningful glance. She was itching, Beck could tell, to lecture him. He joined her in the kitchen and ignored her while he made tea. He poured three steaming mugs, sweetening his own with a generous tablespoonful of honey. His battered guitar was leaning in a corner; he picked it up and strummed idly.

"I prayed for you," said Eurydice. "Every day, I prayed you were safe."

"Thanks, Ma." Beck strummed his guitar a little louder, hoping she'd take the hint.

"Olodumare kept watch over you."

Beck sighed, anticipating what was coming. His father was outside, talking on the phone to Max Griffen, making plans to cycle. His mother had been waiting for this opportunity.

"Your father's head-in-the-box doctor can't explain where you were, and why you don't remember. But you know the truth – you were possessed by an Orisha." Eurydice flourished her knife, silver bracelets rattling on her wrist.

"I don't know, Ma. I don't think so." Beck picked out a melody.

"Your padre told me about las abejas."

"I was hanging out with bees too much. That's what Pa thinks. I must have been feverish all summer and having nightmares about beehives."

"A consulta, Beck. Let me give you one this morning. It will help us understand."

"No, Ma. I told you already. A consulta won't work on me. I don't believe in them."

Beck kept playing guitar and listening to his father's enthusiastic voice, hoping the phone call would end soon, and they could get to work. Eurydice de Famosa's consultas in Cuba were furious, smoky sessions. Participants shouted, cried and occasionally fainted. The distraught and forlorn people who sought a Santerian priest or priestess usually wanted to learn if a grandmother would survive pneumonia, if so-and-so's husband was cheating on her or if a favourite son would marry his desired intended. But although the enlightenment his mother teased out of the ether was accurate more than fifty percent of the time, Beck could never bring himself to believe in the paranormal power of his mother's consulta sessions. He suspected they were nothing more than calculated guesswork. She was hyper-observant, a canny interpreter of subtext and subliminal signs. As a kid, he had never gotten away with anything – stealing spare change for candy, skipping school, smoking cigarettes at a pool hall in Havana. Beck's mother had always intuited the truth, and when he was young this had mystified him. How had she always known? As he grew up, he thought he understood: his guilt had given him away. Whether supplicants believed news would be good or bad, Grandma would live or she would die, the husband was faithful or cheating, the bride-to-be would say *yes* or *no*, their suspicions betrayed the answer. When his mother said faith was required in order to learn the truth, her devotees inevitably abandoned poker faces and revealed, through posture and expression, what they thought the outcome of the consulta would be. Beck suspected that people came to Eurydice de Famosa for answers, already carrying the answers they sought within them, and the santera merely confirmed their feelings. His failure to adopt his mother's faith eroded her happiness; she had returned to her chopping but it was more vehement now, angrier, the knife beating a savage rhythm on the cutting board.

"Fine. You won't do a consulta."

Letting knife fall to board with a clunk, his ma snatched the ajà, a short broom made of palm leaves, from its hook, and began vigorously brushing at the walls, floor and empty air, sweeping away the negative energy he was generating with his mulishness. The side door rasped open and his father entered, grinning.

"Max is coming up later this month. He's getting serious about moving up here – he's been researching real estate, and he had questions about Lanark, Almonte and Carleton Place. He asked about you, son. I told him you're feeling much better." Matthew pushed his glasses up his nose and noticed his wife's ill-tempered swatting.

"Why don't you let your mother do a consulta, Beck? What harm can it do?"

"Oh come on, Pa." Beck stood up, and leaned his guitar in the corner. He picked up his tea and gulped it down thirstily, in three long swallows. "We were supposed to be packing up the cabin today. If I thought I was going to be monkeying around with a consulta, I would have stayed at the farm."

Eurydice swept near her son's head, narrowly missing him with a martial ajà stroke.

"Don't underestimate the power of your mother's faith, Beck. I learned early on what amazing stuff it is. For an entire year before we were married –" Matthew swept a hand through his thin hair, preparing to reminisce.

"Please don't tell me that story again." Beck let his head sag on the tired stem of his neck. Weariness radiated from his bones. A delicate prickly heat crept across his forehead and he broke out in a sweat. An oddly familiar sensation woke inside him. Light in the cabin strobed and his skin began tingling. There was a rushing in his ears that amplified even as his vision faded, his parents blurring into masses of dark, hairy bodies, an ordered chaos of veined wings, sculling. Trickles of moisture collected in his hairline and dripped down the curves of his jaw. The fever was his system attempting to purge him of toxins, and every drop of perspiration held foreign compounds. He could smell it; his body was sweating out the bees.

A hand gripped Beck's wrist, and he concentrated on the pressure of those fingers, breathing in and out, until the worried faces of his parents materialized, covered in tiny bright yellow beads, like pellets of pollen. He heard the tattoo of his own rapid heartbeat, *da-dug, da-dug, da-dug, da-dug*.

"You see – you see?" Eurydice berated Matthew. "He refuses the consulta, and right away, this."

"I'm okay." Beck pried his mother's hand from his wrist, and dried his face with his shirt sleeve. "I drank my tea too fast, that's all."

Weeeeoooo, weeeeoooo, weeeoooo! The wail of a siren came from far away, and then swiftly sounded much closer. It crescendoed, blasting the cabin with calamity, until an ambulance sped by outside, red-and-white lights flashing.

"Did you – how did you call an ambulance?" Matthew gaped at his wife.

"No seas ridículo. I didn't call for it." Eurydice hurried out to the porch, and Matthew and Beck trailed after her. A crunch of gravel filtered through the trees, and abruptly the siren ceased.

"It's gone to Marjorie's house, poor old thing," Matthew said. "Should we go over, do you think?"

"No," said Beck, too quickly, and his father turned to him, looking confused.

"Why not? Your mother might be able to help," said Matthew sharply.

"They're professionals. Let them do their job," Beck said.

"You trust these people you call professionals," Beck's mother waved a contemptuous hand at the ambulance, "and not your own mother."

"Melissa needs help." Beck reached for his shabby work jacket. His backpack was slumped beside his cot, and he crammed clothes into it as he spoke. "I'm going to see if she's cool with me moving back into the spare room. The three of us in this cabin – I can't. I need space."

His mother wound herself up to respond, but his father shushed her.

"You know what, Eurydice? He's right. This cabin is tight quarters. He'll be happier over at the farm. But stay out of that bee yard, Beck." Matthew clapped his son on the shoulder. "I'll take care of buttoning things up here."

The moment he stepped outside Beck felt better. His bicycle, a second-hand ten-speed, was resting against the side of the cabin. He straddled it like a horse and rode it hard onto the road. The ambulance blocked his view of Marjorie's house and he passed without slowing. Glorying in the increasing strength of his limbs, he pumped the pedals, pushing himself hard, and covered the distance to the farm in record time. Panting, he wheeled his bike around the side of the house and left it there, dropping his backpack beside it. Wind rushed off the lake, bringing with it a fresh scent – molecules of live fish, wet scales exposed to air. Above the shore a pair of hawks played in the gusty weather, climbing in slow spirals and plummeting in speedy descents, wings tilting on invisible roller-coaster draughts. On a whim he decided to walk down to the lake. He passed the flower garden, a trapezoid of earth spiked with dead flowers and brown grass, mottled with the dark purple spots of fallen petals. As he gained the dirt road that led to the boat ramp, a quick movement in the reeds caught Beck's eye. He halted, skidding on pebbles. A scrap of plaid shirt on a stooped back, a stubbly face swerved in a posture of elusion. It was Joseph, sneaking up the hill through a screen of young poplars, like an animal avoiding detection.

The lake was a mess of choppy indigo waves. Wind and water filled Beck's senses. He opened his nostrils and tilted his head back, inviting the lake to wash through him and clean out bits of bees left hanging on his insides. Wind pulled leaves from trees and scattered them, their fire-colours muted by clouds obscuring the sun. A string of ducks wavered along the far shore. The whine of a motorboat sliced air and crossed water, until the wind changed direction and whisked the mechanical sound away. He heard a snatch of Melissa's voice and Joseph's blunt response. She emerged on the boat launch, startlingly beautiful, the striking slope of her nose, the fullness of her mouth, her purposeful eyes. The wind flicked her hair into streamers, dark banners moored to her skull. Beck smelled her skin: floral soap and sweat. She clutched his forearm.

"I was at Marjorie's just now," she confessed.

All at once, and unaccountably, Beck felt dizzy. He imagined he was careening through a forest, branches whipping his face, pursued by nameless danger.

"I know you didn't want me to. But I really need help getting the hives back together, and Joseph's being a dick, and you're not up for it. I figured I could convince Marjorie. But she was in bed, really sick. Her hand is infected. Three times the size it should be, and purple. I called an ambulance, and they've taken her to the hospital."

Intense, organic humming in his ears muted the sound of Melissa's voice.

"Beck? What's wrong?"

Squatting down, Beck filled his palms with lake water and splashed his face. “I’m sorry,” he said. “I’m having a rough day. That’s too bad about Marjorie.”

“Yeah.” She frowned. “Weren’t you supposed to be helping your folks out today?”

Beck straightened and levelled a serious look at Melissa. “You know what? It’s not working out, the three of us in that cabin together. Pa has started siding with Ma. They think I should let her do a consulta. And I just . . .” He struggled to finish the thought. “I don’t want some occult reason for my missing time. It was better when Pa thought I had a brain tumour. He’s back to wanting things to be more mystical – he’s even started photographing auras again. Anyway, I came to ask if I could move back into the spare room. I’ll get to work right away. And as soon as I can, I’ll help out with the beehives.” Water dripped from his chin and beaded on his eyelashes. Melissa puffed at wisps of hair blowing in her face, and tucked them firmly behind her ears. He paused patiently for her to finish, and spoke again, low and earnest. “I completely understand why you wouldn’t trust me, but I’m asking you to give me a chance. I know I’ll get better faster here, with you and Daphne.”

“Are you going to stick around?”

“Believe me, I never wanted to leave. I wish I could promise whatever happened to me won’t happen again, but I still don’t understand it. I *want* to stay. I *want* to be with you.”

She jerked her chin downward, a sharp confirmation. Energy leapt between them. Beck stepped forward. They kissed, and pulled apart smiling shyly, as if they had met only moments ago. On the way up to the farmhouse the wind was at their backs, blowing hair around them like blinders, hiding everything in the periphery.

Sixteen

Every October, Melissa's father used to tell her the story of Cinderella. It was an obvious connection: ripe pumpkins in the fields were his mnemonic. The way Charlie Makepeace told it, Cinderella was a fable about the change of seasons. In the fall, nature's fairy godmother transformed plain green trees, and magically they wore a fabulous, ornate ball gown of orange, yellow and red, accessorized with brilliant blue skies and frost slippers. It lasted only a few short moments, then with the *bong, bong, bong* of an unseen tower bell at midnight, the gorgeous leaf-gown was gone, leaving shredded brown rags in its place. The trees were still beautiful, but it was a ragged beauty, tattered scraps of fleeting glory withering in clumps of dead grass. Locked in a chilly garret, the trees wore dun and linen until their spring-prince came. Cinderella always had to wait out a brutal winter, watching her bitchy stepsisters' failed attempts to stuff outsized feet into a delicate shoe, before some anonymous Mister Wonderful figured out who she was in spring.

On a cold morning that smelled like spruce and damp rot, Melissa fed Hotay and pushed her fingers into the donkey's thickening coat. Walking past piles of compost and brown, empty fields, she took a deep breath tinged with decomposing plant parts and yawned. Almost hibernation time. Joseph had covered the outbuildings with blue and orange plastic tarpaulins, defending old roofs. Sleet, ice and snow would come soon. She could sleep in, read under the covers, get up and knit crafty Christmas presents. Some nights Beck slept in the spare bedroom and other nights with her, but they were living in the same house. When she woke and he wasn't beside her, a jolt of alarm compelled her to tiptoe across the hall, and make sure he was still there. Ordinarily Beck's parents would have left for Cuba by now; their cabin was too cold in winter. But Matthew and Eurydice had decided they weren't ready to leave their son. They planned to rent a cheap motel room in Lanark, with a kitchenette.

The back door of the farmhouse slammed. Daphne picked her way to the henhouse, weaving between furrows, carrying a square cutting board piled precariously high with a mountain of russet-red and bottle-green fruit peel. Melissa intercepted her sister, and together they tossed peel inside the chicken coop fence. The birds cackled, running on lizard-legs to peck up the treat. The grass was coated with crunchy white frost, and steam rose from sun-warmed fences.

"Jill's going to be home in the next day or two," Melissa said, even though they both knew it.

"I can't wait to hear about her trip." Daphne glanced wistfully at the farmhouse and banged the cutting board against a fence post. The last of the fruit peel dropped into the chicken enclosure. "I'm worried she'll be pissed about the beehives."

"It was an accident. She won't be angry, just determined to get them going again."

Daphne peered toward the damaged bee yard. "I don't understand why Beck's so slow to fix things up. It's my fault the hives got trashed – I get that. But last spring all he wanted to do was keep bees. I didn't tell you, but I was covering his livestock chores so he could spend all his time over there. Now, when we need him, he won't go anywhere near the hives. And you know what's even weirder? You're not mad about it."

Melissa met Daphne's gaze and they pondered each other seriously for a long moment.

"Okay, you got me," Melissa said, throwing her hands up, resigned. "You deserve to know what's going on. I promised Beck I wouldn't say anything, but you're too shrewd. All this summer, while he was gone, Beck thinks he knows where he was."

Daphne lifted her chin, and cocked an amused eyebrow. "Oh yeah?"

"Yeah, and brace yourself, because this is kind of *X-Files*."

"Hit me," said Daphne, with a little leap to demonstrate how ready she was.

"He thinks he turned into a bee colony and lived in a hive all summer."

Daphne jerked backwards, and held the cutting board up like a shield. She craned her neck and surveyed the fields, as if Beck might be wandering toward them, delusional and requiring a straitjacket. She coughed up two abrupt chuckles, and smiled tentatively at Melissa.

"It's a joke, right? You're yanking my chain?"

"Not a bit. He honestly thinks he was a bunch of bees. All summer, for real."

Whipping her gaze around to the farmhouse, Daphne spluttered. "Do Eurydice and Matthew know? Did he tell the doctor in Toronto that? He knows it's psychotic, right?"

"I'm not sure about the doctor. His parents know. Matthew wants him to see a psychiatrist, and I think Eurydice's kind of *trying* to believe it? I mean, other than hallucinating for three months straight, he's acting completely normal. Oh, except he keeps trying to get me to see bee vectors."

"Bee vectors?"

"He thinks he can see these traces, like gold lines, between bees and their hives."

Daphne pursed her lips and whistled.

"Don't say anything to Jill, or Joseph, obviously." Melissa sighed. "And now I'm going to have to confess that I broke my promise not to tell you."

They traipsed back to the kitchen, where the island was taken over by an industrial dehydrator; the countertops were jammed end to end with baskets of apples and pears to preserve, and neat lines of sterilized Mason jars. A battalion of food for the frozen months ahead marched along pantry shelves: canned beets, tomatoes, pickled cabbage and beans. The front doors closed with a bang and Beck entered the kitchen, smiling.

"Goats are milked," Beck said. "I should start putting the hives back together."

Daphne and Melissa exchanged a brief look of concern.

"You told her." Beck goggled at Melissa, his black eyebrows soaring.

"It wasn't her fault. I wrenched it out of her." Daphne sidled over to Beck and placed a hand on his elbow. "And I totally get it. It was me who first called you Bee-brain, remember? I was getting frustrated you weren't fixing up the hives, but uh, under the circumstances, I understand. And I think Melissa's right – you should stay away from bees. Whatever happened to you this summer, bees aren't good for you. They're like your drug."

Beck's shoulders sank. He ran a hand through his hair, replicating Matthew's nervous habit. "I'm getting a CT scan in Toronto at the end of the month."

Melissa jiggled her head, negative. "You're way too healthy. I don't believe for a second you have anything physically wrong with you. It's something psychological, I bet."

"Yeah, cheer up, Beck – you're nuts! That's the best explanation. But you're in good company." Daphne hooked her arm through his and produced her most maniacal grin.

Melissa took Beck's other arm. The three friends gazed out the back window, contemplating the fields where they worked together. Inspired by the atmosphere of honesty and adopting an air of nonchalance she didn't feel, Melissa briefly told Daphne and Beck about Balvinder Singh's faltering testimony and the reopening of her father's case. "So fair warning, the cops are going to be coming around soon," she finished. Beck kissed her forehead, his eyes unfathomable.

"Oh-oh. Nuh-uh. Jill's not gonna like this," said Daphne.

"Well she's going to have to suck it up." Melissa bristled. "Come on, let's plan this harvest banquet. It's hanging over my head. I want it to be the best one ever."

They sat at the counter and brainstormed, Melissa taking notes on a paper bag scrounged from the recycling bin. They hashed out a pollination-themed menu and tweaked it until they adopted a final version. Melissa would make a carrot pumpkin soup served with baked pita chips and a lemon artichoke dip. Daphne agreed to cook the main course, roasted eggplant and sweet potato with cheddar cheese gratin, seasoned with garlic and chili peppers. Beck suggested Joseph could barbecue trout from a local fish farm and serve it with a tangy almond sauce.

"Joseph said he wouldn't help," Daphne reminded Melissa.

"He'll change his tune when my mother gets home. Joseph does what Jill tells him to."

They would ransack the greenhouse and make a vast quantity of garden salad with a raspberry vinaigrette dressing. Dessert – honey-coated canned peaches and yogourt with sugared pistachios – would be Beck's contribution. Almost every food on the menu wouldn't exist without the pollination work of bees.

With the menu finished, they fell to idle chat and jokes. Daphne performed an uncanny impression of Hotay waiting to be fed, a combination of toothy brays and impatient head tosses, inducing hysterical laughter in her friends. Melissa felt a surge of hope and happiness. Sitting between her sister and her lover, she indulged a childish wish for the three of them to be the farm's only residents.

A week scampered past, and when the harvest banquet was only two days away, Melissa was swamped with tasks. She pictured the Lanark United Church hall, stark and echo-empty, and realized with a start she'd forgotten entirely about decorating the venue. She found Joseph and asked him to do it. He shook his head at her slowly, his countenance registering disgust. God, but he could be a cantankerous asshole. She made a couple of phone calls and convinced a friend who taught at a local elementary school to assign her grade three classroom an art project: cut-out cardboard bee decorations. *Delegate, delegate, delegate,* Melissa's mother always said, *it's the key to great management.* Melissa was hunched in front of the office computer, cursing, trying to design the paper menus, when the slam of a car door outside the hedge distracted her. Light crunch of footsteps on the path, a feminine *oof,* thump of luggage landing on the porch. Jill Makepeace was home. A vague foreboding kept Melissa in the desk chair for a moment's reluctance, and in those few seconds, Daphne ran through the house, flung the front doors open and screeched.

"You're home! Oh, Jill, you look fabulous!"

Melissa slipped into the front hall. Her mother and Daphne were hugging each other with pure affection. She felt a flash of jealousy, witnessing this perfect reunion of mother and child.

When people compared Jill and her biological daughter they sometimes guessed, even out loud, that Melissa was adopted. Jill was compact and round where her daughter was bony; light where her daughter was dark. Daphne and Jill released each other at last, and Melissa absorbed her mother's melanin-altered appearance; freckles had linked up under the equatorial sun and been joined by dozens of brown, asymmetrical age spots. As she embraced her mother, she tried not to notice the tears of joy Daphne was wiping away, or regret how Jill's second welcome-home hug would be a shorter, drier affair than her first.

"Oh, my dear girl, my Melissa. I have seen so much, lived so much, learned *so much*. Farming practices, cooking, animal husbandry – you name it – Central Americans are *much* more holistic in their approach to farming than we are. There's so much to show you, so much to share. I can't wait to survey the farm and show you everything we simply *must* change."

All of this burst from Jill before her luggage had crossed the threshold.

"I would love to hear all about it. I am so unbelievably busy until after the harvest banquet, and then let's walk the farm together for sure. I'm making up the banquet menu right now, actually."

Jill tossed her blond hair. "Isn't that *typical*. I'm gone for an entire *year*, then I walk through the door and *right away*, you have more important things to do."

Melissa's mother could summon tears. They filled her eyes, and watery evidence of emotion spilled down her sun-flecked cheeks. Melissa inhaled for five beats and exhaled for eight.

"Sorry, Mom – you're right. The menu can wait. Let's go have some tea. Beck's living here again, in the spare room, but he's out in the fields right now, harvesting."

"I'll see him soon enough. I'm so happy to be with my girls."

They went to the kitchen. Jill enthused about Guatemalan companion planting and the crucial role of the small family farm. Daphne listened, beguiled, cradling her chin in her fists, asking pertinent questions and hanging on every word. Melissa concentrated on not saying the wrong thing when her mother stopped for a breath. It was hard to listen while troubling topics crowded her thoughts – the return of her twitchy behaviours, Beck's unexplained missing months, the wrecked bee yard, the pollination-themed banquet, the deleted emails and the reopening of her father's missing person's file. The privilege of being an only biological child nudged at Melissa; she wanted her mother to herself. After an hour of Jill's breathless stories from Central America, Daphne went outside to feed the goats. Alone with her mother at last, Melissa hesitated, not knowing where to begin. They stared at each other over the kitchen island.

"From what I can see, the farm looks good, sweetheart. You've done a wonderful job, running it while I was gone." Jill beamed.

"Thanks, Mom, that means a lot. It hasn't been easy. As you know, Beck was gone all summer." Melissa held up a hand to stop her mother from cutting in. "He still says he doesn't know where he was, and don't ask him about it. He gets squirrelly if you do."

"Are you two together again, if you don't mind me prying?" Jill took a demure sip of tea.

"We are – yes, I'd say we are." Melissa felt a rush of affection for Beck, and an unexpected need to confide in her mother: she was in love. But they were interrupted.

The back door opened too quickly and slammed into the wall. Joseph stepped inside. He froze at the sight of Jill perched on a stool at the island, and acknowledged Melissa with a quick, irritated nod. His shirt was fresh and his pants were clean – unusual, for a workday. Jill took him in with enormous, fluid eyes, and produced a tremulous smile.

"Well, Joseph, there you are. How good to see you. Here I am, back from *paradise*. I was just telling Lissy, the farm looks terrific. I'm so grateful to you all for taking such good care of it in my absence." One of Jill's legs was crossed tidily over the other, and her small foot turned, a casual rotation.

Joseph stared as if a spotlight were illuminating Jill at centre stage.

"Would you mind coming back later, Joseph? It's not a good time. We're getting caught up," said Melissa. Why couldn't he see it was a private moment, and leave of his own accord? Joseph nodded curtly and stumped back outside. As Jill watched him go, her face plunged into a frown, and she aged a decade in seconds, round cheeks sagging into jowls.

"You didn't have to be rude. Have you two had a falling-out of some kind?" Two spots of crimson appeared below Jill's glittering eyes.

"Not really. He's been more of a crank than usual though. Like, an animal gets into the bee yard and destroys all the hives, and he wants to write off beekeeping forever? I've been begging him to help out with harvest festival and he refuses to have anything to do with it."

Melissa hadn't realized how much Joseph was getting on her nerves until her frustrations came pouring out to her mother. For years her relationship with Joseph had been coasting on his pleasant, avuncular interaction with her when she was a child, and she was struck by how much her friendship with him had deteriorated. Little things he did had begun to annoy her disproportionately – smoking too close to the farmhouse, idling his diesel truck and filling the front lawn with fumes, depositing his dishes in the sink, assuming someone would clean up after him.

"It's likely he had more work with me gone, and resented it a little. It's only natural; Joseph's always had a curt exterior, but underneath all that, he has a good heart. Now, Melissa, you have that distracted look, like you're burning to tell me something important. What is it?"

Disconcerted by how easily her mother could guess her thoughts, Melissa's lower lip spasmed and she fought off the compelling impulse to puff and tuck.

"I wasn't going to say anything until you'd been home for a couple of days, but seeing as you already know something's up – I've been talking to Constable Hickey." Jill inhaled sharply through her nose and clunked her cup of tea onto the counter, but Melissa pressed onward. "Some of the testimony placing Dad in Lanark and Almonte after he disappeared has been retracted, and some invalidated. It changes the case enough that the police are reopening their investigation and making it active. Constable Hickey said she'd swing around once you were home to talk about it."

Jill's expression was unfathomable. She lifted her cup, put it down without drinking and busied herself adjusting the gauzy folds of her floral skirt. With the thumb and index finger of her right hand she pinched an empty place on her left ring finger. She licked her rose-pink lips and rubbed them together. Making a visible effort to stay calm, she spoke evenly.

"I have been working a lot on *myself*, Lissy. On *self-actualization*. I hope you will gain an understanding of where I am in my *life journey*. I am *freeing* myself from the wreckage of my past. I'm not carrying burdens that don't *belong* to me. I *respect* myself these days, so I pick up only what I can *handle*. And I don't have space in my consciousness for this right now."

Daphne opened the back door and charged breathlessly into the kitchen. Oblivious to the heavy energy hanging in the room, she threw her arms around Jill's shoulders and kissed her cheek.

"Mmmm, I'm so happy you're here. Got someone else who wants to see you," Daphne sang.

Beck's silhouette filled the door frame, and he winked at Melissa before moving to hug her mother. "Hello, Jill. I wasn't particularly helpful while you were away. You probably heard. I'm trying to make up for it now."

"Beckett Wise, I'm sure you couldn't help whatever it was that kept you away. Melissa is very pleased you're back, and so am I. Hail, hail, the gang's all here! Now would one of you please enlighten me about this fascinating theme for the harvest banquet? Daphne mentioned it on the telephone the other day, but I want to hear all the details, and I'm keen to jump in and help."

Beck came to stand behind Melissa and began massaging her neck and shoulders, pinching and kneading with both his hands. She shivered with pleasure. Daphne provided Jill with an animated explanation of the pollination theme, rubbing her belly to demonstrate gustatory ecstasy the banquet was sure to induce.

"I can't get over how chill and happy you look," Daphne gushed.

Jill smiled. She uncrossed her legs, sprang off the kitchen stool and executed a girlish pirouette, flourishing her skirt as she twirled.

"Do you think I look great, *really*? I'm eating an *entirely* raw food diet. Well, with *some* exceptions. And I'm running, of course, and my yoga-slash-meditation regime is very strict. I was given a new mantra by my guru, and it has made *all the difference*."

"You really do look good," said Melissa, and she grasped her mother's hand and squeezed it to demonstrate her sincerity. The same determination that powered her mother's zany passions had benefited Melissa as a lost little girl, a bewildered child whose father had run off. This was the same woman who had rescued Daphne from a life of violence, penury and neglect. This was the parent who had stuck around; Melissa let love and admiration swell in her heart for her intrepid, courageous mother. "I have to make a run into Lanark – it's a delivery day. I'll be back in a couple of hours. Mom, the big bedroom is all made up for you."

Outside, the old pickup was sitting beside the work shed, loaded with boxes of fresh produce. Melissa caught a whiff of tobacco smoke and looked around to see Joseph, lingering outside the kitchen door, waiting for the all-clear to go inside.

Driving to town, the flush of forgiveness fading, Melissa became preoccupied with her mother's strained reaction to the reopening of Charlie's case. She wanted her mother to be the kind of storybook heroine who relentlessly pursues the love of her life. She wanted to forget any evidence her parents' marriage had been unhappy; there had to be another reason for her father's disappearance. She delivered produce to three restaurants and two grocery stores, and when the truck was empty except for a few battered cardboard boxes, she pointed it home. Passing the hospital, she decided on a whim to stop and visit Marjorie. The beleaguered old woman would probably be relieved to learn her bees were hale and hearty, and not "all dead," as she had feared.

Melissa felt magnanimous as a nurse led her to a cramped, curtained-off space in a four-bed hospital room. Marjorie looked pale, shrunken and washed-out against institutional blue sheets. Only her eyes were alive and they pierced Melissa with antagonism.

"Your bees are okay," Melissa said defensively. "I checked them, and they're fine."

"I changed my mind. Tell Beck to come see me. I'm the only person who understands. It could happen again, and I can recognize the signs." Marjorie's chapped lips met over dry, rotting teeth.

"He's fine. He's eating well and gaining weight." Melissa heard possessive pride in her voice, as if Beck were an adopted animal, or a foundling.

Marjorie's eyes glinted and she spoke slyly, glancing at the nursing station in the hallway, concerned she might be overheard. "He should eat honey. It's a perfect food. A body could survive for a long, long time on nothing more than honey and water."

"Oh really? I doubt that."

"Well, you don't know everything. It's the truth. The *pharaohs*, the pharaohs in *Egypt*, they were buried with sealed jars of honey, food for the afterlife. I bet you didn't know that, did you? I could write a book filled with all the things you don't know about honey. There's honey that can heal wounds, and honey that will take you on a magic carpet ride. *Mad* honey, made from bees that suck on fields full of . . ." Marjorie sought a word desperately, clutching the bed rails with gnarled claws and holding her head inches from the pillow. She had violet sacs under her eyes, and her hair swirled and twined like a headdress of white snakes.

Melissa regretted making the visit. At the hallway station, two nurses were glaring at her for upsetting a sick old woman. She flashed the nurses an obsequious smile. "Fine. I don't know anything about honey. I just came by because I thought you'd be relieved your beehives aren't toast."

Marjorie plucked at her sheets. Her eyes roved out the window, took in the dim, whitish sky and then found Melissa again and bored into her. "I saw the goings-on when your father was still around."

"Oh, the 'goings-on' again. Whatever you're dying to tell me, please just spit it out."

"Charlie liked his drink, just like my Albert," said Marjorie.

"That's nothing new to me. I know my father drank."

"I used to ski around your place, on the trail that goes through your farm. I saw Joseph down by the dock that day, with a big old fish on his line." She opened her rheumy eyes wide, mimicking awe. "But it sank."

A patient's alarm bell rang, *bing, bing, bing, bing*! A vile odour seeped through the ward, and it felt to Melissa as though the temperature had dropped ten degrees. She knew without asking what day Marjorie meant, but it didn't make sense. The old woman was out of her mind with fever.

Bing, bing, bing, bing!

"Can somebody help me, here?" a weak voice quavered from behind a green curtain.

"Lots of shouting, over at your place. Charlie drunk as a skunk."

"Right, that's enough for me thanks, Marjorie. Get better, okay?" Melissa forced herself to add, before pivoting and charging out of the room.

Seventeen

The night before the harvest banquet Beck slept curled around Melissa's back, one arm draped heavily on her rib cage, a reassurance. At five thirty, her alarm sounded. Beck slipped out of bed and went downstairs. Drowsily, Melissa slid her hand along the warm, flat empty space where he had been, remembering the way he used to show up in the minuscule hours of the morning. She was drifting back to sleep when the door hinges creaked. Daphne entered in pyjamas, sat down heavily at Melissa's feet and tugged the curtains open. Looking outside vacantly, she spoke in an uncharacteristically soft tone.

"She seems happy. Positive. Stoked to be home."

"Yeah, yeah, I know. She had a great time."

Daphne spun a finger meditatively in a lock of hair, winding it like thread on a spool. "My mom and I used to choreograph these dance show routines – with, like, costumes and makeup. I wish we'd made videos. We were actually pretty good."

Melissa studied her sister's profile in the feeble morning light. Daphne rarely talked about her life before adoption; this revelation felt like a clunky, poorly timed effort to elicit compassion for Jill. Melissa guessed Daphne meant she was being unreasonable and spoiling what should have been a joyous homecoming for their mother.

"Please. It's not like I don't appreciate her."

"It seems like you resent her. Like you haven't forgiven her for your dad leaving."

"Way off base," Melissa warned, stamping on the conversation spark before it could ignite.

"Sometimes," Daphne said, her voice louder and edgier, "when my mother was high and being mean, I thought my father left because my mother was a selfish bitch. Like if she'd been nicer, he would have stuck around and protected me. Instead I got kicked around by her boyfriends."

In the awkward pause that followed this confession, Melissa tried to compose and voice a condolence, but it wouldn't form, and dissolved unspoken. Silence thickened.

"You must wonder why your father left," Daphne said at last.

"I don't wonder. I heard their arguments. I know why he left."

"Because . . . ?" Daphne lifted a hand, inviting an answer.

Melissa's heavy exhale turned into puffs. She suppressed the accompanying tucks by gripping the sheets. "Admit it, Daph. Jill's not easy to live with. It was super harmonious with her gone, and don't tell me you didn't notice."

"It was nicer without you two squabbling all the time."

"What are you getting at? The banquet is today, and yes, the pollination theme was a hot ticket, so it's sold out. At five o'clock this afternoon, two hundred hungry people are going to clamour for food we haven't prepared. Check the clipboard in the office – you'll find a dozen loose ends and last-minute touches no one's signed up for. Like beeswax candle centrepieces and fresh flowers, which were your ideas." Melissa's tongue darted to a rear molar and started its compulsive inventory.

"Jill can't change who she is. If you would just let her be herself, maybe you wouldn't be so irritated with her all the time."

"Okay so suddenly you're, what, my therapist?"

"I'm just saying. Our moms weren't perfect. But our fathers could have stuck around."

Daphne left, closing the door gently behind her. Melissa rolled over and glared out the window. Her father wasn't like Daphne's, an irresponsible duty-shirker. The comparison made her uneasy. Her father was the fun-loving, easygoing parent, and her mother, uptight and self-centred, had driven him away. Daphne wasn't waiting for her father to find her because she knew he would never come back. Melissa's fantasy of her father's return kept him alive, preserved his status as the good guy. And it wasn't far-fetched – it *wasn't* – but the longer he stayed away, the more a nasty possibility gnawed like a cutworm on the green stem of her hope. Had Charlie Makepeace chosen freedom over his family?

Some time later, Melissa startled awake, the top sheet pressed between her knees. The centre of her pillow was uncomfortably hot, and she felt queasy. What was wrong with her? Today of all days she should have sprung out of bed, agenda squarely in mind. Her eyes felt puffy, her mind vague and unfocused. Smiling his crooked smile, her father stepped out of the past, ambled into her room and plunked himself down on the bed. Lifting his elbows to mimic wings, he flapped, pushed his breastbone forward proudly and crowed like a rooster. Twelve years since he'd gone missing, and she still longed for his easy company, lighthearted laughter and goofing around. Out in the hallway, Jill banged the master bedroom door open and thumped into the bathroom. Downstairs the kettle whistle screamed. The rough idle of Joseph's pickup truck reverberated through the walls. Melissa pushed up to her elbows; the sky was a flat steel pan, the sun a hazy circle. She closed her eyes and tried to remember what it had been like, padding downstairs in socks to join her father where he used to perch, bleary but grinning, by the kitchen window. Memories of him were like tombstones, marking buried moments in time, and Melissa visited them solemnly, her attention directed reverently to the past.

Late winter. She is out in the fields with her father, far from the farmhouse. She is seven years old, holding his hand, his skin sandpaper-rough and black with engine grease. Here and there the greyish snow has melted, smears of brown earth showing through the last tired layer of ice. She hopscotches from one dirt patch to the next. When the distance is too far, her father grabs her free hand and swings her slight body in the air. She loves the feeling of being airborne, kicks her heels up as she gains altitude, shrieks when he lets go. She flies for two seconds and then crashes, laughing. Overhead, a V of geese honks and flaps its way south. Her father freezes, motioning for her to be still. On the ground is a robin, brown jacket and orange-red bib, pecking and pulling at an insect in the dirt. He whispers, "There's old Robin. You know better times are coming when he shows himself in spring."

Back in her bedroom, Melissa scrutinized the memory. Had her father only meant that winter was over, or had he hoped the robin augured relief from drawbacks more sinister than slippery roads and extra clothes? He had wanted the bird to be an omen of luck changing for the better, she is sure. An urgent knock cleaved her from the past, and Daphne spoke through the closed door.

"You picked a bad day to sleep in, boss. Your troops need discipline."

"Is everyone here already? I'll be down soon."

The antique oval doorknob rotated. Daphne swung the door in slightly, just wide enough to push her lips inside the room.

"Eurydice came to help. She's got vegetables on every flat surface. I don't know about you, but I think we should get the main course rolling before fussing with sides. There's a hundred eggplants to cut and seed, and four blocks of cheese to grate. Where am I supposed to get that done – the henhouse? I tried talking sense into her, but Eurydice's in a mood. I need her out of my hair."

Daphne's lips retreated.

Melissa swung her feet onto the chilly hardwood floor, yanked on jeans and warm socks, threw on a sweater and hurried downstairs. Beck, sipping tea by the window, rolled his eyes and lifted one shoulder, conceding both his mother's eccentricity and his inability to influence her. Jill and Joseph were huddled in a corner, pouring themselves coffee. A veritable dump truck–load of produce dominated the room. Daphne hadn't exaggerated: the double stainless steel sink was crammed full of lettuce; the counters were invisible under stacks of cucumbers piled three deep; and there were pyramids of peppers, radishes and parsley. Eurydice, presiding over the chopping block island, was slicing radishes into translucent, red-rimmed rounds, her lips puckered defiantly.

"Gang's all here," Melissa announced, falsely cheerful.

"Pa's swinging around to pick me up, and to load the peaches and honey. But first he's bringing Marjorie home from the hospital," Beck said, his expression sour. "She's been discharged. She gave the nurses Pa's name and number. There was no one else to bring her home, so Pa said he'd do it."

"Joseph and I are leaving too," Jill said, edging around the melons toward the back door, Joseph sliding behind her. "We're going to set up the barbecue and pick up the trout. I'll come back this afternoon to ferry food over to the hall."

As Melissa had predicted, Joseph had agreed to help with the banquet when the request came from Jill. Now that her mother was home, the farmhand's disposition had returned to its previous state – still sullen, but more amenable and affable. Daphne hesitated near Melissa in the hallway, humming a nervous, uptempo tune. Eurydice snatched a bunch of radishes from the top of a heap and smacked it down on the cutting surface. With a flourish of a broad knife, she set to furious chopping. Melissa took a step toward her.

"Thanks so much for helping out today, Eurydice. But the salad construction has to move into the dining room, so Daphne can work on the main course."

Knife rattled against wood, staccato and precise. Little pink-edged white circles stacked up. Eurydice took another bunch of radishes and plopped it on the chopping block. Melissa reached out and touched Beck's mother's arm. Eurydice recoiled as if she'd been burned, slammed the knife down beside the radishes and glared at Melissa.

"Ma's got one of her bad feelings today," Beck explained. "An intuition something negative's going to go down. She doesn't get them often and they really throw her off. But just last night, we heard that my grandfather Luis's cancer is in total remission. So everything's cool, Ma."

Eurydice sniffed in displeasure at this appeasement.

"We can manage without you," Melissa offered.

Eurydice flicked a hand impatiently. "Staying busy is better," she said. Scooping a quantity of radishes into the crook of an arm, she grasped a small cutting board and wove around Daphne into the dining room.

"Are your mom's heebie-jeebies for real?" Daphne breathed.

"You'd be surprised," said Beck. "But you know, vague prophecies, no concrete timelines – it's easy to claim the next bit of bad luck was the reason for the freaky feeling." He screwed up his mouth dismissively, but Melissa could tell he was uneasy.

"So why are *you* nervous?"

Beck sighed. "I guess I'm in a weird mood myself. Just ignore me."

Daphne raised a quizzical eyebrow, but Melissa shunted superstitious misgivings aside; work for the banquet had to begin in earnest. She cooked down an enormous pot of carrots she had peeled the previous day. Daphne plugged her phone into the stereo, started a playlist of energetic, upbeat tunes and assembled dishes of eggplant. Beck hauled up boxes of peach preserves from the basement pantry. Matthew slipped in the back door and settled on a stool by the window. Melissa didn't notice him at first, and she was startled to see him there, transported to the kitchen. Frowning, looking drained and distracted, he gazed out at the lake. Melissa turned down the music volume and Matthew seemed to wake from a trance. He drove a hand through his thin hair and cleaned his spectacles.

"Coffee? That was really kind of you, to bring Marjorie home from the hospital," Melissa said.

"You know," he answered slowly, "I don't recall giving her my telephone number. I suppose it was a good thing she had it. Her house is strange." Matthew glanced furtively at his son, then back at the lake. Beck looked uncomfortable, his complexion wan, his expression strained.

"Strange how?" Daphne asked.

"I can't say, exactly." Matthew examined his hands. "She's a little old lady, living alone, so I imagined her place would be odd. But there's something sinister about it. If I photographed it in black and white the pictures would be, I don't know – sad, I guess. She hustled me out, quick as she could, crabby as heck. She insists she's coming to the banquet tonight. I said we'd take her."

"Is that a good idea? Shouldn't she be resting?" Beck's pallor beneath his dark skin had a greenish tinge. Melissa was surprised to see him cover his mouth with a hand and lean forward, as if he were about to be sick.

"I guess the company will do her good," Matthew said lamely. "That's what she claims, anyway."

Beck's goodbye to Melissa was remote and tentative. It was an unsettling beginning to an important day, and the uneasiness of the morning lingered with Melissa as minutes and hours ticked down to the harvest banquet.

Eighteen

After his father dropped him off Beck worked alone all morning in the echoes of the cold, empty church hall. Shivering, he scooped peaches into small white ceramic bowls, ladled spoonfuls of plain yogourt from a two-gallon white plastic tub over the orange fruit, then drizzled honey and sprinkled sugared pistachios on top of the yogourt. In the afternoon Melissa, Daphne, Jill and Joseph bustled in, along with a gaggle of the United Church Ladies' Auxiliary, and the crash of folding tables being erected resounded deafeningly. Beck struggled with a growing sense of perturbation that culminated when his parents arrived, flanking Marjorie. He avoided them by ducking into the kitchen and offering to help. He felt unwell, and wondered if he was coming down with a flu bug or the first cold of the season.

At five o'clock the crowds descended in earnest, bodies coming and going. Beck sidled out to the parking lot and leaned against the old farm truck. He watched people flow in and out, entering and exiting a large three-dimensional cuboid structure by way of a small rectangular aperture. All the bodies were more or less the same size and shape, acting independently of each other but engaged in a greater common purpose. They weren't bees, and this wasn't a hive, but the impression persisted. Even the sound was hive-like – unless he listened carefully and picked out the timbre of a specific voice, the collective noise was a loud, even buzz. He imagined them naked. Clothing removed, they would be a mass of pinky-brown blobs. And the females were doing the bulk of the work. Loath to go back inside, Beck edged around the outer corner of the church hall to where Joseph was presiding at the barbecue, flanked by men dressed as he was, in rough work coats and jeans. One man's job consisted of wielding a squeeze bottle of water, spraying it intermittently into the coals for effect, sizzle and smoke. Another man held a bowl of brownish sauce and a brush. Joseph frowned importantly, patting the fish with a big stainless steel spatula, flipping each fleshy pink fillet. The grass was dotted with more men slouching in white plastic chairs, drinking beer from the can, making pronouncements about the weather and waiting to be fed. Drones, Beck thought. Sperm bags with appetites.

"Think you can avoid me?" said a quivery voice.

Beck took a broad step away from Marjorie, who had snuck up beside him. Her outfit, a Sunday-best pantsuit, smelled of mothballs. A white pearl orb was nestled in each of her stretched, lined earlobes. A bandage on her left hand bore puce-coloured stains.

"Oh hey, Marjorie. Sorry I haven't come over to say hello before now. I've been kind of out of it. I heard you were sick and in the hospital."

"Sepsis, from this cut on my hand. You're not fooling me, Beck. I know you remember."

Remember what? Beck pitied her. Marjorie was deteriorating and not taking care of herself. Her funky bouquet was overpowering, a sweetness masking putrescence. Beck struggled to find something cheerful and heartening to say, and then Daphne rushed out to the barbecue area and rescued him.

"Beck, there you are. Melissa wants you inside."

He smiled at Marjorie. "See you later."

Inside the hall Beck blinked, his eyes adjusting to the semidarkness of the cavernous interior. Eager diners were collecting at rows of collapsible tables accommodating hundreds of cheap folding chairs. Circles of gold light surrounded beeswax candles set in clunky square candleholders, two per table. Friends stood chatting in clusters on the perimeter of the room. Outsized cardboard bees were duct-taped to the walls, rendered in watered-down acrylics on hexagonal backgrounds, a child's name printed carefully on each paper stinger. Bee mobiles hung at the serving window, crafted with black and yellow construction paper and liberally coated with glitter-pollen. Beck spotted a reporter, a television news camera perched like a black plastic parrot on his shoulder. His father was circulating with a bulky Nikon, capturing images.

A kid motored past at knee-level in a bee costume, then another. Beck scanned the hall and found about two dozen three- and four-year-olds ducking under the tables and slamming into the chairs, their chubby legs stuffed into black tights and ending in fuzzy yellow socks. They wore identical black-and-yellow striped sweaters, and strapped around their shoulders were wire-framed wings of white nylon, adorned with more glitter. Antennae fashioned from pipe cleaners bobbled on small heads as the kids careened around adult legs, their miniature knees dusty from imperfectly mopped floors. Beck stared until a bee-costumed kid noticed him and skidded to a stop.

"Bzzzz! Bzzzz!" The kid screwed up his face in mock insect-anger. Beck raised his palms defensively, warding off the bee-boy, and examined the tables for people he knew. He found his mother sitting beside Jill Makepeace. Eurydice was using her hands to illustrate some anecdote, the drooping sleeves of her blouse wafting over open flame, but Jill wasn't going to let his mother ignite; an unobtrusive tanned and freckled arm hovered beside the candle, tactfully preventing the combustion of his mother's clothes. He smiled and looked for Melissa, finding her at last on the raised stage, fumbling with a microphone and amplifier. Daphne was there too, and a young woman from the local Beekeepers' Society in a white zip-up beekeeping suit, clutching a hat, gloves and veil. Daphne waved a scrap of paper at Melissa and pointed to Beck. Melissa motioned for him to come and join her, and with a slight slide of his chin, he refused. God, she was gorgeous. His vision telescoped, omitting everything in the hall but her. Then the reporter zeroed in on Beck, and a bright camera light flared, leaving purple spots of damage in his sight.

"Hi, Beck. You're the beekeeping expert, right? Melissa said we could get a quick segment from you about the destruction of your hives and how it relates to this banquet?"

Panic gripped him. A loud mosquito-whine in his ears built to an anxious pitch. He felt his heart pounding, and the hall began to blur at its edges. Onstage, he saw Melissa snatch the microphone. "Turn this thing on," he heard her command, as if she were right beside him, and the clamour of everyone else in the room was filtered out. He swivelled his head to find his mother. When he did, Melissa's voice faded, and it was only Eurydice's strident tone he could hear. Across the table, Jill's mouth moved, but Beck picked up only what his mother was saying. She was divulging her belief that her son's soul could migrate between bodies. "He could have become a bird," she was saying, "like a Canada goose; but not a *flock* of birds. Do you see? If he became an entire hive, it's because the hive is an organism, made up of other organisms. A superorganism." A goose? Appalled his mother was publicly expanding upon her esoteric theories, Beck felt his skin erupt in bumps, and his pores prepare to sprout feathers. He produced a squeaky honk from his tight throat. Melissa's amplified voice filled the hall again, obliterating all other voices and aborting Beck's illusion.

"Good evening! Would everyone please take a seat? You'll be lining up for the appetizer soon. I'm Melissa Makepeace, the organizer of this event."

Applause, some catcalls. The reporter swung camera and light away from Beck, and as if a pressure valve had been released he deflated and sagged into a chair. He had just hallucinated he was turning into a *goose*. The possibility that he was a fraud, an unintentional charlatan with a delusional anxiety disorder, filled Beck with confusion and alarm. Where had he been for the whole summer – exactly how fucked up *was* he? Onstage, Melissa was fumbling with the black loops of the microphone cord, stepping over it in tall leather boots, slim jeans and a teal sweater. Her dark brown hair was loose, tumbling around her as she moved. She addressed the crowd, talking about bees and pollination and the banquet menu, and as he watched her Beck started getting aroused, an erection tightening his jeans even as he wrestled with doubts about his sanity. Melissa trusted him, and his parents trusted him. The doctor from Toronto, Max Griffen, trusted him. Dr. Griffen was there for the banquet as well, sitting with Beck's father, beaming. All of them were gambling on his honesty. What a profoundly shitty thing he was doing to the people close to him, wasting their time and mental energy on his bee delusions. Melissa introduced the beekeeper onstage as Joyce Deacon, handed over the microphone and leapt off the stage. She came to his side and lowered herself gracefully, flashing him a reassuring smile, flooding him with desire.

Joyce Deacon made a mock-surprised noise and donned her bee hat and veil. She put her gloves on and with a startling crash, "Flight of the Bumblebee" blasted from big speakers in the hall. The frenetic piano music disconcerted Beck and his cock softened. He flattened his palms on the table and engaged his leg muscles, preparing to flee. His nerves were jangled and his body overcompensated and manufactured adrenaline – but the music was for the kids dressed as bees. They mobbed the stage and surrounded Joyce, who made a show of pretending to smoke them to protect herself. A collective vocal swoop rose from the audience, *Awwww*! The child-bees formed two disordered circles, one moving clockwise, the other counterclockwise. Small striped bottoms waggled furiously and the children stumbled, struggling to coordinate their little legs and avoid wire-and-nylon wings flapping in their faces. A redheaded girl kept backing into the boy behind her, much to his annoyance. Just as the piece of music reached its dramatic conclusion, the bumped boy's patience expired, and he gave the redheaded girl a two-armed shove, knocking her down harmlessly onto her behind. Her outraged wail was drowned out by laughter, and the bee dance dissolved into a playschool mêlée. Parents rushed to collect costumed kids from the stage. The screaming redheaded bee was escorted outside by her father. When the ruckus had dwindled, Joyce stood alone onstage once more. She removed hat and veil and smoothed her mussed hair. Melissa covered Beck's hand with hers and he blushed. He felt unworthy of her affection, and selfishly wanted it anyway.

"I'm an apiarist," said Joyce, "which means I'm a person who keeps bees. When I heard about the wrecked hives at Hopetown, I understood how devastating the loss was. I've been there myself; my hives have been knocked over and raided. Honey is delicious, and humans aren't the only animals who will risk stings to get some. In that sense, I think of beekeeping as a two-way street. Sure, we take a percentage of the honey the bees work so hard to create. But we also do our best to keep them safe from other predators, and provide lots of nectar-producing flowers for them to feed on. I'm grateful that this farm's misfortune has forced us all to think more about bees and pollination. Melissa asked me to get up here and talk to you folks about what I do, so here goes."

Joyce launched into an explanation of the basics of beekeeping. Beck tuned her out and surveyed the hall. At the next row of tables he caught the eye of a guy he recognized from high school, Steve Langevin, a popular athlete three or four years older than him. Steve gave him a comical insect-salute, fluttering his hands like small wings.

Onstage, Joyce was wrapping up. "Let's all bow our heads in a moment of gratitude for the humble, industrious honeybee."

Into the ensuing silence came coughs, clanking from the kitchen and screams of the redheaded girl from outside the hall. "I have to go," Melissa whispered in Beck's ear, and he nodded. Steve filled the chair Melissa had just left, smiling broadly.

"Beckett Wise. I was talking to your mom just now. She says you were gone all summer, pretending to be a beehive. I always knew you were crazy. But this banquet is a cool idea. Plus, Melissa's a total babe. So you've got good taste, I'll grant you that."

Beck scanned the hall for his mother. He had to stop her from blabbing about him to everyone she met. But he couldn't find her, and the sound of the kitchen gong, a resonant metal triangle, rang out. The hall filled with the scraping of chairs and the bustle of people lining up.

"Finally," said Steve, and he jostled Beck to join the hungry press of people.

Melissa's carrot pumpkin soup gave off an irresistible spicy, comforting aroma. Beck let the queue propel him forward while Steve chattered in his ear about his prowess at hockey, his wife's interest in snowmobiling and the house they had bought in Lanark – such a bargain, needed a new roof but the yard was enormous and there was a double garage. Beck feigned interest. He admired Melissa's concentration as she served two fragrant ladles of soup per bowl, wisps of steam rising like beckoning fingers from the pot. Daphne finished each bowl with a drizzle of translucent green olive oil and a sprig of fresh thyme. Back at their table Steve kept talking; he was taking his wife to Jamaica next Christmas, expensive but a guy's gotta keep his woman happy and she wouldn't stop pestering him about it, the money would be better spent on an ATV in his opinion but what could you do? The Ladies' Auxiliary, wearing frilly aprons, deposited baskets of warm pita chips on the tables and glass dishes brimming with a delicate green coulis of artichoke, lemon and sea salt. Beck was conscious of evading Marjorie. He could sense her watching him balefully from a table near the main exit, and he wondered if she had designer drugs from the hospital lingering in her system, or had suffered a small stroke. Her hostility toward him was bemusing, and at the same time he felt he deserved it.

Finished his soup, Beck lined up for the main vegetarian course: layers of purple-sage eggplant slices and deep orange buttery mashed sweet potato flecked with fresh ground pepper and specks of green basil, topped with melted aged white Ontario cheddar cheese. Steve cut in line behind him, still talking. After loading up with eggplant they followed the omnivores outside to where Joseph was serving fresh local trout at the barbecue with a skim of tangy sauce, merest sprinkle of coarse salt. There was drop-in pond hockey every Sunday in the winter and if Beck wanted to play, Steve would lend him a stick – he had a pail full of them in his garage, which was a double garage, and good thing too, because both he and his wife drove big all-wheel-drive SUVs. Inside the hall, the tables were now dotted with wide stainless steel bowls of garden salad – crisp lettuce and cucumber, crunchy sprouts, grated beets, capers, sliced radishes and borage flowers. A cruet of pink raspberry vinaigrette flanked each salad bowl. Beck ate studiously, grunting in the right places while Steve spoke around his dinner. Soon they were both poking at their plates, spearing the last shreds of food with their forks.

"I still don't get your angle," Steve said.

"What do you mean – what angle?"

"The big mystery man thing. Running away for a summer. Faking you were abducted or whatever. It worked, obviously. I mean, you got between *her* sheets."

Steve jerked his head at Melissa who, relieved at last from her kitchen duties, was swooping down beside them with her dinner. Beck said nothing.

"I guess everyone's desperate for entertainment," Steve said snidely.

"Speak for yourself," said Melissa, around a mouthful of eggplant.

Steve scowled, picked up his empty plate and left without saying goodbye.

"What was that about?" Melissa asked, and at the same time Beck became aware of a cloying, funeral-parlour smell.

"Oh, Marjorie. It's good to see you up and about. Thanks for coming," said Melissa.

"Some, apparently, are happier than others. To see me."

Beck didn't comment. Marjorie stood a fraction too close, leering at him like a gargoyle. She was just a lonely, sick little old lady, yet she unnerved him.

"I have to go serve dessert," Beck mumbled, and Marjorie's face twisted unhappily. She wrenched her body around to watch him go, and said something else, but the hubbub in the hall, silverware scraping on plates, shrieks of laughter and mothers shouting at their kids, drowned her out.

Beck slid large metal trays out of a double-wide industrial refrigerator while the dessert line snaked around the hall. Two silver-haired, white-aproned ladies in cardigans shuffled in and gave him a wide berth while they fussed over stainless steel coffee and tea dispensers, and straightened rows of white ceramic mugs. The small bowls of honey-glazed peaches gave off a subtle aroma. He was proud of the dessert's presentation – a yellow-orange star of peaches, a dollop of pure white yogourt, six or seven plump sugared pistachios, glistening glaze of honey. It looked like each bowl held an edible flower. He smiled pleasantly as he served. When everyone had their dessert, he rejoined Melissa and was deeply relieved to find that Marjorie had settled elsewhere.

The gentle chiming of spoons in ceramic dishes filled the hall. Muted, mellow evening light angled in through propped-open rear doors. The redheaded girl had stopped screaming at last. Jill Makepeace took the stage and spoke into the hush.

"Let us acknowledge the farmers, cooks and everyone else who helped make this banquet such a marvellous event. And of course, the bees." Jill tapped her hands together, joining in general applause. "Tonight I have a special treat for you. As some of you may be aware, I recently returned from several months in Guatemala and Ecuador. I have put together some of my best pictures of the organic farms I visited while I was in Central America. A guided virtual tour, if you will, of my remarkable adventure."

Beck missed the next part of what Jill had to say because Melissa dragged her chair closer to his and he caught her scent: clean hair and wet leaves. He leaned over and kissed her neck. She swung around, hair delicately brushing his face, kissed him full on the lips and returned her attention to the front of the hall. Beck stared at the back of her head, wishing he could burrow through her soft brown hair, trepan her skull and examine her thoughts. On the white wall behind the stage, bright tropical images flashed one after the other, clusters of pink tubular flowers, rows of green lobed leaves, bodies clad in rainbow-coloured clothes bent double under blazing sun and bluest sky.

"What I learned in my head and felt in my heart," Jill was saying, "was that pollination is *miraculous*. I think natural miracles occur all around us, all the time. And honeybees are a perfect example of a *miracle*. If, after the delicious dinner you've enjoyed this evening, you are *inspired* to help us out with an offering, in the form of a donation, we will reward you by getting our beehives up and running again. Anything and everything helps. The donation box is located beside the exit doors as you leave. Thanks for celebrating harvest with us, and good night."

Clapping, table-thumping and whistling greeted Jill's speech. Beck used the ovation to withdraw from the hall. It was dark outside, new moon and smattering of stars, the air cool and sweet. Behind the church hall was a humble and outdated children's playground. An old-fashioned metal slide ended in a sandpit, and three simple swings hung from a single peeled log, wooden planks suspended on knotted ropes. He sat in the swing farthest from the exit doors. A bright exterior light shone on the parking lot, sinking the background into blackness and hiding him from view. From inside came the tinkling of a bright melody. Beck closed his eyes and listened. When the music ended, he watched people file out to their cars and depart. He was waiting for his parents to whisk Marjorie away so he could return to the hall without the risk of being confronted. A woman with blond hair came outside, accompanied by Natalie, whose farm bordered Hopetown. They moved deliberately into the darkness, and the blond woman, who looked vaguely familiar, checked over her shoulder, making sure their conversation was private. Neither of them realized Beck was within earshot.

"Jill's not bothering to hide it anymore," said Natalie. "Except maybe from Melissa."

"That poor girl," said the blond woman. "She might be the only person in Lanark County who doesn't suspect they're together. And I'm sure she can't remember how bad things got, with her father. Just between you and me, and I really shouldn't discuss this outside the precinct –"

Ah. The blond was Susan Hickey, the cop. She looked different without her uniform. Beck held the swing ropes tightly and swayed his upper body toward the women.

"Of course not," said Natalie eagerly. "But you know I won't tell a soul."

"Right. Well, let's put it this way. If the father of my kid went missing, I'd be interested in the outcome of the investigation. I mean, a little girl loses her father, I don't care what a wretch he was, you cooperate with police, right? Even if it's only on the kid's behalf. You make phone calls, you make an effort."

"I know what you mean. It's really sad. And Melissa's got other problems. I guess Beck – you know, her boyfriend who was gone all summer? He's telling some story about turning into a beehive. He's either a complete loon or a terrible liar. I don't envy her, either way."

"Mmm," Susan agreed. The women wandered into the parking lot, got into separate cars and drove away. Leaning on the swing, Beck watched bats fly, swishing in unlikely parabolas, snapping up an insect feast in the margin where light met darkness. A dog barked in the distance. He sat with his thoughts in turmoil until he couldn't stand another moment of immobility, and then he bolted. His legs spirited him away from the people-hive and his feet crunched fallen leaves on the road. Above him clouds gathered, obscuring the stars, and the night opened up.

Nineteen

Beck slipped out after Jill's presentation. Melissa watched him go, feeling sorry for him and vaguely responsible for his discomfort. The bee theme was popular, but it had shone a spotlight on Beck, the farm's beekeeper, who disliked being the centre of attention. The Lanark Ladies' a cappella group sang, the bee kids went back onstage for a hilarious encore and still Beck didn't come back. The television reporter wanted his interview, but no one could find Beck, and the reporter left the banquet venue scowling. The hall emptied and cleanup toil began. Annoyance crept in, souring the end of what should have been a one-hundred-percent successful evening. Jill politely excused herself from a small crowd of admirers and cornered her daughter.

"Where's Beck – did you have an argument with him? For heaven's sake, Lissy. You should have communicated how *important* it was that he stick around. His parents had to take Marjorie home, thank goodness, or they would be *frantic.*"

"Beck's an adult," Melissa said, feeling cross and contrary. "He can come and go as he pleases. He probably got tired and walked home, or caught a ride with someone."

The crowd trickled away, leaving compliments in its wake. Working alongside Daphne in the church hall kitchen, up to her elbows in slick, brown dishwater, Melissa's pique ballooned into anger. Beck was a lousy friend and an even worse employee, stealing away when she desperately needed him to contribute, after begging to be part of the farm again. A headache budded in her temples and bloomed as she heard the infernal clatter of Joseph folding plastic chairs, and resounding clangs as he collapsed tables and slammed them against the walls. When the dishes were done Melissa pushed a filthy mop around the speckled linoleum, which only seemed to spread the dirt around more evenly. She chewed at her lower lip. Beck had slunk off, leaving the rest of the staff with all the unenviable, inglorious tasks.

It was almost midnight, the transformative pumpkin hour, when Melissa and Daphne clambered into the back of the farm truck and sat with their backs against the cab, surrounded by cardboard boxes of food and dishes. Up front with Joseph, Jill was in a bubbly mood, smiling and giggling. At what? Melissa had never known Joseph to crack a joke. Daphne put her arm around Melissa's shoulders.

"A night to be proud of, my friend. People won't forget that meal anytime soon. Those bee kids, adorable, a stroke of genius. And Jill's presentation was perfect, right?"

Melissa grunted. At home, Joseph unloaded the truck, dumping boxes beside the farmhouse, and then deserted them. "I'm done in," he claimed, and he decamped to his trailer, leaving Melissa, Daphne and Jill to carry everything inside and pile it in the kitchen for the night. A final box of candles, serviettes and condiments had been left outside. Melissa sighed and went to retrieve it. Hefting the box, she paused for a moment to breathe in a cleansing draught – and an inky silhouette vaulted from the shadows. She dropped the box, sickening crunch of broken glass, and swung her right arm, fist clenched. The figure dodged her punch.

"It's me, sorry."

"You jerk! Where did you go – how did you get here?"

"I hitchhiked partway and walked the rest. I'm sorry. I couldn't stay."

He took a tentative step toward her. She stepped back.

"Can you shed some light on why you fucked off in the middle of the biggest event of the year, an event that meant a great deal to me?"

"I got flustered. It was too much. I apologize, truly."

"What was too much? Trying to understand, but failing." Melissa wasn't about to let him off the hook without watching him thrash on its sharp end for a minute. But as her eyes adjusted to the darkness, she saw Beck looked downcast, and it diluted her rage.

"I don't know. All the talk about bees and beekeeping. It's not getting easier, wondering where I was this summer. I'm still getting flashes of being inside a beehive. I see another bee's face in front of mine, these enormous eyes surrounded by hair. A mouth with mandibles, and hanging –" Beck used his fingers to demonstrate the various dangling bits of a bee's mouth. "I hear her, this queen voice, ordering me to do things." He gulped.

A chill spread like ice water over Melissa's scalp.

"Beck, you weren't in a beehive, okay? It isn't possible."

"I know. So that means I was out of my mind. What if I hurt people when I wasn't myself? I could have done anything – could have killed someone, for all I know." Beck shuddered. His anguish was genuine, his contrition sincere, and Melissa relented.

"I understand your bee ordeal, or whatever, can't have been easy. Honestly, the way you are now, spacey and strange, is exasperating. But even though you left too early, the banquet was a success. So I forgive you." Basking in a warm, expansive wash of self-congratulations for her beneficence, Melissa swept her hair back and waited for Beck's gratitude.

"I don't need your forgiveness, Melissa," Beck said irritably. "I'm grateful to be working on the farm, and it's good to be together again. But it's not like I'm dead weight. I've been working as hard as Daphne, and as hard as you. Why is it so difficult for you to put yourself in someone else's shoes for a minute? Sometimes I get the impression we're all letting you down. None of us are meeting your expectations, me especially."

Melissa's headache returned, the pain augmented by prickles of exhaustion. Dropping to one knee, she righted the cardboard box and groped for its contents in the wet grass. As she found items she threw them forcefully into the container – jar of ketchup, broken beeswax candles, plastic bag of serviettes – her temper flaring into a tantrum. *Nerve of the guy – leaves the banquet – knows how important!* She straightened, puffed hair out of her eyes and balanced the box under an arm to tuck loose strands of hair behind her ears. Beck moved closer and touched her back with a gentle hand. She flinched.

"Okay. I'm going to sleep at the cabin tonight. I'll see you tomorrow."

He walked into the night.

Melissa took the cardboard box inside and shoved it on the counter.

Daphne and her mother had gone up to bed already; she could hear water running in the bathroom. Her cheeks burned. She had neglected to thank everyone who had helped out with the banquet. It was unforgivable, not acknowledging any indebtedness formally, onstage, or personally, afterward. Her hair was lank and heavy but she blew at it anyway and tugged it with tired hands. She was touching her teeth with her tongue and scratching at the seams of her jeans when her mother padded into the kitchen, cinching the belt of a rose-coloured silk kimono.

"Lissy, what are you *doing*? I thought you were *finished* with those nervous tics!"

Jill moved to grasp her daughter's hands and force her to be still. Melissa jerked her body away from her mother's touch. She couldn't speak until her tongue finished tapping her teeth, *canine, bicuspid, molar, molar, done*.

"Please leave me alone."

Melissa was utterly wrung out, but her mother was flushed and excited. Jill hadn't removed her makeup; there was a complex dusting of powders on her eyelids and cheekbones. Her eyelashes were black and clotted with mascara, her lips a slick, unnatural hot pink. Perfume hung around the folds of her kimono, a spicy cinnamon-based fragrance that tweaked memories of childhood evenings in the room where they now stood. Winter evenings, holding a cup of hot chocolate dotted with mini marshmallows, Melissa sitting on a high stool, skinny legs hanging in midair, sock feet kicking at the counter. She could picture her back-then mother wearing a low-cut cotton print dress covered with an apron, the strings tied tight under her breasts. Jill as equal parts farm wife, country cook and sexy-sitcom mom, tossing her head to laugh at jokes Melissa was too young to understand. Flirting with a shadow, a grizzled man in grease-stained plaid. Jill fluttered her hands.

"For heaven's sake, if you're tired, go to bed. I'll clean all this up. No wonder you're having an attack of nerves. The banquet has *worn you out*. It was a huge success, sweetheart. Truly, well done."

Jill stood on tiptoe to deliver a perfunctory kiss to Melissa's chin, and swished out of the kitchen, perfume wafting. Melissa traipsed upstairs a few minutes later. She summoned the energy to wriggle out of her clothes and fell into bed. When she woke up, the house was cold and the darkness complete. One arm was pinned under her body where she had collapsed, and with the circulation restricted, the hand had gone numb. She flopped from side to side, fingers tingling as blood rushed back into arteries and capillaries. In the stillness of the farmhouse, she heard quiet voices. She sat up in bed and listened, coming eventually to the bleary conclusion that a radio had been left on downstairs, tuned to some obscure midnight interview. *Mmmph.* She fell onto her pillows, pulled covers over her head to muffle the sound and tried to slip back to sleep. She was almost there, her eyelids drooping, when she heard a thump from the master bedroom, followed by a little squeal. The murmuring resumed, but now Melissa had an auditory bead on the source.

Her jeans and sweater lay where she had shed them, crumpled beside the bed. She put them on. Carefully, she opened her bedroom door and crept through the hallway, wooden floors cold under her bare feet. Creak of a metal bed frame, weight shifting on old springs. A mumble too quiet to distinguish. Rustle of bedding, frustrated masculine exhalation. Then, as if a radio dial had been nudged to produce clean, clear reception, Melissa heard her mother speaking. ". . . asking about Charlie. She can't leave it alone."

Low grumble of a man's voice, a mutter too soft to distinguish, then Jill again.

"It would crush her. He was a drunk, you know as well as I do."

Stumbling in reverse, Melissa retreated. A traitorous floorboard creaked underneath her weight.

"Oh my god, Joe, there's someone in the hall!"

Stingy luminescence from a sliver of moon shone through a staircase window. Taking exaggerated, silent-film stealthy steps, Melissa passed framed photographs of the farm through the seasons, faded in dim light to black-and-white. The orchard in spring, fruit trees in bloom; the chicken coop in autumn, mossy roof littered with leaves; the farmhouse in winter, a foot of snow icing the railings and gables. Regaining her room she pushed her door closed, climbed into bed and, like a naughty child, feigned sleep. There was distortion in her ears, static, a between-frequencies broadcast of crackle and fizz. Beyond this noise, the door to the master bedroom squeaked open and hollow, heavy footsteps clomped downstairs. She heard the familiar click, swoosh and slam of the front doors. Her bedroom door shuddered open and her mother whispered urgently, clearly trying not to wake Daphne, "Are you awake?"

"Of course I am. You just heard me in the hall. It's none of my business, and I don't want to know. Good night, Mom."

"Let's talk about it, sweetheart."

"Stop wheedling and go away."

"Don't be brutal, Lissy. It's not –"

"Not what I think, right. Just go away, please."

The temperature dropped overnight. Moisture on hillocks of dead leaves and brown grass froze, covering the ground in a textured coat of hoarfrost. Overhead, the first arctic cold front of the year had given rise to anemic, sulky clouds that released a fine, powdery dusting of snow, changing the season in spite of the calendar. Although her sleep had been disturbed, Melissa woke early. She slid her limbs into long underwear and found a favourite flannel shirt. She planned to spend the day outside, alone and brooding, insulating outbuildings and buttoning up the farm until spring. Downstairs, she lit a fire in the living room hearth, and the warm comfort of crackling flames soothed her. She was pouring boiling water over coffee grounds when the kitchen door opened and Joseph sauntered in.

"I wouldn't say no to a cup of that."

Not embarrassed, or guilty. Had she heard her mother say *Joe?* Not *this* Joe. Inconceivable, that her mother would sleep with the bachelor farmhand with his obstinate habits, rough appearance and social awkwardness. Joseph was practically a hermit. He didn't have a girlfriend or a group of guffawing, beer-swilling buddies. He was just Joseph, living in his trailer, thankful for a place to park. Joseph, who used to yell at her to stop climbing the apple trees, then gently carried her home when she fell out of their branches. Melissa reached for another mug and transferred the steaming ceramic cone over. The aroma of fresh coffee mingled with the reassuring smell of woodsmoke. They both watched the descending water level in the paper filter. From upstairs came the sounds of feet hitting the floor, doors opening and closing, and a toilet flushing. Melissa removed the cone and handed Joseph his cup of coffee.

"It's about time you knew, Lissy." A line of crimson climbed from Joseph's threadbare shirt collar to his weathered face. "It was a natural thing, me and your mother."

She held the ceramic cone in the air. Coffee dripped onto the floor.

"I don't believe it."

"Your father had been gone a long time."

"How long? A month, a *week*?"

"I don't know exactly. Longer than that. A year, anyway."

Joseph slurped coffee and glared from under bushy eyebrows, daring her to defy him. Melissa's breath came in shallow gasps. Joseph, her father's friend; Joseph, who had always been here, lurking in the wings.

"When did you two screw – when I was at school?"

Joseph's mouth tightened like the top of a drawstring bag, and he didn't answer.

"Wow. Just, *wow*."

"Now, Lissy. I admire your mother very much. She and I have always been good friends."

Joseph was talking to her like she was still eleven years old, in the placating tone adults use to tell half-truths to children. It occurred to Melissa that she had underestimated Joseph. She had been humouring him for years, having long ago decided to condescend to the farmhand, given what she perceived as his low intellectual and emotional intelligence. He was a halfwit she could order around without consequence. A halfwit with a *dick*. Melissa warmed to her outrage.

"Oh, I get it. You guys are like, besties, with benefits. So why not tell me before, if it was so natural and cool? Why not tell me *before* I discovered your little secret?"

"Ah, well, we didn't know for sure . . ."

"You didn't know for sure if Dad was gone for good. How nice, very cute. And if he had come back, what would you have said to him? *Sorry for fucking your wife, Charlie. We thought you were never coming back*."

"We knew he was never coming back."

"*How*? How could you know that? How can you know he's gone for good, even now? He could be living somewhere far away, as himself or –" A flash went off in Melissa's head, a bright explosion. "You guys were probably fooling around before he left, and that's *why* he left!"

Joseph placed his coffee cup on the kitchen island. He spread both hands on the butcher block surface and braced himself, deliberately bulging out his trapezius and biceps, trying to make himself look bigger and threatening. He was pathetic. A coward and a bully, an absolute frigging idiot. This was all he had, this pitiful reliance on his fading physical strength. Melissa was taller, younger and infinitely smarter. She let her disdain for him show, and his lips broadened smugly in what she guessed was an imitation of how a strong man behaves, an impression of a tough guy.

"I always wanted to tell you the truth about your father, but Jill wouldn't let me. Charlie was an alcoholic – a drunk. Chances are he's dead now. Your mother put up with a lot back then. She deserves to live her life. She's allowed to find happiness."

The word "alcoholic" rattled like a paper bag full of broken glass. It was valid; Melissa felt the truth of it click into place with a *snick*. She skimmed over it.

"Oh he's dead? Why haven't we had a funeral, then? He could be –" She faltered, the rims of her eyes burning with acidic, unshed tears.

"He could be what – a beehive? Get a grip, Melissa. I heard everyone last night, talking about Beck's stupid excuse for pissing off all summer. Charlie isn't hanging around here disguised as a hive of bees, or a pack of wolves. He drank himself silly and wandered off to die. He's at the bottom of a lake somewhere. For a long time now, miss, you've needed a good dose of reality."

Joseph snorted deeply, producing a wet, phlegmy sound, the emptying of sinus cavity contents into throat. He hacked up mucus and gathered it on his tongue. Grizzled cheeks chewing on this mass, he pirouetted and stormed out the back door. She heard him expectorate the vile contents of his mouth onto the dead grass. He clumped back inside and she gawked at him in disbelief. His never-laundered plaid work jacket had smooth, oily places where dirt had accumulated over the years. Was this man really her mother's lover? In the past, Melissa had evaluated other candidates: that suave, flirtatious realtor who came around the farm every spring, or the gruff bearded man from Perth who played banjo at the farmers' market, winking at Jill when she passed. One of those guys, she could picture with her mother. But not Joseph.

Jill entered the kitchen in a good-mother costume, a white terry cloth bathrobe and striped multicolour knit socks. Gone were the sexy kimono and come-fuck-me makeup from the night before. Her face was pale and wobbly; her cheeks and lips trembled like the top of a pudding, but she went to Joseph and put a tender hand on the sleeve of his filthy jacket.

"Don't be *angry*, sweetheart."

Jill reached out and Melissa dodged her mother's touch, afraid of lashing out physically if their bodies came into contact. She rushed blindly through the downstairs hallway and threw open the double front doors, rage surging from her chest along her arms. She turned and slammed the doors as hard as she could. There was a cracking and splitting, the sound of something solid breaking at its core.

Melissa gained the pickup truck, started it and revved the engine. The angry cough and growl of the exhaust brought her grim pleasure and she drove away, remembering how much she used to hate it when her father left, and how things had been strange and wrong when he was gone. Charlie had usually vanished for a few days at a time. *Gone on a bender, off on a tear.* Asking questions about where her father was had only resulted in making her mother cry; there were never any answers. When he had returned, with flowers and chocolate for Jill, he'd always told his daughter a funny story about where he had been and what he had been doing, delivered with an unsteady smile.

"I was kidnapped by a hippie caravan. They forced me to play tambourine and dance around the campfire. I escaped while they were washing their clothes in the lake – guess they'll have to find another tambourine guy."

"Dad*dee*, you were *not*. Where were you, really?"

"Okay, okay, you got me. I was fishing, and I hooked a big one, a monster, so big he dragged me all the way across the lake, water-skiing on my bare feet. Took me a couple of days to walk home from the other side, but here I am."

Until the final time, when her father hadn't materialized with a scruffy beard and a fanciful story, but had stayed gone. Melissa had used her imagination to colour in the grotesque black-and-white outline of his absence. She had invented ideas that had slowly turned into facts, as days had become weeks and he hadn't come home.

He went hunting and lost his way. He was living in a cave until the weather warmed up. Armed only with a pocketknife and his hunting rifle, he was subsisting on venison, clothing himself in the rough, tawny hides of the animals he killed. Or maybe he had been asked to go on a Top Secret espionage mission for his country. Disguised as an elderly anthropologist, he had to keep his identity unknown to ensure the success of the mission. He knew his family was making a terrible sacrifice, worrying and wondering where he could be, but they would understand. Once the assault rifle–toting, moustachioed foreign dictator was deposed, her father would return, and a parade would be held in his honour, with people throwing candies.

But he hadn't come home. The cold snap had ended. February had turned to March and then April. Snow had melted and leaked away. Her mother wouldn't talk about her father, and Melissa cried at night. The early spring landscape was bleak. Ridges of old, dirty ice lined the roads and pathways around the farm, coated with sand and studded with dog crap. Piteous piles of last year's leaves emitted a wet, organic stink, and still her daddy didn't walk through the gap in the hedge or rattle up the driveway in his old truck. After her bedtime, her mother and Joseph sat up talking in the kitchen. She heard them murmuring, discussing things she wasn't supposed to hear.

At school Peter Linniman, whose father was a police officer, said, "The cops are searching for Charlie Makepeace."

"Shut up, they are not."

"Are so. My dad told me he's looking for your dad." Peter stuck out his chest, swaggering.

"My dad's on a business trip," Melissa lied. "It's just taking longer than he thought."

"So how come your mom doesn't know where he is?"

Melissa ran across the playground to the swings, fighting the urge to weep.

Flowers nudged their way out of the ground and pale green tree buds thrust their way into the world. Her mother sat on the edge of her bed and comforted her. Her father's absence was a perforation, a rip through which joy and security seeped.

Melissa had allowed her mother to become her ally. *It's okay, Lissy. We can run the farm without him, we're going to be just fine.* She had taken the hateful day she'd lost her father and shoved it in a safe recess, an inaccessible alcove of her brain. The entire memory had faltered and faded. Her father was gone but spring had arrived, filling her days with warmer things like bicycle rides and canoe trips. Secretly Melissa had known her father would come home one day. He would walk in rumpled and dirty, with an abundant beard, filthy hands and a fantastic story. She had created a magical incantation, a spell to bring him back. For the incantation to work, she had to chant it perfectly in her head, then puff at her hair (three times – the magic number), and tuck it snugly behind her newly pierced ears (three tucks – the charm). It might not work the first time, or the hundredth, or the thousandth, but eventually the trick would bring her father home.

Twenty

The white farm pickup truck jolted into the cabin driveway, its suspension loose and squeaky. Beck was sitting by a fly shit–speckled window, reading a self-help paperback his mother had picked up at a church bazaar. It was a dingy morning. He was bushed from the harvest banquet, his legs rubbery from walking to the farm and then back to the cabin the night before. Light snow was falling, a half-hearted, thin powder. Naked birch trees shivered among the spruces. His father was in Lanark, shopping for cross-country ski gear with Doctor Griffen. His mother was kneading bread dough, singing to herself, ignoring him. He was reading to prevent himself from obsessing over Marjorie's hostility at the banquet. The olfactory memory of the old woman lingered in his synapses, and his senses kept drifting to her dilapidated house, through a tangle of trees and thorny shrubs. The thought of her made him uneasy, but he couldn't stop thinking about her. Mentally exploring what he knew of Marjorie, Beck found his knowledge of her family and personal history inexplicably amplified. Her husband, Arnold, was dead, and there was a son – Thomas? Had he known these things, previously? Why did he know them now? Marjorie had never confided any details of her personal life to him.

Outside, Melissa parked the truck and turned off the engine, creating a sudden hush. She sat in the driver's seat and stared at the cabin. Beck pondered what she saw – a neglected bungalow, dark green paint peeling from weathered wood. A ghost of the unbearable otherness that had driven him from the banquet swept through his body, and he knew that since being bees, he was travelling on a different orbit than everyone else, including Melissa. He had provoked her benignly, unintentionally, and in the aftermath of his nebulous bee trauma he was likely to do it again and again, piss her off without meaning to. Beck peered through the dirty glass, mentally composing polite ways to ask her to leave, wishing that in the absence of a welcome she would leave on her own. She might have come to ask him to find somewhere else to live for the winter. But he wasn't going to make it easy for her by going outside and joining her in the truck. She could say whatever she had come to say in front of his mother.

"Why is Melissa here?" Beck's mother asked, without looking up from her dough.

"Search me."

Eurydice's head snapped up.

"Don't be rude. Put your book down and go welcome her."

He flipped the book over and balanced it on the window ledge, then stood and waved weakly at Melissa, waiting for her to notice him.

"Ahora!" his mother bellowed.

Shoving his feet into a pair of workboots, Beck went out to the truck. Melissa didn't acknowledge him. Cold air nipped his skin, and clear fluid began to leak from his nostrils. He was close to turning around and going back inside when he became aware that she was crying. He realized he had never seen her cry. It was unsettling. She wasn't sobbing; her cheeks were wet and her features were distorted, as if she were made of soft clay and a giant's hand had pinched her face. He opened the truck's rusty old driver's side door, *clunk, squuueee*!

"Don't ask me why I'm here," she said thickly.

Touched by her anomalous vulnerability, he reached over her lap and undid her seat belt. She allowed him to help her out of the vehicle, and this fragility astonished him more than her tears. It couldn't merely be fallout from their argument – had she been attacked, or assaulted in some way? Was she sick? He kicked the truck door shut and escorted her into the house. She was unsteady on her feet, almost tottering. It could have been Marjorie on his arm, so diminished was Melissa.

His mother, her hands by some wonder instantly clean, dry and free of bread dough, eased Melissa into a chair and pressed a steaming cup of tea into her hands. Beck stood on the threshold, arms dangling at his sides. His mother went back to kneading as if no one had arrived and nothing were amiss. Both women ignored him. He glanced anxiously around the cabin for a task or a purpose. The back door was enticing. Five minutes earlier, he had been content to read and nap to pass idle hours; now he found himself contemplating a refreshing walk in the brisk air. He'd never seen Melissa so distraught, yet he sensed he shouldn't pry into her reason for coming. The thing to do, he decided, was accept her presence until she was ready to divulge why she was there. Beck retrieved his book from the window ledge, hauled a clunky stool to the wood stove and sat a friendly distance from Melissa. He imagined the Wise family cabin from her perspective. His parents were minimalists: the cabin was sparse and strange, the bare plywood counters lined with plastic tubs and dusty coffee-tin containers of dry goods. The beds – three single metal cots covered with charcoal army-issue wool blankets – were topped with thin, sepia-stained, coverless pillows. A circa 1970 collapsible card table served as both a working and eating surface, metal legs and Formica top. Pictures of saints rendered in lumpy oil paint, the frames encrusted with seashells and beads, hung from an assortment of nails driven into the walls. A few prints of his father's scenic photographs were tacked up here and there. Beck opened the book, found his spot and settled into pretending to enjoy the fire and the tea.

"What the hell are you reading?"

Beck flopped the paperback closed so Melissa could read the front cover, *Discovering the True You: Ten Paths to Self-Knowledge.* She gaped at the title. Unaccountably, it dried her tears and brought a smirk to her lips. Telltale dimples beside his mother's mouth revealed that she too was amused. He narrowed his eyes and slid them between Melissa and his mother.

"What is funny, exactly?"

The women couldn't answer. His mother cackled, and Melissa bit her bottom lip. Gathering his dignity, Beck placed the book upside down on his leg and stared grimly at the cast-iron wood stove, edges of the door glowing red like tongs in a forge. He concentrated on the roar of fuel being consumed, hiss of gases escaping, sizzle of moisture evaporating in the stovepipe chimney. Melissa's features betrayed a struggle to be serious.

"I doubt your book has a chapter for bee people," she said gently.

"No. There might be a chapter in here for you, though."

Melissa shook her head sadly. "No self-help book is going to fix what's wrong."

"Hey, now. Last night was tough, but it's nothing we can't figure out."

"It has nothing to do with you," Melissa said. She slouched in her chair and lowered her voice to a murmur. "I was thinking Eurydice might be able to help. I need to know about something that happened twelve years ago."

At this, Eurydice perked up, her eyes flickering with interest.

"¿Quieres una consulta? I could do a reading. But you must be open, and willing." Beck's mother made a fluid gesture to accompany the offer, suggesting she doubted these conditions would be met.

Beck stared at the top of Melissa's head. What did she hope to discover, and why was she desperate enough to try a reading? Last year, when he'd described his mother's consultas, Melissa had sneered and rolled her eyes. "If you don't believe in the divination process, a consulta reveals nothing," he said. "If you want answers, faith is crucial. Is this about your father?"

"I want to know why he left," she said quietly.

Beck thought about what he'd overheard after the banquet and guessed what Melissa might be hoping to find out. He resolved to stay mute about the gossip; addled and distracted, he might have misunderstood. His mother had returned to thumping bread dough, but he could tell she was wholly attuned to Melissa's every word and gesture.

"What do you remember about that time?" Beck kept his tone even, unobtrusive.

"Only that my father thought he was a failure. That's all I know for sure."

Melissa's answer was evasive, and she glanced around the cabin mistrustfully; she was withholding crucial details. His mother would never agree to do a consulta with a subject like this, because the margin for failure, for misinterpretation, was too great. Eurydice dusted flour from her hands, and reached for a tea towel to cover the pasty ball of dough. From an upper cupboard she took a wicker-wrapped liquor bottle, a white candle jammed in the aperture. She flicked a match, lit the wick and with an exaggerated sigh, lowered herself heavily into an armchair. Candlelight cheered the cabin; low, dense clouds had transformed midday into an atmosphere of dusk. Melissa's hair was uncombed, and there were puffy half-circles under her eyes. She was lovelier than ever, Beck thought. Burning wood in the stove popped and settled, spitting an orange ember onto the brick hearth where it quickly cooled to black. Crows argued on the cabin roof, chastising each other in atonal squawks and caws.

"A person who cannot be found wishes to stay hidden," Eurydice said shrewdly.

"I know that," Melissa said. "My father doesn't want to be here, obviously. I get it."

"And yet your search continues."

Melissa raised her shoulders and jutted her chin. "I have new information. There's a good reason my father stays away. Last night . . ." She faltered, and her lips fluttered, shaping soundless words. "I had an argument with Mom," she finished miserably.

"When you fight with your mother, you lose the blessing of God," Eurydice said flatly. She lifted heavily veined hands and let them fall to her knees. Silver and turquoise bracelets collided with soft *tings*.

"Ma," Beck warned, but his mother's advice hadn't angered Melissa; she sagged in defeat, as if the source of her malaise had been identified.

"I only want to know if he's alive. For some reason, Mom is offended by that. It's like she wants me to forget he exists. I mean, existed. I'm always wondering if he's still out there, or –" Melissa swallowed, and glanced briefly at Eurydice. "The police have been searching since he disappeared, and his truck plates are red-flagged. No one has seen him. I know there's a chance he could be dead."

Eurydice nodded agreement, and inhaled slowly. Melissa leaned forward, widening her eyes, and all at once Beck appreciated just how eager she was for answers, and why she'd come to the cabin. She was hoping for a glimpse beyond the veil of death, and believed his mother's connection to the spirit world might give her access to such mysteries.

"If your father was dead, Jill would know," Beck said reasonably. "I mean, there would be some record, and officials would have contacted –"

"Even in death," Eurydice interrupted, "Charlie's intention may have been to stay hidden."

Melissa nodded passively at this bizarre implication. A heaviness flattened her shoulders and her eyes shone with recognition. "I hate believing he was that unhappy," she mumbled.

"What does that mean? Are you saying he could have killed himself?" Beck asked.

"It's possible," said Melissa.

"Surely he would have left a note," said Beck, remembering his own hastily scrawled explanation before his body had recast itself as bees.

Eurydice's lips softened into a small, sympathetic smile. "So much thought and energy devoted to an absent person. Meanwhile, you spurn those who are present."

Melissa shifted to hide her face behind her hair, and worked her tongue around her teeth, the way she did when she was upset. Her hands crept across her lap and she picked at the seams of her jeans. The candle flame tilted and shot a wisp of black smoke north, toward the farm. Eurydice sat up rigidly, tracking the smoke with her eyes. Outside, a twig snapped. Beck twitched and checked uneasily over his shoulder. Just a squirrel, he thought, or a rat in the compost pile, but he was seized by the irrational suspicion that another soul had entered the cabin and was observing them with sinister intent. His mother sensed it too; spreading her fingers flat on her thighs, she rotated her upper body left then right, as if she might catch the phantasm unawares. Raucous cawing outside the cabin abruptly ceased. Lifting his mug to take a reassuring sip of sweet tea, Beck caught a whiff of an off-putting but familiar perfume. Gorge rising in his throat, he thumped the mug down on the windowsill. Melissa fidgeted and exhaled loudly, breaking the spell. She tipped her chair sideways, reached out and covered his hand with hers.

"I'm really sorry about last night," she said. "It was super selfish of me to be angry, just because you needed to leave."

"It's fine," Beck said. "Consider me unspurned."

"Spend your time pursuing ghosts," Eurydice intoned, "and ghosts you will find. Supplicants of my faith don't seek to have their wishes granted. You say you want a consulta, Melissa, but you don't want to know God's will; you want to be right."

Melissa recoiled in surprise and her nostrils flared. "Thanks for the advice," she said, waspish once more. "I thought you and Matthew might have heard rumours about my father, back when you first bought this place, but I guess not. You sound exactly like Jill, telling me to leave the past behind – easier said than done, especially after the charming discovery I woke up to this morning. Joseph and my mother are together," she announced haughtily.

Beck and his mother exchanged a significant glance. Jill and Joseph's closeness had suggested intimacy for years; it was startling, and poignant, that Melissa had failed to notice.

"As in, romantically together," Melissa said pointedly.

Eurydice studied her own hands. Beck became interested in the progress of a pale brown spider, lifting and placing thin legs precisely as it ascended the elaborately carved frame of a photograph. Disgust contorting her features, Melissa stood and, leaving her tea untouched, snatched her coat from her chair and exited the cabin in a dramatic huff. In the wood stove, the fire had burned down. Wisps of cold air were seeping into the cabin, but Beck's mother was flushed. A gusty breath escaped her lungs, and she hung her head. Beck blew out the candle and brought his mother a glass of water. He opened the stove and pushed two sticks of dried birch onto the hot coals.

"Are you okay, Ma?"

"Go on," Eurydice said, shooing him away with a torpid motion. "Leave me now."

When Beck joined her on the road, Melissa said, "Don't pity me."

"I'm not; I don't. Let's go for a walk."

She bounced her head *yes* and started out to the south, back toward the farm past Marjorie's house. "Not that way," Beck said, and with a light touch to her elbow he redirected Melissa, executing a half-turn so they faced north, toward Lanark. She complied without objection. She was wearing a pair of red-and-blue-striped mittens she had knit herself, with small holes here and there where she'd impatiently lost count of stitches. He reached for her hand and she let him clasp it. The snow had dwindled to an intermittent dusting. Gusts of wind blew fine powder in swirling patterns over frosty gravel. The landscape was barren; the road was lined on both sides with paper-white skeletons of trees. Melissa halted their progress, rotated to confront him and put a hand to his chest.

"I was rude to you last night. I have to tell you, since you've been back . . ." She hesitated and exhaled sharply three times, her breath streaming in misty clouds and freezing in midair. Jamming loose strands of hair behind her ears, she sniffed rhythmically, two short inhales per set, *snff snff; snff snff.* Beck reached to comfort her but she flinched, tore the mittens from her hands and scrabbled at her jeans with bare fingertips. She spoke through clenched teeth.

"I've never told you. I used to get these nervous tics, when I was a teenager." Melissa coughed up a choked sob, masquerading as a wry laugh. She wiped her leaking nose, covering the back of her hand with a slimy film. "Since you've been back, they've started again. I thought they were gone forever."

Beck was astonished. Melissa truly believed he had never noticed the neurotic things she did when she was nervous. He started to say he knew her better than she gave him credit for, but words were too much clutter and instead he kissed her, tasting salt on her lips. He tried to pack the kiss with meaning, *I know all about your tics, they're part of you, I love you, don't be afraid.* They pressed their bodies together, her puffy down coat sighing into the scratchy nap of his father's old lumberjacket. Beck felt his skin fitting around him, like it was tailored for an entirely human body. For the first time since he got back he felt free from the errant thoughts and desires of something different, free from indulging in pretend memories. The bee part of him felt dormant, gone, maybe for good.

Twenty-One

Abruptly it was austere, grim November, with nothing obliging the occupants of the farmhouse to go outside, and no chores to grant them distance from each other; there was a paucity of merciful, time-consuming labour. It was the worst part of the calendar to host tension and discord, a month marked by lack of colour and merriment, a wealth of frigid wind and days leached of laughter. Traditionally at the farm November was a month for books and board games, cooking and cleaning, but instead they bickered and shut themselves in their rooms, or contrived to spend long hours away from the house. Beck and Melissa enjoyed protracted mornings in bed together and went hiking or drove into town, their absence forcing Daphne into the role of Jill's companion and confidante.

The exposure of Jill and Joseph's relationship wreaked havoc in Melissa's psyche, but everyone else, to her chagrin, settled comfortably and much too quickly into accepting the romantic partnership. Melissa confronted Daphne with the revelation and then pounced on her sister's unsurprised reaction.

"Did you know about them? Because if you did, I swear I will never trust you again."

Daphne put her face in her hands and peeked from between fingers. "I knew they were friends. I knew they hung out together. I didn't know they were lovers."

"It started before you even got here. The sneaking around." Melissa grimaced.

"Be fair, though. Jill had to get on with living her life."

"You just don't see it, do you? How selfish she is."

"No, I don't. No one in my life has been more generous to me than Jill. And I don't mean with room and board and employment. She gives me time, attention and love. I am sorry your father left, I truly am. But no way am I going to diss Jill for this."

Daphne set her jaw, and Melissa caught a glimpse of the inflexible, strained child her sister had been when she had first come to them. As ever, Melissa thought sourly, her own complaints dwindled into insignificance beside what she knew about Daphne's past. She felt a familiar surge of resentment: the shadow cast by Daphne's fraught history deprived Melissa of the right to be an occasional malcontent. "But honestly," Melissa muttered. "Your bar is pretty low."

Daphne's features hardened into an inscrutable, stony mask. "No mother is all lollipops and rainbows. If you'd known mine – if she hadn't overdosed – you would have liked her. My bar only seems low because yours is so impossibly freaking high."

Melissa began using the subject of Charlie Makepeace as flint and tinder to start blazing fights, ambushing her mother before coffee and breakfast.

"Tell me the truth. Did you delete emails between Dad and Balvinder Singh?"

Rubbing sleep from her eyes, Jill glared balefully at her daughter.

"I don't know what you're talking about, and I won't be treated like a criminal. My relationship with Joseph is not a crime, Melissa, in spite of what you've decided."

Jill's tan had faded, leaving behind a tropical residue, light brown blotches on white skin. She was distracted, drawn and conspicuously silent on the topic of her beloved New Age pursuits. On many days Joseph's diesel truck would idle on the road, Jill would hurry out to join him, and they would drive away. Melissa didn't care where they were going and never asked.

"I notice Joseph never comes in the house anymore," Melissa remarked acidly one morning as her mother rushed to join the farmhand in his truck. Beck was seated at the kitchen counter, studiously minding his own business. "Why not? Is he embarrassed?"

Jill paused on the threshold. "Why would Joseph subject himself to your caustic attitude? Your behaviour is *atrocious*, Melissa, and Daphne agrees with me. I think counselling sessions are warranted, but you're doing the books, so you know how ill we can afford a hundred dollars an hour. Especially after the loss of the beehives and the honey crop. I've ordered three colonies for spring, by the way, and if Beck can't keep them, I expect you to pick up the slack."

Jill exited, shutting the front doors carefully in an exhibit of control. Beck glanced at Melissa and pressed his lips together briefly, before capitulating to a comment.

"I never thought I'd hear myself say this, but remember what my mother said? The thing about fighting with your mother, and losing the blessing of God?"

"So I'm supposed to defer to Jill, no matter what? That's old-school morality, and I don't buy it. She isn't the authority on everything, forever."

"True. But you don't have to pick fights with her."

Melissa sniffed, and fell silent.

Beck gained both weight and a modicum of confidence in the bee yard. He rebuilt three Langstroth hives, shrouding them in tarpaulins for the winter months, and was poised to insulate the single remaining active hive once the honey inside it was harvested, a task forgotten and then delayed, but nevertheless necessary.

"I can't get close enough to them to harvest. The buzzing," Beck quavered.

Melissa struggled with disbelief. How could Beck continue to be frightened of an occupation he had once adored? But his fear was tangible, a stark trepidation that commanded respect, so on a cold, clear morning she went alone to the last living hive, armed with instructions and advice from Beck. Despite the near-dormancy of the colony she suited up and pried the lid off the surviving hive with a sharp bee tool. She loosened the frames and hefted them. They were heavy with honey. The bees were down in the brood frames and didn't protest as their precious payload was pilfered. Two at a time, she moved full frames to the extraction shed, and while she waited beside a row of space heaters for the honey to soften and liquefy, she peered out the window, reflecting on Beck's reluctance to be close to bees, and wondering what unaccountable experience had stolen his love for beekeeping from him.

Melissa took off her hat and veil. She uncapped the comb, pressing the heated knife along the perfection of wax hexagons, and placed the frames in the electric centrifugal force extractor. She pressed the *on* switch and the drum spun, fast and faster, until it was a blur of silver and gold, stainless steel and honey. While the extractor whirled, she was reminded of Marjorie, who had sold them this machine and taught them how to operate it. Sure, the old lady was irascible, and vaguely disconcerting, but she was all alone, and had recently been gravely ill. Perhaps because of the proximity of her beehives to her house, Beck wouldn't consider coming with Melissa to drop 'round and make sure Marjorie was coping.

"You realize it's unreasonable, right? Being afraid of an old lady's house?"

"Go by yourself, if you want to go. You don't need me to chaperone."

And she would do it, Melissa promised herself, but each time she found herself driving past Marjorie's house, another priority trampled all over the good intention. One day in the middle of the month she set out toward Lanark for a meeting of the Organic Growers' Cooperative. Beck had taken the bus to Toronto for his CT scan and EEG. She was accelerating away from the farm when a police cruiser passed in the opposite direction, right-hand turn signal blinking. She braked to a stop and watched her rear-view mirror. Sure enough, the cruiser turned into the farm. Executing a three-point turn, she went home and parked beside the work shed. She meandered slowly toward the front porch, where Constable Hickey was engaged in conversation with Jill.

"He must have gone to Lanark, or Almonte. Where else would he have gone?"

Melissa recognized a shrill edge of hysteria in her mother's voice.

"That's exactly what we're wondering," Constable Hickey exclaimed brightly. "Where else, right? I mean, there aren't that many places he *could* have gone. Let's go back over your statement from twelve years ago. Charlie had no plans to travel, or go ice fishing, or skiing, or anything else. As far as you knew, he was going into Lanark to run some errands and coming straight home again."

"Nothing has changed. He went to Lanark, he must have," said Jill.

"Aha. That's the probability. But everyone who says they saw him there, or in Almonte, has either died or withdrawn their testimony. So we've got to start fresh with the day he disappeared, and rethink this thing."

Melissa skulked out of sight beside the porch, holding her breath.

"This is going to come off as insensitive, but I'm sure it's in my original statement," Jill said loftily. "Charlie was very drunk when he left. Slurring his words and stumbling."

"Did you try to take his keys from him?" asked Constable Hickey.

"What? Don't make this about *me*!"

"Just think back and try to remember," the police officer said, mollifying. "We can't look for Charlie under every rock and behind every tree. Anything that gives us a direction, a focus, would help. It might be something that seemed insignificant at the time. An old friend he was thinking about visiting, or a debt he needed to pay. I'll nip 'round and put the bug in Joseph's ear, too. It's interesting – his statement from back then matches yours exactly."

"That's because Joseph was here. He was right here with me, when Charlie drove away. Joseph tried to stop him. He told Charlie not to drive and Charlie drove anyway. Personally I think it's crystal clear what happened. Charlie crashed his truck and didn't survive."

"Sure, seems like a reasonable conclusion," said Constable Hickey. "Except – where's the truck?"

An uncomfortable pause spooled out.

"Okay then, thanks for your time, Jill. Here's my card. Be sure to call if you think of anything at all. In the meantime, I'm going to check around the pubs, see if there's any regulars who might have seen Charlie after he vamoosed. Have a good day."

Jill closed the front doors. Melissa caught up with Constable Hickey beside her cruiser. A frisson of intuition made her glance back at the house; Daphne was watching from the living room window, her distressed visage framed in a pane of glass. Melissa gave her a thumbs-up, *everything's okay*, before turning her attention to the cop.

"Thanks for coming by," Melissa said.

"Just doing my job," said Constable Hickey. She inserted her thumbs in her loaded leather belt and looked past Melissa, eyeing the farm critically, a slow surveillance. "We searched this entire property, back then. You won't remember – you were at school. Conducted the search on snowshoes. Combed the fields, separated this farm and the neighbouring ones into a grid. A few volunteers showed up, but not enough. Took three days. Put out an APB on the truck and drove the side roads searching for it. Big snowstorm blew in the night he left, which didn't help. Lots of vehicle accidents, including a fatality on Highway 7 out near Perth. Our manpower was stretched to the limit. I knew your dad, and I liked him. He enjoyed his booze, no secret, but he was always nice. Polite and respectful. Can't blame your mom for being convinced he crashed his truck driving drunk, though. Suspended his licence once myself," she sighed.

A flash of red over by the bee yard drew Melissa's eye. It was Joseph, on the path between his trailer and the house. The distance was too great to tell for certain, but it seemed as if he had spotted the police officer and hurried to hide in the bushes. Constable Hickey saw him too, and when his jacket had sunk into the scenery, she raised an eyebrow at Melissa.

"They're together, did you know? My mother and Joseph. They have been for a long time."

"I guess I knew that," said Constable Hickey, firming up her lower lip. "Or I figured it might be true. Complicates things a little, eh? But like I said, our investigation back then was comprehensive. I talked to both of them myself. There's circumstances, and then there's facts, and in this job you gotta keep 'em separated. Don't lose hope, kiddo. We may figure this thing out yet."

Constable Hickey lowered herself into the cruiser and sat behind the wheel, poking at a display screen. Over in the trees along the electrified bee fence, Joseph's red jacket bobbed back into view. He was loitering, Melissa guessed, waiting for the cruiser to leave so he could debrief with Jill. Mulishly desirous of thwarting the tête-à-tête she imagined Joseph wanted with her mother, Melissa walked toward him, and grinned with satisfaction when he retreated once more.

Late in the afternoon Beck called from the Lanark bus station, and Melissa drove to town to pick him up. She met him at a pizzeria. They chose a back booth, orange Naugahyde bench seats, rough wooden tabletop, a sleeve of watery lager each.

"There's no tumour," said Beck, when the waiter withdrew. "And the EEG was normal too."

Tears welled up and Melissa patted them away with a stiff paper serviette. "I'm so relieved. I didn't realize until right now how worried I was."

"Yeah," said Beck glumly. "But, you know – now what?"

"You can get on with your life. Put it behind you and move on," Melissa said, implying with her tone it was obvious, the only rational conclusion.

"Easy for you to say. There're only a couple of possibilities now, and I don't like either of them," said Beck. "First, I came unhinged this summer and had a long, unwitnessed, delusional adventure. And second," he lifted his glass, drank half the contents and returned it with a *smack* to the table, "it really happened. I became a beehive, regardless of what you are about to say – that it's illogical, irrational and contrary to natural laws. I've examined the problem from every angle, believe me. Apply Occam's razor, and my cells made a quantum leap. I turned into bees."

They drank and chatted until the waiter arrived with their pizza. Beck ate slice after desultory slice, and Melissa grappled with accepting what the man she loved had no choice but to accept. She finished her beer and, surfing its effervescent lift, knocked a half-eaten pizza slice from Beck's hand. Grasping his greasy fingers tightly in hers, she met his eyes and spilled the contents of her thrumming heart. Melissa told Beck she loved him, and he said he loved her too.

It wasn't until Beck was asleep beside her and snoring gently that Melissa flashed on her failure, once again, to visit Marjorie.

Twenty-Two

In November, Max Griffen resigned from his job at the clinic in Toronto. Again and again he had counselled patients complaining of depression to take chances and make changes in their lives. The time had come for him to take a spoonful of his own medicine. His life was in flux. The usual arguments for staying on the treadmill were much less compelling in light of his divorce.

He had found a house on Bridge Street in Almonte, a village that captured his imagination and catered to his fantasy of becoming a distinguished, silver-templed, small-town doc. The house was two rambling storeys of classic red brick on a corner lot, wrapped in a white porch and tied with ivy ribbons. The kitchen had been modernized with stainless steel and tile, but the bedrooms were antique, wallpapered, one in stripes and another with sprigs of flowers. The floors were the original scuffed hardwood. He could imagine his kids there. It was big enough to include both a medical practice and a private home. He had hesitated for a day, wondering if it were a silly romantic notion, then woke up wishing he lived there, and bought it.

It was an old, quirky building. He discovered its vagaries one by one, like characteristics in a new friend; places where frigid air slipped under doors and seeped through walls, creaky stairs, startling midnight noises. On a cold, sunny day he went on the bicycle ride of his dreams, rolling down swaths of open asphalt, criss-crossing endlessly through bucolic scenery. His kids came up for a weekend and to his relief they were charmed by the town and house, unhappiness about their parents' broken marriage mitigated somewhat by the spark of a fresh experience, a vista beyond a newly opened door.

Nights grew long and dark. Max stayed up late, slouching in an armchair and roaming the internet on his laptop, the screen's artificial glow the only light in the room. Occasionally he pondered the strange case that had been his impetus to move to Lanark County. He was relieved to receive test results confirming no dire malignancy was causing Beck's symptoms. The bee story was an intelligent, elaborate hoax, tied to a paranoid fantasy, and out of his jurisdiction as a general practitioner. Theoretically he could distance himself from the Wise boy entirely and let the case fade into history, but for his growing friendship with Beck's father.

When snow began to fall, the cycling season ended, and Max convinced Matthew to take up cross-country skiing. During the gap season between the two sports, snow accumulated incrementally on the trails, and in this interim Max helped outfit Matthew with skis, poles, boots and bindings. Together they studied videos about push-and-glide techniques and discussed the relative merits of traditional waxed skis and no-wax fish-scale systems. On dry days they jogged rural roads, boosting their stamina and endurance. Matthew and his wife had moved to a motel in Lanark, and when Max swung by to pick up his friend, Eurydice stared at him shrewishly through the window.

"Does it bother your wife that you and I do sports?" Max pushed his fingers into black neoprene gloves and pulled a wool toque over his ears.

"She worries," Matthew said.

"What's she worried about? We're going for a run, not skydiving. The worst that can happen is you sprain an ankle."

"She has premonitions. You'd be amazed how often she's predicted the future."

Max made a noncommittal noise and changed the subject. Matthew's predilection for magical thinking was bolstered by his wife's religious beliefs. Since the medical community had failed to produce a concrete explanation for Beck's lengthy absence, his parents had resorted to believing that a miracle had occurred. Not wanting to offend his friend, Max repressed protests of charlatanism that bubbled in his brain when Matthew spoke of things like animism and astral projection.

At last the winter storms rolled in, heaping snow on southern Ontario in blizzard after blizzard, covering barren rock and denuded trees with layers of frosty white. When snow on the trails was deep enough, Max and Matthew went skiing every day. A trail around Crescent Lake, a couple of kilometres past Hopetown Farm, became their favourite; it had plenty of dips, climbs and S-turns. They always skied aggressively, tucking when they careened downhill and double-poling for speed on the flats. Matthew wasn't as fit as Max. One frigid day, Max waited at the top of a long uphill section, watching his friend struggle up the incline. When he caught up, Matthew was gasping and leaning on his poles. He glared at the doctor.

"What's your secret? You must be taking performance-enhancing drugs."

"No secret. It's all practise and technique."

"But I'm doing everything right – sitting back, using my poles, gliding on both skis – and you're still slaughtering me. It's obvious you're cheating. I just can't figure out how."

Max glided to the side of the trail. "Ski ahead of me for a minute. I'll watch what you're doing and see if I can tell what's making you inefficient."

The trail began at a roadside pullout, then meandered alongside flat fields before climbing gradually through a wooded area to a ridge above Crescent Lake. From there, a skier could choose to turn right or left, and circumnavigate the lake either clockwise or counterclockwise. The highest point was on the far side of the lake, and it was there that Max and Matthew were stopped, poised to descend the steepest incline. At the bottom of the hill there was a tight turn to negotiate around a rocky outcropping, before the trail led through a clump of trees and came out beside the remains of an abandoned log building that might have been an old homestead – a simple wooden rectangle with a collapsing pitched roof. Matthew teetered anxiously at the apex of the hill, then set his skis in the tracks and pushed off, accelerating instantly.

"Plant your poles! Bend your knees!"

But Matthew had lost control. He was hurtling downhill while standing up straight, windmilling his arms like a vaudevillian in a silent film. Max held his breath and watched. When he reached the turn at the base of the descent, Matthew transferred weight, throwing his body to the left, trying to force the turn by wrenching his limbs in the direction he wanted to go. His right ski careened off the track and lodged in rocks on the right side of the trail, halting his progress on that side with a jolt, while his left ski continued to describe the sharp turn he was committed to making.

There was a smothered snapping sound, like a muted gunshot. Matthew's body crumpled into soft snow at the trail's edge, black silhouette on white, a reverse chalk outline with a sickening abnormality to the angle of the lower right leg. Max shoved off from the top of the hill, leaning forward to increase his velocity. At the bottom he neatly veered and made a tidy double-edged stop beside his fallen friend. He released his skis and knelt down. Matthew was groaning between gritted teeth.

"I think I broke something – *mnahhhh*!"

"I'm certain you broke something."

Matthew's right boot was still in its binding. Releasing the ski would mean either compromising the injured limb, or removing the boot from Matthew's foot. Both were likely to be painful procedures. Max shivered, sweaty workout gear cooling against his skin. He chose to free Matthew's foot from the boot as gently as he could, and started by manoeuvring the boot's cover zipper open, then loosening the inside laces as wide as they would go. He dug a hole in the snow below Matthew's ski, and eased the boot into this hollow, exerting the smallest amount of pressure possible. Matthew cried out in agony as his foot came free.

"I think you've fractured your fibula."

"Hnnnnmm!"

Opaque clouds that had been gathering overhead, squatting lower and lower to the ground, began to release gouts of wet snow. *Oh, great.* Max blinked fat flakes from his eyelashes and assessed their predicament. The base of the steep hill was the farthest point from the trailhead, so they were as far as they could possibly be from help. It began to snow in earnest; a torrent of white blanketed the sullen spruce trees and masked the lake. But there was a dark smear visible through the snowstorm – the boarded-up building by the trail.

It was big enough to have housed an extended family, or perhaps it had been a little school. The roof sagged in the centre like a saddle, but the walls, constructed of wide, chocolate-brown snugly fitted horizontal logs, were still intact. The windows had been nailed shut and covered with plywood boards. Max squinted through the screen of falling white and made out a shape that might have been the entrance, blocked, like the windows, by solid lumber. He had given up on entering the building and was mentally designing a stretcher, young evergreen boughs lashed together with strips of ripped fabric, when he spotted a weakness; in the back corner, closest to the trees, there was a gap above the foundation, a place where a plywood patch had been pried away. It might have been a coal scuttle at one time. The edges of the hole were scarred, as if the logs had been damaged by a crowbar. Who had been so keen to gain access to the interior of this old structure? Teenagers, Max thought, looking for a secret place to party. He estimated the distance he would have to drag Matthew's body from the ski trail to the corner of the house: not far, maybe five metres.

"Matthew, I'm going to get you out of this snowstorm, then I'm going to go for help."

"Oh damn, hmnnn . . ."

"I'm going to pull you across the snow, and it's going to hurt. I need you to help me cross your broken leg over your good one." With a clean lift-and-drop, Max adjusted the patient's broken leg for transport. Matthew screamed. "Sorry, sorry! Now keep your arms glued to your sides, and I'll haul you by the armpits. I know it's hard, but try to relax."

Max dragged his friend through deep snow, pulling the injured body as smoothly as he could, sinking down to his knees with every step. Snow and ice filled his ski boots, and the log wall seemed to inch farther away as he battled toward it. In the distance he heard the high scream of a snowmobile. He pictured finding matches, or even a flare gun, inside the old building. The broken leg would heal, but shock and hypothermia could kill Matthew, whose groans had ceased – had he passed out? Max dug at the base of the building, beside the hole in the boards, using his hands as shovels. The snow was wet and sticky, ideal for sculpting, and he shaped it into a pile and tamped it down, constructing a ramp. He positioned the patient so he would be easy to drag through the opening, supine, arms above the head. Lowering himself onto his belly, Max squeezed through the hole.

Inside, the forsaken shelter stank of mouldy wood saturated in piss, both rat and human, with subtler notes of decay, dried feces and mildew. If this was how it smelled in here in winter, Max hated to imagine the stench of the place in the heat of summer. It was dim, but enough daylight came through cracks to discern that the space was one large room, with tall piles of random debris stacked against the walls and in the corners – unhygienic, but at least Matthew would be out of the wind and snow. Max scuffed the dirt floor with a boot, checking for sharp rocks, nails or broken glass. Satisfied the path was clear, he reached outside, grasped Matthew's wrists and hauled his friend over the crumbled foundation. The patient was grimly silent.

Max tugged his cellphone out of his jacket pocket. His expectations were low. If he could place a 911 call, he could give precise directions to their location and wait with Matthew for help to come, but naturally, there was no cell service. Max weighed his options. The patient was out of imminent danger, but he urgently needed treatment, and until he got it, he needed to stay warm. A blanket – there could be something, some insulating layer, in the heaps of refuse stacked against the walls. Max began picking apart the piles, looking for anything warm, like old burlap sacking or newspapers. He dismantled two stacks of junk that yielded nothing more than broken boards, rusty tin cans and beer empties. He was about to give up when he saw something coloured, a fold of faded red-and-blue fabric, peeking out from a bunch of garbage. *Sleeping bag?* He grabbed the material with both hands and yanked, expecting it to come loose, but whatever it was seemed to be caught, or maybe frozen. With an aggressive wrench, Max freed the fabric thing. It was a decrepit men's ski jacket, sewn in a dated pattern of broad, V-shaped stripes. Extending from the collar were several cervical vertebrae – the spine of a human being. Max immediately checked the bottom of the jacket. Yes, there they were, the sacrum and pelvic bones.

He dropped the jacket-clad partial skeleton and whirled around. Had Matthew seen? No. The patient's eyes were closed, his body reclined. He moaned, softly. Turning his back on Matthew, Max placed jacket and bones in a shadowy recess, hiding them from view. *What's worse than waiting for help, alone, in winter, with a broken leg? Waiting for help alone in winter with a broken leg in the company of recently discovered human remains.* Max removed his cross-country ski jacket and woollen base layer, put his jacket back on and forced the base layer, still warm from his body, over Matthew's head. Matthew extended his arms helpfully, like a toddler being dressed in the morning. Wool shirt tugged in place, Max arranged his friend's body in what he hoped was a comfortable position, repressing an urge to glance toward the dead person wrapped – *not just wrapped, it's stuck in there, whoever it was died wearing that thing* – in the old jacket.

"Right. I'm going to ski to the car, call an ambulance, direct the paramedics here and ski back. You're going to be here for an hour, maybe two. Meditate, try to relax, keep breathing. Can you do that?"

Matthew nodded, his eyes closed.

Max squirmed out the opening into the snowstorm. At the trail, he planted Matthew's skis and poles upright where the accident had happened, then clipped into his own skis and raced back to his vehicle. The sticky snow, ideal for construction, made the ski a challenging slog, and in spite of lending his warmest layer Max was panting, overheated. Adrenaline pumped through his body and his mind rushed ahead, creating a rescue itinerary and formulating an accurate description of Matthew's location. A snow-covered, car-shaped lump took shape in the storm. Max stowed his ski gear, brushed the car off, got in and started the engine. He turned the heaters up to full blast, and checked his phone: one bar of service. He called 911 and reported Matthew's accident, then hung up and called the non-emergency number for the Ontario Provincial Police in Lanark.

Two stretchers were dragged off the Crescent Lake ski trail that afternoon. The first was loaded into an ambulance, destination Perth & Smiths Falls District Hospital. Police covered the second with industrial grade translucent plastic and secured it in the back of a windowless van. This stretcher contained human remains that Max and the police had found in the old building, including a skull and enough bones to almost completely reassemble a skeleton.

Max drove partway to Lanark in convoy behind an ambulance, the van and a police cruiser – siren blaring, roof-mounted lights flashing and revolving. The driving was dangerous. Snow was still falling, thick and fast. As he passed the motel where the Wises were staying, Max spotted a wavering figure standing by the road: Eurydice, bare-headed, snow accumulating in her hair. His headlights picked out her wide eyes and frumpy, makeshift winter costume: old-fashioned men's snow boots and a baggy insulated car coat. He pulled over. She got in and slammed the passenger door.

"Come on, Doctor – vámonos."

"What were you doing outside? How did you know I was coming by?"

Eurydice stared stonily ahead. Max could tell she wasn't going to explain how she had come to be standing there, so he navigated onto the road, skidding in slippery snow.

"His leg is broken, that's all. He's going to be fine."

As if this reassurance insulted her, Eurydice rotated, presenting him with her back. Night was falling; the road was a tunnel of white streamers on a black background. Pinpoints of headlights bounced soundlessly through the streets, red taillights fishtailed around corners, wheels spun at intersections. Max stopped under a covered walkway in front of the hospital. Eurydice flung the car door open and paused.

"It is interesting, Doctor," she said calmly. "We both give advice. But the difference, in this country at least, is that your advice is heeded, while mine is ridiculed."

Eurydice exited the car in a graceful swoosh and left the door ajar. As if activated by her intention, the hospital's automatic glass doors slid open, and she sailed into the building. Loath to leave his heated vehicle, Max sprawled across the passenger seat and tugged the door shut. How was it that Eurydice had been waiting outside at the motel? He hadn't given the police or paramedics her phone number. It struck him that she might have some kind of extramundane insight into her son's bee delusion, an apprehension overlooked by the medical community. He shivered and let the speculation slip away. Damp with melted snow and half-dried sweat, Max was chilly, and wanted nothing more than a hot shower, a big meal, soft pyjamas and his bed. But the cops had asked him to come by the station and help fill out incident reports on Matthew's accident and the ski-jacket skeleton. Sighing, he manoeuvred his vehicle through slushy, near-deserted streets to the two-storey brick police station.

Constable Hickey met him in the foyer and introduced herself. She was in her mid-thirties, almost his height and twice as substantial. She ushered him into her office, applying lip balm and chatting cheerily about the gruesome discovery.

"The presence of a skull means access to dental records, which will make matching up this guy's head with his history a cinch, basically."

"How do you know this skeleton is male?"

"Fashion." She gave Max a stagey, conspiratorial wink.

"I'm sorry?"

"No woman would wear such a hideous coat."

"A woman could have borrowed that coat, to stay warm."

Constable Hickey's peppy smirk became a scowl.

"That's unlikely, Doctor Griffen. Anyway, I just have a feeling. You get a feeling about these things – those bones belonged to a man."

"Do you find a lot of dead bodies in Lanark County?"

The constable pressed glossy pink lips together.

"Thank you for your cooperation, Doctor Griffen. I'm going to ask you to keep this discovery to yourself, for now. When we find the identity of the deceased person, we'll be notifying next of kin first, then putting out a formal bulletin. Good night."

Max drove to his house on Bridge Street. The roads, mercifully, had been ploughed. The abandoned building with its gory contents appeared again and again in roadside shadows – his mind conjured it around every corner; it lurked behind a white veil in every field.

A year later, when Max took up painting, the old building on the Crescent Lake trail would be his first subject. For a year, the log-frame structure and surrounding scenery would be the *only* thing he painted. He would capture it from every angle and in every season, canvases piling up on his porch: the building in winter, half invisible beneath snowdrifts; in spring, obscured by puffy seed heads topping weeds; and in summer, defended by thickets of thorny plants, burdock and Scotch thistle. In every painting, Max would include the ghost of bones hidden behind log walls.

Twenty-Three

twelve years earlier

Not quite noon. His vision was blurry, he had the hiccups and he desperately needed to take another piss. *Damn Irish cream.* Charlie Makepeace laced his coffee with liqueur at Christmastime, and here it was February, and he couldn't break the habit. He got a gateway buzz from his morning tepid cup of coffee, heavily diluted with festive creamy alcohol, leading him to crack a first beer before ten o'clock and spelling bad news for his afternoon. *Tomorrow, I'll drink my coffee black,* he promised himself, every day. But the next morning, without fail, the Irish called from his work shed. Good thing Jill still hadn't figured out where he kept his flats of cheap beer, in a cardboard box above the automotive supplies. He threw his empties directly into the recycling barrel and covered them with plastic oil containers, so no one knew how much beer he was drinking these days. A violent hiccup raised tastes of hops, sugar and bile. In front of him on the workbench was the oil-and-grease-encrusted carburetor from the farm utility truck. His intention had been to clean the thing, but now he couldn't recall where the cleaner was, and his rag bucket seemed to be missing as well.

Charlie spun on his heels. His work shed kept spinning after he came to a stop. Toast, that was what he needed. Warm bread, to sop up all the liquid in his stomach. And hey – some of those old dishtowels were ripped, permanently stained, unfit for wiping kitchen surfaces, so *boom*, missing rag bucket problem solved. Charlie fumbled with the zipper on his soiled plaid jacket, but the darn ends wouldn't match up. Swaying, he squinted down at his fingers and pinched the little metal bits. One part wouldn't fit into the other. He couldn't figure it out.

Whatever. It was a bitterly cold day, but the farmhouse was close. He opened the shed door and stepped into the startling temperature of minus twenty-two degrees Celsius, with sudden blasts of even chillier wind. He remembered to pull the plywood door closed; the time last month when he'd left it ajar was still fresh in his memory – all his beer frozen, cans ruptured at their pop-tops. A sticky, smelly mess, not to mention all the wasted beer.

The snow underfoot was smooth and compressed. Styrofoam snow, kids called it, an apt moniker: it squeaked like Styrofoam when you walked. A half-smile played on Charlie's lips as his footsteps peeped comically. He could hear music playing inside the farmhouse, a guitar strumming in three-quarter time, accompanying an earnest, plaintive female folk singer. A waft of a sweet, buttery aroma met his nostrils. *Jill must be baking.*

Charlie composed himself outside the kitchen door before entering with the overly gentle, forced caution of a drunk person trying to seem sober. An unusual scene was unfolding in the dining room. A man and woman were dancing, turning and turning to the song's lilting beat. They twirled around the table, laughing as they bumped into a chair, then a wall. The woman was his wife. The man was Joseph Sommerton, whom Charlie had brought home from the bar and hired as farmhand more than a decade ago. Charlie had left the back door wide open; a gust of frigid air reached the dancers and they startled, then sprang apart forcefully, like boxers in a ring.

"Charlie, what the *hell*? You *said* you were going to town to get a new *tractor* battery today!" Jill shrieked.

Had he planned to get a new tractor battery? That did sound familiar. Somehow that job had been forgotten, and he was doing something else instead. Cleaning the carburetor.

"Whatever, Jill. Don't freak out. I'm cleaning the carburetor. What the, what the hell, are you guys –" Charlie hiccuped, then burped "– doing?"

"Oh my *God*, you're drunk already. It's only *lunch*time. Get *out* of here, and don't bother coming back until you're sober."

Jill was overreacting and hysterical, as usual. Charlie raised his chin and waved vaguely at Joseph. "You're the one – *hic* – dancing around, with, with *him.* I – *hic* – happen to be cleaning the carbub, the barcub, the carburetor. *Hic*!" His throat hurt from trying to squish hiccups back into his body.

"You *idiot.*" Jill stomped into the kitchen and thrust a finger in Charlie's face. "We would all *starve* if it weren't for Joseph. I am so *fucking tired* of your drinking and lying. I'm *sick* of covering for you, doing all the work and trying to balance the books, when you spend *everything* on booze."

Charlie recognized this rage. It spewed from Jill when she was frustrated with his drinking. The best reaction was contrition; he should offer her a sincere apology and promise to do better. Then she would relent and say that she loved him. But his wobbly reasoning argued that this time was different. He was pretty sure that dancing with Joseph changed things. He was allowed to be the affronted party, for once.

"What're you – you're dancing – and, what's going on, anyway? What're you doing with my – *hic* – wife?" Charlie lurched toward Joseph. "I did you a favour, and now you're in my house . . ."

Joseph puffed his chest and confronted Charlie.

"Listen, Chuck, why don't you come to a meeting with me?"

Charlie waggled an index finger under Joseph's nose.

"Uh-uh. I told you. None of your, evanzeli – ejanveli – evanzellizing."

"It's not *evangelizing*, you fool," said Jill. "Joseph wants to help you, God knows why. But you won't even *try*. Not for me, or Melissa, or the farm. And it's *over*, Charlie."

Her words pealed out, deep and even, like funeral bells. But she had said them before.

"I just want a piece of toast," Charlie mumbled. She always made such a fricken big deal.

"It's *over*! I'm packing your stuff and throwing you out. Get the hell out of my life, Charlie. I can run this farm without you. It'll be *easier* without you."

Charlie turned his back on Jill and Joseph. He grasped a serrated knife in one hand, a loaf of whole-grain bread in the other and slowly sawed thick, uneven slices. He heard the thump of Jill's feet ascending the stairs, and the rattle of drawers opening and then slamming shut.

"I think she means business this time," said Joseph.

"Aw, come *on*, I'm just – hungry, man. I just gotta . . ."

The toast popped up. Charlie slathered two trapezoid slabs with uneven quantities of butter and lumpy orange apricot jam, getting as much on his fingers as he did on the toast. From the hallway came a cacophony of crashes and bangs. Joseph charged out of the kitchen. Charlie leaned over the sink, taking huge bites of toast and smacking his lips. Crumbs adhered to his ten-day-old beard. He chewed with half-lidded eyes, peaceful and bovine. More noises in the hallway, the sound of glass shattering. Joseph returned.

"That's your stuff she's throwing."

"Wh – aaat?" Charlie stuffed the last piece of toast in his mouth, then staggered to the lower landing of the staircase, where a pile of his broken belongings was accumulating.

"Jill, get down here and, and talk this out."

"Fuck you!"

Joseph left through the front doors and Charlie let him go without a challenge. It started to seem real: his marriage was over, Jill was kicking him out. She was throwing everything he owned down the stairs. He rocked back and forth, holding the polished wood banister, pleading with her to stop. A framed picture crashed into the wall behind him. Overcome, he charged upstairs and grabbed her wrists, but she threatened to call the cops so he let go.

"What about Melissa?" Charlie challenged, taking a tack that had proved successful in the past.

"Believe me, I *am* thinking of what's best for our daughter."

That sobered him up. He got himself a cup of cold black coffee and guzzled it, a headache tightening around his skull. He cast about for options, anxiety fluttering in his chest. He wondered if his parents were still alive, and where they lived. If he could find them, maybe they would take him in, though the indignity would be unbearable. He tried to remember his father's stony face and an image came to him: the old man's craggy chin jutting above the black leather whipping belt he had employed in his drunken rages, administering beatings because Charlie had misbehaved, or for no reason at all, his mother crying pathetically in the next room.

Not his parents, then.

He had friends, of course, married friends, with children. He could stay on a couch in the basement of a friend's place until Jill calmed down and took him back. One by one he considered them, buddies from high school who might agree to offer sanctuary. But for each potential friend, Charlie could imagine a reason why the man might refuse him. Gary, for instance – Gary and his wife had a newborn, for chrissakes. Mike and Janet had their own problems; he didn't want to contribute to the demise of someone else's relationship. Brian was a bachelor, but he drank too, and Charlie owed him money. He dimly recalled a public argument at Mal's Restaurant in Lanark. Brian had come over to his table to demand repayment of a drinking debt. In the end, Charlie had thrown a couple of punches, and now he wasn't allowed back into Mal's Restaurant, which was a drag, because Melissa liked to eat there.

A chill settled over Charlie and a black hole gaped in his mind. Under his tool bench in the shed there was a bottle of expensive Scotch, a Christmas gift from a restaurant owner who bought Hopetown Farm produce. He had been saving it for an emergency, and now relief washed over him as he summoned up his man cave, with its trusty wood stove and cache of beer, the rear cans coldest from being stored against the draughty wall. Kicked out: if ever there were an excuse to get stinking drunk, this was it. He felt satisfaction at the thought of how sorry Jill would be when she found him blacked out on the bench seat of his truck. She would feed him a hearty dinner while she read him the riot act and set him straight. He would come clean with Melissa, confess to her small, sweet elf-face, those big brown-green eyes and rosy cheeks. His daughter's innocent smile would prevent him from drinking *ever again*, after this one last time. The knowledge of how it would disappoint Melissa to have a drunk for a dad – that would be the thing that would keep him sober. Today, though, he would tie one on. A final, glorious spree.

Abandoning Jill to her wrath, Charlie returned to his work shed. He stoked the fire in the clunky wood stove until metal creaked and groaned. Soon he was warm enough to remove his plaid coat and, shrugging it off, he realized the exterior fabric would make excellent rags for cleaning grease chunks from the carburetor. He took scissors and methodically cut cotton strips from the coat, exposing blue satin quilting underneath.

Charlie kept his Scotch consumption civilized – poured into a cracked glass instead of swilled from the bottleneck. He refilled his glass every ten minutes, and soon the amber liquid was half gone. Beside his glass of Scotch he kept a can of beer to slake his thirst. An old CD player, coated with sawdust and grime, kept him company. He chose a New Orleans bluesman's gravelly voice and complaining guitar as the soundtrack for his bender. He worked diligently, as if cleaning the carburetor would prove his worth. It was important to watch the clock too, because Melissa got home from school mid-afternoon, and he didn't want her to see him like this.

While he was replacing the carburetor, Charlie accidentally knocked a beer into the truck's engine bay. The beer spilled, and the can lodged beside the motor, too far down to reach, so he left it there and weaved to the cardboard box to get another. He put his plaid coat back on. It wasn't as warm as it had been, with the outside layer of fabric snipped away. The clock said 2:16 p.m., less than two hours until Melissa got home. There was no way he would sober up before then. The truck was fixed – he could go for a drive. He opened the shed's bay doors, snagged a six-pack by the plastic rings, tucked the rest of the Scotch under his arm and grabbed his chainsaw with his free hand. He stowed everything in the back of the truck, then got in the driver's seat and turned the key in the ignition. To his delight, the old beast fired up right away. An initial cough of black-and-blue smoke hung around the taillights. Throwing the truck in gear, Charlie reversed out of the shed, shivering and talking quietly to himself.

"Preddy dang col' out, gotsta bundle up."

He left the truck spluttering in the driveway and returned to the shed for more clothes. A few incongruous items hung from hooks behind the door: black canvas work coveralls, a red-and-blue ski jacket. Charlie stepped into the coveralls and zipped the jacket on top of them. A ragged toque and a pair of paint-stained leather work gloves completed the ensemble, and he stumbled back outside. Joseph was leaning on the driver's door of the old truck, arms folded across his chest, a hand-rolled cigarette hanging from a corner of his mouth.

"Where you headed, Chuck?" Joseph's cigarette bounced as he spoke.

"None of your business, dancy pants."

"You make it my business, if you're fixin' to drive drunk."

"Can't all be saints like you."

Charlie reached around Joseph and opened the heavy truck door, which struck the farmhand, hard, on his shoulder. With a grunt, Charlie heaved himself into the driver's seat, but distributed his weight unevenly and nearly fell out of the truck. On his second attempt he wound up centred in front of the steering wheel. He slammed the door and tried to give Joseph a menacing stare, but the movement went farther than he anticipated and his head hit the window with a dull *thud*. Sheepishly, Charlie rolled the window down far enough to speak out the aperture.

"Not gonna *kill* anyone. Gonna take the back road, go get some *fire*-wood. 'S not like I don't do anything around here. Where do you think all the, all the *fire*wood comes from?"

Half a kilometre from the farm, a private road wound through ranch-land and past abandoned summer homes. It snaked past Crescent Lake and came out on the other side of Bow Lake, along the way passing plenty of deadfall you could pick up for firewood. In summer the road was two dirt ruts, and in winter it wasn't ploughed, but occasionally someone with a four-by-four would drive through, blazing a trail for others. A thaw at the beginning of the month followed by this extreme cold snap meant the private road would likely be cement-hard and drivable. But first, Charlie had to drive the main gravel road that ran past the farm.

"Don't be stupid, Charlie. Turn the truck off."

Charlie clunked the truck into reverse and revved the engine, hard. The truck jounced backwards a few metres and halted with a lurch. He slammed it into drive, careened forward and sped onto the gravel road. *Done this drive a zillion times*, he thought. Anyway, he didn't even pass another vehicle between the farm and the unmarked intersection where the Crescent Lake road began. With a rush of boozy elation, he cranked the wheel and roared off the main road, misjudging his speed. The truck rammed a tree trunk and stopped dead. Charlie's head snapped forward on impact and smacked the top ridge of the dashboard. Bright lights popped and fizzled in his vision, and a bell in his head rang *ding-ding-ding-ding*! He vomited onto the steering wheel.

Warm puke dripped into his lap. Pain radiated in his head and neck, but he was conscious and everything on his body was working. Charlie unbuckled his seat belt, *which I was fucking wearing*, and slid out of the truck, letting the driver's door swing open and leaving it that way. Boots slipping on the icy surface, he skated to the front of the truck to evaluate the damage. The grille was punched in six or eight inches, and the tree was embedded in the engine bay. Steam hissed in a vertical column; the radiator was probably screwed. *So what? I'll get her running again.* Steadying himself with a hand on the truck, he made his way to the box and retrieved his chainsaw. The beer and Scotch were still there, whisky bottle unbroken and cans intact. A negative thought niggled, and with a sinking feeling, Charlie remembered there was no gas in the chainsaw.

No big deal. He could collect deadfall by hand. *Said I was gettin' firewood – gonna get firewood.* A bolt of pain lanced his skull behind his eyes. Wincing, he lowered the chainsaw to the ground and snagged the six-pack in one hand, Scotch bottle in the other. Blue-and-yellow lights strobed as he ambled into the woods, his gloves forgotten. The throbbing in his head was a metronome for his feet; he stepped in time to pulses of pain, eyeballs bulging with cerebral pressure. When the discomfort became too great he stopped to drink a beer, leaving the empty can hanging on a twig like an inebriated Hansel.

What deadfall Charlie could find was frozen to the ground. He tried pulling logs free, sadly noting the absence of his gloves. His bare hands quickly became stiff and useless, and he used his teeth to open the Scotch. He spat the cap out and tipped the bottle, but his lips wouldn't close properly and whisky trickled out the corners of his mouth, wetting his face, alcohol stinging abraded skin. Painstakingly, he retrieved the cap and closed the Scotch with his palms. *Be nice to have those gloves – nah. Too far to go back.*

Charlie plunged farther into the woods. Pain danced along his brain stem. He threw up again, retching and spitting on dirty snow. The heap of sick steamed, and Charlie was tempted to plunge his hands in it to warm them up. Instead he moved urgently onward. As if in a fairy tale, an abandoned, boarded-up house revealed itself. The booze kept panic at bay, but benumbed fear penetrated his mind; he was damn cold, had to get out of the cold. He stumbled to the building's nailed-shut front door and heaved his weight, threw his shoulder into a plywood board. He slammed it over and over, *ka-wham, ka-wham*, but failed to budge the plank. He trotted around the structure, searching for a weakness.

In the southwest corner he found a board nailed in at ground level. It was compromised by age; a wide horizontal crack ran through the wood. Charlie kicked, and was temporarily blinded by an explosion of keen agony, but encouraged by fresh splitting at the nail holes. He kicked and kicked, grunting with exertion, and the energetic movement warmed him up. Circulation returned to his extremities. He stopped for more Scotch. Eventually he was able to reach down with his near-useless, frozen-slab hands and pry the board from the logs, revealing a small opening. He knelt on an icy ridge, inserted one foot and then the other into the hole and wriggled inside.

He found himself in shadow. Vague shapes wavered in muted winter light that filtered between cracks in log walls. His head ached like a bastard, and his nose and cheeks burned with frostbite. All he wanted to do was sleep, cover himself up and sleep. Unconscious, he could forget Jill's anger, Joseph the traitor and guileless Melissa, whose pure heart would be broken by this mess.

Charlie bumbled inside the building. Nothing made sense. Junk was mounded against the walls, towers of broken furniture and garbage, some almost reaching the drooping roof. There was nowhere comfortable to lie down. His buzz was fading and he needed sleep. A flattish surface in a stack of scrap had the look of a bunk bed. Charlie squirmed into the space, snugging in, jamming knees to chest. He drew the sleeves of his coat over his red, raw hands, and thrust his feet in and out like pistons, trying to get comfortable. The motion dislodged the precarious jumble above him and it settled, pinning him in place. He couldn't move, but he was tired, so tired, and the world spun 'round and 'round. He was happy when the merciful arms of oblivion embraced him.

Twenty-Four

twelve years earlier

Charlie's jalopy was wrapped around a tree, steam rising from its busted radiator, driver's door hanging open. His chainsaw was sitting in a snowbank. Joseph whistled through his teeth, but he wasn't surprised. He didn't even get out of his own truck, a newer red Dodge four-wheel-drive diesel, to investigate. Palming the wheel, he turned around expertly, reversing so the rear bumpers of the two trucks were close. Joseph had a tow bar and winch assembly; once it was detached from the tree, he could tow Chuck's manual-transmission beater back to the farm. Slinging the chainsaw in beside his own tools, he set about hooking up the winch to the smashed vehicle. The hood of Charlie's truck yawned obscenely, displaying a tired, crusty engine.

Each of Joseph's exhales lingered, hanging in the frigid air of an uncomfortably cold day. His nostril hairs stuck together with each inhale. He tried to put the details of the accident together: drops of blood on the dashboard, vomit congealing on the steering wheel, forgotten chainsaw. The alcohol Joseph had watched Charlie toss into his truck was missing. Joseph sniffed the air for smoke, and peered into the forest for evidence of a campfire, but he didn't call for Charlie by name. *Why didn't you call the police?* Joseph would later be asked repeatedly, and he would return to this frozen place in time, when another train of thought might have chugged him along toward different choices. Charlie and the booze were gone. Was he supposed to follow an impetuous drunk through a forest?

Joseph Sommerton was a simple man, confronted with a simple problem: a broken truck. The driver was an adult, out doing his own thing, in a forest not far from his home.

Joseph started his truck and left it running. He turned on electric power to the winch, listened to the scrape and howl of bending metal. Pungent automotive exhaust fumes mingled with the stink from Charlie's blown radiator. Splintered wood and crushed car parts were solidly meshed, fused together on impact. Joseph turned off the winch, climbed in his truck and gunned the engine, revving it hard to pull the old wreck free of the tree. Squeaking, crunching and cracking sounds ricocheted around the empty clearing. Without warning the broken truck came free, and Joseph's truck bucked forward, jolting onto the main road. Gripping his steering wheel, Joseph controlled his speed and came to a stop with both trucks straddling the thoroughfare. In his side mirror he saw the hood of Charlie's truck bounce crazily, like a demented laughing clown mouth.

One witness. It would take just one person, driving by at that moment. If someone happened by and asked questions, Joseph was prepared to tell the truth. Maybe this imaginary, hypothetical witness would ask the crucial question: Where was the driver of the wreck? And Joseph would answer *I don't know*, and eyebrows would be raised, and the business of searching for Charlie would get underway. But fate intervened on that brutally cold February day. It wasn't unusual in such a remote area, at such a bleak time of year, for hours to pass without a soul rolling down the rural road. People with plenty of groceries, firewood and common sense stayed warm and dry in their homes, darning socks, repairing small machinery, watching television, napping.

Joseph didn't rush. He edged the two trucks onto the snowy shoulder, unhooked winch and chains, drove around the wreck and backed up to its mangled front end. To stay warm he kept his body in motion, preparing Charlie's truck for a tow, ensuring the stick was in neutral. Retrieving Charlie's chainsaw, Joseph gassed it up from a red and yellow plastic jug of emergency fuel he kept in his truck and mixed in a splash of two-stroke oil. Three feet from the ground, the tree trunk Charlie had struck bore witness to the collision: raw yellow wood was exposed like a vivid beacon. Joseph pulled the chainsaw's rip cord. It started up right away, a mechanical scream breaking icy silence on the lonely road. The saw whined and roared as Joseph cut the struck tree down, limbed it and sawed the trunk into sections. The sound of a chainsaw was common enough, unremarkable in this area. And if Charlie were nearby, surely he would hear the chainsaw and return to the wreckage of his truck? Joseph expected the inebriated man to lumber out of the woods, but seconds and then minutes ticked by, and Charlie didn't appear. Joseph carried trunk sections to his truck and heaved them in the box, one by one. If someone came along and asked what he was doing, he would say, *I'm just cleaning up this mess.* Charlie made messes and Joseph cleaned them up; that was how things worked at Hopetown Farm.

Joseph stood back and surveyed his handiwork. The ground was frozen; tracks made by Charlie's truck were indistinguishable from the rigid wheel ruts of others who had parked there. A freshly culled tree wasn't an unusual sight, and the barometer in Joseph's truck showed pressure falling fast; a snowstorm was imminent. By the time anyone came out here to investigate, stump and sawdust would be covered with fresh snow.

Back at the farm, Joseph bumped around the house and onto the Bow Lake access road, dragging Charlie's truck behind him like a toy on a rope. There was no one around. He drove uphill, then spontaneously and without reflection backed down the boat launch. It was slow going, reversing eighty metres down to the lake with Charlie's truck hitched to the back of his own. Leaf springs complained, and hot air whooshed from vents in the cab of his modern, well-maintained vehicle. Halfway down he took a break, and left his engine idling while he packed a white square of paper with loose tobacco, rolled it professionally with one hand, wet the adhesive strip and stuck the finished product in his mouth. He lit the cigarette with the glowing orange circle of his vehicle lighter, then finished backing down the hill until Charlie's truck was perched on the frozen rim of Bow Lake. Smoke wreathed Joseph's head while he parked, rummaged in a red sheet metal tool kit and extracted a wrench. He sauntered to the open mouth of Charlie's truck and removed everything he could quickly salvage for scrap: the battery, the filters.

Joseph let the stubby brown end of his smoke drop to the snow. He unhooked hitch and chains and gave the wrecked vehicle a shove. As if it were eager to comply, it slid down the ramp and smoothly out onto the lake, but to Joseph's astonishment the ice didn't crack immediately. The old crippled truck sat there, its crushed front end staring back forlornly at the shore. It could have been Charlie himself, standing on thin ice, mutely pleading with his friend to save him.

Joseph's pulse was nicotine-increased, but he felt an evenness of spirit. He couldn't have planned it better. Charlie's truck had rolled out far enough that when it sank, it would sink nice and deep. A minute of peace passed. Geese flew high above the lake, their honks far away and faint. When the ice broke at last it cracked like a gunshot, then split open with a smacking sound. And down she went. Ice and water swallowed her up. Chuck's old truck sank ceremoniously, her parts disappearing one by one like a time-honoured ship, now the passenger rear tire, now the chassis, now the front end. Joseph was glad he had remembered to roll down the windows; water rushed into the cab, facilitating its descent. Great air bubbles blorped to the surface as the ton of metal sank. Before it was gone completely, Joseph's scalp tingled a warning, and he heard a quiet cough from the top of the boat launch. He whipped around to find the source, his heart racing.

Albert's widow was up there on the berm, leaning on old-school ski poles, wearing a dark pink crocheted toque and a hip-length gold-and-brown winter jacket. Grey braids, encased in frost, swayed against her chest. She was skiing, determined, gazing off past the farmhouse. Had she seen anything? He felt a surge of panic before he realized it wouldn't matter, even if she had. Everyone knew she'd been off-kilter lately, Albert's widow, what was her name, Marianne, was that it? No, Marjorie. She had Jill's permission to cut through the farm and access cross-country ski trails around Crescent Lake, and she did so once or twice a week, but he'd already seen her three times since Sunday. How much was the old bitch cutting through? It was too cold for skiing; she was probably bored and snooping around.

But no, she was skiing past, had already passed, was descending onto the proper trail, and soon all he could see was her crocheted hat. He looked back at the lake, gauging what she might have seen: rim of metal, glint of glass. Most of it was underwater, but you could still tell what it was. Seconds later a final air bubble rocked the ice, and the truck submerged completely. A hole and cracks on the ice surface were the only evidence; even the ripples had already dispersed. Bow Lake was calm once more. Ice would form again, now. Joseph watched the pink hat bob through the orchard. Should he track Marjorie down and find out what she might have seen? But how could he explain, what could he possibly say? He looked back at the lake, and when he turned around again, she was gone.

Twenty-Five

It was the twenty-first of December. Melissa wished for quiet winter days, but Beck's parents were still at the Lanark motel, bored and restless. Beck had assured them he was fine, but they were determined to hang around Ontario until after Christmas, as if making it through the holidays without incident was the litmus test for their son's normality. Matthew, on crutches, was devoting his days to photography and spent many afternoons perched down by Bow Lake, swaddled in a parka and peering through a telephoto lens. Melissa had asked Eurydice to check in on Marjorie, but Beck's mother reported the septuagenarian would only crack her door a few centimetres, insist she was fine and brusquely retreat. Beck warned Melissa that his mother's boredom spelled trouble; she was hounding him to do a consulta. So far he had successfully dodged her attempts, but he didn't know how much longer he could hold out. Matthew and Eurydice ate dinner at the farm once or twice a week, and the previous night, over creamy potato leek soup, when they had announced their purchase of airline tickets to Cuba for early January, Melissa had done a poor job of concealing her delight.

"You're going to Cuba, fantastic! There's nothing to do around here in the off-season, anyway. And honestly, I'm not used to so many people hanging around over Christmas."

"You'll have to excuse my daughter's rudeness," Jill had sniffed.

Beck's parents had shifted uneasily, and left the moment the dinner dishes were cleared.

Tensions were running high at the farm. Melissa and her mother fought frequently and Joseph avoided everyone. Even Daphne was less buoyant, the poisonous atmosphere corroding her relentless, iron-clad optimism. Joseph continued to live in his trailer and some nights, to Melissa's open and vocal disgust, Jill slept out there with him. In the privacy of her bedroom, Melissa and Beck talked about agricultural land prices and the possibility of starting their own farm.

Snow piled up. Beck claimed it insulated him from bee thoughts, which receded in the daytime but lingered maddeningly in his subconscious, he complained, converting his dreams to bee-centric nightmares. He had reduced his honey intake to a tablespoonful of the amber medicinal variety in his tea at bedtime. "You're normal now," Melissa told him, "normal and boring, like the rest of us." Beck said he wished it were true, and confided he was haunted by singular episodes from his childhood. Did every child imagine they could fly, he wondered, and feel the experience in detail, feathers rippling in the wind, talons tucked up tight to the ellipse of an avian torso? Melissa had no answers for Beck's weird questions. He had a new pathological aversion to small, poorly lit spaces, a late-onset claustrophobia. Waking at night he thrashed under the covers, sweating and terrified, until he realized where he was, and she soothed him. Then he couldn't fall back to sleep, for fear of some intangible horror. When he closed his eyes, he said he entered a lightless, confined space behind his eyelids, a place neither hive nor human, an imaginary organic cell where he was a hapless prisoner.

On the winter solstice snow fell overnight, and they woke to a fresh blanket of pure white. Delicate ridges of sparkling snow balanced on every tree branch and along every fence. They were resigned to the inevitability of Christmas, but only Daphne had mustered festive energy, baking gingerbread men, hanging fresh cedar and pine boughs in doorways and singing carols in the shower. Joseph was the farm's reluctant decorator and its resident foul-tempered grinch. He clomped around, smoking and scowling, stringing coloured lights and hanging glass balls in broad evergreen branches. He propped a wooden cut-out of a fat, jolly Santa on the lawn, and Jill tied luxurious cream-red-and-gold-plaid bows to the porch railings and posts; the casual visitor would never guess how unreachable the joys of the season were to the occupants of the festive, twinkling farmhouse. On this day especially they would have to fake it, because Jill was insisting an annual tradition must go forward: a candlelight cross-country solstice ski party around Bow Lake.

In-house enthusiasm for the event was feeble. They prepared for it mechanically – Melissa setting out torches at the ski trailhead, Daphne stirring cinnamon into an enormous pot of apple cider. In the afternoon Joseph made a rare appearance, barging defiantly into the kitchen through the back door and prompting Melissa to storm toward the front. In a show of solidarity, Beck joined her. Melissa snatched her puffy orange down parka, stuffed her arms into the sleeves and covered her loose hair with a coarse-knit toque. Beck buttoned up a black wool coat and wound a striped scarf around his neck. He had grown a short beard, and a not-too-scraggly moustache. They tightened the laces of felt-lined snow boots. Jill's shrill laughter rang out from the kitchen, and Melissa grimaced with displeasure. They waded through diamond drifts toward the bee yard.

"All this snow will help the bees survive, right?" Melissa glanced at Beck, sidelong.

"Yeah. I can picture them, clustered in a ball around the queen to stay warm. But you know, it's getting harder for me to believe I was a bee colony last summer. I'm starting to forget what it was like. I guess that's a good thing."

Melissa deactivated the electric fence, kicked a white ridge aside and pushed the gate open. With their supers removed, the empty hives crouched, waiting for fresh occupants in spring. Beck cleared a path to the active hive, excavated around it and squatted down. He pressed a cheek against black, heat-absorbent roofing paper wrapped around foam insulation panels. Melissa kneeled beside him and put her opposite ear to the hive so they faced each other. She placed a hand gently on his knee. He wasn't crazy, she was certain, but the more convinced she became of his sanity, the more she longed to know where he had been all summer.

"Okay, but you had to be somewhere. What did you eat – where did you sleep? And what about seeing the gold trail things, the vectors?"

Beck didn't answer. The clean, astringent smell of spruce mixed with waxy hive scents and mingled pleasantly with Beck's body perfume, his skin, his cells. She leaned in for a kiss. He closed his eyes and their warm mouths met. Simultaneously, Melissa heard the crunch of tires on roadside ice, and a car parked alongside the hedge. Her eyes fluttered open and the kiss dissolved. Car doors slammed. She rose, and through the gap in the hedge she saw the yellow, blue and red racing stripes of a police squad car.

Two cops in formal hats and jackets emerged on the front path, one a man with silver sideburns, the other Constable Hickey. The cops walked stiffly, shoulder to shoulder, yellow stripes along the seams of their dark blue trousers moving in a synchronized swing, left, right, left, right. Inadvertently they brushed tree branches as they passed, setting precariously balanced snow tumbling in miniature avalanches: small, dramatic puffs of white. They climbed the porch steps and rang the doorbell, oblivious to their observers.

"Stay here." Melissa squeezed Beck's hand. Clumps of snow sticking to the wet wool of her mitten melted in his bare palm. "I'll go see what this is about."

Melissa stepped back to the house, fitting her boots into depressions she had tamped down on the way out. She heard Jill answer the door and exclaim in tense surprise when she saw it was the police. The cops were side by side on the threshold, holding their hats respectfully, hands crossed at their waists, a solemn, official posture.

"There's no mistake, Mrs. Makepeace," the male cop was saying. "The remains are without a doubt those of your late husband, Charles Everett Makepeace. We're very sorry."

Melissa went rigid.

"Can we come in, Jill?" Constable Hickey asked kindly.

Melissa's mother didn't answer.

"Yes, come on in," Melissa choked out, her voice taut as a guitar string, and the cops swivelled their heads. The male cop squinted at Beck in the bee yard. Beck raised a reluctant hand, acknowledging his presence.

Jill protested weakly, but the police officers shuffled inside. Melissa shepherded them through the foyer. "No, you don't have to take your boots off, the sitting room is to your right." Jill, her features wooden, whisper-shouted over a shoulder, "Joe? Joe!"

Assiduously wiping their polished black boots, the cops tromped into the living room and stood by the mantelpiece, near the family photograph. Melissa sat on the cracked leather couch. Stunned, she looked at the photo. Her father's smile was compromised, a diamond with a flaw, his joy tempered by melancholy in contrast to her mother's camera-conscious smirk. Young Melissa was the only genuinely untroubled subject of the portrait. Her father was dead – *he was dead*. She puffed at her hair, but she was still wearing a toque, so her quick exhales moved nothing but air. She tucked anyway, her fingers shoving bumpy wool to get at her ears. Jill entered the living room warily and perched on the edge of the overstuffed armchair, her eyes darting now to the front door, now out the window. She seemed to be expecting another visitor. Constable Hickey coughed delicately and cleared her throat.

"You ladies know me, and this is Constable Vic Murray. We regret bringing this news. I'll lay it out for you. Three weeks ago, two men were cross-country skiing about two kilometres east of here, when one of them broke his leg."

"For heaven's sake, I *know* that. It was Matthew, Beck's *father*, who broke his leg, and Beck *lives* here." Jill twined her fingers in her lap.

"Right, that's right. So, Dr. Griffen dragged Matthew into an abandoned building out by Crescent Lake to keep him out of a snowstorm while they waited for rescue. Inside the building, Dr. Griffen found – uh, human remains. We asked the doctor not to share news of his discovery until the identity of the deceased had been determined. The site had to be thoroughly searched, and the body examined for cause of death. This process is now complete and dental records have confirmed – it's Charlie."

Melissa's features were strangely askew, and her hands groped for traction on her thighs. Jill closed her eyes and took forceful breaths. The police watched them intently. A strained silence ensued.

"He died of exposure," Constable Murray volunteered at last. "He froze to death. There were no signs of foul play."

"But why wasn't that building searched, back when he disappeared?" Jill's voice was like the bleating of a lamb.

Constable Murray fiddled with his hat.

"A fair question. When you reported your husband missing, we based our investigation on the information you supplied at that time. Your husband reportedly left in a rusted circa 1980 white Ford pickup truck, licence plate MLS 783, destination Lanark. We concentrated our efforts on locating this vehicle. Several other witnesses corroborated your claim that your husband was in Lanark. After forty-eight hours, when we hadn't located the vehicle in question, we conducted an extensive search of this property and drove rural roads in the area looking for the truck. There are many abandoned buildings and sheds around here. Without the proximity of his truck, we had no reason to believe Charlie would have sought shelter so far from a main road."

Constable Murray shifted uncomfortably. In the distance Hotay brayed, tragic and plaintive. The leather couch creaked underneath Melissa. Joseph's diesel truck chugged to life beside his trailer, and Daphne entered the kitchen through the back door, whistling.

"So you gave up looking for him because you couldn't find his *truck*?" Jill's tone clearly accused the police of incompetence. Constable Hickey frowned.

"In your statement to police at that time, you said you and your husband had disagreed. Your conclusion was that your husband had left subsequent to a domestic dispute. You suspected Charlie would be at one of the bars he frequented, Lanark Landing, or the Almonte Arms. Unfortunately, other customers of those establishments mistakenly claimed they had seen Charlie, leading us on a false trail. So no, we didn't look for him out near Crescent Lake."

"Joseph's leaving," Melissa said. "I hear his truck."

"Who is Joseph?" asked Constable Murray.

"Joseph has never done *anything* but help out around here," Jill said quickly.

"But you were sleeping with him," Melissa said, "and Dad found out."

The police officers glanced at each other. Constable Murray eased a cellphone from his coat pocket. "I'll take a statement, Melissa, if that's all right with you."

"It's not all right with *me*," said Jill, raising her chin.

"To be clear, Melissa isn't a minor. You can't prevent her from providing us with a statement, and any attempt to do so would be an obstruction of justice," said Constable Hickey. Joseph's truck roared past the hedge in front of the house and accelerated away from the farm. Melissa gestured hopelessly out the window.

"Let's start with Joseph's last name," Constable Murray began, typing into his phone.

"Sommerton," Melissa supplied.

"Your father was a *drunk*!" Jill shrieked, gripping the faded armrest of her chair. Constable Hickey's right hand dropped to the gridded black metal handle of her sidearm.

"Charlie was an *alcoholic*, who made our lives miserable, and for your information, *officers*, Charlie was *stinking drunk* the day he left, and he was *driving* his truck – driving *drunk*. You'll find his truck wrecked, at the bottom of a lake, or wrapped around a tree somewhere. Oh, for heaven's sake. I'm not sticking around for this." Jill rose regally.

"Jill, finding Charlie's remains has opened up an official investigation. We're going to get to the bottom of this. You'll be wanting to learn the truth about what happened to your husband, I'm sure," Constable Hickey stood up, "but we'll leave you for now. This news must be a shock. Come by the precinct tomorrow, and we'll discuss this matter in more detail."

Melissa closed her eyes.

The day was an especially cold one, metal squealing when she descended the school bus stairs, her cheap boots sliding on icy hardpack as the bus pulled away. In a backpack slouching from her shoulders she carried a tin lunch kit with a knot of plastic wrap and discarded sandwich crusts, and a dog-eared Hilroy notebook, xeroxed math homework poking out from between the pages. Thin, gritty blues music penetrated the crisp air, a radio station amplified on her father's boom box. Tangy aromas lingered around the ramshackle work shed – motor oil, paint thinner, stale beer. The slatted wooden door hung open a few inches and Melissa nudged inside. Ghosts of her father lingered; there was an empty bottle on the ground and a pile of greasy rags, the same blue plaid fabric as her father's winter work coat, heaped on the workbench. Signs of him, but no Dad. Back outside, she spotted Joseph's truck, streaks of fire-engine-red paint showing through layers of winter highway sand and grit. It was parked pointed uphill on the boat launch road.

A firm hand on her shoulder brought Melissa swirling back to the present and into the farmhouse. Constable Hickey's eyes were soft and sympathetic. "I'm really sorry," she said. "We had hoped for a different outcome, obviously. But no more wondering where he is."

Melissa watched numbly as the police slid their hands into black leather gloves and squared their hats in place. They offered final condolences and let themselves out, walking briskly between the decorated trees on the lawn. Their backs vanished through the gap in the hedge. She heard the cruiser's engine start and listened until it faded.

Jill sniffed primly. "The solstice ski is cancelled."

"Fine. I can't talk to you right now. Please go hang out in Joseph's trailer."

Jill stomped upstairs and slammed her bedroom door. Melissa felt cemented to the couch. Daphne, her lips crooked, entered the living room tentatively and sat down beside Melissa.

"What's going on?"

"They found my father's remains – he died. He's dead."

"Oh, Melissa, I'm so sorry." Daphne jiggled her knees and clenched her hands into fists. "I know what it's like to lose people."

The floor tilted. Melissa was surprised all the furniture didn't slide into a corner. Pieces of her life rearranged and settled in new, unrecognizable places. Daphne's life would tilt now too.

"Everything's going to change," she told Daphne. "Nothing can stay the same."

Daphne's mouth trembled, but the rest of her went curiously static, as if the music playing in her head had ended. She flicked her gaze toward the staircase, and Melissa guessed she was concerned about their mother.

"Go to her," Melissa said. "She needs you." With a grateful, cheerless nod, Daphne squeezed Melissa's hand and went upstairs to Jill's room.

The wait was over. Her father would never surprise her and saunter through that gap in the hedge, weaving uncertainly, wearing a fragile, tenuous, hungover smile, thin as the coloured glass of old Christmas decorations. The phone would never jingle with a "charges-reversed call from Charlie Makepeace," released from jail, or returned from overseas. Melissa's best hopes and worst fears about her father's homecoming died at once: he would never introduce her to his second family – a better, loving family who appreciated him; or limp into the farmhouse, pale and bald, losing a battle with cancer.

She put her coat and mitts back on and went outside where the sun shone, blinding and brilliant, on fresh snow. The bee yard was empty; Beck must have walked down to the lake. Dislodging the broad red plastic blade of a shovel from a snowbank, she cleared the porch stairs, then shovelled the front walkway. She was digging a path around the back of the house when a vehicle sped by toward Lanark, and she looked up to see her mother's car, which had been parked by Joseph's trailer. Was her mother going after Joseph – leaving her and Daphne alone? A current of disbelief shocked Melissa. She tossed the shovel aside and tramped down the main road to Joseph's charmless, tacky, beige-and-brown fifth wheel.

Wolf Spirit, the trailer declared, as if an aluminum box of crap rolling down a highway could possess something so exalted. Dirty, trodden snow around folding metal steps was dotted with cigarette butts. Parallel ruts where Joseph parked his truck were icy and bare, but she went up the steps and pounded on the flimsy door anyway, first with a mittened fist, then with exposed knuckles. Ragged squares of duct tape were plastered over holes in the screen to keep mosquitoes out, and a musty stink of stale smoke and canned food clung to the trailer. A heavy padlock hung from the door's simple latch. Where were they going, her mother and Joseph? They had made her father miserable, and then death had swallowed up his secrets. A robin in springtime, pecking at muddy, half-frozen ground. *It means things are going to get better, Lissy.*

She returned to the house, huffing blasts of frozen breath, stumbling every few steps in the snow. She wanted to be with Beck and Daphne in some urban locale, a dance club or restaurant, where they could be young and carefree. She wanted to break loose from the shackles of the stone building where she had spent most, too much, of her life. As ornery and contradictory as it was, she wanted a drink. In the living room she found Daphne sobbing mutely, hands clenching at empty air, her mouth contorted in a rictus of pain.

"She packed a suitcase," Daphne sobbed. "She's gone."

Melissa put her arms around her sister. Numbness deepened; she was anaesthetized, receding down a tunnel, away from the rough textures and bright colours of her feelings. She scarcely reacted when Beck's parents appeared in the foyer, Matthew navigating with the clumsy thumps of a plastic foot cast and crutches, the lenses of his glasses obscured by condensation. He opened his mouth but failed to speak, and sagged against the door jamb. Eurydice, her eyes enormous, made a loud announcement.

"Marjorie – the old lady – our neighbour."

"We had a Christmas hamper for her, some food and candles," Matthew said, recovering. He peered through moisture on his lenses, and leaned on his crutches, the top half of his body pitching forward. "She didn't answer her door, so we went inside to make sure she was okay. And she's dead."

Silence inflated, filling the foyer, the hall, the staircase. At the back of the house the kitchen door opened and closed. Footsteps approached, and then Beck was there, crowding into the front hall with his parents, innocent and bemused. Matthew's face contorted, and when he spoke, the sounds he made were strangled.

"Beck, have you been to Marjorie's place lately? It's strange, but some of your clothes are there. In her house."

Twenty-Six

Left alone in the bee yard, one of Beck's panicky episodes had threatened, and he had hurried down to the lake, seeking the rinsing, purifying balms of wind and water. He was irrationally relieved the police weren't looking for him, even though he hadn't done anything wrong. He had been momentarily curious about the purpose of their visit, but had pushed the interest away and meditated by the lake, purging bees from his brain. At last, feeling calm, he had ventured back to the house, and to his surprise his parents were there. They told him Marjorie was dead.

She was dead.

His father called 911, and insisted Beck accompany him and his mother to see what they had discovered in Marjorie's house. Melissa seemed off, remote and troubled, but she kept a protective arm around a desolate and crying Daphne and mouthed at him, *Later*. His parents escorted him to the Volvo and he went without protesting, resigned to their stern purpose. He wondered vaguely why the police had come to the farm with news of Marjorie's death, and why Daphne, who had barely known the old lady, was mourning her.

From the outside Marjorie's house was a cool, white cocoon, already in darkness on the shortest day of the year, the setting sun blocked by trees to the west. A wretched guilt enveloped Beck, and looking toward the old woman's apiary, he confirmed a suspicion he'd been nursing like a dirty secret for weeks: her hives weren't insulated. Supers were still piled on top of brood boxes; inside, he knew, bee colonies were clustered and imperilled, staying in motion to keep warm, but December had been sharply cold, and bees were probably dying in there. His father parked in the driveway behind Max Griffen's car.

"What's the doctor doing here?" A surge of doubt and alarm – was Marjorie truly dead?

"Max was with us when we found her. He was going to do a little unofficial house call, to make sure she was coping."

Beck fell in reluctantly behind his mother, and they edged past a tangle of branches. His father straggled behind on his crutches. Eurydice turned the silver knob and pushed the front door open. The singular, disagreeable smell engulfed Beck immediately, a cloying sweetness wrapped around decay. He recoiled, and rapidly covered up his fear by doing a one-eighty and pretending to help his father navigate the stairs. They filed one by one into Marjorie's sitting room, where Max Griffen was studying the photographs hanging on the walls. The doctor spun around as they entered, his expression a mash of pity and confusion that made Beck want to turn and run from the house.

"Her body's in the bedroom. I closed the door. Good thing she heats with wood, and we're having this cold snap. She's been dead for three, maybe four days. Say, Beck, what do you make of this?" Max beckoned, directing Beck to the narrow, panelled hallway leading to dimness at the back of the house.

Beck hesitated. "Why is it so dark in here?"

"There're only a couple of light bulbs. She wasn't taking care of herself, or her place."

Max was right; it was cold in the house, almost as chilly as outside, and everything was dirty. Unwashed lace curtains hung in the sitting room windows, their grimy fabric filtering weak remnants of daylight. Max was waiting for Beck to join him, but there was pressure behind Beck's eyeballs and a lump of sick in his throat. He took two tentative steps, then stopped and retched. His mother removed a framed picture from the wall and held it close to her face, the dusty glass surface almost touching her nose.

"Beck, this person looks like you, *exactly* like you, when you were a boy."

"I'm not feeling well."

"I get it – the smell is overpowering. It's not her – I don't know what it is. Beck, you really need to see this," said Max.

With a gargantuan effort, Beck swallowed his bile and went around the corner into the dusky hallway. Max was peering into an alcove, a space perhaps a metre deep and two metres long, tucked into the wall across from Marjorie's bedroom. In the alcove was a single bed built with two-by-fours and plywood. The sleeping surface was a piece of ochre camp foam, pockmarked with dime-sized holes and stained with irregular blotches. Lumped on top of this makeshift mattress were a pair of men's jeans, a dirty sleeping bag and a worn, frayed T-shirt. Max picked up first the jeans, then the shirt. He shook them out and held them up for Beck's inspection. Against his will, and contrary to common sense, Beck recognized them.

They were his.

He lurched to the bathroom and hurled his stomach contents into the tarnished porcelain toilet, which was also familiar. He knew the sight of the cracked tiles on either side of the toilet bowl, and the greenish build-up of accumulated grunge in the grout. He knew the dust clumps on the painted baseboards, and the carapace of a large spider in a corner, legs curled under its thorax in death. His vomit splattered toilet sides and seat, and his eyes rolled wildly around the washroom: vinyl shower curtain hanging from three plastic rings, cheap polyethylene tub surround, rusty water marks dripping from a chipped faucet, vice-grips clamped to the valve where a hot water tap should have been. Wiping his mouth with the back of his hand, Beck stood and confronted a warped mirror with chipped edges. Above the mirror, someone had used plastic clothespins to clip a bunched-up, light brown towel to a poor-quality oblong light fixture. Gulping down another wave of sick, he reached up and tugged the towel, nightmare squeal of violins in his head, urgently hoping he was wrong. The towel had evidently been designed to obscure the mirror; it unrolled, releasing tiny grey corpses of long-dead flies and exposing a hand-drawn hexagon pattern in dark-brown marker.

"Beck, are you all right in there?" Max shouted. The door opened, a hand thumped against the wall, located the light switch and flicked it on. The bathroom light bulb was red, and the dingy space transformed into a cell where Beck had been imprisoned. He straddled the toilet and threw up again. He was intimate with this room, and at the same time he had never been in it before. At least, not like this, while he was conscious. Not in possession of his wits.

Max edged around Beck's splayed feet. With firm, reassuring hands, the doctor held his hair back and steadied him as Beck continued to be sick. When his stomach was empty, Max ran cold water over a worn washcloth and wiped his face and the back of his neck. From nearby he heard his mother sounding off in livid Spanish. The resonance of her protests washed around him, blood roared in his ears and that singular, overpowering stench mingled with the smell of his puke.

"What's going on? Beck, did you eat something questionable?" His father asked from the hallway. "What's all this stuff out here?"

Beck brushed Max's hand away and reeled into the hall. He felt cold and clammy in his extremities and feverishly hot in his core. He dropped to his knees beside the cruddy alcove bed and blinked at the low ceiling. The alcove interior was decorated like the towel in the bathroom; an amateurish hand had painted crude three-dimensional hexagons in shades of deep orange and brown on every surface visible from the bed. Another towel, the same light-brown shade as the one above the bathroom mirror, was staple-gunned to the joist where the ceiling met the main wall. The towel was rolled up and tied with hemp string. Afraid to see, but desperate to know, Beck untied the strings. The towel unfurled, revealing a drawn-on pattern of honeycomb cells. His father crouched beside him and peered into the gloom.

"What a curious set-up. She wasn't a fastidious person, was she? What was the purpose of having a bed in the hall like this?"

"Unbelievable," Max said distractedly, kneeling down next to Matthew.

Beck felt faint; his sickness was altering, becoming systemic shock. Muttering under her breath, his mother pushed past and barged into Marjorie's bedroom. Beck glimpsed two bright blue staring eyes above an exaggerated rictus. Ignoring the dead body, Eurydice yanked dresser drawers open and rifled through them. "What's this?" said the doctor, and he withdrew his cellphone, turned the flashlight app on and trained a bright cone of illumination underneath the alcove bed. Dots of reflected light glinted from between the bed supports, vertical two-by-fours hammered in every six inches. Max handed Beck his phone and reached under the bed, jostling stout glass containers that clunked heavily. Max withdrew a jar and held it in the lurid crimson bathroom light, tipping it one way and then the other. The contents were viscous. It was darker than most varieties but it was honey, of course it was honey. It was the medicinal honey Marjorie had enthusiastically promoted, extolling its virtues, gifting Beck jars of it, feeding him some every time he came around. A paper label affixed to the jar had lettering in two languages. In English it said "deli bal." Beck couldn't decipher the other written symbols, squiggles and dots.

This sinister set-up was his beehive. It was inconceivable, but undeniable. He had been trapped here in his missing months. *But, but, but,* his psychological defences screamed, *what did I eat, where did I shit, why don't I remember her being here, what about the vectors, how could this place have fooled me*? On hands and knees he crawled into the sitting room, balled up in the fetal position and groaned. His father hobbled behind him on his crutches, *thump-thump, thump-thump*.

Clutching the jar of honey, Max entered the sitting room and peered at the photos again. "This young man, in these photos – are these pictures of *you*, Beck? *This* person looks like you, but it can't be. No wait, this one is Beck for sure. What do you make of this honey, Matthew? There are cases and cases of it, under that bed back there."

"If she weren't dead, I swear, I would kill her," Beck heard his mother say.

"What is that? Eurydice, what *is* that thing?"

The doctor's voice was strangled. Though he wished himself a million miles away, Beck couldn't prevent himself from opening his eyes.

"I found it in her closet."

Floating in midair, supported by his mother's hands but so big it blotted her out, was the triangular head of a giant insect. A curved black proboscis extended from the head like an inverted rhinoceros horn. Realistic bristles surrounded two shiny black ovoid eyes, and segmented antennae crooked left and right from the top of the thing. An empty sac of fabric and nubbly bands of orange-and-black material dangled underneath it. Beck saw this monstrosity, and a floodgate opened in his mind. A montage flickered behind his blind eyes, collected images from his time away: antennae rubbing, slick cells of larvae, hum and brush of a hundred thousand wings, a creature both familiar and alien descending upon him in dark, glutinous closeness, extending a long, flexible tongue filled with sugary nutrition. He latched his lips onto her lingual extremity and sucked. She was his queen, the centre of the universe, his sun, emanating information and inspiration. Everything flowed from her. She was the heart of the hive.

Twenty-Seven

"Come on, let's get out of here. Let's go rescue Beck," said Melissa.

Under a cloudless late afternoon sky, fading to purple where the sun had sunk below the horizon, the old truck swerved and skidded away from the farm. Its winter tires had been around for too many seasons. Beside Melissa, a diminished Daphne rubbed eyes swollen with tears. *He's dead,* Melissa thought over and over. She spared only a brief, mournful thought for Marjorie, who had been old after all, and recently hospitalized. Melissa had officially lost her father forever, but Daphne's sorrow surpassed hers in its intensity. To her astonishment Melissa felt relief spread over her body, like a soothing cream rubbed into dry, chafed skin. The big question in her psyche, which for years had spiralled like a long, intricate cadenza, had at last rejoined the orchestra and resolved, concluding with a triumphant minor chord. She had her answer at last, but it opened up a new question. Her mother, who was Daphne's mother too, had sped away from the farm with a suitcase full of hastily gathered garments. Melissa pictured the padlock hanging from Joseph's trailer door. Why were they leaving, and where had they gone? She knew what lay ahead for Daphne now, the waiting and wondering: Had the parent she loved best abandoned her?

The truck fishtailed in front of Marjorie's house. Daphne yelped and clutched at the dashboard, but Melissa managed to control the pickup's swinging trajectory by nosing into a snowbank. Daphne hiccuped, the aftermath of weeping, and Melissa touched her back, solicitous.

There were two cars in the driveway, the Wises' and Max Griffen's. Melissa's plans raced ahead. She and Daphne and Beck would escape the old woman's house as soon as they could. Together they would drive to town, listening to upbeat music, bolstering each other's spirits with levity – forced cheer, if they couldn't muster authentic optimism. They would find a crowded pub, and Melissa anticipated the blissful annihilation of her roiling soul as alcohol merged with her bloodstream. Climbing the tumbledown porch they heard the muffled shouting of a woman, pitchy and overwrought, and a man's exclamations, guttural and tortured. Like the cascade of disaster at the close of a horror movie, the shortest day of the year was elongating, grievous incidents unfolding faster and faster as night approached.

Daphne pushed the door open, revealing a madhouse. Beck lay on the floor like a dropped puppet, his limbs splayed haphazardly. Max and Matthew hovered nearby; they seemed reluctant to touch Beck or interfere, as if he were dangerously infectious. Eurydice's features were engorged with distress. The situation, whatever it was, had rendered her post-verbal; she gestured to the rear rooms of the house and pointed to a hideous lump on the floor, an oval thing like an oversized rugby ball, but black and fuzzy. Daphne halted in the doorway, but Melissa went to Beck and knelt beside him. He had vomited recently; she could smell it on his breath and see it on his clothes.

"Please get me out of here," he pleaded, and he clutched at her arms, like a drowning man desperate to be hauled out of a cold ocean.

"Help me, Daphne – we have to get him outside."

Glaring at Matthew and the doctor, who both seemed paralyzed, Melissa negotiated a shoulder into Beck's armpit and Daphne did the same on his opposite side. Together they lifted him to a delicate stance, and supported him as he took fragile steps, like a cripple or an invalid. They piloted him along the road and heaved him into Melissa's truck, where he toppled sideways on the bench seat and lay there, trembling. A rough Mexican blanket was draped over the passenger seat; Melissa tore it free and covered Beck, tucking it around his limbs. "Thanks," he whispered. She closed the truck door and confronted Max, who had come out of his trance and followed them outside.

"What the hell is going on?"

"It's – I truly can't explain it. You have to see it for yourself. If you read the notebook – there's a book we found, a diary. It's unbelievable. I don't know where to start. Give me the keys to your truck, and I'll take Beck over to his parents' place. Her body's in the back bedroom – don't go in there."

The front yard was cloaked in shadow; the path to the house felt like a burrow. Melissa and Daphne re-entered the bizarre scene to find Eurydice arguing with herself while holding a photograph, and Matthew reading from a spiral-bound notebook, his eyebrows arched dramatically over his spectacles. He glanced up, and spoke in fragments.

"Some kind of travesty. Really messed up. Some strange honey."

He pointed vaguely toward the bedroom, and thrust the notebook at Daphne, who accepted it and began reading. Wrinkling her nose – there was a foul odour in the building, deeper and more pervasive than the lingering smell of Beck's vomit – Melissa went to the dark recess she had noticed the day she had found Marjorie sick in bed. She must have been distracted that day, because she had failed to observe a rudimentary honeycomb pattern painted on the sloped ceiling of the alcove. Red light from a bare bulb in the bathroom illuminated a towel stapled above the bed, also marked with hexagons. Melissa's thoughts crept along sluggishly, like a primeval beast. She lifted the towel and ran the palm of her hand over raw wallboard. The alcove smelled like stale urine sprayed with cheap household cleaner. Matthew hobbled up and handed her a jar of honey.

"Max found this underneath that bed-thing. There must be fifty jars of this stuff under there, some of it old, some of it fresh."

Melissa took the jar and tilted it. A dark orange substance shifted behind the glass. There was a label on the jar, but not enough light in the gloomy hallway to read it. "It's honey – so what? She kept bees. There's a stash of honey in a cool, dry place. Why is everyone freaking out, and what's wrong with Beck?"

"That's Turkish writing on there, according to Max."

An alcove, honey, hexagons, a notebook. Beck's father wanted her to connect the dots, but Melissa didn't see how these disparate things lined up, or how they had reduced Beck to a cowering heap. Matthew leaned in close, his hot breath blasting her face.

"This honey is a drug, Max says, with hallucinogenic properties. Some of it has spilled under this weird bed. Can't you smell it? And there are some of Beck's clothes here, and pictures of him when he was young. Let me show you what Eurydice found, in Marjorie's closet." Matthew manoeuvred past her, returning to the front room, and Melissa went after him. It *did* smell putrid in Marjorie's house, a mysterious, biotic smell, like the treacly buds of a swamp plant.

Daphne was engrossed in the notebook. Matthew poked a heap of black material with the rubber tip of a crutch, and it flopped on its side. Melissa inhaled sharply – the thing was a papier mâché headpiece, a giant mask painted and adorned with stout hairs, as if from a wild boar. The antennae were made of wire and shiny black duct tape. Beside the mask was a piece of fabric, a textured yellow-and-black cape of sorts. Melissa picked this garment up, pinching it between reluctant fingertips. Coarse hair had been glued to the fabric and sewn-on sleeves ended in black gloves. Leaning against a wall was a set of transparent wings, constructed from wire and plastic film.

"But nobody could be fooled by this! It's a costume – it's obviously a costume." Melissa lifted the wings, and tossed them on the couch contemptuously.

Eurydice emitted a howl of pain, a mother's anguish. Matthew accidentally released his right crutch and it fell to the floor. He thrust his fingers through his hair and pressed his spectacles into his eye sockets. "Max thinks Marjorie could have drugged Beck with this honey. His symptoms, the amnesia, the weakness, the malnutrition – they could all be attributed to the toxicity of this stuff, this mad honey."

Melissa would have laughed, if not for Beck's collapse, his state of shock.

"She was over seventy, small and frail. She couldn't have kept Beck here all summer. I don't care how messed up you can get on this honey. Right, Daphne?" But her sister didn't look up from the pages of the notebook.

"I know, I know, it seems impossible," Matthew said. "But Beck's clothes are here, and she has pictures of him since he was a toddler. Pictures from way back when we first bought the place next door." He pointed at Daphne and the notebook. "It's unthinkable. Read her journal. I only skimmed it. I have to get Eurydice out of here before she falls to pieces."

Eurydice dropped the photograph she was holding and retrieved

Matthew's crutch. Her eyes were unfocused and bloodshot. She brandished the crutch like a weapon and swept her gaze around the squalid room. Matthew gently took his crutch from her and they left, not bothering to shut the front door. Carnival music, the maniacal lilting of a hurdy-gurdy, played in Melissa's head. This wasn't Beck's beehive, it couldn't be. But something sinister had happened here. There was a wicked secret, a hidden truth, like the terrible proximity of her father's corpse. Instinct should have tipped her off, she thought wildly, and let her know her father's bones were close; she should have heard them rattling in her sleep, demanding to be discovered. Melissa shuddered. Marjorie's dead body lay close by. Maybe some of that odour of putrefaction was her molecules, suspended in the air, coalescing into her ghost. Daphne had backed up to the wall and sank to the floor by a window. Melissa joined her, and together they pored over the notebook.

The pages were crinkly, over-inked with dense writing that sloped to the right. The writer had pressed the pen hard into the paper. Daphne flipped to a page near the beginning.

We named him Thomas, this eighth baby, this survivor. He is perfect, the very image of his father. Every mother protects her child, but I will go beyond protection for Thomas. I will smooth his path in the world, I will give him my blood, drop by drop, if I have to. I will sacrifice myself in any and every way for this child. I told Arnold I would kill for our Thomas and he said calm down Marge and I said seven miscarriages, seven dead babies. Seven, before we had one that lived. I would kill for Thomas, absolutely, I would.

Marjorie had a son. But she never spoke of him – her child, after a series of dead children. "Dead, all dead," Marjorie had moaned. But not dead bees, as Melissa had assumed. She had heard what she expected to hear. The dead were *b-bees* – babies.

Grainy, inexpert photos were scattered on the floor. Melissa collected a few within reach and handed them wordlessly to Daphne. Arnold, Marjorie's husband, was easy to identify, but there were also blurry, indistinct images of a boy and a young man, pictures taken too remotely from the subject. Some were surely Beck, and others were almost certainly a different person, weren't they? Why would Marjorie have childhood pictures of Beck in the first place?

"Is this Beck? It must be," Daphne tapped an image of a young boy and a yellow dog.

"No, it can't be. He met Marjorie only a couple of years ago, at the Beekeepers' Society meetings," Melissa said, examining the photo. She returned to the notebook and fanned brittle pages, skipping to the halfway mark. They leaned over it again.

Arnold you shit how could you leave me? We're alone, me and Thomas are alone and he misses you, he's going crazy missing you, he can't control how it's ripping him up! Your dying hurt our son and I would murder you myself for what you're doing to him, murder you over again, better than a lousy car crash ever could. They gave me valium at the hospital, out of sympathy for the poor pathetic widow, but I won't drug myself. I'll feel the pain. You used to say I was tough. Well I am tougher than you ever knew! But our Tommy is crumbling.

Pages crinkled under their fingers. There were long descriptions of beehives, garden plans complete with schematic drawings and rants about members of Marjorie's family. They scanned for the capital *T* for Thomas, reading passages about him as they found them.

By the time he was thirteen Marjorie's son had been a troubled kid, swearing at his mother, blaming her for "*this shit life in this shithole.*" The notebook flopped open to an especially battle-scarred page, penned more viciously than the others and spotted with blurs that might have been tears. Thomas had run away from home. He had caught a ride to Toronto with an older boy known for illicit drug use and vandalism. Marjorie had pursued them, following her son to the big city with not much money and nowhere to stay. She got a bed at a downtown hostel and walked up and down Yonge Street, asking questions, showing strangers a picture of Thomas. It took her three days. She visited dozens of emergency shelters and soup kitchens, but she found her Tommy, bedraggled and hungry, and convinced him to come home. Within a year he was gone again. His absences became more frequent and longer, and the drugs he took got harder. At just twenty years old, they read, Thomas had died of an overdose in a Toronto alley.

Daphne was crying again. Melissa guessed Thomas's story reminded her sister of the life she'd known before this one. They tipped their heads to touch, and huddled together, like much younger girls enduring a dramatic domestic crisis. Melissa wasn't anywhere close to tears, and her tics didn't flare up. She was angry. She kept reading because she wanted to learn it all, learn everything, so she could be as furious as she needed to be. What had Marjorie done to Beck?

I could have saved Tommy from anything except himself. He was attacked from the inside. I never saw that coming. All dead. I go to the bees and I talk to them – I tell them things. That's how it is now, just me and the bees. I won't be chased off this Earth and denied my days because they all went and died on me. My bees don't need me, but they're company, and I can learn from them. I went to a Beekeepers' Society meeting. A pack of fools, but I sold a dozen candles, and maybe I won't go crazy from talking only to bees.

They were shivering, but they kept reading. Marjorie had been managing her solitary life when an interesting couple moved in next door, a Cuban mother, photographer father and their baby boy. They had bought the property in spring, and over that summer they had fixed up the broken-down cabin. Marjorie had watched the Wises through the trees, casually at first, then carrying binoculars and a camera down a trail she hacked through the forest. The trail led to a tree stump where she sat and spied on the little family. Her new neighbours' son had smooth, tan skin and shiny black hair, like a raven's wing. Amazing – so like Thomas! Marjorie had guessed the Wise boy's age, and calculated he must have been born within weeks of Thomas's death. Her son's spirit was strong, Marjorie confided in her journal. Thomas had come back. His spirit had found the body of this boy, and travelled here to be close to his mother.

As the Wises' child grew, Marjorie perceived Thomas emerging, like a parasitical insect pupating inside its host. Beck was quiet, just like Thomas, thoughtful and introspective. He had the same lean musculature, gangling, tending to skinny. In her journal, Marjorie was harshly critical of Eurydice, Beck's "lousy mother," who chased him around with snacks, complaining she could count his ribs and berating him for his ungrateful indifference to food. How like her Thomas this child was, Marjorie marvelled, how precisely the same as her very own son. But instead of nagging Thomas to eat, she, Marjorie, had nourished her son with his favourite foods. That was the best way. If this boy were in her care, he would thrive. She longed to nurture the spirit of her son inside this new vessel.

Marjorie's house was freezing; cold wind blew through the open front door. Daphne got up and kicked it closed. From outside came the rough, scratchy sound of her truck's motor; Max had returned. Melissa stood up, but stayed focused on the notebook. She turned pages, scanning for salient points.

It's my boy. He's my baby. God sent him back to me, put him right into my hands. Thomas looks out of those eyes, Thomas talks out of that mouth. He's mine, and I will have him again.

Marjorie confided a drug habit to her journal. She consumed a daily dose of a rare Turkish honey called deli bal, made by bees that fed exclusively on rhododendrons and azaleas. Her brother Stanley, who had been in the navy, had found himself docked for weeks in the Port of Istanbul. Bored, and keen to profit from smuggling black market goods, Stanley had met a man in a hookah lounge near Taksim Square who had promised he could triple any investment in a little-known, unrestricted drug, deli bal, honey made by bees in the hills surrounding the Black Sea. Convinced, Stanley had invested heavily, and sailed home with dozens of cases of the dark honey, hoping to sell it at inflated prices. But in Canada no one knew what deli bal was, and no one wanted to pay for it. The cases sat in Stanley's basement until he died – young, of heart disease – and Marjorie inherited the mad honey. Hooked, she had planted rhododendrons and azaleas in the rocky, acidic soil around pine trees close to her bee yard, and started producing her own supply of delirium-inducing deli bal.

We met in person at last. A miracle – he wants me to teach him about my hives. I give him my special honey when he comes to visit. He trembles, and sweats, and talks about being bees. I tell him hive-stories and explain the dances. Sometimes he sleeps. Deli bal is perfect food, but it makes you sleepy. Thomas is inside the boy-man who calls himself Beck and thinks he is bees. Life spirals around and through. I take deli bal too, and then my baby and I, we are the bees.

Melissa handed the journal to Daphne carefully, as if it might explode. What if the whole time he was gone, Beck had been right here, as close to the farm as her father's remains? Could she have saved them both? Melissa punched her thighs, disgusted she hadn't tried hard enough to find the people she loved. Her father's death and Beck's lost time twisted around each other like a double helix. She started to puff, but no physical ritual could keep this pain at bay. Daphne riffled through the notebook.

"Oh, man. No way – there's stuff about your dad in here."

With a whirling sense of vertigo, Melissa put a hand on the wall to steady herself. Daphne pulled a dirty curtain open, and holding pages in faint light, read out loud: "'Went to Lanark. Still no word of Charlie Makepeace. Three weeks now he's been missing. I keep thinking about skiing through the Makepeace place that day, and watching Joe sink Charlie's truck. Guess if Charlie's gone for good, it leaves Joe in the clear with Jill. I know what those two get up to when Charlie's in his cups. Guess I could say what I saw, but to hell with people, and to hell with the cops, who gave up on Tommy and let him die on the street. I cried and I begged, and they wrote my son off like he was nothing. They'd do the same with Charlie. He's not rich or white enough to warrant their time and money.'"

Daphne closed the journal and placed it delicately beside the macabre costume on the couch. "We'd better leave this here for the police," she said. On cue, the wail of sirens reached the house from the road toward Lanark, and built rapidly, until a fleet of emergency vehicles arrived in a deafening, caterwauling lament.

Gasping for air, Melissa let Daphne lead her outside. Bright red-and-white lights flashed and swirled, and squads of capable, uniformed rescuers trod on Max's heels as he led them to Marjorie's unfortunate husk. Melissa's old pickup truck grumbled in the snow, with its scabby rust patches and dozens of dings, so much like her father's vanished vehicle, the one she'd been searching for since he left. A snatch of conversation returned to Melissa, a scrap of something Marjorie had said, and she heard the old woman speak through time with a fierce, malicious twinkle in her eyes.

If you're searching, look no farther than your own backyard.

Twenty-Eight

She *thought* she saw it. Doesn't necessarily mean Charlie's truck's in the lake." Constable Hickey leaned an elbow on the precinct's laminated front counter and thrust out a hip. "Thing is, Marjorie Hill was a bit unbalanced. Tell me again what she said, nice and slow."

"She said I would find what I was looking for in my backyard. And then at the hospital, she said Joseph had a big fish on the line, and it sank. She meant my dad's truck – I'm sure of it."

Constable Hickey straightened, crossed her arms and pursed shiny lips. "Well, it's in that journal of hers, too. Tell you what. I've got a hunch the truck's down there, and I put stock in hunches. Not every investigator does, but me, I get a feeling about something and I think, must be a reason why I'm feeling it. But let's just say, for argument's sake, she saw what she said she saw, and the truck's in the lake. Lake's frozen solid. Even after it thaws, it'll be too cold to dive, even with wetsuits, until April." She rocked heel-to-toe, considering. "I'll have to get an official go-ahead, but when the ice melts, and the water warms up a little, we'll come out and have a look-see."

At the farm, Beck folded into himself. Aside from consoling Melissa when she told him about her father's lonely demise, he hardly spoke. He played guitar but didn't sing, and couldn't abide any mention of Marjorie. At night, he fell asleep only when Melissa held him. He gripped her hands and buried his head in her neck. He had nightmares, thrashing so violently she was obliged to roll out of bed and cover her head in self-defence.

"It was me that cut her hand," Beck said suddenly one morning. "The day I got away from her. She left a bee tool beside me. The deli bal must have been wearing off. I attacked her, stabbed her with the bee tool and bolted. Stuff's coming back to me now."

"Good, that's good you're remembering. I'm here for you, you know."

"I know."

Matthew and Eurydice postponed their return to Cuba, and came for dinner most nights, but the meals were dour affairs. The palpable explanation for Beck's lost summer had flattened Eurydice; heavy chagrin hung around her like a shawl. Matthew wanted to dissect the minutiae of Beck's ordeal, and Daphne and Melissa took turns shutting him down, until everyone chewed in silence. Christmas passed them by, and afterward they shuffled around the farmhouse in bulky socks and sweaters, despondently putting decorations in boxes.

Jill and Joseph stayed away. In brief, terse phone calls Jill explained she needed *time to process* the news of Charlie's death, and declined to say where she was living. Daphne didn't sing in the shower or whistle while sweeping the floors. Melissa ransacked her mother's room, emptying Jill's closet and dresser drawers. Whatever she expected to find, a memento of her father maybe, or damning proof of her mother's duplicity, it wasn't there. Of everyone Melissa knew, only Max was chipper and inspired, investigating the pharmaceutical particulars of the honey he'd found in Marjorie's house and calling her from Almonte with enthusiastic reports.

"The hallucinogen in deli bal is called grayanotoxin. It's astonishingly potent and causes everything from numbness and nausea to cardiac irregularities, fainting and seizures. I've sent samples away for chemical analysis. I doubt there are traces of it remaining in Beck's bloodstream, but do you think he'd agree to –?"

"No." Melissa glanced at Beck, curled up by the fireplace, wrapped in blankets, his eyes hollow, his skin translucent. She lowered her voice and moved to the kitchen, whispering harshly into the phone. "The kidnapping, the drugged-on-honey thing, that's only the start of it. He's trying to come to terms with being stalked his whole life. And maybe she hurt him in ways he isn't ready to talk about."

Daphne and Melissa conspired to distract Beck. Daphne professed a new enthusiasm for snowshoeing, feigning interest at first, and then authentically keen. She urged Beck and Melissa outside on daily snowshoe expeditions around the perimeter of Bow Lake, and physical exertion in sub-zero temperatures pumped blood to their cheeks and cleared their heads. At a thrift store in Almonte Melissa found a board game based on an epic television series, with complex rules and a cloth bag of die-cast medieval pieces, and they played it in the evenings by the fireplace, occasionally coaxing a smile or wry remark from Beck.

In February a lawyer named Henry Anderson got involved with Beck's case. He called and requested a meeting, saying he was acting on behalf of the estate of Marjorie Hill. Melissa explained that Beck was declining to talk about his captor, and she would personally ensure he wasn't forced to.

"But my client has bequeathed a certain legacy to Beckett Wise," said the lawyer. "Would you be willing to mediate at a meeting? I need to convey the legal ramifications of this inheritance to him."

Melissa convinced Beck to agree to the meeting. Henry Anderson showed up promptly at ten the next morning and rapped smartly on the front door. Slickly professional, he removed a calf-length expensive-looking wool coat to reveal pleated pants and a pinstriped, button-down shirt. He asked for a glass of ice water and sat sipping it, right knee folded primly over left, one unseasonable leather tasselled shoe tapping in midair, holding a manila envelope in an age-spotted hand. Melissa shepherded Beck into the living room. Henry Anderson extended a hand for shaking which Beck ignored. After this awkward introduction, Henry shifted his water glass, ice tinkling gently, to a coaster on a makeshift side table, and employed both his hands to fiddle with the envelope. Melissa had asked him to refrain from saying Marjorie's name, and Henry was careful to follow this instruction.

"I found this," *this* was the well-handled envelope, held aloft, "tucked into the corner of a leather blotter on, uh, her desk. It's my client's last will and testament. As I mentioned on the telephone, this document has fascinating legal ramifications, specifically in the form of a bequest for Beckett."

"Go on," Melissa said.

Beck's chin was tucked down near his chest. He picked at a hole in his jeans.

"She left Thomas her house, her land and her beehives." Henry brandished the envelope and stroked it possessively, then reclined and produced a wide, satisfied smile. He jiggled his knees, waved the envelope again and sipped more water.

Melissa stared, uncomprehending, while the lawyer waited for a reaction. What were they supposed to feel – pleasure at Marjorie's generosity toward her son? Sorrow, at the futility of her unfulfillable wishes? Some other inscrutable emotion? Melissa lifted a bemused shoulder. Beck stared past Henry Anderson out the window to the porch, as if the man hadn't spoken.

"Surely you understand the implications?" Knee jiggling, toe tapping.

"I – we – don't. You'll have to spell them out."

Henry cleared his throat. "At the time my client composed this document," he palmed the envelope with one hand and patted it with the other, "she believed Beck to be the reincarnation of her son Thomas. Her diary makes it clear. She understood her biological son Thomas to have died long before. Therefore logically . . ."

"She left everything she had to Beck," Melissa breathed.

An invisible hand yanked Beck's hair at his crown, and his head jerked up. "I don't want it. I don't want anything to do with that house, or those hives."

Beck hadn't spoken vehemently about anything since the winter solstice, and Melissa was startled by the rawness of his sentiment. She stared at Beck's reddened face until she found a flaw in the lawyer's logic.

"She – your client – wasn't in her right mind, when she wrote that. And a will isn't legal, I'm pretty sure, if the person who makes it is insane at the time of its writing."

Henry's thin smile reappeared at this dropped gauntlet, and he warmed to the debate.

"My client wrote this last autumn, after a stay in hospital. There are witnesses, doctors and nurses, who can attest to her sanity at the time this will was drawn up. I can assure you these were my client's wishes upon her death. Her journal states unequivocally that she believed Beck Wise to be the reincarnation of her son Thomas. Reincarnation is a spiritual belief, and spiritual beliefs don't constitute insanity." Henry produced a starched handkerchief from a pocket and blotted his nose.

Melissa thought about what the inheritance might mean. Beck's parents could annex the property; it was adjacent to their land, and would double or triple their acreage. Or they could sell. Marjorie's old house wasn't worth anything, but the land could be sold, and provide financial compensation for Beck's suffering. She started to talk about these possibilities, but Beck had turned inward again, the light dimming in his eyes.

"What happens if he doesn't accept?"

"He would have to sign paperwork formally refusing her estate. The land and house would revert to the provincial government. And you should know, if he accepts, there is the matter of this year's property taxes, which must be paid by the new owner within ninety days."

"He needs time to consider." Melissa handed the lawyer his hat and coat and escorted him out over a quiet protest from Beck: *I don't want any of it.*

Winter days blew past. On a clear morning, Max swung 'round and took Melissa cross-country skiing, to the abandoned building where he'd found her father. It was heartbreakingly close to the farm, she thought, when they came around the corner and the walls reared up. But it was desolate, too. Her eyes stung. They leaned on their poles and gazed at the fortress of stacked logs. Plywood had been removed from the main entrance while the police completed their investigation, but had since been replaced. The hole where Max had slipped through with Matthew was boarded over and nailed shut.

"The police say this place is going to be demolished in the spring," said Max.

"Is that where he got inside?" Melissa pointed, and Max nodded. Pathetic, she thought. Undignified. Crawling on his belly for refuge from the cold. Her anger flared, and she spat in the snow.

Laughter carried up from frozen Crescent Lake, where locals had shovelled rectangular hockey rinks and a skating oval. Bow Lake was frozen too. In her nightmares, Melissa saw her father escape from the window of his sunken truck and swim to the surface through turbid water, only to find himself trapped under a dense, blue-black layer of ice, eyes panicky, cheeks bulging. They skied away from the log building, her father's tomb of twelve years.

The police got a warrant to search Joseph's trailer, and in mid-March a white law enforcement van parked outside the farmhand's forsaken former home. They broke in with a crowbar, but found nothing incriminating, not even a stack of motive-establishing love letters.

"It's a boring, dingy bachelor pad," said Constable Hickey. "I got the go-ahead, by the way. We'll search the lake for your dad's truck when the weather warms up." Before they left, the police wrapped the trailer in yellow POLICE LINE – DO NOT CROSS tape. Melissa stayed long after the van had gone, watching the garish tape ripple and snap in the wind.

"Where do you think they are?" Daphne asked Melissa over breakfast one morning, pouches of fatigue under her mournful eyes. "And why don't they ever call?"

How should I know? Melissa wanted to scream, but she shrugged and put a consoling hand on Daphne's shoulder. She gazed out at the lake, where answers might lie, drowned under the ice. If her father's truck was down there, and Jill and Joseph knew it, Melissa doubted they would ever return. How could the same tender mother who had raised her daughter diligently, and rescued and nurtured Daphne, have condemned her husband to death? The contradiction was baffling, like trying to fit a key into the wrong lock.

"We have each other. I'm not going anywhere, and this is your home."

Daphne placed her head in the cradle of her folded arms. Melissa leaned over and hugged her sister, and just then Beck entered the kitchen. He put a hand on the small of Melissa's back, and reached out with the other to comfort Daphne, completing the circle. The three of them created something that filled in hollow spaces at the farm, like dirt tamped into holes.

At the first hints of spring, farming began. The labour was overwhelming now that Joseph was gone, so Melissa interviewed seasonal workers and hired a couple from Australia who brought strong, happy accents and hearty enthusiasm to the fields. Beck's mood improved with days of digging, staking, planting and cleaning, and his smile flashed more often. Circles of bluish water pooled on top of the Bow Lake ice, and hungry deer browsed in the compost pile. The goats ran in sudden spurts, stretching stiff limbs. Hotay rubbed against the rough boards of his lean-to, tufts of his winter coat snagging on splinters and fluttering like moths.

On the second day of April a short convoy of police vehicles rolled onto the farm, two cruisers, and a pickup truck towing a boat trailer. The boat was a simple aluminum vessel with an outboard motor, the word POLICE painted on the bow. A quartet of wetsuit-clad cops launched the boat expertly while Melissa, Beck and Daphne observed from the dock. Melissa was disheartened to learn Constable Hickey wasn't part of the dive team but was attending to her ordinary duties in Lanark. It seemed like bad luck to proceed without the officer who had been involved in the case since its inception; but then again, Melissa was conflicted about precisely what a fortunate outcome to this watery exploration would look like. If they discovered nothing but rocks, fish and a spare tire or two, would it be a letdown, or a victory? On the other hand, if the truck was down there, it would mean she had skimmed the surface above it each summer, enjoying lighthearted, refreshing swims, oblivious to rusty evidence screaming silently at her from below. And it would corroborate Marjorie's account of the day Charlie died, implicating Joseph, and by association Jill, in covering up her father's death.

The lake sparkled, glints of sun reflecting off a gentle blue chop. Two divers splashed off the dock. A third sat on the gunwale of the boat, farther from shore, and fell in backwards. They surfaced every so often, futuristic amphibians, lips stretched wide around rubber mouthpieces, eyes hidden in plastic goggle-bubbles. Melissa chewed her lower lip, suppressing with wearisome effort the compulsion to count her teeth with her tongue. It was still morning when a diver's arm surfaced, his hand curled in a victorious thumbs-up.

Two days later, a police cruiser and tow truck reversed down the boat launch. Melissa, Beck and Daphne left the fields and sat on the embankment beside the canoe, spikes of weeds poking their legs. Melissa wore a pair of owlish dark sunglasses. One of the cops zipped himself into a wetsuit and donned diving gear, while another spooled out a coil of fluorescent nylon tow rope with an industrial iron hook tied to one end. The diver waded into the lake, rope snaking behind him. The tow truck operator, a man in his fifties, sported a tatty baseball hat, his belly spilling past a stained Toronto Blue Jays T-shirt. Melissa wanted her father's truck towed up beside the flower garden, and she told the operator so. Her plan was to fill the drowned vehicle with earth and plant a memorial garden.

"What d'you want it up there for? It's gonna be in crappy condition when I drag it out. I can take it to the scrapyard, just as easy. Flat rate's a hundred and twenty bucks. Gotta pay for my gas."

"Just do it, please."

Shaking his head, the operator set to work attaching tow rope to truck chain. Melissa rejoined her friends in the weeds. Beck stroked her hair, pressing it flat to her spine. Black ants tickled her exposed skin and she flicked them off impatiently. Daphne hummed a nervous song and tapped a brisk rhythm on her knees. Out in the lake, the diver connected the rope to rusty remains. The tow truck operator started up his winch engine, yawned and checked his wristwatch. Metal chain rattled and squealed, and the stink of diesel hung in the air. Charlie's truck rose. The top of the cab breached the surface evenly and quietly, like the smooth, silvery-wet back of a cetacean. A swell formed in front of the cab and then burst upward. The maw of the truck's open hood gaped toward the shore, a giant mouth dripping slimy, dark-green algae. Two glassy green-and-white orbs emerged, the headlights, blank eyes blinded by pond scum cataracts. Underwater, rust-locked wheels scraped against the boat ramp. Brown water poured out the windows. The truck protested its return to land, moaning as it bumped over concrete ramp ridges.

Once the truck was dragged entirely out of the water, two latex-gloved and solemn uniformed officers examined the lifeless carcass. They prodded here, slid a hand along there. The acrid stench of rolling tobacco startled Melissa and she sprang up, searching for Joseph, but it was wafting from the tow truck operator, a smoke dangling from his lumpy red fingers. He scratched the hairy exposed underside of his convex gut, snatched the frayed ball cap from his head and bowed toward her slightly in an apologetic salute.

A week later Melissa's mother called the farm at last. Jill's voice shook. She and Joseph were living in Toronto and they had been happy, *very* happy, until the police had called them both in for questioning. Charges might be laid against them, Jill said, her voice wet with tragedy. The cops had suggested she hire a lawyer. Worry was making her sick. She had lost fifteen pounds, and Joseph was smoking a pouch of tobacco every day. Jill didn't ask how Melissa was or inquire after Daphne. She was still talking when Melissa gently hung up the phone.

Twenty-Nine

"The assistant crown attorney called before we left this morning." Daphne leaned over to whisper in Beck's ear, and their adjacent steel-and-red-plush seats creaked underneath them. "Joseph and Jill each got six-month suspended sentences for withholding evidence."

Beck wrenched around and squinted at black theatre doors. Melissa was in the lobby, returning any moment. The film was about to start.

"But they left him in the woods to die," Beck said.

Daphne tilted her head rhythmically. "Mm-hmm – but the police aren't going to pursue it because they can't prove anything. Melissa's dad was drunk, and he wandered into a remote forest without a hat or gloves on the coldest day of winter. So technically, his death was accidental. Also, because Jill had kicked him out, a case could be made for suicide." She exhaled heavily. "There's something else. Joseph has lung cancer. He's got a few months to live, maximum. Shh, here she comes."

Melissa edged to her seat, the empty one beside Beck, halfway up the orchestra section in the centre of the row. Sitting down, she compressed her tall frame sideways to fit the inadequate space, knees pressing against the curved seatback in front of her. She stared at the curtain, folding and refolding a shiny paper program in her lap. Beck felt perspiration pool in his armpits and trickle down his sides. He listened to the jabber of conversation and watched the audience arrange itself in geometrical rows, bodies streaming up and down the aisles, stopping and rotating, scanning for empty spots. Matthew and Eurydice were part of the audience too, in a pair of front-row mezzanine seats. As the house lights dimmed,

Beck second-guessed his decision not to join his parents up there, where he could have discreetly escaped the theatre if necessary. There was a final round of movement while stragglers hurried to get seated. Someone coughed, someone sneezed. Onstage, a woman emerged from the wings and a spotlight followed her across the polished wood stage to a podium. She wore a black dress, a colourful shawl and a large golden beehive pendant. Towering crimson velvet curtains swished open behind her, revealing a massive blank screen. Professor Barbara Beauchemin waited silently until the whispers of the audience hushed to nothing.

"We wrapped up production of this film two months ago." She coughed gently. "Since then, millions more bees have died. Beekeepers are up in arms, launching multi-billion dollar lawsuits against the chemical companies responsible for manufacturing bee-killing products. Allow me to explain how this affects you. One in every three bites of food you eat is courtesy of bees. Strawberries, beets, onions, peas, peppers, watermelon . . ."

The professor listed foods for a long time. Each time Beck thought she was concluding, she was only taking a breath to resume her litany. "Apples, mangoes, allspice, cherries, peaches, plums, almonds, nectarines, guava, pomegranates, pears, currants, rosehips, every kind of berry, eggplants, grapes, broccoli, cauliflower, tangerines, sunflowers, walnuts." When it seemed there were no more fruits or vegetables left to name, the professor's list petered out, and she surveyed the audience solemnly.

"It turns out there's a lot we don't understand about our little black-and-yellow friends. It seems we have been taking them for granted. I teach quantum physics. In my field, we are constantly discovering what we don't know about the world and revealing our ignorance about the universe. The natural world contains countless phenomena we still don't understand, secrets we have yet to learn. It's a field of miracles."

What Professor Beauchemin said rang true, and Beck sank down self-consciously in his plush chair. On sun-dappled days he continued to see bee vectors, golden filaments of light and movement, where no one else could. Max speculated these were nothing but lingering illusions, a dwindling consequence of consuming toxic quantities of deli bal, but Beck had another theory. Through the narcotic portal of deli bal, he had immersed himself in the realm of the honeybee perfectly and completely. He had gone to the world of bees like Lucy to Narnia, and his journey's existence in his physical, cellular memory was beyond question. He knew the world of bees, its geometry and geography, its society, parameters and physics. His recollections of being bees existed as clearly and truly as his human memories. Being bees was something he could draw on, an artistic skill like playing music or writing stories. It was a beautiful place, and terrible too, and his explorations there would never leave him. Tentatively, Beck had asked his mother about other experiences he held inside him, like touching his wet black canine nose to Conchita's, and soaring over rows of vegetables on borrowed black wings. Both felt as real as being a humming colony inside a hive, golden tendrils extending to flowers.

Beck's imprisonment in Marjorie's house had affected Eurydice profoundly. She was less demonstrative of her faith, more quietly certain of her beliefs. She had placed her hand, heavy with silver rings, on the side of her son's head, and gazed into his eyes.

"In your mind, these episodes are real. So how are they separate from other experiences you remember, and believe are real? Once any moment has passed, it becomes part of our story and lives inside of us. Real to you is real enough."

Beck understood his mother meant Marjorie too. After reading Marjorie's diary, Eurydice had counselled Beck to search his heart and find sympathy and forgiveness for his captor. "Try to understand her pain, mi hijo, a mother's desperate love for her son. She wanted so badly for you to be her Thomas, and she tried to make it true. I forgive her."

In the theatre, Melissa found Beck's hand and squeezed it.

"*Becoming Bees* is a leap into a quantum world," Barbara Beauchemin was saying, "a world immediate and all around us, but also invisible and elusive. Everything is part of everything. Particles move much more freely than we ever imagined. It's only our human consciousness that makes us perceive the world as being made up of separate, unchangeable entities. In reality, our cells are constantly dying and being replaced, and matter is moving much more freely than we think. We are all connected to every other living thing. To behave accordingly, to afford nature the same importance and reverence we afford ourselves, is an act of faith. Let us hope we all find the courage to believe in this interconnection, and thereby rescue our planet."

The professor paused for effect.

"*Becoming Bees* was a collaborative effort. It wouldn't have been possible without the financial assistance of many individuals and organizations. I'm going to acknowledge them now. Our deep appreciation goes out to the National Film Board of Canada, the University of Toronto's Entomological Society, the Nature's Trust of Ontario, the Canada Council for the Arts . . ."

Melissa and Beck pushed their shoulders together. She sighed, and for a jarring second Beck thought she had puffed at her hair; but her nervous tics were gone, "in remission," she said. She spent time at the end of every day in the memorial flower garden she had planted for Charlie Makepeace, crowded with pink bee balm, lavender spikes and foamy white borders of alyssum. Daphne and Beck often joined her there. Like Beck's lost summer, Melissa's anguished months of learning the truth about her father were receding and softening, as better days accumulated.

"Ladies and gentlemen, please enjoy the world premiere of *Becoming Bees*."

Barbara Beauchemin glided offstage, and low house lights faded to black. Softly, then with mounting insistence, the theatre filled with the buzzing sound of thousands of bees. Fear gripped Beck. He clutched his forearms and their hairiness, flesh and sinew reassured him. Melissa pressed on his knee, as if holding him in place. The buzzing intensified, and Beck's heart raced with frenetic bee tension. A vibrant image of golden comb, slick with amber honey, blasted onto the screen. His sweat glands opened up; he was a human colander of fright. He closed his eyes and saw his bee-days behind the lids. His bee-memories matched the true-to-life images on the movie screen, no mock-up cardboard hive walls, no cellophane wings. Beck felt his body, singular and complete, and though it scared him, he believed to his core that there was a time when it hadn't been so.

The dramatic opening beehive footage and soundtrack faded out, and the film cut to an interview with a scientist. Beck opened his eyes. *Becoming Bees* was a documentary, a blend of interviews, nature footage and hive-cameras, focusing on colony collapse disorder. A good deal of the film's content was devoted to the possibility that bees use a fourth dimension to navigate for nectar. It was a seductive, poetic portrayal of honeybees, an embrace of the beguiling romance of the hive.

The film ended to a standing ovation, and the lights came up. Beck congratulated Barbara and left the theatre, emerging from darkness to blink in bright sun, like a hatching insect. Beck's parents sought him on the sidewalk. His father looked rumpled and happy, his mother serene; they were creating a market vegetable garden on the acreage Beck had inherited. Matthew, lean and tan from cycling with Max, had documented the destruction of Marjorie's house in photographs, as well as the clearing of her land with a bulldozer and the relocation of her hives to Hopetown Farm. Beck was slowly recovering; to his astonishment, he was beekeeping again.

One day in May, Melissa had gone to the bee yard. She had suited up, torn off black roofing paper and Styrofoam hive insulation and checked frames. Most of the hives had been healthy, but underneath the final lid she'd found a holocaust; frames marbled with mould and littered with dead bees. She had searched for Beck and found him on his hands and knees, planting garlic.

"You have to come and see this hive. It's disgusting. The brood frame looks like chocolate pudding, and there's a stink coming from it that makes the chicken coop smell like roses."

A stillness had come over Beck, and he had pressed his hands into the earth.

"Sounds like foulbrood," he had said at last.

"Well are you coming, or not? I don't have a clue what to do."

He had followed her, visions of being sequestered in Marjorie's bee-prison hanging before him like heavy curtains. He had suited up, inspected the frames and confirmed it was foulbrood; the hive would have to be burned to keep the disease from spreading. Together they had moved the infected hive into an open field. Melissa had handed Beck lighter fluid and matches, and soon a crackling fire had popped and snapped, sending black smoke and sparks swirling up to a cloudy sky. They had stood by the fire until it was a circle of scorched earth. Watching the flames, the sombre curtains in his mind had parted, and Beck had found he was able to separate his trial in Marjorie's bizarre prison from the miracle of the honeybee.

And then at last it was summer. Beck gloried in the hallmarks of the season he had lost – scorching sun, heat ripples over the fields, grasses bending in hot breezes. The air was alive with the flight of insects and the drift of feathery plant seeds. Beck was in the bee yard. The sky was hazy with pollen and he was immersed in an incessant busy drone. Melissa and Daphne were in a distant field picking fat cherry tomatoes, and the Australians were on the other side of the house, weeding the herb garden. A carload of tourists pulled up outside the hedge. Metal doors opened and slammed shut. Voices spilled out – children's tinny demands and their parents' harried reprimands. Strangers slipped through the gap in the hedge. A dog barked, and Beck saw a golden retriever bounding around the kids like an overgrown puppy. He replaced the frame of comb he was holding, gently extracted another and held it up to the sun. Hotay, tethered in the shade of the orchard, brayed.

"Whisky, Whisky!" the tourists called.

Beck held the hive frame over his head. Sunlight filtered through perfectly even hexagons. More barking, more children shouting. Beck scanned the lush fields and saw Whisky bolt around the side of the farmhouse. The shaggy dog soared over a fence and made straight for Hotay. The donkey rotated his hindquarters and delivered a lightning-fast, accurate kick to the dog's rib cage. Sharp cries of wounded dog, clatter of Daphne's bucket hitting the ground, sight of Melissa and Daphne running to where Whisky's family members were bellowing and shrieking and gesturing over the fence, pointing to their injured pet. Whimpering, the dog limped back to its owners, creeping close to the ground on lowered legs. In the bee yard, Beck bobbled the frame he was holding and almost dropped it. He snagged it with an open palm before it hit the ground, crushing bees between his hand and the frame.

The bees stung him – they *stung* him! Two stings on his hand, more as he staggered away from the bees' ferocious defence of their hive, sharp flashes of pain exploding in the crook of his elbow and on the back of his neck. He gained the porch and took refuge in its farthest corner, swatting at his tenacious attackers, blinking in shock and surprise, and panting in the humid air.

"Oh, *Whisky!* Poor Whisky!" the children bawled.

Beck leaned against the porch railing, amazed by the intense pain and dimly aware of Melissa arguing with the visiting adults. He inspected his right hand in wonder. Red welts were rising. Stingers hung from inflated flesh.

"That donkey should be shot!"

"Oh yeah? We should charge you with trespassing!"

"If my dog dies, you'll have a lawsuit on your hands."

"If your dog dies it's your own damn fault."

"Who the hell is in charge here? I want to talk to your boss."

"I *am* the boss. You can take your dog, and your family, and leave. Now."

Pain blossomed from Beck's stings like flowers, petals of agony opening around the stamen of his fingers. Sounds of car doors closing, tires spinning on thin gravel, acceleration of a motor. Melissa joined him on the porch and Beck presented his hand triumphantly.

"The bees stung me."

"And this is a good thing?" Melissa smiled wryly.

"I think it means it's over. Nothing can shift me anymore. I want to stay right here."

They kissed, Beck spreading his bliss through the conveyance of their tongues. Daphne called up to the porch, "Okay, lovebirds, la la la, I'm gone to hang with Hotay," and whistled gaily as she walked away. A speck with wings buzzed close, and Beck turned from Melissa to follow a trailing, winding path that rose and fell, then settled on the bushy purple flower of a giant burdock. The insect's weight bent the stem and the plant bowed, like a butler welcoming a guest to a hall. His view of the bee was miraculously magnified, her front legs working at globes of orange pollen, the inquisitive curve of her antennae probing the air. Fields and flower beds were cross-hatched with undulating gold lines, strung out across the front lawn and converging, streaking the air between the house, the bee yard and the gap in the hedge.

Acknowledgements

Mad Honey was a long journey from concept to realization, and many thanks are due.

To Will Stinson for his never-ending faith, support and love.

To Carolyn Swayze for her wisdom and persistence. To Paul Vermeersch, Noelle Allen, Ashley Hisson, Jennifer Rawlinson, Tania Blokhuis and everyone at wonderful Wolsak and Wynn for believing in the book and showing me the ropes.

To canny and unflinching editor Jen Sookfong Lee, my heartfelt thanks and deep respect.

As a manuscript this story passed through hugely talented literary hands. I am indebted to Madeleine Thien, Rick Meier, Lynn Henry and Patricia M. Dupuis.

A big thank you to Jen Hale for an astute and meticulous copy edit.

Thanks to the beekeepers who hosted me in their apiaries and shared their love of beekeeping: Tom Brown of Hopetown, Ontario; Frank Blom of Kamloops, BC; and Brian Richards of San Miguel de Allende, Mexico.

I owe a debt of imagination to Adam Frank, whose October 31, 1997, *Discover* magazine article "Quantum Honeybees" about the research of mathematician Barbara Shipman inspired the character of Professor Barbara Beauchemin.

Thank you to the Banff Centre for Arts and Creativity, and to the wonderful writers who patiently workshopped a few early chapters of *Mad Honey*: Eva Crocker, Armand Garnet Ruffo, Syed Hussan, Pamela Rhae Ferguson, Stephanie Jimenez, Sara Marinelli and Kimberley Alcock.

And last but not least, thanks to friends who cheered me on, listened to me fret and read early drafts, especially Donna Bishop, Heather Saya Hughes, Suzanne M. Steele, Shelly and Rebecca McKerchar, Todd Collier, Shauna Tsuchiya, Norah Ashmore, Judy Petersen and Lynne Stonier-Newman.

Katie Welch writes fiction and teaches music in Kamloops, BC, on the traditional, unceded territory of the Secwepemc people. Her short stories have been published in *EVENT Magazine, Prairie Fire, The Antigonish Review, The Temz Review, The Quarantine Review* and elsewhere. An alumnus of the Banff Centre's Emerging Writers Intensive, she was first runner-up in UBCO's 2019 Short Story Contest, and her story "Poisoned Apple" was chosen as Pick-of-the-Week by Longform Fiction.

Katie holds a BA in English Literature from the University of Toronto (1990). Her daughters, Olivia and Heather Saya, share her passion for nature and outdoor recreation. Katie loves to cycle, hike and cross-country ski with her husband, Will Stinson, and they are creating a remote home on Cortes Island, in Desolation Sound.